WELCOME, PLEASE LEAVE

ROGUE ENTERPRISES
BOOK 3

JOHN WILKER

Rogue Publishing

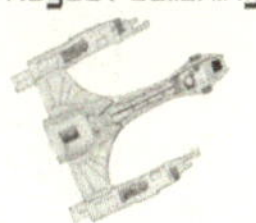

Cover art by: Ana Voltz

V 1.0

ISBN: 978-1-951964-29-0

For Tyler Morrison

You're about to embark on a fun adventure!

When you're done reading, I hope you'll take a minute to leave a review!

If you liked the story and want more, joining my newsletter is a great way to get free samples, and exclusive short stories, and other goodies.

PREVIOUSLY ON...

In our last adventure, the team found themselves, as usual, neck deep in galactic politics. How does that keep happening? The Commonwealth Governing Council would surely like to know so they can put a stop to it.

With everything going on in the galaxy, more and more societies are thinking about going it on their own or even forming new coalitions outside of the Commonwealth.

That's not great for the Galactic Commonwealth, of course, as they lose members and tax revenue. The Peacekeepers, still weakened from their battles with the renegade Janus and his mutant warriors, can't keep up.

While trying to do a job—security escort—for a separatist movement speaker, the team stumbled into a plot to destabilize the Commonwealth. It seemed several members of the Harrith government and military hadn't forgiven or forgotten the plot to force their society to join the Commonwealth (*Space Rogues Book 1*, don't you know). Even the separatist speaker was in the dark!

While part of the team dealt with one side of Harrith

society wanting to destroy the Commonwealth, the other part of the team worked to convince the Harrith to help the GC's Governing Council by sending a delegation to Tarsis.

Harrith society, after all, had been stable for centuries... Maybe the Commonwealth could learn a thing or two.

PART 1

CHAPTER ONE

"THIS PLACE IS NICE," Nic said. "Like one of those vids from Wil's world where people lived in the dirt and rode around on animals."

The Heritage City Spaceport was little more than a two-kilometer-wide circle outlined by a meter-tall concrete wall. A lone two-story tower stood at the northernmost part of the spaceport, a series of dishes and comm antennas surrounding it.

Oberon was Earth's first extrasolar colony, and Heritage City was its capital. The Earth Government Alliance's first colony had gotten off the ground faster than Wil would ever have thought. He'd forgotten how determined humans could be when they set their minds—and planetary economies—to something.

The road from the spaceport into the city was nothing more than a kilometer-long packed dirt track wide enough for a pair of grav trucks to go both ways. Unfortunately, no such vehicle was on the road today, so they were walking.

Situated in the middle of a five-kilometer crescent of beach that hugged the coast, with the spaceport to the northeast, slightly inland, Heritage City was along the shore of the world's only ocean.

"It is only two years old," Zephyr pointed out. She gestured ahead of them to the span of two- and three-story buildings made largely of prefabricated components.

Behind them, a cargo shuttle lifted off from the spaceport, its lift engines roaring as they pushed the heavy vessel into the sky.

"I kinda like it," Wil said. He pointed toward a low mountain range beyond the city, covered in whatever passed for pine trees on the planet. "A nice little cabin up there in the woods." He draped an arm around Cynthia's shoulder. "You can chop wood, right?"

Shaking her head, his wife said, "Dream on, wilderness man. You wouldn't last a week without climate control."

He shrugged. "Could be a rustic cabin with modern touches."

"Remind me what we're doing here," Bennie said as he kicked a rock ahead of them. Like Nic, he was in his earth-tone-colored tunic and trousers—what passed for a uniform among the Knights of Plentallus.

"You were in the briefing," Maxim said. Bennie turned to look up at his much taller friend, saying nothing. The big Palorian sighed. "We've been hired to escort the newly minted ambassador to the GC on a tour of the Commonwealth before depositing him safely on Tarsis."

"Where he'll be sworn in by the Governing Council," Zephyr added.

The Brailack hacker bobbed his head. "Ah, right. Just as boring the second time." He ducked out of the bigger man's reach just in time. He grinned as he darted ahead.

"The pay's good," Wil pointed out, even though Bennie was no longer listening. After their last job fell through, funds were lower than he liked. Since going *legit* as Rogue Enterprises, he'd been trying to take only above-board jobs. The pay wasn't always as good.

He turned to Bennie. "Not like you and your underling bring in much money." He looked back at Nic. "No offense."

She shrugged. "I keep telling him we should charge for our services."

Bennie shook his head. "I've told you before, apprentice, that Knights of Plentallus don't charge for services rendered. We help where needed, and if citizens feel inclined to support us, they do."

Nic turned to Wil, expressionless. "They rarely do."

Zephyr clucked at her friends, pointing ahead of them. At the edge of town was a small group of people, apparently waiting for them.

Bennie perked up. He turned to Wil. "This is an Earth colony. You think they have those crunchy red things, cheezos?"

"Cheetos, and I doubt it." Wil ran a hand through his hair. "I shoulda asked earlier—maybe they could have imported some. Haven't had Cheetos in way too long." He gave his little green friend a pointed look. "They'd last longer if someone didn't sneak them."

Bennie made a face.

THE GROUP of humans that met them at the edge of town were all well dressed in what Wil assumed must be the fashion back home. He looked down at his standard shipboard attire and shrugged. He'd never been able to keep up with fashion. It was harder being thousands of light years away.

"Hi, folks. Wil Calder." Wil extended his hand.

One of the men stepped forward. "Branson Carlisle.

Ambassador to the Galactic Commonwealth." He shook Wil's hand. "It's a pleasure to meet you all. I've heard so much about you." Looking at the assorted aliens, his gaze fell on Nic. "I don't believe you were in my briefing. Hello." He reached out to pat Nic's head only to have his hand batted away with a growl. Carlisle recoiled. "So sorry."

Bennie had a hand over his mouth to control his laughter. "This is my apprentice, Nic'ole Thot'la."

"Nic," she offered. "Not a child."

"Technically a child," Bennie corrected. He did not look at his angry apprentice's face.

Cynthia put a hand on the younger woman's shoulder.

Ambassador Carlisle smiled. "Well, it's nice to meet you, Nic. Sorry I tried to pat your head." She nodded once. He took in her outfit, then Bennie's. "I look forward to hearing more about your order." He turned to the group. "Forgive me." He motioned another man forward. "This is my aide, Bruce Hawkins."

The man behind the ambassador stepped up. He was at least ten years younger than his boss and significantly more fit. Nothing like what Wil thought a junior bureaucrat would look like. The man stuck his hand out.

Wil shook the offered hand. Firm grip—too firm. "Nice to meet you." He turned to the others. "My team: my first officer, Zephyr. Tactical, Maxim. Tall and shiny is our engineer Gabe. Green and surly is our hacker and resident Knight of Plentallus, Bennie. His apprentice, Nic. And last but not least, my wife, Cynthia. All around ninja assassin badass."

"Assassin?" Hawkins asked, eyebrows crawling up his forehead.

Wil shrugged. "For good."

"A good assassin?" Ambassador Carlisle asked.

"That's a thing," Wil insisted.

"The best," Cynthia said with a grin. She turned to the gaggle behind the older man. "And they are?"

Carlisle eyed her a moment, then turned and introduced the rest of his entourage, but since none of them were coming with on the job, no one on the team paid much attention.

The team was following Carlisle and his aide back to the government building when Cynthia leaned in to Wil. "Something is flashy about that aide, Hawkman."

"Hawkins, and flashy?"

"Yeah, him. You know...smells bad, not quite right."

"Fishy. Why? What's up?"

The short whiskers near her nose twitched. "I can't put my finger on it, but...I dunno. He's too smooth to be an aide. Too fit, too."

Wil grinned. "I'm smooth and fit."

"You are neither."

He made a noise. "Strong handshake, too. I'm guessing maybe ex-security or something. Maybe that's what's got your Spidey sense on edge?"

She shook her head; her left ear twitched. "Maybe."

The group stopped outside a three-story building surrounded by what was eventually supposed to be a lawn. A few stubby blades of grass were visible in patches on either side of the walkway that led to the double doors. The colonists planted saplings along the walkway. Someday they'd provide lovely shade.

Hawkins broke off from the group as they made their way into the building. Wil watched him open an unlabeled side door and vanish inside.

"Heritage City was the first city on Oberon. There are two more now," Carlisle said. He pointed to a large map on the wall opposite them. Heritage City sat along the coast, the largest of three dots. Another dot to the east on the other side of the small mountain range was labeled New Denver. One to the south and slightly east was labeled York.

He guided the group to a staircase. "I have refreshments set up on the patio. The governor would like to meet you all."

THE ROOFTOP of the Oberon planetary government building offered an expansive view of the fledgling city from the spaceport inland to the coastline and ocean beyond. A handful of automated fishing boats bobbed just off shore, shut down for the evening.

The governor, it turned out, was a fan of Wil's.

"By the way, Captain. The new president sends his regards," the ambassador said.

"That the Canadian guy? From an island or whatever?"

The older man nodded. "Vic Douse, from Prince Edward Island, yes. From cabinet minister to prime minister to leader of the Earth Government Alliance. Quite the career path."

"Impressive for sure. Nice guy?" Wil asked. He smiled. "I mean, he's a fan of mine, so we know he's got impeccable taste."

The governor and ambassador shared a look.

"Probably knows somebody," Bennie offered. All three men looked at him. "What?"

When no one said anything, he looked around. "What?"

Wil shook his head. "That's not how Earth elections work." When he got raised eyebrows from the other two men, he added, "Mostly."

The ambassador chuckled. "The president is, in fact, a big fan of yours. He was read in as prime minister and put everything Canada had behind forming the UEGA. I doubt we'd be this far with the Galactic Commonwealth if anyone else had won the election. He's followed your story ever since."

Wil nodded. "So, I have a fan club?"

Zephyr leaned over to Maxim. "He's going to be unbearable for at least a week."

"Two is my guess." He looked across the seating area as Wil was regaling the governor with the story of their time aboard the *Siege Perilous*, the massive dreadnaught run by a machine intelligence from the far side of the galaxy. The governor was leaning in, eyes wide, elbows on his knees. Maxim watched the pair. He was pretty sure Wil had said that the other man was Kolien or Kelpien...Korean, that was it. It was interesting to see another type of human. There were so many. Palorians had a much more limited genetic variety.

Cynthia joined Gabe at the edge of the building. "Humans everywhere, as far as the eye can see."

"Unsettling," the team engineer said. The pair looked out over the city and sea beyond until Gabe cocked his head. "Interesting."

"What?"

He pointed. A block away there was a cluster of half a dozen droids doing who knew what with a couple of humans. It looked like they might be helping erect a scaffold in front of a two-story building with a coffee shop on the ground floor.

"Droids," the Tygran woman said absently. "That is interesting."

Gabe nodded and then turned to the larger group. "Excuse me."

Governor Shen turned from Wil. "Yes, Gabe?"

"There are droids here."

The governor joined Gabe and Cynthia, looking down the street. He smiled. "Yes, indeed. Arcadia has been instrumental in helping get Oberon off its feet so quickly. Your people are intensely industrious."

Gabe inclined his head. "I would like to go down and say hello."

The governor turned, extending an arm toward the door to the stairs. "Of course."

"Okay if I come with?" Cynthia asked the droid. Gabe nodded. The pair headed for the exit.

As Gabe and Cynthia exited, a young man brought a tray of drinks and snacks to the seating area.

"How're things back home?" Wil asked as the governor picked up a glass of what looked like... "Is that...beer? Real beer? Not grum?"

The other man's grin was ear to ear. "An IPA from my favorite brewery in Southern California." He picked up a pint and offered it to Wil. "I have a keg or two brought in on the diplomatic shuttle." He sat back down and leaned back in his seat. After taking a sip, he sighed. "So good."

Wil took his own sip. "Oh, damn."

Bennie watched the exchange and then said, "I thought you said grum was like beer." When the team had gone to Earth a few years ago, the only way he could blend in was disguised as a child. Wil had insisted it would blow their cover if he was seen drinking beer.

Wil offered the Brailack his glass. Bennie took a sip. Savored it. Then, he drained half the glass. Lowering the mug and licking his lips, he said, "Wow. That's way better than grum." He offered the glass, but Wil waved it off, reaching for a fresh pint off the table nearby.

Nic reached for the offered glass. Bennie pulled it away, making a clucking noise. The young Olop bared her teeth, crossing her arms and leaning back against the seat.

"No beer for children," he smirked.

Zephyr and Maxim shook their heads.

Turning to the governor, Wil said, "So. What's the good word from home?"

Maxim picked up a pair of pint glasses, offering one to Zephyr, keeping the other.

The governor adjusted his position on the outdoor sofa. "You remember that Earth First movement?" Wil nodded. "Mostly gone. Or at least minimized."

"That didn't take long," Wil said. He took a sip of his IPA, relishing it.

The other man nodded. "It didn't take long for politicians to see which way the tide was going. Those yahoos kept burning bridges left and right until no self-respecting politician would touch their cause. Those already in office found something else to occupy their time."

"Tide?" Maxim asked. "What does the motion of your world's moon have to do with anything?"

"Public opinion," Wil offered. Maxim's mouth formed a line. He nodded.

The governor continued. "Once the Earth Government Alliance fully unlocked the archive you provided, things improved for everyone. Quickly. Power is abundant. Food is growing where it never could, meaning there's more than enough to go around. Obviously, our space exploration program has accelerated beyond anyone's wildest dreams. There are more volunteers for emigration to Oberon than we can accommodate."

Wil took another sip, then said, "Glad to hear. I was a bit worried you all were going to embarrass me. Or destroy the planet."

Ambassador Carlisle, who'd been tapping away at a tablet, looked up at that but said nothing.

Bennie's wristcomm played a little tune. "Oh, uh, I'll be right back. Something I need to take care of."

Wil looked at his friend suspiciously. So did Nic.

He smiled as he got up. "Just be a microtock."

As he headed for the staircase, Bruce asked, "He always suspicious like that?"

Wil nodded. "That's nothing."

A BLOCK from the Heritage City government building, Gabe and Cynthia approached the work crew they'd seen from the roof. "Excuse me," Gabe called out. The droids near the coffee shop stopped and turned as one. "Hello."

A four-legged load lifter stepped forward. "Greetings, Gabe. It is an honor to meet you." It placed a rugged manipulator against its chest. "I am Onyx Quad."

Gabe bowed his head. "This is my colleague, Cynthia," he introduced, extending his hand toward her.

She smiled, inclining her head. "Nice to meet you, Onyx Quad."

Gabe gestured to the scaffold and human crew standing nearby. "I do not wish to delay your work; I was surprised to see Arcadians."

A dull gray bipedal bot approached from around the side of the building. Cynthia thought it might have been a residential service bot. "I am Tycho Aloft."

Gabe turned to Cynthia. "Tycho Aloft was on the governmental affairs sub-committee on Arcadia when I was there."

She made a thoughtful face.

Tycho Aloft dipped its head in acknowledgement. "Indeed. After the last election, I found myself dissatisfied with government service and sought a new vocation."

"How did you end up here?" Cynthia asked.

"I heard that Arcadia had made political inroads with the

people of Earth and were embarking on several collaborations. Of the available choices, helping to set up the human's first extrasolar colony seemed the most rewarding. I am pleased that I was not incorrect in my assumption. The people of this planet are remarkably kind," Tycho Aloft replied.

Onyx Quad bent its front legs, dipping its torso. "The humans have proven to be interesting partners. Helping them to establish this colony has been a worthwhile endeavor. They have no preconceived ideas about synthetic intelligences."

Another droid rolled forward on a pair of knobby tires. "I am Ajax Table."

"Ajax Table?" Cynthia said under her breath.

Via Cynthia's earpiece Gabe said, "Many emancipated droids consulted dictionaries to determine their names via random selection." She looked at him and nodded her thanks for the explanation.

The wheeled droid nodded to Gabe. "We have met before. On Arcadia."

Gabe inclined his head. "It is a pleasure to see you again, Ajax Table. When last we met, you were part of President Mitch's cabinet."

"Like a reunion," Cynthia quipped.

Ajax Table nodded. "Yes. When his term was complete, Mitch was given leave to seek partners for Arcadia. We were all members of the trade delegation to human space. Once we learned of their efforts to establish their first extrasolar colony, we offered our services."

"I'm sure they appreciate it," Cynthia said.

Ajax Table nodded. "They seem to. In exchange for our labor and expertise, they have provided parcels of land for Arcadians to establish homesteads."

"Construction on the first arcology begins next year," Onyx Quad offered.

Gabe cocked his head. "Are many Arcadians planning to emigrate?"

Onyx Quad bobbed as it bent all four legs. "It is nice to have options. Our people should not be limited to just one world." Looking over its shoulder, it added, "We should return to work. It was enjoyable to meet you, Gabe."

Cynthia consulted her wristcomm. "We should get back. Wil says they're on their way down from the roof."

Gabe nodded. "I am pleased to see Arcadians outside our home world. Be well."

BENNIE EXITED THE GOVERNMENT BUILDING, looking around until he spotted Gabe and Cynthia up the street. He headed the opposite direction. A quick look at his wristcomm confirmed that the person he was here to meet was two blocks away.

"I wasn't sure you were going to make contact," he said as he reached his destination. The human woman was standing in front of a café that closed after lunch. She looked up and down the street before saying, "I wasn't sure I was either. I saw your ship come in. I almost didn't." She hadn't made eye contact with him. Looking at the table next to them, she asked, "You have it?"

Bennie nodded. "Of course." He reached under his tunic to one of the many small pockets sewn into the inside. He produced a data chip. "Your tech should be able to read this." He held it out for her.

She reached out for the chip.

Bennie pulled the data chip back. "My fee?"

"Oh, yes. Right," she stammered. She fished out one of the devices the humans liked to use instead of wristcomms.

He watched her fumble with it until his wristcomm beeped.

He checked the banking app, confirming the transfer. He held out the chip. "Enjoy."

She took the chip, quickly putting it in a pocket. "Thanks." She turned and headed away from him.

He smiled and turned to head back to the government building. His wristcomm beeped again. It was Wil letting them all know that it was time to head back to the ship.

He met Cynthia and Gabe outside the building. The former eyed him, eyebrow raised. "What were you up to?"

"Nothing."

"That seems unlikely," Gabe said.

Before Bennie could answer, the rest of the team and their clients exited the building.

"WELCOME TO GNO NEWSTIME. I'm Xyrzix." The newscaster's hairless blue head dipped.

"And I'm Klor'Tillen," the pale green Brailack said, "in from the cold to help my friend Xyrzix behind the desk." He beamed and turned to the other journalist.

Looking at his small cohost, he said, "Indeed, it's pleasurable to have you here in the studio." He turned to the camera pickup. "The newest soon-to-be full members of the GC, the humans of Earth, will be taking their place among the council's representatives."

Klor'Tillen nodded. "Yes, we're told that the hoo-mon...?" He shook his head. "That's not right. Hugh-men. I think that's it. Their ambassador will be making his way to Tarsis soon to be sworn in." He turned to another camera pickup. "While most see this as great news, bringing new blood, as it were, into the Commonwealth, others are not so optimistic."

Picking up the story, Xyrzix said, "Indeed. We've received

reports of a few Tier 3 worlds demanding a temporary moratorium on new GC memberships."

"I wonder why?" the Brailack anchor said from his side of the desk.

The other news anchor shrugged. "In other news, the Florkelball tournament on Qwazino Three ended in a sudden death overtime shot that also resulted in bloodshed among the rival fans."

"Sudden death, indeed," Klor'Tillen quipped with a chuckle.

"Dark, my friend...dark," Xyrzix said.

CHAPTER TWO

"HERITAGE CITY SPACE CONTROL, *Ghost*. Requesting departure clearance," Cynthia called from her station behind and to the left of Wil's pilot station. She turned to look at Wil, who was looking over his shoulder, and gave him a nod.

"Powering up repulsorlifts." He slid the throttle lever forward, feeding power to the repulsors mounted in the front of each of the two engine nacelles. The *Ghost* rose, balancing on columns of gravity-repulsing energy. The ship teetered a bit.

Bennie clucked without looking up from his station.

"Just a little wind," Wil said, adjusting the power to the repulsors. Until the atmospheric engines kicked on, the *Ghost* could do nothing but balance on the power columns of energy pushing her higher and higher into the air.

"Uh huh," the Brailack hacker said, still not looking at Wil.

Once the *Ghost* reached an altitude of one hundred meters, Wil pushed the atmospheric engine throttle forward one position. A loud boom echoed through the ship as the overpowered engines roared to life, pushing the ship forward.

"Love this part," Wil whispered.

He continued to feed power to the engines and the repulsors, forcing the ship higher and higher. The *Ghost* had not been designed with aerodynamics in mind. Her wings couldn't generate lift; her center of gravity was well aft of her middle. It took a careful balancing of her repulsorlifts and atmospheric engines to keep the ship in the air, let alone get her out of the atmosphere.

"Space control wasn't thrilled with the noise," Cynthia reported.

"They never are," Maxim said from the tactical station just forward and to the right of Wil's flight command station. He was also grinning.

The crew watched as the pale pink clouds of the Oberon sky thinned. The sky darkened from light blue to black. Stars appeared. Wil shut down the atmospheric engines as he brought the sub-light engines up to half power. As always, there was a brief second of freefall when the atmospheric engines cut out and before the sub-light engines ramped up.

The bridge hatch opened, and Ambassador Carlisle walked in. "Already in orbit? Impressive."

Wil smiled. "We're full of surprises."

Zephyr turned. "You and your aide get settled? Quarters to your liking?"

The older man inclined his head. "Indeed. Your guest berths are...cozy."

"That's one word for them," Bennie said.

Wil glared at the little green hacker. "If you'd stop going in there to do God only knows what..."

"I'm sorry, what?" Carlisle's face paled.

"What?" Bennie said, studiously facing forward. "Oh, look, we're about to collide with the freighter."

Wil turned his attention back to the screen a moment before the *Ghost*'s collision warning alarm sounded. He pulled the flight controls hard to the right while stomping on the left foot pedal, kicking the *Ghost*'s tail end out and around before pushing the sub-light throttle forward. The ship accelerated, the larger ship growing in size as it slid to the top of the primary display.

Wil glanced over his shoulder to see the ambassador clutching the sides of the bridge hatch, knuckles white. "Sorry." The other man gave three short nods.

Wil turned to Bennie, glaring.

Zephyr cleared her throat. "We're probably far enough from the gravity well to jump to FTL."

Wil shook his head, then glanced at one of the displays mounted near the main display. The *Ghost* was indeed nearing a safe FTL distance. Jumping to Faster Than Light speed near a gravity well was never wise and almost always deadly.

Wil looked over his shoulder to Cynthia, who nodded that they were clear to depart. He eased the sub-light engine controls back to zero. After flipping a few switches and confirming the FTL system was online and ready, he reached for the slider for the FTL drive.

He pushed it all the way forward. On the main display at the front of the bridge, the stars stretched into rainbow lines swirling around the ship.

Zephyr stood. "Ambassador Carlisle, we'll be having dinner in a tock."

The older man stepped to the side of the hatch to let Zephyr pass. As the others filed out, Maxim remained in his seat.

Once it was just the two of them, Wil looked at his big friend. "Something on your mind, pal?"

The big Palorian man leaned forward. "I've made the final arrangements. For the joining ceremony."

Wil beamed. "Well, it's about damned time." He stood and crossed the small distance between his station and Max's, offering his hand. The big man clasped Wil's forearm as Wil returned the gesture, the GC's version of a handshake. He leaned back against the back of Zephyr's station, crossing his arms over his chest. He was beaming at his friend.

The normally stoic Palorian special intelligence operative was grinning like a kid in a candy store. "The betrothal band was delivered to the warehouse just before we left."

Wil's eyebrows shot up. "That some kind of weird warrior sex thing?"

"It's a bracelet, you classless backwater bumpkin." Maxim's grin hadn't budged. "It's a Palorian tradition that the oldest male in a family is bound with the family band to his life mate. Fathers make them when their firstborn arrives. They hold on to them until the firstborn is ready."

Wil moved back to drop into his seat, turning toward Maxim. "Like a family wedding band—a ring. But like, custom made? By your dad?"

The other man nodded. "Each oldest son makes a band for his oldest son, etcetera." He smiled. "My father has been harassing me to finalize plans for some time now. I think he was getting tired of holding on to it."

Wil made a face. "I mean, you've been kind of a bridezilla about this whole thing." He raised a hand to keep his friend from replying. "So, what're the plans? What're we doing? On Fury?"

"Gods no. That place is a dren heap." Maxim shook his head. "Once we wrap up this job, I've got us booked at a small resort on Qwazino Three." He leaned forward in case somehow Zephyr was listening. "It's a quaint little place on a lake. Reminds me of the Rioldro shores on Palor. She'll love it."

Wil smiled at his friend. It was good to see Maxim finally solidifying these plans. The big man had been waffling from idea to idea for ages now, and Wil knew it was grating on

Zephyr's nerves. Apparently, wedding planning for Palorians was a guy thing.

He stood. "Well, I'm happy for ya, man. Let's get ready for dinner."

"BENNIE, don't hog all the bacon," Cynthia scolded. The team and their guests were crowded around the table in the kitchenette on the starboard side of the ship's common deck. It was a tight fit when there were six of them. Eight made it a bit too cozy.

"This is really good," the ambassador's aide said. He scooped up a forkful of eggs.

Wil nodded. "It's gotten easier since Earth stopped being a protected backwater." He scooped up a forkful of eggs. "Was so hard to get in and out with eggs and bacon. I used to have to land in shitty little backwater towns and sneak to the nearest Costco—which was never that near.

"Don't forget the Cheebos," Bennie added.

Wil nodded. "Cheetos, and yeah, other than yipsee sticks, nothing compares."

"You smuggled Cheetos off Earth?" Bruce asked. "Cheetos?"

"Several times," Maxim confirmed. "Always exciting."

Bruce shook his head. "Of all the things to risk life and limb for..."

Wil waved him off. "Not that big a risk."

"You said Earth was a protected planet," the other man said.

Wil shrugged. "Yeah, but it wasn't like they parked a command carrier in orbit. Most of the time, the nearest PK ship was light years away."

"Doesn't seem very protected," Ambassador Carlisle said. He took a bite of eggs. "Please pass the salt."

Wil looked at Zephyr. She inclined her head. "Even before events drastically diminished Peacekeeper forces, there were more protected worlds than we could maintain any permanent presence at."

Bruce cocked his head. "That's right," he pointed at Maxim, "you two were Peacekeepers." He accepted the salt from Bennie and handed it to his boss.

Zephyr inclined her head again. "Just so. Anyway. We couldn't maintain a presence in every protected system, so command carriers and cruisers were given random patrol routes. Since you never knew when a ship would arrive, most criminals didn't risk it." She looked at Wil. "Most."

He grinned. "Hey, if it weren't for Lanksham breaking the rules, I'd be a well-preserved corpse drifting in space around Neptune."

Maxim picked up the explanation after. "Peacekeepers had strict, no warning, no mercy orders for protected systems. That and the unpredictability of the patrol schedules did a pretty good job at keeping those worlds safe."

"Amazing," the ambassador said. "All these centuries, sentient, spacefaring life has been all around us." He shook his head.

"Anyway. I've got some options I want to go over with the ambassador on this whole tour," Wil said. He tapped his wrist-comm, activating the bulkhead-mounted display across from the kitchenette.

"Oh no," Zephyr said.

Bennie groaned.

Nic looked at him. "What?"

"Multimedia presentation time," Maxim answered. Bennie groaned again.

"I hate you all," Wil said. He grabbed his plate and headed for the seating area. He looked over his shoulder. No one was following. "Now."

Ambassador Carlisle and Bruce exchanged a look, the former turning to Cynthia. She shook her head. "He likes to do presentations when planning heists—jobs."

Maxim looked at Bruce and nodded toward the lounge space. "Might as well go get comfortable."

Once everyone got comfortable, Wil started. "Our job is to show the ambassador around. A quick trip through the GC. Show him the highlights as we make our way toward Tarsis for the swearing-in ceremony."

Bruce Hawkins raised his hand. "We don't want to see just any planets."

The ambassador nodded his agreement. "I'd like to see what the GC has to offer. As you know, Captain, you're still the only human outside our limited sphere of influence. Earth knows only what we've been told about the GC from your reports, what the Arcadians on Oberon have shared, and what the GC representative that came to Earth brought with her. We—I—want to know what it's really like out here."

Wil nodded. "I figured." He updated the display. "We're on our way to Fury, but that's not a place you need to see."

"Why?" Carlisle asked.

"Because it sucks," Nic offered from the dining table. She and Bennie were perched on stools at the table. "So gross and boring. Sand everywhere."

Bennie glowered at his apprentice.

Wil cleared his throat. "Anyway." He updated the screen. "Fury isn't important. Mari Sava is on the way. It's interesting."

"A minor Olop colony," Gabe offered.

Wil nodded. "Nothing too fancy, but it's on the way." He

nodded to Nic. "Plus the Olop are nice. It'll be a good first stop. Nothing too over the top."

"Very well. That sounds like a good first stop," the ambassador said.

"After Fury, I figured we could head to Gulveig," Wil said. He slid the presentation to the next screen that showed a blue-green world with a thick brown band along the equatorial region.

"No," Zephyr said.

Wil frowned. "Why?"

"Hulgian colony," Gabe offered.

She consulted her wristcomm. "Fwillundrah Rao starts in a week. Every major city will be an orgy."

"That could be fun," Bennie said. Everyone turned to look at him. "What?"

"Couldn't the Hulgians be a powerful ally to Earth?" the ambassador asked. "Perhaps it would be—"

"No," Zephyr repeated.

Wil swiped the screen on his own wristcomm, updating the display. "Okay, Tro Ella." They had a pretty okay relationship with the Trollack. Wil called them catfish people, but not to their faces.

Cynthia raised her hand.

Wil sighed. "What?"

Nic leaned over to Bruce. "About now, he's wishing he'd asked for help with the presentation."

Wil heard her and glared at the young woman.

Cynthia shook her head. "Nothing. I was voting yes."

Wil took a deep breath, looked at the ceiling, and released it.

"What about Burrziira?" Bruce asked. "The Burzzad are highly advanced. They could be valuable allies to Earth."

Wil waved his hand. "Too far. Would take a few weeks at least. What about Draji Rix?"

Bennie made a choked-sounding noise. Everyone turned to look at him again. "I may have an outstanding warrant or two..." When everyone kept staring, he said, "Ten. Ten warrants."

"What the wurrin did you do to them?" Maxim asked.

"I thought he was some kind of noble protector space wizard or something?" Carlisle asked.

Zephyr leaned over. "He is, sort of. Before that he was—" she looked at Bennie, "still is—a hacker with questionable morals."

"Hey!" Bennie said. He looked indignant.

Maxim raised an eyebrow. "Really?"

"Okay, fine." The Brailack hacker reached for a piece of bacon. He made a slashing motion with his free hand. "But no Draji Rix."

WIL OFFERED Ambassador Carlisle a tumbler with a dark brown liquid in it before he sat. Everyone else was either asleep or busying themselves elsewhere in the ship. The common deck lounge was quiet. The lighting was at fifty percent.

Carlisle took a sip. "This is good." He swirled the glass, letting the single ice cube clink against the glass. "Space bourbon?"

Wil smiled. Zephyr hated it when Wil put *space* in front of things. He nodded. "D'nini Schlufluk."

"Bless you," the other man said.

Wil smiled. "No, D'nini Schlufluk is what this is." He held his glass up. "Closest I've found to bourbon." He took a sip, closing his eyes to savor the peaty flavor. "Don't ask me what it is. I have no idea."

The ambassador leaned back, absentmindedly plucking at a

thread sticking out of the arm of the sofa. "You ever think about coming home?"

"Home?"

"Earth."

Wil shook his head. "No. Been back a few times. A lot of times, actually."

"Costco runs," the other man said with a nod.

Wil dipped his head. "Nothing for me there." He waved a hand to encompass the ship. "Plus, I've got a family here. And a badass spaceship." He filed away Carlisle's use of *Costco runs* for later. It was a little too accurate. He'd have to ask James just how much information Earth's government had on him.

Carlisle ran his free hand through his mostly brown hair. Gray was appearing at his temples. Wil figured the gray would accelerate once the man settled into his role on Tarsis.

"What about you? Ready to not be on Earth?" Wil asked. He held up the bottle, offering a refill. Carlisle nodded.

"Tell me about Tarsis." Carlisle raised his glass, letting Wil fill it. "I mean beyond the official stuff."

Bennie came in from the corridor that led to engineering and the computer core. Without saying a word, he grabbed a spare glass, poured himself a drink, and hopped up onto the sofa next to the ambassador.

Wil grinned at his friend and said, "The Tarsi are assholes. They're snooty and superior." He shrugged. "But they did bring the Palorians in line and give them a purpose. Then they formed the Galactic Commonwealth." He took a sip. "And they've held it all together. Until recently."

Bennie took a sip of his drink. "Brai would be a very different if not for the Tarsi. But also, yeah, they really are assholes."

"How so?" Ambassador Carlisle asked.

The Brailack hacker took another sip. "We were constantly under threat from neighbors. We're not exactly a race of warriors. The Tarsi showed up with Peacekeepers, and like that, we had a chance to flourish. So long as we paid our taxes." He raised his glass.

Carlisle smiled. "Know what I did before being tapped to represent our home world to the rulers of the galaxy?" Wil shook his head. "In-house counsel for one of the largest pharmaceutical companies in North America. I'm used to dealing with assholes." He held his glass out.

Wil tapped his own glass against both of theirs. "To assholes." After a sip, he added, "Quite the promotion. I'm sure you'll do just fine then."

"Donations to the winner of the election have long-reaching results." Carlisle smiled.

Leaning back, Wil said, "Get in good with the Tarlak. They're cousins of the Tarsi, usually in service roles. They'll be your best allies."

"Good to know. And the council itself?"

"Bigger assholes." Wil grinned. Bennie nodded wordlessly. "Well, most, not all. Some of them are just trying to make the galaxy a better place. Others...well, politicians are the same whether they have two legs or four." The other man chuckled. "Lately, things have been a bit up in the air."

"I've heard. Rumor has it, you and your team had something to do with that?" He raised an eyebrow as he took another sip of his Schlufluk.

Wil inclined his head. "Well, we were just transportation mostly."

"Mostly?"

Wil grinned. "Mostly."

"You think the council will make the changes the Harrith are proposing?" the ambassador asked.

"If they know what's good for them. I don't think most folks know just how close to collapse the GC is," Bennie said.

Wil nodded. The other man was more informed than he had expected. While it wasn't a secret that the Harrith were helping the Commonwealth, the council was doing its best to spin the other race's involvement. "He's right. The Harrith will be excellent teachers, I think." He set his glass down. "They welcomed Earth into the fold, though, so clearly they're still making the occasional mistake."

The other man chuckled and raised his glass. "Can't keep humans out."

Will slapped his knee then stood up. "On that note, I believe my wife is alone in our berth. I should fix that."

Carlisle finished his drink and handed the tumbler back to Wil. "Indeed. I have some reading to catch up on."

Both men turned to Bennie. The Brailack downed the last of his drink and reached for the bottle. "I've got nothing else to do right now."

Wil shook his head and headed for the kitchenette, Ambassador Carlisle following him.

After putting the glassware away, Wil opened the hatch to the main staircase, letting the ambassador go up ahead of him. He looked over to the sofa and Bennie. "We'll be arriving on Mari Sava around midmorning. Don't be too hung over."

Bennie held up the tumbler without looking back at Wil.

CHAPTER THREE

MARI SAVA WAS a lush green world. Technically, it was a moon orbiting a massive gas giant. Most of the surface was covered with enormous trees. The rest was two large oceans.

The colony's spaceport was a thick permacrete slab fastened to the trunks of several dozen of the big trees that had had their tops removed. Each massive trunk was fused to the platform at a molecular level.

"This is different," Zephyr said as the *Ghost* settled onto the pad.

"They did ask our tonnage," Maxim pointed out.

"I wonder what larger ships do?" Bruce asked from his perch near the bridge hatch. The *Ghost*'s bridge had no visitor seating.

"Likely shuttle goods and people down," Bennie said. "Cargo shuttles, even fully loaded, only weigh a little more than the *Ghost*." He pointed to the primary display where a midsize cargo shuttle, slightly larger than the *Rocky Nontee*, was lifting off. Bruce half shrugged.

"These trees are something else," the ambassador said. "I

wonder what else they use them for? Do they export the lumber?"

Wil put the ship into standby. "Let's find out."

"You've never been here?" Bruce asked.

Wil shook his head. "Nope." He snapped his fingers. "No, wait. We did a job here once." He looked at Zephyr.

The Palorian woman scrunched her brow ridges, then nodded. "A hold full of...let's just say power converters."

Bennie bobbed his head. "Oh, yeah." He looked around, rubbing his little three-fingered hands together. "I wonder if... what was her name? Well, whatever it was, wonder if she still lives here."

Wil made a show of ignoring the team hacker. "Gentlemen. If you'll come with Cynthia and me. I called ahead to make an appointment with the governor."

"Very good," Ambassador Carlisle said. "Do you know the governor? Personally?"

Wil shook his head. "No. We dealt with her lieutenant the last time we were here. Nice fella. Looked a lot like Logray from *Return of the Jedi.*" He turned to Bennie. "Do not get arrested or cause a scene of any kind." He turned to Max and then Zephyr. "Can one of you?"

His first officer nodded. "Yeah."

Bennie made a face. "I do not require a chaperone. I am a fully vested Knight of Plentallus and a grown adult." He puffed out his chest.

Maxim shook his head. "Come on, Knight of Plentallus. Let's get Nic and Gabe and hit the town."

Outside the ship, a trio of Olop were waiting at the foot of the boarding ramp. When Wil led the ambassador and Bruce down, one of the little teddy bear people stepped forward. "Greetings, Captain Calder. It is pleasurable to see you and your crew again. Welcome back to Cuhroh."

Wil inclined his head. "Good to see you, too, Lieutenant Governor." He bent down to offer his arm. The smaller being clasped Wil's forearm as he clasped the furry little man's forearm. Standing, he gestured to the two men standing behind him. "Lieutenant Governor Crispin Tu'holla of the city of Cuhroh, please meet Earth's first ambassador to the GC, Branson Carlisle, and his aide Bruce Hawkins."

The lieutenant governor turned, offering a light-brown-with-white-striped arm to the ambassador. "An honor. Governor Ski'Fallo is excited to meet you." He turned. "If you'll follow me." The two other Olop who were with the lieutenant governor stepped aside. Looking over his shoulder, he said, "Dru and Vuor will remain here in case the rest of your crew needs anything."

BENNIE WATCHED WIL, Cynthia, and the two new humans depart from the top of the *Ghost*'s boarding ramp. "Okay, they're gone. Let's go." He had only taken one step before a pale purple four-fingered hand clamped onto his shoulder. "Hey!"

Maxim said, "Do you even know where you're going? Last time we were here, we barely left this district."

Bennie smirked. "If you recall, I did not stick around with you sleamohs."

Maxim crossed his arms and stared at his small friend.

"I have an innate sense of —"

"He already has the map on his wristcomm," Nic interrupted.

"Horrible child," Bennie hissed. "I should replace you with one of the new recruits."

The Olop girl rolled her eyes.

"We can offer ideas on destinations if you'd like," one of the two Olop waiting below called up. He reached up and touched one of his teddy-bear-like ears. "Couldn't help but overhear."

Maxim looked at Zephyr. "I'm going to stay aboard with Gabe. Make sure the ship's secure and catch up on some reading."

After giving her partner a kiss, the ship's first officer led Bennie and Nic down the ramp.

"Why, hello there, young one," one of the waiting Olop said. "I'm Dru." He offered his arm.

"Uh, Nic." She exchanged handshakes with both escorts.

The other escort—Vuor, he said his name was—looked Nic up and down. "Interesting outfit."

Nic puffed up a bit. "I'm a Knight of Plentallus. Trusted guardian of peace and justice in the galaxy."

Zephyr looked at Bennie, expecting him to fire off a quip to deflate the young woman's pride. Instead, he was beaming with pride.

The light-gray-furred man rocked on his heels. "Okay then."

Zephyr sighed as Nic visibly deflated. She cleared her throat. "We aren't expecting to be here long. Would it be possible to see something of your commercial core? The last time we were here, we didn't have time to explore beyond the spaceport neighborhood."

"Of course," Dru, the shorter of the two, said. He was dark brown with spots of pale orange fur.

"Can you tell us about these trees?" Zephyr asked as the group made its way to the edge of the spaceport landing pad.

Bennie fell in next to Nic. "That was well said." He moved off before she could reply.

"Oh, yes," Dru replied. "The hoskee trees, native to Olop-nal, grow only in very specific conditions. When our people learned of this moon and its soil composition, we seeded the entire surface several cycles before the first colonial transport arrived."

The edge of the landing platform had no railings. An open-top air car waited, hovering, at the edge of the pad. The group made its way one by one into the vehicle.

Once seated, Zephyr asked, "How long ago was that? These trees are enormous."

Vuor, at the vehicle's controls, looked over his shoulder. "Two hundred orbits."

"So short a time."

Dru bobbed his head. "Hoskee trees grow quickly, reaching full maturity in as little as one hundred orbits."

"How do you build if the trees are still growing?" Bennie asked.

The air car pulled away from the landing area, dropping straight down—to the shock of all of its passengers, except Nic, who seemed to be enjoying the plummet—before accelerating toward a clump of the thick trunks.

"Hoskee trees reach their full thickness halfway through their maturation cycle. So, we're able to build into them as well as anchor things to them at that time. We just plan for early construction to spend the next fifty to one hundred orbits rising higher off the ground," Vuor said. "It can take some planning, to be sure," he added.

The air car wove between several trunks that looked like they'd had apartments and commercial buildings carved into them.

Dru looked over at Nic. "I imagine life on a ship must not afford you many opportunities to climb."

She shrugged. "Not really. I lived in Dae before this."

The other Olop nodded. The capital of Olopnal was as much glass and metal as it was nature and hoskee trees. A true blending of nature and modern technology.

CUHROH'S GOVERNMENT complex was a series of structures strung between several massive hoskee tree trunks. The trip from the spaceport to the complex took the group through myriad districts, some entirely built into the enormous trees, others completely modern looking glass and metal structures supported on and between the massive trees.

"And this is a client colony?" Ambassador Carlisle asked.

Tu'holla nodded. "Our home world, Olopnal, is about eighty or so light years from here. There are many Olop colonies. Mari Sava is the most distant, however."

"I see. And do you export the lumber from these, what did you call them?"

"Hoskee trees."

"Yes, hoskee trees. Given how much weight these trees can support, I would assume lumber made from them would be like steel beams."

The lieutenant governor again nodded. "We do. The southern continent is reserved for lumber production." He turned in his seat. "Many Olop vessels are made from hoskee lumber."

"Vessels like spaceships?" Wil asked. That was news to him. He knew that ships in the GC were made from a variety of materials, but he always assumed they were all metal alloys of some sort. He realized he'd never actually seen an Olop ship before.

"Indeed. Our freighters and sector security vessels in particular. All hoskee lumber. It is, as you say, Ambassador, quite strong."

"I didn't know that," Cynthia said. "You mentioned it taking two hundred orbits. How do you sustain the production?"

The lieutenant governor inclined his head. "Indeed. Our

farming operation rotates crops. But also, don't forget how large a hoskee is. We get quite a bit of lumber from each tree." Turning in his chair, he said,33 "Here we are."

The luxury transport came to a halt and then lowered to the small landing pad attached to the building. Their pad had space enough for a dozen air cars similar to the one they were in.

Governor Ski'Fallo met the group at the top of the steps. "Ambassador Carlisle, it's a pleasure to meet you." She smiled, her white teeth contrasting with her jet-black fur.

"The honor is all mine, Madame Governor," Carlisle said. He introduced Bruce and then asked if there was some place the two could speak. He looked at Bruce. "I won't need you for this; feel free to remain with Captain Calder and the others."

Wil looked at Bruce and caught the slightest flicker of annoyance on the other man's face. The aide had expected to be in the meeting. Was he normally included in these types of meetings? Wil shrugged. "Come on. Let's find a place to grab a drink." He looked at Cynthia and added, "I bet space teddy bears have happy hour." He ducked almost in time to avoid her punch. "What was that for?"

"That was for Zephyr," she said with a crooked grin.

THE TRIO LEFT the governmental center, following the winding suspension walkways that wove between the giant hoskee trees. They passed countless Olop as they went until finally Wil stopped a passing woman. "Excuse me, is there a bar or restaurant anywhere nearby?"

She looked Wil up and down and then said, "Two levels up." She pointed behind him toward an open-air lift of some sort. They had walked right past it without noticing. "Then I think you'll come this direction and should see it."

While Wil and the Olop woman chatted, Cynthia turned to Bruce. "How long have you worked for the ambassador?"

Wil passed them. "This-a-way."

Everyone fell in behind him.

Bruce turned to Cynthia next to him. "A little over a year. I joined his team when he learned he'd be going off-world to represent Earth."

Wil looked at the open-air framework, marveling that they'd walked right by it. He spotted the controls where the old woman said they'd be. After pressing the button, he watched as a cage like contraption rose from below.

"What's that like?" Cynthia asked as they all boarded the lift.

As the platform rose, she continued, "Being the first official off-world mission."

They followed Wil to a structure carved into the tree. He nodded appreciatively. The Wood Lizard was just as divey as Wil liked his bars.

The barkeep looked up when the group entered. "Welcome, travelers." He grinned, bearing tiny sharp teeth. "I've always wanted to say that." He waved into the room. "Take a seat wherever you like. None will be comfortable."

Bruce looked at the chairs around the table Wil selected. They, and the table itself, looked as if they'd been made for children. He looked around. Small furry children.

Cynthia and Wil each took a seat and looked at Bruce. "Sit."

The bartender arrived. "What can I get you all?'

Bruce eased himself into the remaining seat. "What's good?"

The little man nodded and left.

Bruce looked at the others, his mouth working like a goldfish. "I...uh. Didn't expect that."

Wil shrugged. "I'm sure it'll be fine."

Cynthia leaned forward, her elbows on the table. "You were saying? The first off-world mission?"

The ambassadorial aide nodded. "It's exciting. I'm eager to see what the galaxy has to offer humanity."

Her ears twitched in a way that Wil recognized as irritation. He saw her tail jerk left and right a few times. Having seen both signals often enough, he leaned away from his wife. She set her glass down. "I don't know that I'd look at it like that. Humanity would do well to learn from those who've been around a little while longer."

Bruce crossed his arms, ready to reply when the proprietor returned with a tray of drinks. He handed one to each member of the group. "I think you'll enjoy these."

Bruce looked at his glass.

"A radiant dream," the Olop man said. Then he turned and left.

Bruce turned back to his glass. The drink was blue with splashes of yellow and orange that seemed to move about of their own accord. With a shrug, he took a swig.

Wil looked at him. He nodded as he picked at something on his slacks with his free hand. "Of course. Earth has much to learn. But we also have much to share."

The Tygran woman pursed her lips but said nothing.

CHAPTER FOUR

"THIS IS INCREDIBLE. They hollowed out this tree and built the market inside it." Bennie spun in a slow circle as the group walked through the main entrance of what their guides called the most spectacular shopping district the city had to offer. They weren't exaggerating.

"This grove of hoskee trees is one of the oldest in the city," Dru offered. "This shopping center is only ten cycles old. Originally, this tree and the tree connected to it were the government center. This stand of trees was the center of the city."

Vuor nodded. "I used to live in tree one-two. It was not a glamorous residence."

Nic scrunched up her face. "Tree one-two?"

The other two Olop nodded. "This is tree one-one," Dru said, waving to encompass the market and the tree they were in. "From that tree," he gestured toward where tree one must be, "the original settlers counted outward in concentric circles. The current governmental complex sits across trees eight-six and eight-seven."

"I didn't notice that this forest was particularly circular," Bennie said.

Vuor and Dru both chuckled. "It is not. The original addressing system was not the most well thought out, but it stuck." The shorter of the two offered his wristcomm screen. On it was a series of wobbly-misshapen concentric circles. "It does, however, support a cottage industry of mapmakers."

"You ain't kidding," Bennie said.

The group stopped at a vendor. Vuor picked up several cups. He handed them out. "Mojupi berry juice."

Nic's eyes went wide. "I haven't had this since I was a kid."

"You're still a kid," Bennie said. She made a rude gesture. He looked around. "Anyway, where's the good stuff?"

"The good stuff?" Dru repeated. He rubbed his chin. "Well, two levels up is mostly homewares, and there's a vendor that makes the most amazing rugs—"

"No," Bennie interrupted.

"Oh, well," Vuor looked around. "On level minus three, there's a great clothing vendor that—"

"No." Bennie shook his head. "The weapons, tech, that kind of thing."

The two Olop government workers exchanged a look. Zephyr sighed. Nic rolled her eyes.

Bennie wouldn't rest until he found whatever passed for a black market on this world.

The Brailack hacker looked around and then smiled. "There we go." He headed off without waiting for the others.

Zephyr sighed and turned to their guides. "He's eccentric."

"Heard that!" Bennie shouted. He reached a ramp that spiraled up and down the hollowed-out trunk. Each level had a landing. He set off downward, pushing his way through the crowd of Olop moving between levels.

Nic was following the group, taking in the sights. She'd been a little kid when her parents died. The three of them had lived in Dae her whole life up to that point. Her memories of the city were vague at best.

The town her grandmother lived in was much smaller. This was more Olop in one place than she'd seen in one place in a long time. Her train of thought was derailed when someone bumped into her.

"Oh, excuse me," she stammered.

The woman she collided with smiled. "It's quite all right, youngling." She cocked her head. "Are you all right? Are you lost?"

Nic shook her head. "No, ma'am. Just a little overwhelmed. It's been a while since I've seen so many Olop in one place." As far as she knew, there were no Olop living on Fury. None that she'd ever seen, at least.

The woman smiled. She was wearing a smart business suit, her fur trimmed and brushed smooth. "This market is one of the largest in the city now. Lots of people." She looked Nic up and down. "That's an interesting outfit."

Nic's facial fur rippled. "I'm a Knight of Plentallus."

"That sounds fun, like an after-school activity," the woman said, glancing at the luxury model wristcomm on her arm. She seemed to have already lost interest in Nic.

"I'd better catch up with my friends," Nic said. She added, "It was nice to meet you."

"You too, dear," the woman said, hurrying off in her original direction.

Nic headed down the ramp, spotting Zephyr, the tallest person in the market by far. The group was two levels down the ramp. It looked like they were nearing what seemed to be the lowest level.

She shook her head. Of course, the sketchy part of the market would be at the lowest level. Olop liked to climb, so she guessed it made sense that the black market or whatever they called it would be where few Olop would want to go.

She heard Zephyr ask Dru, "What is this?"

The Olop man looked around. "I think it must have been where the environmental systems were kept when this was the governmental complex." He looked around. There were half as many stalls as on the upper levels. "Why is it so dark down here?"

Bennie pointed to the thin material that was draped from hooks around the enormous trunk's inner perimeter. "Keeps folks from noticing what's going on without actually hiding it." He nodded. "Clever."

The team's hacker walked over to a stall and immediately launched into some sort of negotiation.

Dru turned to Zephyr. "He's interesting."

She shook her head. "That's one word for it." She spied Nic joining them. "Thought you got lost."

The young Olop shook her head. "Just taking it all in. Nothing like Dae."

Vuor nodded. "Indeed. Olopnal, for all its glory, is far more industrialized than many like. Most people here are from homeworld. They wanted something a little closer to our ancestral roots."

Nic looked around. The stalls were freestanding but secured to the trunk's inner wall. She'd seen and been inside hoskee trees on Olopnal. Dae had several older neighborhoods of the massive trees. But their guide was right; there were more trees in this city than likely still remained on the entire Olop home planet.

Zephyr looked at her wristcomm. "Wil says it's time to go." She whistled. "We're leaving."

"I'll catch up!" Bennie shouted, not taking his eyes off the vendor. They were engaged in what looked like a staring contest. She shook her head. He'd return to the ship with some random, and entirely useless, piece of technology that he got for a bargain. There were even odds he'd leave it at the spaceport.

Turning to Vuor and Dru, she said, "This has been enlightening. Thank you."

The pair bowed. Dru said, "Of course. We'll take you back to the spaceport."

"WHERE HAVE YOU BEEN?" Wil asked as Bennie crested the cargo boarding ramp, walking into the *Ghost*'s cargo bay. "And what the hell is that?"

The Brailack hacker was carrying what Wil thought was a vacuum cleaner crossed with a guitar.

Bennie set the thing down. "I don't recall what she said it was called."

"Then why did you..." Wil shook his head. "Never mind. Stow it and get ready for departure."

Bennie gave a mock salute and picked the whatever-it-was up. Wil sighed, watching the team's hacker cross the hold. He looked at the ceiling. "Zee, go ahead and start the preflight."

The overhead speaker crackled. "Copy that."

Bruce, leaning against the staircase that connected the hold with the common deck above, said, "Run a pretty loose ship, Captain." He was smirking as he glanced up at the mid-level landing where Bennie was struggling with his latest acquisition.

"Not a military ship, Mr. Hawkins," Wil said with a smile. He tapped his chest. "Not a military man, either, for that matter." He started up the stairs. "Pretty sure you knew that, though."

"Why do you say that?" Hawkins asked, following Wil up the steps.

Wil caught up to Bennie, picked up the whatever-it-was, and continued on up to the B deck hatch.

Wil opened the hatch. "I assume someone back home must have read you in."

Bennie followed Wil through the hatch. "I'll take my…my… Just give it to me." He held out both hands.

Wil handed the space vacuum to Bennie and then turned to Hawkins. "Right? CIA, FBI, some other alphabet agency? Whatever the world government created."

The ambassadorial aide smiled. "Guilty. We got a briefing from some agency or another." He smiled. "They know a surprising amount about all of you."

From the sofa, Nic looked up from the tablet she had propped up on her knees. "What'd they say about me?"

Bruce shook his head. "Nothing. They didn't mention you."

Maxim chuckled. Nic spun her head to look at him. He fell silent.

Bruce waved his hand. "Nothing personal, I'm sure." He turned to Wil, voice lowered. "Kinda weird you've got a kid on your crew."

"I'm not a kid!" she bellowed.

Wil gave a half shrug. "She's an old soul."

"Captain, we're cleared to depart," Zephyr announced over the ceiling speakers.

Wil looked up. "I'll be right there." He turned to Bruce and then Nic. "Behave." He walked to the forward hatch that led to the corridor that connected the forward and aft sections of the ship. The thick doors slid apart.

As the doors slid closed, securing the common deck, Bruce turned to Maxim. "Why does he look at the ceiling like that?"

The big Palorian shrugged. "It's a Wil thing."

"THE KID WAS RIGHT," Bruce said. The familiar brown sphere of Fury was growing on the main display at the front of the bridge. "It is ugly."

Ambassador Carlisle and his aide were standing on either side of the bridge hatch. The former had wanted to see the planet that the first human to leave the Earth called home. He was not impressed.

Wil nodded. "She ain't much to look at, but she's home." He adjusted their approach as Fury's space control network came into range. The ghostly green navigation aid was visible on the main screen to guide him down to the surface.

"Space control has asked us to give them an orbit to clear a freighter that's holding things up down there."

Wil grunted. The purchase of their building and its spaceport rights was supposed to keep these types of delays from happening. "Sure thing." He adjusted their course, putting the *Ghost* into a holding orbit.

"This happen often?" Bruce asked Cynthia.

She shook her head. "No. Our building has spaceport rights. We've only gotten hung up like this once or twice before. Usually when some freighter captain takes on more weight than he can safely lift with. Messes up the traffic pattern until they get it sorted. Space control doesn't like much traffic in the air so they can get the offender off the deck without any further delay."

He nodded. "Makes sense."

Maxim stood up. "Anyone want a snack?"

"I'd take some yipsee strips," Wil said.

The big man nodded and left the bridge.

Everyone was relaxing, enjoying yipsee strips and a grum when Cynthia's console beeped. She looked down. "We're cleared through to the building," Cynthia said. She added, "With space control's thanks."

"About time," Wil replied.

"Doors at home are opening," Zephyr announced.

Wil guided the *Ghost* into the upper atmosphere. Plasma streamers began to form against the forward shields. "Switching over the atmospherics," he announced a moment before the twin rumbling booms echoed through the ship.

"What's Fury's defensive posture?" Bruce asked.

Zephyr turned in her chair. "While they're not an actual member world of the GC, there is a small Peacekeeper garrison."

"No orbital weapons? Ground to orbit?"

Maxim turned. "You planning on invading?"

"What? No, I was just curious. If they're not a GC member, why do the Peacekeepers have a presence?"

Zephyr shrugged. "Common practice. Fury barely has a functional government. It's kind of a," she looked at Wil, "what did you call it?"

"Rest stop," he said without taking his eyes off the main display.

She nodded. "A rest stop. Most of those who reside on Fury are here because they have no place else to go. In such cases, the Peacekeepers figure that a minor presence can have a calming influence."

Bruce gave a slow nod. "That works?"

"Why do people not want to live here?" the ambassador asked. "I mean, notwithstanding the obvious desert world stuff."

Bennie turned. "Because it sucks. It's dirty. There's little in the way of industry. Most folks here don't have much money. They're all criminals."

"Present company included," Wil quipped. The *Ghost* trembled as it passed through some rough air. "Repulsors coming online now," he added, pushing the repulsorlift control lever forward.

Once the *Ghost* entered the atmosphere, she mostly just fell. The atmospheric engines could brute force the ship into flight on a limited basis until the ship was close enough to the surface for the repulsorlifts in her engine nacelles to have something to push against.

Cynthia watched her husband guide the ship around in a wide arc on a heading giving the spaceport a wide berth and lining them up for the hangar. Turning to the two men near her station at the bridge hatch, she said, "Fury is a safe harbor." She glared at Bennie. "Someplace for people with no place else to go, to go."

"And there's no taxes," Bennie said.

"There very much are taxes," Zephyr said with a sigh.

THE *GHOST* CAME to a stop outside the massive warehouse, her repulsors humming as she balanced on the invisible pillars of energy holding the small warship aloft. The warehouse's large access doors were already fully retracted, waiting on the ship's arrival.

Will eased the ship around one hundred and eighty degrees before adjusting the repulsors to slide the ship backward into the hangar.

"Beep, beep, beep," he said as the ship made its way.

"Don't mind him; he thinks that's funny," Zephyr said.

Bruce chuckled. "Like a delivery truck."

Wil turned, a wide grin on his face. "See, he gets me."

"I propose a new company policy regarding the maximum number of humans on the ship at one time," Bennie said.

"Seconded," Maxim said.

"All in favor?" Zephyr asked.

"Next hand that goes up gets shot," Wil growled.

Bennie's half-raised arm fell to his side.

Wil turned his attention back to bringing the ship's rearward motion to a stop. He had an aft-facing camera view on the main display screen. The automated system of approach lights that Gabe built into the rear wall of the hangar was solid green. He pulled the repulsorlift power lever towards him, reducing power.

Three meters from the ground, he flipped a switch, deploying the landing gear. Articulated birdlike legs unfolded from compartments on either side of the main body in the wing roots.

The ship touched down, the gear groaning as the full weight of the Ankarran Raptor Model 89 settled on them. After a slight forward and backward tilt, the ship settled, her center of gravity establishing itself.

"And we're home," Wil announced. He powered down the flight systems and put his station into standby mode.

Over the loudspeaker, Gabe announced, "Reactor is in standby mode."

"Nice flying, Captain," Ambassador Carlisle said.

Wil nodded, a grin reaching ear to ear.

As he exited the bridge, Bennie said, "He's gonna be unbearable after this."

Wil scowled but turned to Zephyr. "Zee, you mind showing the ambassador and his aide to the conference room?"

The Palorian woman nodded.

Once everyone was off the bridge, Wil walked over to the communication station. He tapped a few commands and turned to face the forward display.

The screen came to life.

"Well, well. The Calder Taxi Company," James Hawthorne said with a smile.

Wil shook his head. "I can already tell I'm going to hate you for hooking us up with this gig."

"Where you at now?"

"Fury."

James' mouth fell open. "You took Earth's first representative to the Galactic Commonwealth, to Fury? The—what did you call it—butthole of the galaxy?"

Wil smiled. "That was before I was a property owner." He leaned forward in Cynthia's chair. "I'm respectable now."

The man on the screen laughed. "So, how's it going? Assume you're not calling to tell me you got the ambassador or his aide killed."

"Not yet, no. But the day's young." Wil got up and moved to his seat. "Just wanted to say hi."

"Bullshit you did," the other man said with a chuckle.

Wil made a face. "Fine. What can you tell me about the ambassador and his henchman?"

His friend adjusted himself in his seat. "What's to say? Carlisle's a bit of an unknown. Big donor to Douse's campaign. Seems like a standup fella."

Wil nodded slowly. "Yeah, he does. That worries me."

Hawthorne shook his head. "So suspicious."

Wil shrugged. "And Hawkins?"

It was James' turn to shrug. "Never heard of him before he got attached to the mission. Met him at a mixer before they left for Oberon."

Wil took that in. "What's your gut think?"

James leaned forward. "Is there a problem?"

Wil shook his head as he shrugged. "No?" His friend's eyebrows both rose. "Nothing specific, but I don't know. He feels both over- and underqualified to be an ambassadorial aide. If that makes sense."

Wil's longtime friend gave a nod of his own. "Sure. I mean,

he probably is both of those things depending on the situation. Shit, the ambassador probably is, too. We're not talking about a cushy job in some European country or something. This job is the face of Earth and Earth's interests in a place with hundreds if not thousands of aliens with a lot more experience."

Wil thought that over. "You're right. I'm probably just being weird about it."

His friend chuckled. "Well, that would track, you being weird." Wil made a show of slowly raising his hand then his middle finger, causing his friend to laugh even harder.

Wil leaned back. "Okay, enough of that. Last time we chatted, you mentioned you were seeing someone. How's that going?"

His friend blushed.

CHAPTER FIVE

WIL STEPPED off the *Ghost*'s boarding ramp as Gabe and Nic were bringing over a gravlift work platform. "What're you two up to? We're not planning to be here very long."

Nic was grinning. "Gabe said I could help him."

"With?" Wil crossed his arms over his chest.

Gabe positioned the lift. "During our departure from Mari Sava, the engineering computer logged an imbalance in the starboard repulsorlift."

Wil looked up at the massive engine nacelle overhead. The repulsor emitter in the forward section looked fine to him. "Serious?" He had felt a little waver on their takeoff and again upon arriving home and guiding the ship into the hangar.

The engineering droid shook his head. "No. Nic and I should have it repaired before you are ready to depart."

"Okay, cool. Let me know if you need anything. Don't want to be here any longer than necessary." As the two nodded, he turned and headed into the building.

Cynthia was waiting for him in the prep area. "I'm going to start loading the ship. I ordered a few things on our way in. They'll arrive in a tock or so."

He leaned in for a kiss and then said, "Sounds good. Hoping we don't have to be here long."

She nodded and headed back into the main hangar complex.

Just before the door slid closed, something heavy clanged to the ground. He heard Nic say, "Oops. Sorry."

Wil was walking into the conference room after stopping to grab a bottle of water from the small kitchenette off the hangar when the room's lighting dimmed and the trim lighting around the ceiling's edge turned red. The sound of metal shutters engaging over the few windows in the building sounded through the building, followed by the clack of thick bolts sliding in place over the front doors.

Zephyr was on her feet in a flash, her pulse pistol up and sweeping the room.

Wil was a beat behind his executive officer, his bottle of water rolling under the conference table as he swept his pistol around the room. He glanced at their guests, noticing that Bruce Hawkins was also on his feet.

"What's going on?" Ambassador Carlisle asked. His eyes darted between the three other people in the room. "Are we... you, under attack?"

Zephyr looked at Wil, who shrugged. "Beats me." He raised his arm, opening the team comm suite. "What's going—"

Maxim burst into the front office area. "We've been robbed." He joined Wil and Zephyr in the small foyer outside the conference room.

A few seconds later, Bennie came down the same stairs, beam saber humming. "What the wurrin is going on?" He looked around, catching sight of his teammates.

"Why are you in your underwear?" Wil shouted, holding a hand up in front of his face. Zephyr turned around to face the other way.

"I was changing clothes! You're lucky the alarm didn't go off thirty seconds later." He scanned the area as he deactivated his saber. With a *snap-hiss*, the beam of energy snapped out of existence.

"I don't care if we're under attack, go—" Wil started.

"What the grolack?" Nic said as she and Gabe came in from the hangar, her own crimson bladed beam saber humming away. She snapped her eyes shut. Gabe was standing behind her, arms raised, forearm blasters deployed, optic sensors glowing red. Wil spied Cynthia behind the pair, her sidearm drawn.

Wil looked at Bennie and pointed at the stairs. "Go put clothes on." He turned to Maxim. "Care to explain?" Turning to Gabe, he nodded. The alarm fell silent, and the lighting throughout the building returned to normal.

Maxim turned to Wil, his face pained. Wil's eyes went wide. His friend gave him the smallest of nods. Wil cocked his head, eyebrow raised. Maxim's eyes also went wide, and he jerked his head down once. Wil groaned.

Bennie vanished up the stairs, shouting, "Gabe, meet me upstairs; we can review the logs."

"Please get dressed first," Gabe called. Bennie didn't reply.

"Okay, well, that was exciting," Wil said. He gestured to the stairs. "Assuming Bennie is presentable, let's go upstairs and figure out what's up."

THE SECOND FLOOR of Rogue Enterprises was mainly storerooms and some homemade lab spaces that Bennie and Gabe had set up for themselves. A thick sparring mat like the one in the cargo hold aboard the *Ghost*, but twice as big, occupied the northwest corner. Racks of practice weapons lined two sides of the sparring area.

Bennie met them on the stairs, coming down from the third floor where the living spaces were. "Good news. Nothing of mine is missing." He was fully dressed in his earth-toned tunic and trousers.

"Did you check your stash room before or after you put pants on?" Cynthia asked.

Bennie held up his arm, showing his wristcomm. "Inventory app. Real time." He winked. Cynthia rolled her eyes. Pointing to a door, he said, "Let's look at the logs. If someone got in, I'm a little concerned that neither Gabe nor I got an alert."

Gabe inclined his head. "That is troubling, to be sure."

Cynthia looked at the two human guests. "Why don't we stay out here? It's not a very big room." She tilted her head toward the training area.

What passed for the company security room was a storage closet with displays covering the entire back wall. Bennie sat on the only chair at a terminal. He immediately set about pulling up camera feeds. His fingers were a blur as he worked. Each screen had a view from one of the dozens of cameras around the building.

Outside in the second floor's open area, Bruce leaned over to Cynthia. "This a common thing? Being robbed? You all said this planet wasn't the best, but I assumed it wasn't, you know, robberies all the time. I mean, if someone robs you guys, what's everyone else doing for protection?"

She shook her head. "First time, actually." She peered across the floor into the security room and then turned back. "Believe it or not, this is the good part of town." She smiled. "Did you ever hear about the time we rescued this cranky drunk wizard? *That* was a bad part of town."

Bruce shook his head. "A wizard?"

Her ears twitched as she grinned. "Not a real wizard. He

was a Knight of Plentallus. The last Knight of Plentallus, it turned out."

The ambassador hitched a thumb over his shoulder. "Like Bennie, that kind of Knight of Plentallus?"

The Tygran woman nodded. "Yup. During the mission, Bennie took a liking to the old codger." She shook her head, remembering that job, Jarek Ruus finding them in a bar and hiring them to help him finish his final quest. "The universe is weird."

"What?" Bruce asked.

She shook her head again. "Nothing. Anyway. I'm sure they'll figure out who broke in and what, if anything, they took."

IN THE SECURITY OFFICE, Zephyr leaned over Bennie's shoulder. She pointed at one of the wall-mounted displays. "Uh, what was that?"

"What was what?" Bennie asked without looking up from his work. The display flipped to another camera. The screen had briefly shown Bennie slipping out of what looked like a secret panel in the hallway between Maxim and Zephyr's quarters and Wil and Cynthia's.

"You know damn well, you little sneak," she growled.

"There!" Nic pointed to an exterior view on a different display. She hadn't seen what Zephyr saw and, knowing Bennie, didn't want to know what the Palorian woman had seen. On the screen, someone in a black tactical outfit was kneeling next to the control panel at the rear of the building.

Zephyr leaned down. "Whatever illicit goods, physical or digital, will be gone by the time we're done with this job." Bennie swallowed and gave a tight nod. His skin was a paler shade of green than normal. "And I'll be filling that crawlspace with expandofoam, regardless." She stood and took a step back.

Maxim looked at her. "What was it?" She shook her head.

Ambassador Carlisle watched the exchange and asked, "What did I—"

"Leave it," Zephyr said.

"Moving on," Wil said. He hadn't seen whatever it was, either, but was certain he wouldn't approve. He pointed to the figure on the screen. "Anyone we know?"

"Average build, bipedal," Maxim said. "Not much to work with. No extra limbs or other features."

Wil nodded. "Be easier if he had four arms or wings. Can't be many races in those categories."

Zephyr shrugged. "More than you might think, but yeah."

He turned. "Really?" She nodded. "Huh."

"Anyway," Bennie said as he followed the intruder with cameras as they made their way through the building, room by room. The intruder moved from floor to floor, stopping at every door, looking in every room.

"He was busy," Nic said as the intruder entered her room. "Hey!" She turned and bolted out of the room.

Bruce pulled Ambassador Carlisle aside. "These are the professionals the government hired?" The other man shrugged. "Unbelievable."

Bennie turned. "Hey. This system is top of the line. Whoever that," he jabbed a finger at the dark-clad figure currently exiting Nic's room, "is, he knew what he was doing and probably had help."

Gabe inclined his head. "Bennie is correct. Whoever that is, they broke through security that rivals most Peacekeeper facilities."

Bruce shrugged. "Then that guy is good."

Gabe made no move but said, "Indeed."

The group watched as the intruder moved through the building. Only upon leaving Max and Zephyr's room did they have something in their hands.

Wil glanced at Maxim, who gave a terse nod. "Indeed."

Zephyr turned to her partner. "What's that box? I don't recognize it."

Maxim opened his mouth and then closed it again.

WIL SMACKED his palm against his forehead. "Damnit." Everyone turned to look at him. "Max, was that the...that... thing, uh, you know?"

Maxim stared at him blankly, then his brow ridges shot up. "Yes! Yes, it is the...uh...oh—"

"How'd they know it would be in our room?" Zephyr asked, cutting off her betrothed. She turned to Maxim. "Why was it in our room?"

"What was it?" Gabe asked. Everyone looked at him. "I can be curious."

"More importantly. Is it valuable?" Bennie asked with a glint in his eye.

Wil held up his hands. "It's, uh, kinda sensitive." Quickly adding, "But we have to get it back. Fast."

Bennie nodded slowly, a deadly serious look on his face. "A weird human sex thing."

Everyone turned to him. "What? No!" Wil said. "Why would you even—You know what? Never mind." He ran both hands through his hair and then turned to Gabe. "How'd they get in?" He hoped that would forestall any further inquiry from the others.

Maxim looked at the team's Brailack hacker. "Why would I want anything to do with human sex stuff?" He shook his head.

Bennie shrugged. "You two are friends."

Maxim's mouth fell open.

Zephyr made a noise. "Anyway."

Ignoring them, Gabe pointed to one of the displays. It was showing a log file. "I believe I have pieced together the hack they used to gain entry into the building." When everyone stared at him, the droid shook his head once. The log file moved to one of the more central monitors; several other files that Wil couldn't decipher joined it. "The intruder used an incredibly sophisticated software suite that disabled all of the DNA scanners, while spoofing the sensors so that the building's management suite did not notice."

Wil looked at the two Palorians, then Gabe. "Sure, that makes sense."

Gabe turned to the captain, optic sensors whirring as they focused.

Bennie picked up where Gabe left off. "Yeah, he's right." He pointed to another text file. "Once inside, he installed a hack," he turned to the team, "which shouldn't have been possible. Once he got that in, he had full control of the building's systems. That's why we didn't get any alerts, and most of the security logs were blank."

"He wanted to erase his presence," the team's executive officer said.

Bennie and Gabe both nodded. The latter added, "Indeed. The hack looks like it was designed to back out of our systems, erasing any sign of it, or his," he pointed to the frozen frame of video, "presence."

Bennie smiled. "Lucky for us, there was no way he could have planned for the improvements I've made to the security system over the years."

"Improvements," Gabe said in a tone that sounded like he thought they were anything but.

Bennie squinted up at the engineering droid. "Anyway. With all the changes I've made, the hack couldn't do its job. Not fully."

Zephyr looked at the ceiling, then turned to the screens. "So that's good, right? We have clues."

Gabe inclined his head. "Yes."

"We know the exact day and time this all went down. We should be able to do a lot with that information," Maxim offered, adding, "We need to get it back." Zephyr turned to him. "I mean. It's obviously important...to Wil."

"Yeah. He's right," Wil said. "We'll need to track this scumbag down." He slammed a fist into his open palm.

Zephyr cocked one eyebrow ridge but said nothing.

"NO DISRESPECT—I'M sure whatever was stolen is tremendously valuable, but you have a job you've been paid quite well to do," Ambassador Carlisle said. The team and their guests were seated around the conference table on the first floor.

Maxim and Gabe had just walked in, having finished a full sweep of the building. The former said, "Nothing out of place."

Gabe nodded. "The building is secure."

Wil nodded then turned back to their guests. "And we're going to do the job," Wil insisted. "Max, Bennie, and Nic will track down our mystery visitor. The rest of us will continue the job." He grinned. "You're only really missing out on Max's company. Bennie sucks, and Nic is a lot like him." He winked at the young Olop. "No offense."

"I used to think you were cute." She crossed her arms and leaned back in her chair.

"You did?" He leaned forward in his seat.

"Is that really the important topic here?" Cynthia said. Wil blushed. Zephyr shook her head, looking away to hide her grin. She'd almost forgotten that the young Olop woman had told her that.

Cynthia continued. "We've got another ship. The four of them can join up with us along the way, when they finish their mission."

The ambassador and his aide exchanged a look before the older of the two finally nodded. "Very well. We can still be on our way today?"

Cynthia nodded. "Of course." She looked at Zephyr, who nodded. "The *Ghost* is almost ready to depart." She cocked her head, sporting a big grin. "I can escort you aboard, if you'd like."

Wil turned to Bennie. "Better get anything you need off the *Ghost*."

The Brailack hacker nodded. He still didn't understand what the urgency was but knew something was up. He could spot something hinky from a plorith away. Wil and Maxim were up to something. He didn't like it when others were up to things that he wasn't involved in.

He turned to Nic. "Come on, apprentice." The young woman scowled as she hopped out of the chair.

Once the others had left the conference room, leaving only Wil and Maxim, the big Palorian leaned into his friend. "Thanks."

"Sure, pal. Hope you all can find our visitor." He patted Maxim's shoulder as he passed. "Your life may depend on it." He chuckled.

"Not funny," Maxim shouted at Wil's back.

Over his shoulder, Wil added, "Oh, and if you can come up with whatever MacGuffin it is you're chasing and let me know. My wife's gonna ask the moment we lift off."

"I will do my best," Maxim shouted at his departing friend.

CHAPTER SIX

WIL STOOD at the bottom of the *Ghost*'s cargo ramp as Cynthia guided a gravsled loaded with consumables up the ramp. The low thrum of the ship's idling engines filled the space.

He looked at Gabe, then up at the starboard engine nacelle. "You're sure you fixed that thing?"

The droid looked up at the nacelle and then down at Wil, who stood a good ten inches shorter than him. "Yes. The diagnostics returned no error codes." He cocked his head. "The ship is in excellent condition."

"You're sure?"

"If I am mistaken, the likely outcome would be our fiery death, in which case you will have little time to be upset with me." The droid tilted his head to the other side, optics spinning as he looked at the captain.

The gravsled slid down the ramp unattended. Once it reached the permacrete, it banked to the right, sliding into the docking station against the wall. Wil watched it, then turned back to Gabe but realized he'd forgotten the retort he had lined up, so he just shook his head.

"Our odds of not dying are increased with my being aboard the ship," Gabe added, hoping it helped.

"We're all set," Cynthia said from the top of the ramp.

Wil nodded. "Are the VIPs all settled?"

She nodded. "The ambassador is his berth. Bruce is inside the building somewhere. Probably looking under the couches or in the closets."

"Okay, I'll find him," Wil said. He patted his mechanical friend on the shoulder as he turned to head back into the building proper. "Glad to have you with us on the A-Team."

Ignoring his friend, Gabe looked up at the ship's cargo bay. "Do you require anything, Cynthia?"

She shook her head. "No. I think we're good. Zee is on the bridge getting us clearance."

The droid nodded. "Very well. I will be in engineering." He headed the rest of the way through the cargo hold, toward the stairs.

Cynthia watched him climb the stairs then turned to look around the cargo hold. Everything they'd brought aboard was secured to the bulkheads and tie-downs that were evenly spaced around the deck plating. Several cargo modules were arrayed like a wall between the sparring mat and the forward section of the hold.

WIL LEANED into the conference room. "You ready?" Bruce slammed his laptop closed. Wil raised an eyebrow. "You found the Wi-Fi."

The other man smiled. "Just checking the ambassador's messages and downloading the latest briefing documents from the State Department." He waved a hand. "Amazing I can open a laptop on this world and access email from Earth." He shook his head. "Still no jetpacks though."

Wil smiled. "Right? Like, jetpacks are so hard?"

"You'd crash into buildings," Maxim said from behind Wil.

"Just that one time." Turning to Bruce, "They're everywhere out here, by the way."

"Really?"

Wil nodded. "Lots of fun. Crashing into buildings notwithstanding." He shrugged. "You ready?" The other man nodded as he stood and collected the laptop. "Get to the *Ghost*. The ambassador is already aboard. Cynthia can help get you situated."

Once the ambassador's aide left, Wil turned to the big Palorian. "Good luck. If you end up killing Bennie, I'll totally understand."

Maxim grinned.

THE *GHOST* ROARED off into Fury's late afternoon sky. Within minutes, the glow of the atmospheric engines was barely visible.

Maxim turned to Bennie and Nic. "I have to tell you something."

"We don't like Wil, either. We support your move to take over," Bennie said without missing a beat.

"I like Wil," Nic said.

Maxim frowned. "That's not." He cocked his head. "What?"

Bennie made a slow hand-wave gesture. "Never mind." He blinked his large black eyes a few times. "You were saying?"

Maxim shook his head, sighing. "We're not going after something of Wil's."

"We're not?" Nic asked.

Maxim shook his head. "Wil was covering for me. That box the thief took. It was mine. A family heirloom. A colla band."

"What's that?" Nic asked.

"Isn't that like, some key part of Palorian bonding ceremonies?" Bennie asked.

Maxim nodded once, surprised that the obnoxious little hacker knew about the Palorian bonding ceremony. "My father made it for me the day I was born."

"Why would anyone want that?" Bennie wondered. He looked up at his friend. "Valuable?"

"Beyond measure, personally." He shrugged. "Other than some semiprecious gems, no."

"How did the intruder know to steal it?" Nic asked.

"Or where it was?" Bennie added.

Maxim shook his head. "No idea. Obviously, someone who knows me, or my family."

Bennie looked at his wristcomm. "We'd better get going. The spaceport's gonna be a roolek this time of day."

Maxim walked to the control pedestal at the edge of the opening. He mashed his hand against the *close* button. The warning klaxon sounded twice before the heavy doors made their ponderous way toward each other.

As the group crossed the hangar, Bennie looked up at Maxim. "So, what's in this for us?"

"I don't kill you," Maxim offered with a shrug. He added, "Or tell Wil you're planning a coup."

"Seems like a good trade," Nic said from the rear of the group.

"You hush," Bennie scolded. He looked at Maxim, who was scowling at him. "Fine."

The Brailack hacker raised his arm, tapping commands into his wristcomm. "I'll get the *Nontee* warmed up." He veered off toward the stairs. "I'll package up the précis Gabe and I worked up and upload to your wristcomms."

Maxim looked down at Nic. "I'll order some supplies, have them delivered to the port."

Nic looked shrugged. "I'll just wait by the door."

"Call a cab, apprentice!" Bennie shouted from the stairwell.

Nic looked at Maxim. "Guess I'll call a cab." She looked down at her wristcomm, pulling up the local transport company's booking system. "So, you're finally doing it?" She didn't look up from her work.

Maxim looked down at the young Olop woman. "Uh, huh. Well, that was the plan."

She made a face. "We'll catch whoever took it. It's what we do." She looked up. "Cab will be here in fifteen microtocks!"

Maxim released a single chuckle. "You're right. It is what we do."

"Make it twenty!" Bennie shouted from somewhere upstairs.

She made another face, her short muzzle scrunching up. "I mean, Bennie and I, Knights of Plentallus." She adjusted the details on her transport request.

Maxim gave a honk-like laugh. "Yeah, you two are the experts."

"Apprentice! Where are my extra shoes?"

She sighed, and Maxim shook his head. "They're probably where you left them! I'm your apprentice, not your shoe caddy!"

Maxim headed to the conference room, where he could pull up the StellarWares portal on the room's large display. He hated placing supply orders; he always forgot something.

WIL PUT his console into standby. It was just him and Cynthia on the bridge. Zephyr was preparing dinner.

"So," his wife said as Wil spun his chair around to face her.

His eyebrows crept up. "So...what? I didn't leave the seat up, did I?"

She smiled, one of her upper canines pulling at her lower lip. "Gonna tell me what that was all about back at the office?" Her tail swished back and forth behind her seat. "That was some of the worst acting I've seen since you made me watch that vid—what was it? *Robot Jox*?"

"A classic," he said under his breath. She gave him one of her very serious looks. He held up both hands, palms out. "Okay, fair, that movie absolutely was hot garbage, but hey, then I showed you *Pacific Rim*." He shrugged. "That more than made up for it." He made a face and leaned back, rubbing his chin. "Let's watch that after dinner."

He was hoping the discussion of giant robots fighting monsters would distract his way-too-smart wife from the topic of the theft at the office.

"Sure, that's fine," she said. She pinned him to his chair with her stare. "But you didn't answer my question."

So much for that.

"Oh, uh. Well."

She leaned forward. "Out with it."

Wil took a deep breath. "The thief didn't take a—did I say what it was?"

"You didn't."

"Ah. Hm. So, well."

Cynthia quirked an eyebrow, one ear twitching.

He frowned. "The thief took a scallop band. Maxim's scallop band."

"Scallop band?"

"You know. For marriages and stuff."

"Ah," she said. "A colla band."

Wil snapped his fingers. "That. Yeah."

She nodded and then shook her head. "Dren." She straightened and took a step back, frowning.

Wil stood. "Yeah." He pushed out of the chair and stepped to the hatch. "Don't tell Zee."

She pursed her lips and nodded. "Let's go see what's for dinner."

CHAPTER SEVEN

"GOOD MORNING. I'm Megan, and here's your GNO Morning Briefing." The blonde-haired news anchor smiled at the camera pickup. "The Peacekeepers have reported that," she glanced down at the tablet before her, "task force Suif Cringo Seven has been reported missing." She turned to another camera. "The task force's last known position was the Ontruum Sara sector performing a routine patrol. At the moment, Peacekeeper Command is reporting that the task force is simply overdue for a routine check-in but not considered missing in action."

She swiped on the tablet, bringing up the next story. "In other news—"

MAXIM THANKED the driver and turned to the spaceport. Bennie was making a busy-looking Quillant man look at his wristcomm. They'd all put copies of the building security feeds on their wristcomms. Bennie and Gabe had cleaned up a few pieces of the video as best they could, making still images to show around. Not that it was proving helpful; the intruder had been clad head to toe in an infiltration suit.

The three of them agreed on the drive from the warehouse to the spaceport that their best shot would be asking around the port about their mysterious visitor. They didn't have much to go on, thanks to the suit—no face, no DNA, or biometrics. Hopefully, the intruder's physique would be memorable enough. Maxim had his doubts but had no better ideas.

Bennie came back to Max and Nic, shaking his head. "This may take a while."

Maxim nodded. "We'll split up. Work our way toward the central lobby. Focus on vendors and anyone who would have been here when our guest would have been leaving."

Bennie and Nic nodded and headed off in separate directions.

Maxim watched them go: Nic toward the market outside the spaceport and Bennie off toward the west entrance. Then he headed off himself, toward the east entrance.

Maxim looked around. The east entrance was for VIPs. He swiped his wristcomm at the reader set in the arched entryway. The Rogue Enterprises building came with VIP spaceport access for when they couldn't take the *Ghost*.

The reader beeped, and the faux-wood doors slid apart. Maxim took a step, then stopped. Why did Bennie choose the public entrance over the VIP? That wasn't like him. Then he saw. Affixed to the pillar next to the concierge desk was a poster. Of Bennie.

Rolling his eyes, he stepped into the VIP section of the massive building. The concierge would be the one to ask about their visitor.

"Hello, sir," the Malkorite woman said, looking up at Maxim. Jeweled earrings that tinkled as she moved her head adorned her large ears. "How can I help you?"

Maxim nodded to the poster. "What did that Brailack do?"

She turned, the jeweled earrings casting prismatic light in all directions and filling the space with the sound of wind chimes. Scowling, she said, "Oh, him." She turned back to Maxim. "He was running a VIP lounge unlimited use access pass scam. Somehow, he got inside our system so that when his customers scanned their bogus access cards, his virus let them in. Went on for months, cost us tens of thousands of credits."

"Some people." He shook his head.

She nodded. "When we caught on, all of his customers screamed at us for weeks as they showed up and were denied entry."

Maxim clucked, shaking his head in actual disgust. He offered his wristcomm screen. "I know it's a long shot, but I'm wondering if you recall seeing this person in the last one or two weeks."

The woman leaned forward, her lips pressed into a line. Her gold-flecked eyes narrowed before she looked up at Maxim. "We don't get many assassins in the VIP lounge." She winked.

Maxim frowned. "I know it's not much to go on, but they stole something incredibly valuable from me." He offered his arm again.

The Malkorite woman reached up and took his arm in one hand. With the other she pinched, zoomed, and rotated the image on his wristcomm. She looked up at Maxim. "Sorry, I don't believe so, no." She shook her head, releasing his arm. "Sorry."

Maxim inclined his head. "A longshot. Okay if I ask around the VIP lobby?" She nodded. "Thank you."

"Good luck," she called after him.

BENNIE STRODE into the public lobby of the spaceport. He wasn't sure if that Malkorite concierge still had it out for him but figured it was safer to let Maxim deal with her.

He looked around. The public lobby was three or four times the size of the VIP entry into the spaceport. Vendors lined the perimeter of the space, a few larger stalls that sold chlormax and baked goods; the rest were locals hocking whatever they had found the day prior, hoping to sell a piece of junk to a tourist. Not that Fury got many of those.

He threaded his way through the circular rows of seats to the cafe in the center. After ordering a drink, he brought up the image of the thief on his wristcomm. "Seen this person before?"

The Guldranii man looked at the image, then turned his long head, allowing the eye on the side of his head to get a look. "A...what? Maybe male of indeterminate species?" The vendor looked at Bennie waving an arm. "Take your pick."

Bennie frowned. "Look, man." He shook his head, composing himself and dropping his voice into his Knight of Plentallus register. "I'm searching for a thief."

The Guldranii man blinked his outer eyes and then the forward set. "And I'm searching for more paying customers, Brailack." He made a shooing motion. "Go bother someone else."

Bennie scowled, his hand falling to the hilt of his beam saber. "Why, you long-headed—" He shook his head. "Never mind." He stormed off, stopped, turned, and came back to snatch his drink off the counter. "I paid for this." He stormed off again.

THE FORWARD HATCH opened to let Wil and Cynthia into the common deck lounge. Zephyr and the ambassador looked up from the tablet they were hunched over at the table in the kitchenette.

The Palorian executive officer smiled. "Dinner's almost ready. Holintuu stew and floomb."

"A feast," Wil said, rubbing his hands together. He nodded to Zephyr. "We're on course to Tro Ella. ETA, three days."

Ambassador Carlisle rapped his knuckles on the table. "Why does that name sound familiar?"

"The homeworld of the Trollack people," Bruce offered from the sofa. He sat the tablet he was reading from down and said, "The planetary capital city is Vablim, if I remember correctly."

Zephyr smiled. "You do." She turned to the ambassador. "We thought it might be worthwhile to introduce you to one of the Tier 2 societies."

Wil, leaning over the pot on the cooktop, looked over. "Plus, there's this festival; it's like a month long. Tons of fun."

The ambassador made a face. "A party? That's what you want to show me?"

Zephyr shook her head. "No. Well, not entirely. The Trollack have been GC members for hundreds of cycles. Seemed like seeing an established society would be good. They've colonized a few worlds but aren't a major power and are okay with that."

"The little fish guys also really can party," Wil said with a grin. He grabbed bowls and plates from the cupboard. "Ready for dinner?"

"It's more than just meeting the Trollack," Cynthia added. She took the plates and bowls from Wil. "People from several nearby sectors attend the Genko Akdool. It's an enormous cultural exchange."

The older human man nodded, grabbing the tablet he and

Zephyr had been working on and making room for the table to be set.

"That does sound like a great opportunity," the ambassador admitted. He watched as Zephyr brought the pot from the cooktop and sat it on the table. "And what exactly is flume?"

"Floomb," Zephyr said. She pointed behind her. "And those are floomb." Nodding to the steaming pot, she said, "This is Holintuu stew."

Cynthia dropped into the seat. "Holintuu is a dish from my world."

"Tyr," Bruce said, taking a seat next to her. She nodded. "I'd love to visit one day. I read all about it in our briefing about the civil rights movement that your engineering droid led."

Wil set the plate of dumplings down and took his seat. He slid a small dish filled with some type of red paste in it. "I like mine with this." He scooped some of the paste and dropped a dollop on his plate.

Bruce smiled and followed Wil's lead, adding a healthy serving of the red paste to his plate. He stabbed a doughy little pocket with his fork and dipped into the paste.

"Oh, that might be—"

Bruce popped the entire dumpling into his mouth.

Wil glanced at the others as the ambassadorial aide chewed the meat dumpling. He got up and pulled a pint glass from the cupboard and filled it with water.

"Ohgawd," came out in a rush of spittle-laced coughing. A flush colored Bruce's cheeks in seconds.

Wil offered the glass. The choking man took it and emptied it, handing it back. Wil filled it and offered it again. This time, more water ended up running down Bruce's chin than down his throat.

"I tried to warn you."

Bruce was flapping both arms.

Carlisle watched all this and scooped the small amount of paste he'd put on his plate onto a knife and scraped it back in the dish.

Cynthia shook her head. "Bo hur paste is...an acquired taste."

Bruce's eyes were watering. He looked at Wil and the again empty water glass. Wil nodded and refilled the glass. He was smiling. "Sorry, man."

Zephyr popped a floomb into her mouth, watching the exchange. She pulled the jar of bo hur sauce closer to her plate.

NIC WOUND her way between stalls, dodging shoppers on their way in and out of the spaceport. The night market around the spaceport's main entrance was as busy as ever.

She approached a vendor selling wristcomms and, from a curtained-off section at the back of the stall, illegal wristcomm mods. She knew the latter from experience. She and Bennie had bought some gray-market multiplexers from this vendor last year.

"Hey, seen this guy?" she asked as she stepped under the stall's awning.

The Tleb vendor looked at her and shook his head. One of his incisors was gold. He glanced at her wristcomm. "What am I looking at? He...or she, is all in black. You can't even see the face." He smirked. "It could be you." From the stool he was perched on, he looked her up and down. Tleb were shorter than Olop, even teenage Olop. "Well, not you, but you know, any one of these taller folks."

"Well, he or she," she shrugged, "they, wouldn't have been in their infiltration suit!"

"Then how would I recognize them?" The little man put his

tiny hands on his hips and let out a *bark-yip* laugh. "Is this some kind of daycare scavenger hunt?"

Nic glared at him. "Thanks for nothing!" She waved as she wandered back into the crowd.

"Rude child," the vendor called.

She moved from stall to stall, stopping at the legitimate and less legitimate stalls. No one had seen anyone that looked like a —what did Wil call the intruder? A ninja—wandering through the market.

She moved to the row directly outside the spaceport. Vendors this close tended to sell tchotchkes and other last-minute needs someone might have: clothes, snacks, gadgets, and more. About to give up, Nic turned toward the port's entrance. Stopping dead in her tracks, she made a slow turn. A young Stilten was staring at her.

She raised her wristcomm. "Adults, I think I have a lead."

"What've you got?" Maxim asked.

"It's street urchins, isn't it?" Bennie asked. "It's always street urchins."

Nic scowled at her wristcomm. "It was just the one time. And they did help."

"Knew it!" Bennie croaked. "Okay, fine. What's your lead?" he asked.

Nic ran a hand over her face. The little Stilten was still watching her. She had no idea why but figured it had to be related.

"Well?" Bennie demanded.

She sighed. "It's street urchins," she said in a low voice.

"What?"

"Fine! They're street kids! Meet me in the outer market." She closed the comm channel and looked at the kid two stalls away. "Hey."

The little insectoid darted around the corner. Nic sighed

and sighed and gave chase. The child obviously knew its way around the market, ducking between stalls to avoid large crowds.

Nic was no slouch herself, having spent plenty of time in the market in the early days of her apprenticeship as a Knight of Plentallus.

Her wristcomm buzzed. In her ear, Bennie asked, "Where are you?"

She tapped her earpiece. "Follow my signal!" She made a left, squeezing between a stall with dehydrated vegetables and a stall that sold shoes. "Stop! I just want to talk. You came to me, remember!"

The child stopped at the nexus of the back of three stalls. "Shh." He put a thick digit to its mandibles.

Nic cocked her head, eyes wide. She squinted, her ears twitching this way and that, worried this was a trap. Between her senses and her training, however, nothing felt off.

"Do you need help? Can you help me?"

The child looked at her, compound eyes glittering. "You're looking for someone. We see everyone. Inside and out."

"Who's we?" Her ears quirked. "Never mind. You can all come out now."

A half-dozen children appeared from all three cloth alleys. Several were behind her. It was a mixed bag of GC races, though many were Quilant. She wondered how a semi-aquatic race found themselves on a mostly desert world. Shrugging, she put it aside. "I could use your help. All of you."

One of the Quilant came forward. "With what?"

She held up her wristcomm. "My friends and I are looking for someone. They robbed us, and we have to get what they took back. It's important."

The Quilant boy, she now saw, leaned forward, big eyes squinting. "Demdi, know this guy?"

A Sylban with an unruly mane of foliage eased around from behind Nic. "Sorry," he apologized in a voice barely above a whisper. He looked at her arm, then the Quilant boy, and nodded.

Nic's eyes went wide.

"There you are!" Bennie shouted as he and Maxim squeezed into the small and crowded space.

"It's okay! They're friends!" Nic hissed as she made calming gestures, hoping the small army of street kids wouldn't all bolt. Especially the Sylban. She nodded to the kid, smiling. "Demdi here thinks he knows our friend."

Maxim turned to the small shrub-like child. He kneeled down. "Demdi, is it?" The Sylban nodded once, his eyes never leaving whatever he was looking at on the ground. Maxim offered his wristcomm. "You know this person?"

The shrub-kid shook its head.

Maxim shook his head and looked at Nic.

She leaned over. "What can you tell us about this person?"

The Sylban boy brightened. "I don't know him. He came out of a Grendel 3400

Sprinter."

Maxim pursed his lips and looked at Bennie, who shrugged.

The boy sighed. "It's a ship. A really shabazz ship. Demdi likes ships. He goes into the port and watches them come and go." He put a protective arm around his friend. "People, not so much."

Maxim stared at the boy. "I don't know what that means."

The Quilant boy cleared his throat. "For three hundred credits, I'll explain."

Bennie turned to the boy. "I like your style, kid. One hundred, and that's all you're gonna get."

"Two—"

"One hundred, kid. We're in a hurry," Bennie interrupted, shaking his head.

The boy looked at his friends and then nodded. "Deal." He nodded to his friend, Demdi.

Demdi looked at Maxim. "The Grendel 3400 Sprinter came eight days ago. It had to circle the spaceport twice to get its approach right. Not a good pilot. Had brand new gravlift motors."

Maxim pulled a face. "Okay, that's great. Thank you, Demdi. Is the Grabble 1900, whatever, still here?"

Demdi shook his shaggy, shrub-like head. A handful of leaves drifted to the ground. "Skinny purple man left in the Grendel 3400 Sprinter two days ago."

Maxim nodded. "Skinny purple man? Purple like me?"

The young boy's eyes darted up and down in a flash. After a few beats, he nodded.

Maxim smiled. "I see. Anything else? Scars or other facial features?" When Demdi just stared at the ground, he turned to the group's spokesman, the Quilant kid. The boy shrugged. "Demdi notices ships. Not people."

Maxim looked around the group. "No one else saw the owner of that ship?"

Head shakes all around.

"Okay, thank you." He turned to Bennie, who just stared at him. "Pay 'em."

"Me? This is your adventure. You pay these little street urchins." The team hacker turned and left. "Come on, urchin whisperer."

CHAPTER EIGHT

AFTER HACKING the spaceport's control computers, they learned that the mystery Grendel 3400 Sprinter filed a flight plan: Fury to Lorstak Seven.

Bennie turned his chair. "Guess we're going to Lorstak Seven."

"Who filed the plan? Did they leave a name?" Maxim asked.

Bennie shook his head. "Just filed under the ship's ID."

Maxim nodded. "Figured. I've actually never been to Lorstak Seven."

Bennie shook his head. "Me neither, but Wil told me all about it."

"That's right," Maxim said. "His vacation with Cynthia."

Nic poked her head around the side of the open doorway. "Someone's coming," she hissed. The three of them were in a small security monitoring room off the main public lobby. The team had been coming and going through the spaceport for so many years, they knew every nook and cranny of the place. This small room was two non-public-but-unsecured hallways off the lobby.

Both men stood and made their way to the door. Maxim stepped over the unconscious security guard. Nic ducked in, closing the door.

Bennie made a face. "What are you doing? Why are you in here with us?"

The small Olop shrugged. "Because the person coming this way is out there."

Maxim watched the two of them. "We want to be out there."

A beep came from the door. All three of them turned to the door.

"I disabled the access control," Bennie whispered.

The door handle rattled. The person outside pounded on the door. "Khron. Khron, you in there? Why's the door locked? You'd better not be doing something gross in there! We've talked about that!"

Bennie looked at Maxim, who shrugged while making a disgusted face as he moved his hand from the back of the chair next to him.

"Khron, come on, open up!" Another series of bangs against the door, followed by repeated beeps as whoever was outside the small security office was trying to use their access card again.

Maxim growled at the door. He strode forward and pressed the control panel. The door slid open. In a flash, he lunged out into the hallway and pulled a wriggling Brailack into the room as Nic slapped the door control, shutting the door again.

"Hey!" the little green-skinned man yelped.

Maxim pulled him close so that he was face to face with the little man. "Hush."

The Brailack technician looked around, spotting Bennie and Nic. "What, what's going on?" He spotted his friend Khron and let out a low keening wail.

Maxim shook the little man. "Focus."

"He's alive," Nic offered.

"How do I know that? How do I know you're not gonna kill me?"

Bennie squinted. "We might."

"Brailack on Brailack violence. The worst," the wriggling friend of Khron complained.

Maxim said, "We just needed some information. You can sit down and count to five hundred."

Bennie opened the door.

"Or?"

"Or we kill you," Bennie said from the doorway. He leaned out. "It's clear, let's go."

"I don't want to die," the new addition to the room said.

Maxim shook his head. "You sit quietly in here and count, or we stun you."

"I'll count. I'll count."

Maxim deposited the technician onto the empty seat. Nic leaned forward. "We'll know if you don't count to five hundred. You don't want to know what we'll do if you don't."

The little man sank deeper into the seat, whimpering and nodding.

Bennie frowned. "You're a testament to Brailack courage."

The other Brailack looked at him. "You're a criminal." The two Brailack scowled at each other.

Maxim sighed and slammed a fist on top of the little man's head, knocking him out. "Brailacks are so tedious."

"Got that right," Nic said. She didn't wait for the two men, heading off down the hallway.

Nic led them back up to the public lobby, avoiding spaceport workers as they went. They exited out into the landing area.

The *Rocky Nontee* was idling on her landing pad when the

three of them reached the small freighter. Maxim eyed the craft. "I can already smell it."

"You're welcome to walk," Bennie said. He approached the ship and stood on the tips of his toes to reach the access panel. He entered a few commands and the forward cargo ramp lowered. "All aboard."

Maxim and Nic followed the team hacker up the ramp into the ship.

"You've been busy," the big Palorian said.

The last time Maxim had been in the *Nontee*'s hold, it had looked like any other cargo hold: bare metal bulkheads, scuffed deck plating.

Now, however, strings of lights were draped around the ceiling, threading between reinforced beams. The deck was painted a pale blue-green color. The bulkheads were a light tan color, like sand.

"You like?" Nic asked. She was grinning.

"I think it looks dumb, but she gets bored on long trips," Bennie groused as he rode the lift platform up to the main deck above.

Maxim shook his head. "I like it. Very warm and inviting."

The young Olop woman bounced on her heels, her facial fur flattening in the Olop version of a blush. "Thanks."

"Lift off in ten microtocks," Bennie announced over the overhead speakers.

Maxim moved to the ladder. "Better get settled in."

"Hope you like the couch," Nic called from the deck below him.

THE *GHOST* ROARED over the fairgrounds that were the

home of the Genko Akdool Festival. The grounds covered several square kilometers.

"Unbelievable," Ambassador Carlisle said. He was standing at the front of the bridge, near the large main display. The grounds were awash in color. The lake in the center of the grounds was full of barges loaded with festivalgoers. A creative use of repulsors and gravlifts caused four waterfalls to flow up to a hovering island covered in foliage and manicured parkland.

The *Ghost* soared overhead on her approach to the Garan Spaceport. Garan was one of the smaller ports outside Vablim proper. The Trollack were parking tourists at the smaller ports to leave Lesla Spaceport, their largest metropolitan spaceport, open for cargo and other commercial traffic. The fairgrounds were several kilometers from the edge of the capital.

"Garan Spaceport is sending our approach vector and landing assignment," Cynthia announced.

Wil nodded. "Better grab a seat, ambassador." He nodded toward Bennie's empty station. Bruce had called dibs on Maxim's station.

The other man looked at the team hacker's station; additional displays were mounted to the bulkhead and ceiling with epoxy. Food wrappers littered the floor under the console. He frowned. "I have to?"

Wil shrugged. "Up to you. You're welcome to stand. It might get bumpy."

The other man approached Bennie's station, head cocked. "I'll stand."

Zephyr smiled. "Good call. Last time I sat over there, my pants smelled like, well, I don't know what, but they smelled like it for two weeks."

The older human man made a face as he backed away from Bennie's station.

Bruce watched the exchange and then asked, "Why don't you make him clean his station up?"

Zephyr shook her head. "We've tried."

"It didn't end well," Wil said.

"He started hiding trash and other things in our quarters." She shook her head at the memory of the rotten Fyolpi he'd put under her and Maxim's bed.

"On final approach," Wil announced.

The Garan Spaceport was a series of kilometer-diameter duracrete circles arrayed around a smaller circle that housed the flight control center and customs checkpoints. Everyone landing at Garan funneled to the center and then out through underground tunnels into the city.

The *Ghost* made a slow pass around the western edge of the port. Her repulsorlifts glowed bright green as they held the small craft aloft. The rumble of the atmospheric engines faded as the ship came in over bay 4.

The nimble pocket warship lowered to her assigned pad, 431. Pad 3 was empty of other ships. The *Ghost* settled onto her landing gear with a hiss.

The cargo ramp lowered, striking the duracrete with a clang. The thick cargo doors at the top of the ramp slid apart.

Wil was the first out. "Okay, everyone remember where we parked."

Zephyr and Cynthia exchanged a knowing look. Bruce chuckled.

The group made their way from their docking ring through a tunnel that led them to the main complex nestled between the myriad docking rings.

"This is a lot," Bruce said as they fell in behind a group of Malkorites.

Zephyr looked around. "What? Customs?" He nodded. "With the GC in its current state, a lot of Tier 1 and 2 societies have beefed up their own customs and border patrol efforts. Used to be you could move pretty freely between systems."

Wil harrumphed. "Now, everyone wants to know who you are and where you've been."

The ambassador took in the space. He smiled at a group of Ruknak that fell in behind them. He looked up, smiling at them. "Hello."

The closest Ruknak, a woman that towered over the group, smiled. Her rocky hide rustled as her expression changed. "Hello. Is this your first Genko Akdool?"

The ambassador's head bobbed. "It is!"

She let loose with a booming laugh. "You're in for a treat. My family comes every cycle." She shifted to let the three other Ruknak lean over to see who their matriarch was speaking to. A child, still nearly six feet tall, said, "Hi! You look squishy!"

"Plora, mind your manners!" the woman scolded. Turning to Carlisle, she said, "Apologies."

The older man chuckled. "Quite all right." He looked at Plora. "Compared to you, little one, I am quite squishy." The little Ruknak grinned and then hid behind a family member.

After a few more minutes of small talk with the Ruknak family, the ambassador turned to Zephyr. "What is your take on the current state of the Galactic Commonwealth?"

The line progressed forward a few steps.

"There should be a VIP line," Wil said.

Zephyr glanced at him, then Carlisle. "I think things are close to a positive turning point."

The older man smiled. "Diplomatically said." Zephyr inclined her head. "What's the nondiplomatic answer?"

Zephyr grinned. "A year ago, the GC was in free fall. Tier 1 societies were withdrawing. Bush wars were cropping up between smaller civilizations. It wasn't looking good."

"Then we came along," Wil said, taking a few steps forward.

He stood on the tips of his toes. They were thirty people from the customs kiosks. "Really need a VIP line," he added under his breath.

"More accurately, the Harrith came along," Gabe said. "They were willing to set aside their well-placed animosity for the Commonwealth and help the Governing Council craft an improved governance model. A more inclusive model."

Wil made a face. "We were there, too."

"Hey, keep up with the line," one of the Ruknaks said.

Wil scowled. "Keep your pants on." He turned and closed the gap between their group and the Malkorites ahead of them.

Ambassador Carlisle nodded. "That was the same conclusion the Earth Government Alliance came to."

MAXIM RUBBED HIS BACK. He, in fact, did not love the couch. The common deck on the *Nontee* was much smaller than on the *Ghost*. As such, all the furniture—a sofa and chair—

were just a bit too small for his frame. Just enough to leave his back aching after a prolonged use, which included a night of sleep.

"Everything on this ship is so tiny," he complained from his seat on the couch, which for him felt more like a chair. He glanced to the side, glaring at the actual chair.

Nic looked up from the tablet she was reading. She had claimed the only other place to sit in the lounge, the overstuffed chair, for herself. It was a nest of blankets and pillows that she burrowed into whenever they were not on the flight deck. "We're small." She went back to reading.

Bennie was in the small kitchenette along the port bulkhead. "Now you know what it's like for us on the *Ghost*."

Maxim looked at his friend. He was going to reply but realized the small hacker had a point. Granted, little folks could get comfortable in bigger seats easier than bigger folks could in smaller. He shrugged. It was Bennie's ship, after all. "What's for dinner?"

"Privlip."

Bennie was moving things around on the cooktop with intent.

Maxim looked at Nic. "When did he learn to cook?"

She shook her head. "He didn't."

"You both can suck it," Bennie said without turning around. He moved a pot from the cooktop and then poured the contents over the top of another bowl. "I've been practicing." He brought the large bowl over to the coffee table in the seating area. There wasn't a dedicated kitchen table on the *Nontee.*

The *Nontee*'s common deck didn't have room for a place to sit and eat. Maxim got up and got the dishware and utensils. "Well, good or bad, thanks for the meal."

Bennie nodded. "So, any thoughts on who stole your bracelet?"

Maxim pursed his lips. After counting to five to avoid smacking the rude little Brailack across the room, he said, "Colla band, and no—they knew what they were looking for, though."

Nic leaned forward, getting a second helping of privlip. "Someone from home? A Palorian, it sounds like."

Maxim took a bite. "This isn't bad." Turning to Nic. "I can't imagine. It's not like I'm not close with many people on Palor. I can't imagine why a Palorian would want my colla band."

"Family?" the young woman asked.

Maxim shook his head. "My parents sent the band. The intruder is too slight to be my younger brother."

"Maybe another Peacekeeper?" Bennie asked.

"Extended family?" Nic offered.

Maxim's eyes widened. "A long and a sorta long list." He shrugged. "But again, why? Why me? Why the colla band?"

His two small friends both shrugged. After that, they ate in silence until the overhead speaker chimed.

Bennie looked up. "Time to go to work." He set his plate down and headed forward. The flight deck was the only thing forward of the common deck lounge.

Nic finished her last few bites, then sat her plate down and followed him. Looking over her shoulder, she said, "Maybe a scorned lover from your time in the PKs?"

Maxim shook his head. "You watch too many of Wil's movies." He grabbed their plates and the bowl with the remaining privlip and headed for the kitchenette. Might as well make himself useful while they flew the ship.

The ship shuddered. "I better not die with these two," Maxim said.

CHAPTER NINE

THE MAIN ENTRY to the Genko Akdool Festival was a massive pavilion lined with information booths and vendors selling food and drink tickets.

"This is amazing," Carlisle said as the group passed through the main gate. Hundreds of people from all over the GC were moving through the pavilion. "I knew the GC was diverse, but..." He stepped out of the way of a pair of Hulgians. "This is something else." He pointed to a group of Ficu making their way out into the main festival grounds, their trio of mobility tentacles moving them quickly into the flow of festival goers. "So many different types of beings."

Wil nodded. "It can be a bit disorienting at first."

Bruce nodded his agreement. He had his CommPad out and was snapping pics of the crowd.

After a stop at the food and drink ticket stall, they made their own way into the festival proper.

Wil distributed the paper tickets—paper, of all things—to the others. "In case we split up."

"Paper?" Bruce held the ticket up. He rubbed the thin material between his finger and thumb.

Wil smiled. "Well, space paper." He continued before Zephyr could make a face. "It composts down to nothing in like two days." He gestured around. "Lotta kids and others who may not have a wristcomm or any other device for electronic tickets."

The ambassador handed Bruce his set of tickets. "Interesting."

Gabe took the ticket from the ambassadorial aide, holding it between two metal fingers. "Tickets provide an enjoyable tactile experience for festival goers." He handed the tiny piece of paper back to Bruce. "Do not spend them all in one place."

The group reached a central nexus of walkways that encircled a fountain that shot pale purple liquid thirty feet into the air. Two Trenbal kids splashed around while their fathers shouted at them to stop.

Ambassador Carlisle watched the family unit with interest, then turned to the group. "So where to, first?"

Cynthia pointed toward one of the pathways. "I think the Celestial Neighborhood."

"Good call," Zephyr said.

"What's the Celestial Neighborhood?" Ambassador Carlisle asked.

"You'll see," Cynthia said, pointing toward the walkway Zephyr was starting down. Gabe and Carlisle followed Zephyr. Cynthia and Bruce fell in behind them. Wil brought up the rear. Cynthia glanced over her shoulder as the two Trenbal parents finally got their kids out of the fountain. The small reptiloids were squirming and screaming with joy as their fathers tried to dry them.

The walk to the Celestial Neighborhood took the group through several other sections of the massive grounds. There was a large area with several ponds where Trollack and other aquatic species could lounge, and what must have been five acres of grassland with large mechanical structures wandering aimlessly around it. Each had dozens of Tleb hooting and hollering from the platforms.

The Celestial Neighborhood itself was a massive dome 200 meters across at the base and four stories at its peak, which sported a six-meter tall orrery of the Apennul system. Tro Ella was a golden sphere that glinted in the sun as it moved through its orbit.

"This is the biggest planetarium I've ever seen," Carlisle said as they entered the building.

"Planetarium?" Zephyr asked.

Cynthia shook her head. "Don't ask. Last time we visited Earth, Wil made me go to one. There was loud music and low-powered lasers accompanying some sort of documentary or something. Ponk Flod or something like that." She hugged herself. "It sucked."

Wil made a choking noise. "No culture." He pointed to a section of floor with enough room for all of them. "Over there."

The lights dimmed, and a voice filled the dome. "The show will begin momentarily." Several hundred beings oohed as the interior surface of the dome shimmered, first becoming a deep black, then slowly filling with shimmering pinpricks of light.

One of the points of light grew in brightness and size until it filled the dome. A large orange star. Planets appeared one by one as they took up their proper orbits. When one of the planets was centermost in the air overhead, the view shifted and zoomed in. Pale greens and blues were covered in wispy white clouds. The lights of thousands of cities glittered like a carpet of diamonds. A new voice filled the auditorium: "Tarsis, birthplace of the Galactic Commonwealth."

The crowd inside the dome oohed and aahed. Wil looked at their two guests. Both were staring straight up, mouths hanging open in awe. He watched as Bruce took a few steps back from the group, sliding between a pair of Hulgians and maybe the Ruknak family from earlier in the day?

He turned to Cynthia to see that she too had just watched the ambassador's aide make his discreet exit. She nodded to her husband and slid into the crowd in pursuit.

"WHY DOES your ship smell so bad?" Maxim said, stepping onto the small flight deck. He'd tidied up the common deck as much as he could, mostly putting everything into the ship's small matter reclamator. Bennie and Nic seemed to prefer fabricating new dishware over cleaning the existing. Who was he to argue?

Bennie was sitting at the pilot's station. "You smell." He didn't take his eyes off the forward transparent section of hull in front of him. Unlike the *Ghost*, the *Rocky Nontee* had an actual transparent canopy at the front of the small bridge. They were on approach to Lorstak Seven. The pale blue and white world filled the forward window. The ship helpfully floated planetary data and other important information onto the canopy as a large heads-up display.

Nic turned to look forward out through the transparent hull at the front of the bridge. "We've been given clearance to land at the Hessaf'as'sev Spaceport." She added, "Nav data is ready for you."

Bennie accepted the navigation data. A pale green arrow like the one on the *Ghost* appeared guiding the ship through the atmosphere toward one of the regional spaceports. According the flight plan they'd gotten on Fury, the intruder's ship landed at Hessaf'as'sev two days ago.

After breaking through the upper atmosphere, the *Nontee* came in over a city that the ship's HUD labeled *Barua*.

"Pretty place," Maxim said from his spot leaning on the side of the open bridge hatch.

"This where Wil and Cynthia vacationed?" Nic wondered.

Bennie shrugged. "Why would I know that?"

"You could have just said you didn't know."

The ship shuddered as a gust of wind shoved it sideways. Maxim braced himself. "This thing needs more seatbelts." The guidance arrow hovering on the HUD was flashing yellow.

Bennie brought the ship back under control. The guidance arrow was green again. The range to spaceport indicator showed only a few more minutes. "I did say that."

The young woman growled, deep in her chest. "No, you didn't."

"Yes, I did."

"I will kill you both," Maxim growled from where he stood.

The small ship's flight deck fell silent.

The *Rocky Nontee* came in over Hessaf'as'sev Spaceport. A green rectangle highlighted their designated landing pad in the forward window. The small freighter flew in over the ring wall, her repulsorlifts whining.

"Look," Maxim pointed out the window. Sitting on the duracrete two hundred meters from their assigned parking place was the Grendel 3400 Sprinter.

"Landing gear deployed," Nic announced.

"We've got you now," Maxim said, grinning. "Whoever you are."

The ship lowered to the duracrete, settling onto its four stubby landing gear.

Nic hopped out of her seat, not waiting for the mechanism that lowered and raised the seats to bring her closer to the deck. "Customs inspector will be here in five." She squeezed past Maxim and headed down to the cargo deck.

Maxim watched her go, then turned to Bennie. "By the way, how'd that last mission of yours go?"

After putting his station and the ship into standby mode, the Brailack hacker looked up at his friend and shrugged. "Oh, you know. Lots of action and adventure, daring dos and such. Tons of beam saber duels and overwhelming odds to overcome. We're Knights of Plentallus, after all. Danger follows us." He shoved his way past the big Palorian.

"Wasn't your last job negotiating peace between two warring tribes on some no-name planet?"

"Yeah, so?"

"So, all that other dren happened?"

They reached the cargo deck. "You think we just walked in and shouted, 'Get along or else?'" Bennie asked. He headed for a console mounted next to the port cargo hatch.

Nic was working on something near the rear of the cargo hold. She was half inside a cargo container. She kicked her feet until she wriggled out of the container dropping to the deck. "One side tried to kill the other during a holiday break."

"What?" Maxim looked at her, then turned to Bennie.

The Brailack Knight of Plentallus shrugged. "Like I said: sword fights, action, and adventure."

Maxim's eyes grew wide. "So, what happened?"

"One side. The–what were they called? Whatever, who cares. Those guys were celebrating their regional high holiday: big feast, dancing, all that. They invited us," Bennie said without turning around. "The other guys, I can't recall what they're called either. Anyway, the attack came, we fought them off, killed every last one of the assassins."

"That part was pretty fun," Nic offered.

Bennie continued. "We had video, and the bodies for DNA testing. The other guys, the scummy ones, knew they had lost the support of everyone in the sector and were about to be attacked, so they sat down and made peace." He turned from the console. "Easy peasy, as Wil likes to say."

Nic hopped down to the deck and closed the cargo container, activating the seal.

Maxim shook his head. "Okay, that is quite the adventure. Seems like killing all the attackers may have been a bit much."

Bennie trotted down the cargo ramp, motioning for the other two to follow. "It's not like there's a rule book." He looked over his shoulder. "Come on. I want to grab a snack before we track down your thief."

Nic passed Maxim. "There very much is a rule book. Several, in fact."

BRUCE EXITED THE CELESTIAL NEIGHBORHOOD. He looked around the crowded festival grounds surrounding the massive building. He spotted a wayfinding sign and used his CommPad to translate the galactic standard into English, then strode off along a pathway that continued deeper into the festival grounds.

Cynthia slipped out of the building, darting behind a group of Multonae waiting for the next showing. She slid past them to catch sight of Bruce walking away from the building. He was almost out of sight. She pursued him, falling in with a group of Tygrans as Bruce pulled out a CommPad, the device humans used instead of wristcomms—she had no idea why—and checked it, looking around until he set off down a side path.

"What're you up to?" She set off after him. One of the Tygrans started to ask who she was talking to but shook his head when she was already gone.

The Genko Akdool fairgrounds was a five-kilometer-long oval almost two kilometers wide. The grounds were divided into sections, each with food halls and entertainment areas. Bruce looked at his CommPad again. The instructions were less than detailed, but he was pretty sure he was in the right zone. He looked around again, sighing. He spotted a being in the tunic of a festival worker. "Excuse me?"

The large treelike being turned. "Yes?"

Bruce held his CommPad up. "I'm looking for the Feegillian smoked sooba vendor." He held the device screen out.

The Sylban man nodded, the foliage around the top of his head rustling. He pointed. "I believe the vendor you are looking for is in that food hall."

Bruce inclined his head. "Thank you." He headed off toward the food hall.

Cynthia watched the exchange from afar. She couldn't hear the two men or see the screen of Bruce's mobile. The grounds were too loud, even for her hearing. A quintet of Brailack crossed in front of her, stopping to take scans of something or other. She tried to scoot around them but they kept moving. "Excuse me," she said to one of the darker green beings. The five little Bennies ignored her, shuffling this way and that.

"Move, you little green shits!" she roared.

The five, meter-tall beings all froze. One of them, a woman, looked up. "Well, I never!" She stomped a foot.

Cynthia ignored them, moving past the group toward the food hall.

Inside the hall, Bruce spotted the Feegillian smoked sooba vendor. He still had no idea what a Feegillian was, or what sooba was, for that matter. The stall was at the end of the aisle of stalls. He made his way slowly around the hall. No one seemed to be paying any attention to him. He reached the back of the smoked sooba stall. Shrugging, he knocked on the door three times, then twice more.

When nothing happened, he looked around again. No one was nearby, and no one seemed to be paying any particular attention to him. He was about to knock again when the door opened a crack. Someone with three eyes looked him up and down.

Bruce's eyes went wide. He was supposed to do one more thing. "Uh, oh. Fuguhlspoof." He leaned forward. "Right? I think that's it." He reached for his CommPad to confirm.

The door opened further. "Come in, already."

Cynthia watched the ambassadorial aide knock on the door of the Feegillian smoked sooba stall. Who wanted smoked sooba? The man looked nervous. She moved a little closer, falling in behind a Hulgian man who was walking by.

By the time she ducked away from her Hulgian cover, Bruce had entered the back of the stall. She stopped at the door. "What the hell is this?"

She made her way to the front of the stall. A sign said it was closed, a handwritten note taped to the metal shutters: *Closed until cooktop repairs complete.*

"Well, then." She headed back to the small building's rear. She didn't know what Bruce was up to but figured it wasn't good.

THE GRENDEL 3400 Sprinter was completely powered down.

"Definitely been here couple days," Bennie said. He had a scanning device in one hand. "Reactor is cold."

"Should we break in?" Nic asked.

"Yes," Bennie said.

"No," Maxim said.

The two men looked at each other, the larger saying, "No. We're not going there. Not yet, anyway." He looked around. No one was paying any attention to them.

Nic moved around the other side of the small craft.

Maxim looked at Bennie. "What can you tell me about it?"

Bennie looked up at his friend. "That it's a ship." When the big Palorian made a face, he said, "We just got here. I'm not the ship whisperer. We shoulda brought Gabe or the slow tree kid, if you wanted a walking starship encyclopedia." Maxim scowled at him.

Nic came back around the ship's nose. "Looks brand new."

"It is," a voice said.

Bennie spun faster than Maxim, which irked the big man, his hand on the hilt of his beam saber.

"Just bought her," the Trenbal woman said. She was sizing up the two men, hand on her hip, just above a pulse pistol.

Maxim looked at her. "You? Just bought it?"

"Sure did. Off some kid in a goofy mask." Her tongue darted out, tasting the air. Maxim's mind drifted back to when he and Zephyr first met Wil. The only human in the GC worked for the Trenbal crime lord, Xarrix, right up until the team had blown the lowlife villain to atoms while saving a bunch of sentient starships he had been hoping to enslave as living freighters.

He shook his head. "A mask?"

"Yeah, real secretive. One of those kinds meant to fool facial recognition and such. Made me pay in VortiCoin." She shook her head. "Had to go to two different bank branches to get that much." She looked at the sleek craft behind the three Rogue Enterprises team members. "Worth it."

"What can you tell us about the 'kid in the mask'?" Maxim asked.

She shrugged. "Not much. Sounded youngish. From what I could see under the cloak, he had a kind of average frame for a Palorian."

"Cloak?" Nic asked. She looked up at Maxim. "Did you pick a fight with some kind of supervillain?"

The big man shrugged. Turning back the Trenbal woman, he asked, "You're certain he was a Palorian? He still here?"

Another shrug, but this time it was only with one shoulder. "What's in it for me?"

Bennie's hand drifted back to his beam saber. "You'd be doing the right thing for a Knight of Plentallus." He'd dropped his voice into his Knight of Plentallus register. "We remember these types of things."

The woman looked at him, then Maxim, then Nic, who made a show of moving her hand to her own beam saber hilt.

Maxim rolled his eyes. "Two hundred credits."

"Three."

"Two, and I don't let these two little monsters do their thing."

Nic bared her teeth as she activated her beam saber. The area was cast in pale red light.

The reptilian woman's eyes went wide. "Okay. Two. He's not here. Said something about picking up a new ride and getting gone before they caught up with him." She eyed the three of them, her hand out expectantly. "Guess *they* is you?"

Maxim nodded.

She put her other hand on the ship. "Stolen? Yours?"

Maxim shook his head. She smiled. "That's all I know. Promise."

He nodded. "Thanks." He turned to Bennie, then Nic. "Come on."

With a *snap-click*, Nic's beam saber shut down.

The Trenbal woman cleared her throat. Maxim stopped.

With a sigh, he turned around and pulled up the banking app on his wristcomm. He swiped up on the screen, aiming at the new owner of the Grendel 3400 Sprinter. Her own wristcomm chimed. She glanced at the screen. "Good hunting." She turned and headed around the other side of the craft.

CHAPTER TEN

IT TOOK Cynthia less than a minute to pick the lock on the rear door of the Feegillian smoked sooba stall. The look on the Tragalallan man's face when the door opened suddenly gave Cynthia a small thrill. She still had it.

Grinning, she pulled the door closed behind her and then leaped onto the man. He had a sidearm still holstered. His hand dropped to the weapon. She dropped her hand on top of his, pressing it against the holstered weapon, keeping it pinned. She wrapped the other arm around the man's neck as she pushed against the wall to slam him into the opposite wall as hard as she could.

The impact shook him but didn't render him unconscious. He rotated as he bounced against the wall, aiming to fall on top of his attacker.

"Living as long as you do, you must've picked up quite a few tricks," she said with a purr as she wrapped her legs around his torso.

The man didn't answer but shifted his hip enough to force her hand that was on top of his to lose its leverage. He pulled the blaster.

"A few," he agreed.

She clucked. Moving one leg to put a foot on his knee, she flipped up and over him. She planted her feet on the door and pushed. The pair tumbled down the stairs just behind his bouncing blaster pistol.

As they tumbled, she said, "Not enough."

The two of them landed in a heap, Cynthia on top. She looked down at the now unconscious Tragalallan. "You guys are usually tougher." She patted the man's slack face, careful to avoid the open mouth and razor-sharp teeth.

Tragalallans were ferocious fighters, this one notwithstanding. She hoped his employers wouldn't punish him for not stopping her.

Standing, she looked around. She and her unconscious friend were in a foyer of some sort. There was only a single door opposite the stairs. No one else was around.

"This better be interesting," she said, crossing the room. She could hear a crowd on the other side of the door: fighting pit? Dance club? Speakeasy? Weapons market?

She eased the door open. "How plain," she said in a hushed voice. She was looking at a room full of gaming tables with a bar at the rear. "A God's felgercarbed gambling den." She shook her head. "How basic."

She stepped into the room, taking it all in. There was Bruce sitting at the bar next to a Hulgian woman.

Cynthia sighed. "We coulda taken his money aboard the ship," she said as she started through the center of the room. It was only mildly surprising to find such a place under the festival. The Genko Akdool brought hundreds of thousands of people from across four sectors. There was probably one in each quadrant.

Taking in the room, she spied several familiar games of chance: Chol, Autvilo, M'Hena, Gra Gek, and even a few games she wasn't familiar with. There was something where four players placed tiles on the table, one end of their tile matching the end of a tile already on the table.

She'd made it halfway across the room when she saw the knife. The blazer of the Hulgian woman talking to Bruce rose enough to reveal a mean-looking dagger in the woman's waistband. She moved her hand to adjust the coat. The outline of a blaster pistol was also just barely visible under the jacket.

Picking up her pace, she could just make out what he was saying to the woman. Something about orbital defenses, then fleet strength. She thought she heard the name Rhys Duch. That couldn't be good. The Rogue Enterprises crew had dealt with the Multonae crime boss a few times. Wil seemed to like him. Cynthia found him pleasant enough, for a moron. She'd worked with him when they both worked for Xarrix. The Trenbal slime bag had kept Duch around, much to the chagrin of others in the organization. When Xarrix was killed, somehow, gods only knew how, Rhys Duch had been able to grab onto, and hold, most of the dead crime boss' operations. She shook her head and continued toward the bar.

She slid up behind the much larger woman. This close, she realized both of the woman's brow horns were blunted, their sharp points sanded off. One had intricate scrollwork carved in it and inlaid with gold.

She put her hand on the woman's much larger hand. The hand that would draw the knife. The would-be killer flinched, likely unaccustomed to being touched.

Cynthia clucked. "Easy, my big friend." She came around the woman's side, opposite Bruce.

Bruce nearly fell off his stool.

She turned to him. "Hi, Bruce."

He said nothing.

The woman turned. "Who the wurrin are you?"

Cynthia leaned closer, purring. "No one of particular note. Just a friend of this lost human." She glanced at Bruce. "Who was—what? Asking about arms? Thought I heard the term 'orbital defenses'?"

The human's cheeks flushed. The Hulgian woman did her best approximation of a grin. "He was. You did."

Cynthia nodded. "Well, he isn't interested anymore."

The Hulgian woman made a noise deep in her throat. "Well, unfortunately for you, your lost—" she looked at Bruce, "—what are you, again?"

"Human."

"Your lost human made an appointment. An appointment that could be very lucrative for my employer." She shrugged. "I'd like to hear him out."

Bruce coughed. "I think, maybe—"

Cynthia felt the woman's body tense. She shifted her weight so that when the Hulgian woman lashed out at her, she easily ducked the elbow. Bruce wasn't as lucky. Her elbow clipped the side of his head, sending him sprawling to the floor.

The low rumble of conversation that had filled the room came to a stop. Those eyes not on Bruce turned to the Hulgian woman.

Cynthia caught the woman's arm, putting pressure on the elbow, pulling the woman from the stool. She spun, pulling the arm further as she moved, driving her other elbow into the bigger woman's back. She rode the woman to the floor.

"You little," the angry Hulgian snarled as she hit the floor.

Cynthia shoved her, putting distance between herself and the other woman. She reached down to help Bruce up.

"You're both dead," the Hulgian woman said as she got to her feet.

The rest of the room was still silent; now every eye in the room was watching the two women.

Cynthia held both hands up, palms out. "Look. I don't know or care what this is. He's with me. We're gonna go." Playing a hunch, she added, "Ask Rhys Duch about me, about us."

The look on the other woman's face was all Cynthia needed. She nudged Bruce. "Let's go."

As they stepped over the unconscious Hulgian, Bruce asked, "Think we can keep this between the two of us?"

Cynthia sighed. "What were you thinking?"

He struck a more defiant tone. "We've read all of Calder's reports, plus we now get GNO. It's a violent galaxy and not everyone is willing to sell arms to spacefaring societies."

She shook her head. "There's a reason for that. She'd have sold you something that could vaporize half of Earth without batting an eye. There's no returns or warranty."

THE HESSAF'AS'SEV SPACEPORT administration building looked like a luxury office building.

Bennie took a bite out of a tube-shaped pastry filled with a bright blue fruit mash. "You guys should have grabbed one of these. So good." He took another bite. A glob of bright blue goop dropped onto the desk in front of him.

Maxim wiped the glob away. They'd lucked out; there was a VIP line in the customs section, which they'd used to breeze through thanks to Bennie's growing status as Knight of Plentallus. Maxim was certain the Brailack was hacking planetary systems one by one to put himself and Nic on some type of diplomatic list. At this moment, he didn't care.

It took them longer than Maxim would have liked to find an unoccupied office that had a terminal Bennie could hack. In the end, they'd stumbled into a spare data analysis office with half a dozen terminals just waiting for analysts.

Nic watched the screens as Bennie worked. She leaned forward, pointing at the screen. "Look! There it is."

Bennie flicked her hand away. "I see it...apprentice." She growled. He chuckled. She wandered off.

Maxim watched a figure in a floor-length cloak walk down the small craft's boarding ramp. He swore, hoping to finally see the person who'd robbed him. The being paused, then looked around.

"A grolacking mask?" Maxim fumed. "What is this? A holodrama?"

"Supervillain," Nic said from the workstation she'd sat down at, one halfway across the room from the two men. She was absentmindedly tapping the keys of the device's keyboard.

"Not a supervillain," Maxim said. He leaned closer to the screen. "Can you—" Bennie held up a hand to silence him.

The team's hacker worked the terminal's keys like a musician, occasionally swearing to himself.

Maxim joined Nic. "So how many attackers did you two face on that peace mission?"

She pursed her lips, then shook her head. "You know, I don't remember. A dozen or two? It's not like we were surrounded and fighting back-to-back or anything." She grinned. "That would be pretty schway, though." The big man nodded his agreement. She went on. "It was this big hall in one of their older neighborhoods. Horrible security, but I guess it meant something to them." A shrug. "We tried to get the Plothriini to keep some of their troops in the area as security, but I guess that was considered bad form."

"Seen that before," he nodded.

"So yeah, big party with food and loud praying and such, then boom, Chuliwama warriors cut the power and set up jammers." She grinned. "We split up and moved around as fast as we could. They didn't stand a chance. Most never even looked up until I was dropping onto them. Once order was restored, the Plothriini wasted no time taking to the local news outlets with scenes from the attack." She put both hands in her pockets. "Plus, all the bodies and stuff."

"Stuff?" Maxim's nose wrinkled.

"Sometimes things get cut off: arms, hands, heads. You know."

"I don't."

She shrugged.

"Got him!" Bennie shouted, drawing their attention back to him. He turned in his seat. "What're you doing way over there?"

THE LIGHTS in the planetarium rose.

Ambassador Carlisle looked around. "That was incredible."

Zephyr nodded. "I thought you'd like it."

"There's so much." He shook his head slowly, then said, "I knew how large the GC was, of course. I knew—know—the number of systems in the Commonwealth and the light years it spans, of course, but to see it..."

Zephyr nodded. "Yeah, it has that effect on people." She smiled.

"Come on. We'll cut through the Harvest Zone—boring—and check out the commerce pavilions. Most every major society in the GC sets up a tent. Like a crash course on the GC."

"At least a crash course in top-selling items from each society," Wil added with a smile.

Carlisle paused and then looked around. "Where's Bruce? And your wife?"

Wil smiled. "Oh. She's keeping an eye on your currently wayward aide." He waved a hand toward the exit. "Come on.

She's got Bruce. We've got to show you the highlights before your appointment on Tarsis. They'll meet up with us."

The group made its way out of the massive dome. The festival grounds were noticeably busier than when they'd entered the dome.

"How many people attend this—what was it called?" Ambassador Carlisle asked.

"Genko Akdool," Gabe offered. He tilted his head. "Two hundred thousand average daily visitors."

The ambassador's eyes went wide. "Two hundred thousand?" He looked around. "A day...? Wow."

"Indeed," the droid agreed. "Genko Akdool is one of the most well-known and well attended festivals in nine sectors."

Zephyr guided the group through a crowd of Stilten who were excitedly chittering to each other about something they'd just seen. "It's considered one of the GC's cultural gems."

"I can see why," the ambassador agreed.

"Cynthia is approaching," Gabe said.

Wil smiled. "Didn't take as long as I expected." He turned toward the approaching love of his life and their client's aide. "Hey, sweetie. You two have fun?"

Cynthia reached Wil and leaned in for a kiss before saying, "Oh, yeah. Tube of arboreals."

Wil pursed his lips, then said, "Barrel of monkeys."

Cynthia nodded. "That. We discovered a quaint little underground gambling den under the Zone Three food hall. Hope no one was craving Feegillian smoked sooba."

Zephyr made a face. "Is anyone, ever?"

Ambassador Carlisle pulled Bruce aside. The two whispered back and forth for several seconds.

Gabe and Cynthia said, "We can hear you." At the same time.

Carlisle turned. "Oh, yes, of course. Sorry." He tugged at his dress shirt before adjusting his blazer. "Bruce was out of line. Apologies."

Bruce, his cheeks red, added, "I was hoping to collect intel."

"By purchasing arms?" Zephyr asked.

Bruce shook his head. "I was going to ask questions, then back out of the deal."

Cynthia clucked. "She'd have killed you for that."

"I know that now."

Wil inclined his head. "No worries." He looked at Cynthia. "Assume it's all good?"

She nodded. "We may want to reach out to Rhys Duch, just to be sure."

Bruce frowned.

Wil looked at his wife. "Duch?"

She nodded. "His operation."

Wil groaned.

"Okay, then. Let's keep moving," Zephyr said.

"WHAT'VE YOU GOT?" Maxim asked, moving to stand behind Bennie.

The hacker rubbed his hands together. "He's good, I'll give him that. But I'm better." Maxim closed his eyes and counted to five. By the time he reached five, Bennie continued. "He took the cash he got from our Trenbal friend and picked himself up a nice little Bormea Vesper Nine."

Nic looked around Maxim. "How did you figure that out?"

"Jealous?" the Brailack hacker asked.

"Not even a little," his apprentice replied.

"Children," Maxim said.

Bennie clucked. "We know our friend wanted to get moving before anyone caught up to him. We know he had cash on hand.

I hacked into the spaceport's local ship registry for any recent changes of ownership that matched with departures between his arrival and ours and were the right ship class."

"You don't think he bought a bulk freighter?" Nic challenged.

Before Bennie could reply, Maxim held up a hand to silence him. Then he put his hand on his small friend's shoulder. "Nice work."

"I know." Bennie looked at Nic and stuck his tongue out.

Maxim sighed. "Any footage of him or his ship?"

Bennie nodded and tapped a few commands into the computer. The screen updated with several windows showing footage from various cameras. The still unidentified intruder moved from window to window, reaching the newly purchased Bormea Vesper Nine.

The new ship was a bit bigger than the last. The FTL engines were mounted at the ends of swept back wings. The intruder entered through a personnel hatch on the ship's side. Stepping up into the craft, the intruder turned and looked out at the spaceport. He reached up and removed the mask a moment before turning and entering the craft.

"Son of a roolek," Maxim swore.

Nic looked up at the big Palorian. "You know him?"

Maxim said nothing for several seconds, his eyes glued to the screen. The Bormea Vesper Nine rose on its repulsorlifts out of the camera's frame.

Bennie rewound the recording, freezing it at the moment the thief removed their mask.

Maxim sighed. "It's my cousin. Tane."

Bennie whistled, saying, "Felgercarb." Under his breath, "Didn't have family drama on my list."

Maxim growled.

Bennie slouched in his seat.

"Why would your cousin steal your whatever-it's-called?" Nic asked.

Maxim shook his head. "I don't know. Let's go find him and ask."

"Do you know how to reach him?" Bennie asked. "Be easier than chasing him around the GC."

Maxim shook his head. Tane hadn't been an active part of the family for cycles. He'd never been particularly likeable, and once he was of age he'd gone into the technical arm of the Peacekeepers. It was unlikely that anyone back on Palor would know where to find the younger man. Especially since he wasn't on Palor.

"Tane's been on his own for cycles now. Since before Zephyr and I were framed by Janus." He rubbed his chin. "I don't think anyone in the family has seen or heard from Tane since then. I don't even know how he'd know I was betrothed."

"Would he know about the bracelet thing?" Nic asked.

Maxim nodded. "Yes. He's my cousin on my father's side. He'd know about the Colla band. I'm sure he's even seen it." He slammed his palm on the monitor hard enough to make the image jitter. "That arrogant little krebnack."

"Why would he take it?" Bennie asked. "You said it didn't have any specific retail value."

"To keep it from me. Somehow, he learned about the joining ceremony. We never got along, and he's always been jealous."

"Of you?" Bennie asked.

Maxim glared at him but otherwise didn't respond.

"We should get going," Nic said. She looked at Bennie and shook her head, making a tsking noise. "We've talked about this."

Bennie turned a darker shade of green. "What?" He looked at her, then at Maxim. "I'm sorry." He turned to his apprentice. "Happy?"

"That you act like a krebnack, and I have to scold you? No." She left the room.

Maxim turned to follow the young woman. He stopped and looked at Bennie. "You are a krebnack." He winked and walked out.

Bennie scowled. "You can't get into the ship without me!" he called out as he shut down the borrowed terminal.

THE COMMERCE PAVILIONS were a sprawling maze of stalls. To Wil it looked like most of the night markets outside spaceports. He looked at Bruce and the ambassador. "County fair vibes, right?"

Both men looked at him. "That's exactly it!" Ambassador Carlisle said. He looked around as they turned a corner. "Is every GC race represented here?"

Cynthia shook her head. "Not even close."

Zephyr added, "Most of these vendors come from all across the GC. There's a circuit and they all work it, more or less."

Bruce nodded his understanding. "We have that on Earth. Vendors who travel around following state and county fairs, Christmas markets, you name it."

Zephyr's eyes brightened. "That's right. You have Garthflak, too."

"Garth—what now?" Bruce asked.

"Space Christmas," Wil offered. He spied the look Zephyr shot his way. "What? That's literally what it is." She shook her head. He turned to the two humans. "Turns out most species have a Christmas-like holiday around the same time of year." He shrugged. "Weird, right?"

The ambassador rubbed his chin. "Really? All around the

same time of year?" Wil and the others nodded. "That's..." He shrugged. "Interesting."

Wil smiled. "Don't think too hard on it. You'll break your brain. I've never gotten a reasonable explanation other than, 'Well, that's certainly interesting.'"

The other man pursed his lips, clearly not ready to let the concept of a shared galactic holiday go.

Cynthia pointed at a stall. "Hey look, they've got Bol Dvesh!" She headed for a stall with a Tygran man behind the counter.

The others fell in behind her. Bruce leaned over to Gabe. "What's bowl vesh?"

The droid cocked his head. "Bol Dvesh is a Tygran snack food. Known to be quite flavorful with a hint of spice. It is a meat product."

Bruce nodded. "Cool. Thank you." He smiled. "You're useful!" He beamed.

"You have no idea how happy that makes me, hearing that."

Bruce slowed. He looked up at Gabe. "Really?"

"No." Gabe increased his pace, moving to catch up with Cynthia.

Bruce watched the droid leave.

The Tygran man grinned when he spied Cynthia and the others. "Welcome friends! Come, come! The best, and only, Bol Dvesh you'll get here at the Genko Akdool!"

Cynthia reached the stall and looked at the various offerings arrayed on the countertop. "You've got Tolpar *and* Ijih?"

The man behind the counter smiled. "I do, plus D'Xera."

"D'Xera?" Cynthia turned to the others. "Wil, he's got D'Xera flavor!"

Wil smiled at his wife. "I don't know what that is."

She turned to the feline featured man. "What province are you from?"

"Anas Ekal," the man said with pride.

She nodded. "Explains how you've got D'Xera."

He smiled. "I'm Marlcolm." He offered his arm.

Cynthia reached across the counter to clasp Marlcolm's forearm.

Wil approached, offering his own arm. "Hi, Wil Calder. Husband."

Cynthia rolled her eyes. To Marlcolm, she said, "We'll take one of each. Wait. No. Two of each."

The Tygran man smiled at the size of the sale. "Of course." He offered Wil a platter. "Sample what you're about to buy?"

Wil took a sample. "How is this a new thing to me?"

Cynthia moved closer, draping an arm over his shoulder. "Bol Dvesh is tricky to make and trickier still to transport. Short of making a trip to Tyr, it's—I thought—nearly impossible to get." She smiled at the other Tygran.

Marlcolm beamed. "It took me several cycles to master the process in such a way that I had a transportable product." He shrugged. "Once I got it, though...Well, here I am."

Bruce reached around Wil and Cynthia to grab a sample. He offered some to his boss, then took a bite. "Wow."

Cynthia gave him a single nod. "Right?"

Wil looked at Marlcolm. "Add two more of that one." He pointed. "We'll snack on these during the evening show."

PART 2

CHAPTER ELEVEN

ACCORDING to the records Bennie dug up, Maxim's cousin Tane took his new Bormea Vesper Nine to Jannav Kenu, a GC-affiliated colony world. Technically a client colony of Multon, but the Multonae were a minority population after losing interest in the world. Now it was a mixed bag of GC races: folks who wanted to get away without actually getting away. Jannav Kenu was distant enough to be mostly free from GC influence, but not so far it lacked creature comforts.

"This place is nice," Nic said as they stepped off the automated tram that connected the floating spaceport to the town of Vlap. The spaceport was a floating platform a kilometer off the peninsula near the center of the lake. The only access was the tram line that connected it to the mainland.

"Think Wil would move the office here?" Bennie asked. "Like Fury but no blowing sand."

"I could do without sand," Maxim agreed. The town of Lwath, where the team's headquarters was located, was next to one of the great drifting dune oceans that rolled across Fury.

Vlap was a fair-sized town on a peninsula that jutted into a large turquoise lake. Not a dune in sight.

"According to this," Nic waved a brochure she'd grabbed when they passed an information kiosk, "Vlap's biggest export is something called a bubong."

"They're already ahead of Lwath, having an export," Bennie said.

"What's a bubong?" Maxim asked.

The town was well lit. Strings of lights crisscrossed the main road they were on as well as the side streets that branched off from either side.

Nic consulted the brochure. "Apparently, some kind of a large crustacean that lives at the bottom of the lake." She shook her head. "Neat." She looked around. "Maybe we'll get to see one? What do you think they taste like?"

Maxim looked down at her. "Not here to sightsee. Or eat the local animals."

She pursed her lips and nodded. "You're right."

"Any thoughts on where we should go?" Bennie asked.

The big Palorian man looked around. The sun was nearly set; the buildings of the town were lighting up. He pointed. "That must be space control." The tallest building in town was several blocks away and featured a top floor that flared out into a large flat circle with a wrap-around floor to ceiling window.

"That or some rich drennog's penthouse. I'd be okay either way," Bennie said.

Maxim scowled. "If it's the latter, we're not robbing them."

Bennie made a face.

The trio walked along the street as locals began making their way to pubs and restaurants along the main street. Vlap was quite popular among tourists. The entire length of the peninsula was pink and purple sand beach dotted with resorts and bars.

As they walked, Bennie noticed a few sideways glances

from people that seemed to be doing their best to look like they weren't looking at Bennie and his friends.

"He's gotta be flogging the engines on that skiff," Bennie said, mostly to himself, as they crossed an intersection. "We keep getting closer, but he's always gone."

Nic shrugged. "The *Nontee* isn't exactly fast. Staying ahead of us wouldn't be that hard."

Bennie nodded. "True. Still bothers me. I mean, sure, the *Nontee* isn't as fast as the *Ghost*, but she's no slouch. Gabe saw to that."

They rounded a corner, the tall building directly ahead of them, two blocks further. Bennie immediately noticed that the string of lights that crisscrossed every street were out on this one. He pursed his lips and looked up.

"Bennie," Nic whispered.

"Yeah," he said. His hand drifted toward the hilt of his beam saber. He looked down, seeing her hand doing the same thing as his.

Walking a few steps behind the two smaller beings, Maxim smiled. He'd noticed the lights, too. When he first met Bennie, the selfish little hacker would have blithely walked into the trap that was likely waiting for them up ahead. Now, though...Now the two Knights of Plentallus were increasing their speed toward the trap? "What're you doing?" he whispered.

Bennie turned with a smirk. "What we do."

They reached the midpoint of the street as a group of ten beings stepped out in front of them. Five more stepped out from the intersection behind them. Both groups were an assortment of beings, but mostly Multonae.

Maxim slid his hand to the grip of his pulse pistol.

"OKAY, that was a helluva last thing to see!" Bruce exclaimed. He moved to clap Wil on the shoulder but stopped; both of his hands were full with bags of things the ambassador had purchased.

"So, they do that, then what?" Carlisle was walking next to Zephyr at the front of the group. "Everyone goes to their hotel or ship?"

The Palorian woman nodded. "They call it the Day's Rest. The larger of the two suns sets as the smaller rises." She pointed to the brightening horizon. "The second sun is a red dwarf. It won't get much brighter than it is right now. The Trollack still call it *night.* To them, it's a time to reflect, rest, and recharge."

"Sleep?" Bruce said, unimpressed with the fish people's convoluted way of thinking about night.

Gabe said, "Trollack sleep only three tocks a day. This time of day is for quieter pursuits and self-reflection."

They were following the flow of festival guests out the northeast quadrant exit. Most guests were branching off toward the mass transit stations.

Wil pointed to a section of the transit area where several ground and hover cars were parked in a row. "Come on. Cab stand is over there. Fastest way to our spaceport at this hour."

"Well, well. What have we here?" a voice said from a side walkway that intersected the one the Rogue Enterprises team was walking down.

Cynthia groaned. Turning, she spied the Hulgian woman from the gambling den. She wasn't alone; a quartet of, presumably, enforcers was just behind her. It wasn't clear what species the other four were; all were in light combat armor, helmets and all. Thankfully, none had Hulgian dimensions. In fact, they were likely Multonae, or Harrith, if she had to guess.

Wil looked at the Hulgian woman and then his wife. "Friend of yours?" She shook her head and turned to Bruce, who blushed. Wil nodded. "Okay, then." He turned to the Hulgian woman. "Look, we're not looking for trouble."

"Your hoo-man friend was supposed to close a deal with me for arms," the bipedal triceratops woman said. "I had plans for the bonus I'd have gotten."

Zephyr shrugged. "And you're thinking you can beat us into doing the deal?"

The bigger woman shrugged. "Nah. I'm not stupid. I know that deal's dead. Now I'm just planning to beat you all to a pulp for the fun of it. Salve my ego a little." She put her hands together, cracking the knuckles of her thick fingers.

Cynthia rolled her shoulders and cocked her head from side to side. "You really don't want to do thi—"

Faster than someone her size should have been able to move, the Hulgian woman lunged in with a flurry of punches. The four armored goons followed, jumping past their boss toward Wil, Gabe, and Zephyr.

Wil pushed Ambassador Carlisle toward Bruce, telling the latter, "Keep him safe. Get him back to the *Ghost.*" He turned to Gabe. "Get 'em to the ship." The droid nodded. Wil turned just in time to catch an armored fist to the stomach, forcing the air from his lungs.

A group of Brailack shoved away from the fight, commenting on how the riffraff always get into trouble on the way out of the festival.

Cynthia dodged one, then two, then three jabs all aimed at her face. She ducked under a right hook and used the opening her opponent gave her to drive her fist under the other woman's rib cage. Before the Hulgian could double over, Cynthia leaped upward, driving a knee into the woman's mouth. She felt teeth give way as her opponent let out a guttural groan. Cynthia let her momentum carry her up and over the other woman's shoulder.

Zephyr ducked and parried as two of the armored goons attacked her. She reached under her shirt to the small of her back, pulling her hand back and holding it between her and the two thugs. She pressed a button, and the device, no larger than her fist, telescoped out into a bo staff.

She grinned. "Let's dance."

WIL DUCKED a punch and delivered a quick jab to his attacker's helmeted face. It hurt. "No fair having a helmet!" He shook his hand.

The other person cocked their head. "Who said life was fair?" He or she leaned back and planted a kick to Wil's chest, sending him sprawling.

Weapons were prohibited on the Genko Akdool fairgrounds. That didn't mean the team hadn't figured out some workarounds. Cynthia had introduced them to a wonderful little device that was invisible on scans, fit in the small of one's back, and when activated, turned into a bo staff.

He activated it and spun it in a wide arc to give himself some space. He still wasn't very proficient but was better than he'd been six months ago.

Wil spun the staff in a series of moves Cynthia taught him. They were mostly intended to intimidate, and based on the other person's body language, they were working. Wil grinned, then stopped his staff's rotation and launched into a series of jabs and powerful swings.

Cynthia danced around the Hulgian woman's tail. "Look, we're friends of Rhys Duch. He's not going to be happy when he hears you attacked us."

"You attacked me first!" the other woman huffed as she completed her spin with an arm out. Her fist caught Cynthia in the shoulder, sending her spinning through the air before landing sprawled out on the ground.

Wiping herself off, Cynthia said, "Really? We don't need to—"

The much larger woman dropped her head and charged. Cynthia leaped up into a flip. She caught the woman's horn, pivoted, and came down straddling her shoulders. "This doesn't have to get ugly. Okay, uglier." She stood and pushed off with all her might, driving the woman into the ground as she rose into the air, spun, and dropped to her feet.

"You there! Stop!" a voice rang out. "You're in violation of the Genko Akdool code of conduct!"

"Oh shit, the cops!" Wil shouted. He took one more swing at his opponent, forcing them to raise both arms up defensively, which gave him a clean target to plant a kick between their legs. They doubled over. Not everyone kept their genitals there, but Wil had discovered that most did. He collapsed his staff and bolted.

A quintet of Trollack security officers was fanning out.

Cynthia and Zephyr followed suit, taking off in different directions. The former leaped over one of the fishlike people as he waved his arms overhead trying to catch her.

The Hulgian woman got to her knees. Seeing the Trollack already putting their hands on one of her men, she rose slowly. Four stunners were trained on her, while the fifth was aimed at her man being cuffed. She looked in the direction Zephyr had gone and scowled.

GABE WAS WAITING for them in the lounge on B deck. "There is an alert throughout the spaceport for you."

Wil tapped the droid's metal shoulder. "That sounds right."

He turned to Bruce and Ambassador Carlisle sitting on the sofa. "You two ready to go?"

The older of the pair looked at Wil, then at Cynthia and Zephyr; all of them were bruised. "Do I want to know?"

Cynthia smirked. "Just wrapping up some business we started earlier."

Gabe raised a hand. "I have begun the reactor warmup. We will be flight-ready in ten microtocks."

The ambassador leaned forward. "Whatever that just was notwithstanding, thank you, Captain. This was a thoroughly enjoyable experience. I believe I have a much wider appreciation for many of the races of the GC now. The good and the bad."

Bruce nodded to the half dozen large bags next to him on the floor. "So much *stuff*."

Wil smiled. "Tchotchkes from every world in the GC. We thought you'd like it. One of the best ways to see a lot of the GC in one place." He looked at Bruce. "And get souvenirs." He was sure the other man got his meaning.

Cynthia patted Wil's stomach. "Plus, the food's good." He winced, certain that one of his ribs was bruised.

Zephyr sighed. "The wait for departure clearance is gonna be long if they're looking for us."

Gabe inclined his head. "Fortunately, they have no descriptions."

Zephyr nodded. "Good news, for sure."

"Plus, they have our friends. I'm sure she's keeping them busy," Cynthia said.

"My money's on at least an hour before we're cleared for departure," Wil said.

Gabe cocked his head. "A ground vehicle is approaching."

Zephyr made a face. "Ship to ship search?"

"Hardly seems restful," Bruce quipped.

The ship's first officer nodded. "Indeed."

Wil headed for the hatch to the stairwell. "Let's see what's up."

A Trollack man in a uniform was waiting at the bottom of the cargo ramp. "Hi there, folks."

Wil looked down at the little purple fellow. Trollack always reminded him of cartoon catfish. Catfish that wore clothes and had spaceflight. He smiled. "Hi there. Can we help you?"

The little officer bobbed his head, his fishy transparent eyelids blinking several times. Up close, Wil heard a faint *squick* noise with each blink. "We're just going ship to ship. There was a disturbance a little while ago; some irresponsible festivalgoers got into a fight."

Wil affected a horrified look. "Really? That's horrible." He looked at Cynthia. "What's wrong with people these days?"

She made a face but shrugged. "I don't know, my love. Some people are just out to ruin everyone's fun."

The little man bobbed on his heels. "Yeah, it's nothing too serious, but we wanted to ask around before ships started lifting off." He paused, then looked up at the ship. He turned his gaze to Zephyr standing behind Wil, then to Cynthia, then to Wil again. His mouth opened and closed several times before he said, "This is the *Ghost*, yeah?" He rubbed his hands on his trousers.

Wil squinted, drawing out his answer. "Yes?"

Bruce and the ambassador came down the ramp and looked at Cynthia, who shrugged. Zephyr came further down the ramp. "Is there something wrong? I filed our landing permits myself."

The little man shook his head. "Oh no, nothing's wrong. Forgive me. It's just..." He looked down at the ground, shuffling his feet. When he looked up, he said, "I'm a big fan."

Ambassador Carlisle stepped forward. "Fan?"

The little customs officer looked at the older human, then

turned to Wil. "This is the crew of the *Ghost*. They helped keep the Commonwealth from full collapse. They defeated the rogue elements within the Peacekeepers over Harrith Prime."

Wil smiled. "We also beat a sentient warship—"

Cynthia put a hand on his shoulder. "Not now, love."

Wil blushed.

The ambassador turned to the couple. "We'd been briefed, of course, but I didn't realize your exploits were quite so well known."

Wil glanced at the older man. "Honestly, I didn't know that either. We do try to keep a low profile." He looked at the little man and smiled. "Mostly."

The little man thrust a hand out at Wil. "It's an honor to meet you, Captain Calder."

Wil clasped the man's forearm. "The pleasure is ours, Officer...."

"Cliko Vebbar."

"Officer Cliko," Wil said. Trollack society used given names for formal greetings among strangers.

When the smaller man didn't immediately release his arm, Wil coughed. "Well, we really should be getting going."

Cliko Vebbar released Wil's arm. "Oh, uh, sure. You're leaving already? According to the logs, you arrived only this morning. There's no way you could have seen the whole festival."

Wil inclined his head. "Unfortunately. Bit of a whirlwind tour for our guest here."

Carlisle nodded. "You have a lovely world, and the Genko Akdool was most impressive. I hope to return one day."

The little fishlike man grinned. "Well. Safe travels, then." He bowed.

Wil waved. "Good luck looking for your trouble-makers."

Once the ground vehicle departed, the group made its way

up the ramp. "I was thinking, if there's time, I'd like to visit a—what did you call it? A Tier 1 world," Ambassador Carlisle said.

Bruce, who'd been pretty quiet since Cynthia pulled him from the gambling den, said, "Yeah, someplace normal. Run of the mill. Your everyday GC world."

"What do you think this is?" Cynthia asked, waving a hand toward the spaceport and festival grounds behind them.

Wil laughed. "No such thing, but..." He reached over to the control pedestal next to the cargo bay doors. As the doors ground together, the cargo ramp rose. He said, "What's perfectly normal on one world is almost a crime on another."

"What about Brai?" Cynthia said. "They're pretty normal."

Zephyr looked at her friend. "Really?"

Cynthia shrugged. "I mean, more or less."

Zephyr reached the stairs. "More less than more," she said under her breath. Louder, she said, "I'll be on the bridge."

Ambassador Carlisle and Bruce reached the stairs. "Brai. That's where your little hacker friend is from, right? He's Brailack?"

Wil nodded. "Don't hold him against them. Most aren't sociopaths." Following the other two humans up the stairs, he added, "Brai's a good idea. Not far from Tarsis, either, so not a long trip to drop you off before your appointment ceremony."

CHAPTER TWELVE

"I'M GULBAR' Te, and this is GNO Morning Briefing." The Burzzad reporter's long neck bowed as the man nodded to the camera.

"We're hearing reports that the Governing Council was busy overnight with a series of unannounced speeches and motions from members on the subcommittee on Harrith Guided Improvements."

He turned. "As you may recall, last year's political upheavals were forestalled when the Council officially invited the Harrith Collective to come and share their insights on governance. The Harrith are one of the few non-GC societies that have thrived on their own for nearly as long as the Commonwealth has existed. Their form of government has one of the highest citizen happiness ratings of any known governance model."

He cleared his throat. "Since then, the Harrith delegation has been actively working with several subcommittees to fix what many citizens saw as shortcomings in the Commonwealth's government.

"Apparently, several of the Harrith proposals have caused

quite the stir within the subcommittees." He turned to another camera pickup. "We'll be back in five tocks with an update."

BENNIE AND NIC didn't wait to hear what, if anything, the toughs had to say; the pair ignited their beam sabers and dove into the group ahead of them. The hum of their blades was broken by screams and shouts.

Maxim's mouth fell open. He watched in awe and horror as the two smallest members of the team dove, twisted, turned, slashed, and stabbed at their attackers. A Palorian man screamed as his hand, still clutching a pulse pistol, fell to the ground. A Stilten made a warbling, clicking sound as two of its left side limbs fell to the ground, cleanly cut off at the elbow, the chitin glowing.

Turning to face the other group of attackers, Maxim said, "I guess I get you guys." He squinted. "Sorry, ma'am. No offense meant."

The Hulgian woman with sharpened horns winked before she broke into a charge, lowering her head. Her nine friends fell in behind her, all brandishing blades of various lengths and the odd pulse pistol, plus what Maxim thought might be a slug thrower in the hands of a lanky Multonae man.

Max smiled and ran toward the group. He leaped into the air, higher than someone his size should be able to. He grabbed one of the Hulgian's horns, pivoting up and over her to land on the large woman's back like he was riding an animal. He pitched forward a bit, sending her into an off-balance stumble. Before she hit the ground, he slammed his fist into the side of the large woman's head three times. Her stumble turned into a dive for the ground.

Moments before the woman that looked like a bipedal

triceratops hit the ground, Maxim leaped off her back toward the next nearest attacker, a Trenbal man with a pair of long knives in each hand.

He dodged left, then right, then slammed a fist into the man's torso, forcing the wind out of his attacker's trio of lungs. While the reptilian attacker fell to the ground, Maxim pulled his own pistol and fired two bolts of supercharged plasma into the man's back, burning a pair of sizable holes into him.

A loud crack sounded, and a piece of the building near Maxim exploded, sending chips of masonry everywhere, including his face. He ducked, which left him open for another Trenbal to tackle him to the ground. The two men rolled, the reptilian one trying to push a savage-looking blade into Maxim's gut. He could feel the blade's point against his abdomen.

Someone nearby shouted. "You're in my shot, Kattor!"

Nic ducked under the reach of a red-skinned, four-armed man. He held a knife in each hand and was windmilling them to try to catch a piece of her. He moved so fast that her beam saber didn't slice through the man's blades as much as deflect off of them while super-heating them at the same time.

The D'nini man grinned. "I'm gonna gut you, little girl." He brought one of the blades to his face, blowing on it.

Nic smirked. "Bring it on, four arms." She took a step back and struck a Lantash Moroo stance, her blade held backwards behind her, her free hand held out in front of her. She beckoned the much larger man toward her. "Show me what you've got."

He snarled and charged, holding all four blades straight out. She sidestepped his first attack, then his second, keeping her beam saber held behind her in the Flumboli stance. His third attack carried him past her. She swung her blade around, tapping the angry four-armed alien on his behind, just enough to singe his trousers.

He scowled. "You little—"

"Stop playing with him," Bennie said as he sliced through the barrel of a pulse pistol, before driving the point of his blade into his opponent's side, hopefully avoiding major organs. He wasn't sure what the person before him was so couldn't be sure he hadn't just stabbed them in the heart. He'd been trying to set a better example for Nic and the apprentices back on Nexuu. It was annoying.

"Fine," Nic said. She leaped up onto the man's back. With a snap, her beam saber blade shut down. She slammed her hilt down on his head once. Both of his upper arms grasped for her. She ducked under one arm only to feel his other hand clamp down on her arm painfully tightly. She slammed her hilt down on his head one more time. The second time was the charm. The big man's eyes rolled back in his head, and he collapsed under her.

Nic leaped off her opponent a moment before he hit the ground.

Maxim rolled under his Trenbal opponent and got his feet under him. He pushed with all his might, sending the scaly attacker flying into Multonae man with the slug thrower. The two attackers end up in a tangled heap. Getting back to his feet, Maxim picked his pulse pistol up off the ground and shot both. He sighed. "You two need help?"

He barely sidestepped a knife thrust from an already bruised Harrith man. The blade sliced through the arm of his jumpsuit and his arm beneath. Just enough to hurt, not enough to incapacitate his arm, thankfully. He dropped an elbow on the attacker's neck, dropping the man to the ground in a heap. "We need one alive," he called out, adding, "Or at least mostly."

Nic turned, letting a Multonae woman's corpse fall to the ground. "You should have said something sooner!"

TWO DAYS OUT FROM BRAI, as everyone was sitting down for breakfast, the *Ghost* shuddered. The lights on the common deck flickered and then dimmed as red emergency lights came on.

"The fuck?" Wil said as he jumped from his seat. He looked at the ceiling. "Computer, report."

"We are no longer in FTL," the sexless voice replied. After Bennie's repeated attempts over the years to impart some personality and a little sentience into the ship's computer—always to disastrous effect—everyone agreed that the default setting was best.

Wil sighed. "Thanks."

"You are welcome."

Rolling his eyes, he headed for the hatch that led to the long corridor that connected the forward section to the larger aft section of the ship. The ship rocked, and he lost his footing, stumbling backward to fall over the back of the sofa in the lounge area.

Zephyr and Cynthia both made it to the hatch, heading forward. Bruce came to Wil's side, helping him up as the ship shook again. "What's going on?" He looked frantic.

Ambassador Carlisle joined them. He helped Wil around the sofa. "Will someone come help us?"

Wil shook his head. "Don't even know if we need help."

The overhead speakers beeped. "Two tangos. Get your ass up here!" Zephyr said.

"Okay, we might need help," Wil said as he reached the hatch. He looked at the ceiling. "Gabe, you in engineering?"

"I am."

"Good." He rushed down the neck toward the bridge. He looked over his shoulder. "Strap in!" he shouted as the hatch closed.

He pushed through the bridge hatch as sparks rained down

from a panel over the tactical station. Cynthia, sitting there, ducked her head.

Zephyr leaped out of Wil's seat at the command console, taking her position at the Ops station. In two strides he crossed the bridge to his seat. It conformed to him as he got situated before sliding into place at the console.

"Any idea who our friends are?" he asked as he pushed the sub-light throttle control forward while pulling the flight controls to the left.

On the primary display, one of the attacking ships, a Malkorite corvette, swooped by, the pair of topside turrets tracking the *Ghost*. Their shields flashed orange with each impact as Wil forced them into a tight turn to put the *Ghost* behind the attacking craft.

"None," Zephyr said, adding, "beyond them both being Malkorite corvettes."

"Have we pissed off the Malkorites recently?" Cynthia asked.

Wil glanced to the side. "Recently? No. Also, babe, feel free to fire any time you like."

She turned, glaring. "Maxim changed the layout of his console. That weirdo!" She slammed a palm on the console. A second later it made a series of beeps. "Oh, there we go." She turned to Wil and winked. Several metallic clanks sounded from deep inside the ship. On the display, a pair of missiles streaked out from the bottom corners, then banked off screen.

Wil glanced at the smaller tactical display attached to the forward bulkhead next to the much larger primary display. Two red triangles were on either side of the ship. A pair of green dots was arcing toward one of the triangles.

"How'd they pull us out of FTL?" he asked as he kicked in the lateral thrusters, putting the *Ghost* into a tight yaw to port.

Zephyr shook her head. "No idea. I'm looking over the logs now."

Wil pulled the controls hard over, twisting the ship again in a tight arc in the opposite direction they'd just been flying. One of the corvettes came into view on the main screen.

"Firing!" Cynthia called out. Another pair of missiles shot out from the lower edge of the screen while bright green plasma blasts leaped from the sides, firing from the nacelle-mounted blasters. The enemy ship's shields flashed orange over and over as the smaller *Ghost* poured high-energy plasma into them. The enemy corvette shot down one of the two missiles, but the second struck it amidships. Several shield emitters exploded along the hull. The energy barrier protecting the vessel flickered before vanishing.

"I'VE GOT YOU NOW!" Cynthia boasted in a deep raspy voice, sending two more missiles toward the wounded target. As Wil brought the *Ghost* more level with their attacker, she added the smaller turret blaster that sat just behind the bridge. A third stream of energy filled the screen, coming from the top to strike the ship's exposed flank.

Wil glanced at his wife. "I love you."

She turned. "I know."

Zephyr rolled her eyes. "No more *War Stars* nights."

"*Star Wars*," the couple answered as one.

A section of the Malkorite ship exploded. The energy wave from the explosion rocked the *Ghost* violently, nearly tossing Zephyr out of her station.

"Captain, shields are down to twenty-seven percent," Gabe informed via the overhead speaker.

Reaching up to pull herself back into her seat, she said, "I don't know why they're so mad at us, but at least there's one less." She snapped her restraints in place. "Could be guns for hire or just randoms that bought old Malkorite hulls."

"Either way, they're toast," Cynthia growled. The sound of the top-mounted ball turret firing punctuated her statement.

Wil glanced at the tactical display to get a read on where the other corvette was and adjusted course. The damaged ship was limping away in a straight line, likely unable to jump to FTL. Cynthia was peppering its friend with plasma bolts from the ball turret.

"There you are," Wil said under his breath as he pulled the sub-light throttle back to zero, then fired the thrusters in the fore and aft section in opposition, flipping the ship end over end. He pushed the throttle all the way forward, sending the *Ghost* back in the opposite direction, right toward the second corvette.

The enemy ship's forward cannons reacquired the *Ghost* quickly, opening fire. Cynthia returned the gesture with all three blasters and a pair of missiles for effect.

The *Ghost* shook and rattled, her shields flashing with each impact.

"I am attempting to boost the forward shields, but it will not last long," Gabe reported.

Wil glanced at the ceiling. "Copy." He twisted the control stick, putting the ship into a spin. He added some thrust, turning it into a corkscrew.

"Babe?" he asked.

"Forward shields failing," Gabe warned.

"Babe?"

"Stop spinning!" Cynthia hissed.

The ship rocked. Several overhead panels erupted; sparks rained down.

Zephyr had both hands on her console. "Damage to the starboard wing!" She had to shout to be heard over the sound of alarms and shrieking metal.

Wil pulled them from the corkscrew and passed close enough to the corvette that he could read the ship's name stenciled across the ship's bow: *Gaart Naarg*.

"Status of the other guys?" he asked.

Zephyr consulted her sensor display. "Their forward shields are nearly gone. Looks like several power fluctuations along her portside emitter array." She glanced back down, then turned to Wil. "Looks like they're trying to circle back and link up with their friend. Maybe get out of here."

"Oh, no you don't," Wil said, mostly to himself. He pulled the controls over, bringing the *Ghost* onto the wounded corvette's tail. The stricken ship's rear turrets, mounted on either side of its centrally mounted engines, swung around to take aim.

"Uh, we don't have forward shields," Zephyr warned.

Bolts of energy shot from the sides of the display, lighting up the other ship's shields. Grinning, Wil turned the ship, rotating it on its long axis, tipping her up on her wing. The enemy ship's weapons fire flashed by on either side of them.

A missile streaked away from the *Ghost* to detonate against the enemy corvette's shields. Their missile was answered with two from the Malkorite corvette. Wil used the foot pedals to kick the ship into a spin, bringing their strongest shields into position. The ship lurched.

"Aft shields at thirty-two percent. Several emitters are throwing error codes," Zephyr announced.

A quick maneuver by the enemy pilot brought one of the ship's turrets to bear on the *Ghost* a moment before their missile impacted, overloading several more sections of the ship. The corvette's engines flared and then died, sending it into a tumble. It tumbled along the same course the *Ghost* was on.

The damaged corvette was growing larger on the primary display.

"Wil?" Zephyr asked.

Wil was frantically pushing controls on his main flight console.

"Will?" Zephyr repeated.

On the forward display, the wounded corvette was still growing larger.

Wil looked up. "Uh, Gabe? I don't have flight control. Flight dynamics are all fucked up up here."

"I am aware of the current state of the ship's systems," the ceiling answered.

"Impact in one microtock," Zephyr announced.

"Dude, we're going to slam our ass into the bad guys," Wil said.

The bridge hatch opened, and the two human guests walked in. Ambassador Carlisle pointed at the display. "Uh, are we going to collide with that other ship?"

"No," Cynthia said.

"Maybe," Wil said at the same time.

"Yes," was Zephyr's answer.

Wil pointed to Cynthia's and Bennie's stations. "Better grab a seat."

BENNIE AND NIC WERE BACK-TO-BACK, beam sabers humming.

"This is so much fun! This trip was starting to be boring!" the young Olop girl said between breaths. The fur on her forehead was matted with blood. Very little of it was hers.

Bennie grinned. He was proud of his apprentice. He'd die before he told her, but it was true. He knew he shouldn't have that attitude, but being forthcoming didn't come naturally to him. Maybe the next crop of apprentices, he'd do better? "Don't get cocky, apprentice," he warned.

"Oh, come on! There's only like three left."

From the mouth of the alley, ten Multonae stepped into view.

Bennie scowled, using his saber to deflect a pipe in the hands of an angry Quilant. When the little man's stubby whiskers vibrated, he howled and swung again. Bennie deflected the pipe again, this time adjusting his swing to bring his blade back down on the pipe, severing it inches from the Quilant man's hand.

He reared back and kicked his opponent, who was busy gaping at the still glowing end of his makeshift weapon. "See what you did with your prideful boasting?" he scolded.

"That's not my fault," Nic protested. "Obviously, they were waiting."

"Children," Maxim said. He had his pistol up and moving in a slow arc between the ten new arrivals, all of whom were armed, and the two remaining thugs from the first group.

"As Wil would say, you jinxed it," Bennie said.

"I don't know what that means," Nic replied.

"Children!" Maxim shouted.

The two smaller beings both turned. Nic snapped off her beam saber, using her thumb to spin the custom dial on the hilt. In the blink of an eye, she raised the hilt, holding it parallel to the ground, and aimed at the Multonae man in the middle of the new group. She pressed the activation switch.

A bolt of supercharged plasma leaped from the hilt. Rather than forming a coherent blade, the bolt continued down the alley to strike the man in the chest. The impact knocked him backward. The remaining nine toughs gasped as one, all stepping away from the smoking corpse of their friend.

"Run!" Maxim shouted, seeing their opportunity. He hustled his two friends further down the alley. "We need cover!"

Supercharged plasma splashed against the walls on either side of them along with a few slugs.

"Why do so many of them have slug throwers?" Maxim huffed as they neared the end of the alley.

Ignoring the big man's question, Bennie turned to Nic. "That seems to have really angered them," he added. "Good shot, by the way."

"Agreed," Maxim said. He was running at half his top speed so as not to lose his two friends. He glanced down at Nic. "Great shot. Especially at that distance."

Nic beamed, but her reply was cut off by a bolt of energy striking the building next to her, sending super-heated masonry in all directions.

Maxim half turned while continuing on. He squeezed off several rounds at their pursuers. "This is a lot. More than Tane should be able to arrange, let alone afford."

"If we survive, we can ask him all about it." Bennie huffed.

"Maybe he got a loan?" Nic wondered aloud.

Bennie looked at her and shook his head.

The trio reached the end of the alley and found themselves on a street that offered little cover.

"Where's a parade when you need one?" Maxim said. He turned left, then right, then left again. "This way." He fired several more rounds down the alley.

Nic turned and fired another shot from her beam saber hilt. She turned before seeing if her aim was true but was rewarded with a pained grunt. Hopefully that would buy them a few minutes to find shelter.

CHAPTER THIRTEEN

EVERYONE on the bridge of the *Ghost* watched as the damaged Malkorite corvette *Gaart Naarg* grew larger and larger on the primary display. Gabe had triggered the lateral thrusters to end their lazy spin, but the braking thrusters were still causing him trouble.

"Can't you blow it up?" Bruce asked from the communication station.

Wil shook his head. "Way too close now. Especially without shields." He closed his eyes.

Everyone else did too. The ship rumbled and then fell silent.

After what felt like enough time for the *Ghost* to crash into the *Gaart Naarg*'s engines, Wil opened one eye. The enemy ship's inert engines were the only thing visible on the primary display.

"We're not dead?" the ambassador asked, opening his eyes.

Wil looked over to spot Zephyr opening her eyes. He turned to look at Cynthia, one eyebrow arched. She shrugged. Turning to the ceiling, he said, "Gabe?"

"I had to perform an emergency purge of the cargo hold,"

the disembodied voice of the team's engineer said. "I will need to run a full diagnostic of the maneuvering thrusters."

"Well, good work, buddy." Wil looked at the others. "Hope no one left anything important in the hold."

"I've got limited sensors," Zephyr said. "The other corvette is gone. They must have jumped to FTL assuming their friends were about to die."

"Know the feeling," Bruce said.

On the forward display, the *Gaart Naarg* seemed to be slowly spinning on the display. Wil couldn't tell if the crippled corvette was spinning or if the *Ghost* was.

"How long for repairs?"

"At least one tock. Two is more likely," Gabe answered.

Wil looked at the *Gaart Naarg* again. "It's a race, Gabe. Make it one. Or less."

"Acknowledged," the ceiling replied.

"DO we still head for the space control?" Nic asked as they rounded another corner. Maxim was bringing up the rear. He turned and sprayed the alley they'd come out of with plasma. Return fire came back, exploding the wall nearest them. Their pursuers seemed intent on keeping up.

"Not much point now," Bennie said. His beam saber was back on his belt. He returned fire with a blaster he'd picked up off a dead Kilden a while back.

"We still gotta figure out where his cousin is." She stopped, looked around, and with a *snap-hiss*, had her beam saber humming. She stabbed the door handle once, melting it and everything behind it in a flash. "In we go." She didn't wait for the two men to follow.

Maxim looked at Bennie. "Authoritative, isn't she?" Bennie

just shook his head and held out his arm for Maxim to enter the building.

Walking into the darkened space, Bennie said, "What is this?" He let the door slam shut, plunging them into pitch black.

From somewhere else in the room, something clunked, and Nic swore.

"It won't take them long to find that door," Maxim said.

Suddenly, the room went from the complete absence of light to what seemed like all the light in the universe; it was strobing, blinking, twirling, and flickering.

"Muhgrolacker!" Bennie swore. "You coulda warned us!" he shouted, holding both hands out in front of his face to try to shield his eyes from the luminous onslaught.

Maxim looked around, now that he could see. The two men were standing on the dance floor of a nightclub. Automated spotlights were sweeping the floor as small strobes went off along the perimeter of the space, casting angular shadows this way and that.

"Sorry!" Nic shouted from somewhere deeper inside the club.

Maxim looked around. "Well, this isn't subtle." He turned to the damaged door and then looked around, spotting a chair someone had left off to the side. He picked it up, blew glitter off it, and wedged it under the remains of the back door's handle. Looking at the damaged handle, he said, "That won't last long."

"Seems like a good place for a final battle," Bennie said. The Brailack hacker and first knight of the reborn Knights of Plentallus turned to the door, then back to Maxim. He activated his beam saber, the magenta glow illuminating his feral grin.

Maxim shook his head. "Yeah, no. No last stands."

The hacker shrugged.

Maxim grinned. "We still need to question at least one of them."

Bennie looked at where Nic was still waiting in the control room in the corner of the large space near the front of the building. "Cut the lights. Stay there and do the blinding everyone thing on my mark."

"Copy that," she replied. She ducked out of sight inside the booth. After a minute the space was plunged back into darkness except for the magenta glow of Bennie's beam saber.

Just in time as muffled voices came from the ruined door. Maxim and Bennie scrambled deeper into the building, the latter extinguishing his beam saber as he moved.

"I HAVE BEEN able to restore several basic systems. We have limited maneuvering. Shields are at ten percent. The starboard blaster is marginally functional," Gabe said as he entered the bridge.

The team and their guests had maintained a watch on the bridge, only leaving to grab snacks or use the head. The enemy ship hadn't so much as flinched in the hour they'd been waiting for Gabe to effect minimal repairs.

Wil rubbed his chin. "Then let's go say hi."

"Come again?" Cynthia said.

"I assumed we'd be, you know, getting the hell out of here," Bruce said.

His boss, the ambassador, nodded.

Wil smiled. "I don't know about you, but I'm kinda curious about who they are. They did attack us."

"By pulling us out of FTL," Zephyr added.

"So, they knew our route," Bruce said. He looked at his boss. "That's definitely not good."

Wil slapped his palms on the arms of his chair, careful to

avoid any of the controls, after what happened last time. "So... let's go say hi."

After a pause, he turned his chair around. "That would've been more dramatic if we'd docked first."

Cynthia nodded but said nothing.

"I will remain aboard the *Ghost* unless you need me," Gabe said from the ceiling. "There is still much repair work to be completed."

Wil nodded. "Copy that." He pulled his seat into the flight console and powered up the maneuvering thrusters to bring the *Ghost* alongside the crippled corvette.

The *Ghost* moved alongside the damaged corvette. Using one of the side-mounted cameras, Wil lined up the *Ghost*'s port airlock with an airlock on the corvette that looked undamaged. He nudged the ship closer, the distance on the top of the screen ticking down by the half meter until it read three meters. The only design flaw the Ankarran Raptor Model 89 had, as far as Wil was concerned, was that her wings made pulling alongside other ships difficult. You either had to use the docking tube at its maximum length or tilt the ship off axis to the other vessel.

"Activating docking bridge," Zephyr announced. On the screen, a flexible umbilical telescoped from the *Ghost* toward the *Gaart Naarg*'s airlock. The flexible connector rotated on its axis to line up properly with the other ship.

Wil turned his chair toward the rear of the bridge. He slapped his hands, carefully, on the arms of his command chair. "Okay, let's go say hi." He stood.

"Much better," Cynthia said, rising to follow him. Zephyr and their two guests brought up the rear.

The group headed down the stairs on either side of the security hatch that led down the neck toward the rest of the ship.

"I've wondered where these go," Bruce said as the group

reached the forward section of C deck. "What's down here?" He looked around.

Wil pointed. "Bathroom."

"Well, I'll be," Ambassador Carlisle said. "I've been going all the way back to the crew area." He walked over and pressed the release on the door and peered inside when the hatch slid away. "Huh. Nicer than the one in my quarters."

Bruce nodded to the much more robust-looking hatch opposite the one to the head. "And that?"

Wil grinned. "Playroom." He pressed a palm against the reader plate next to the hatch and waited for a beep to acknowledge that the computer had verified his identity. A series of clunks announced the release of the security locks. Then, with a hiss, the armory doors parted down the middle and slid apart.

Wil didn't wait for the doors to fully open, stepping into the armory as the lights clicked on, illuminating the individual alcoves that each member of the team used to store their combat gear.

Bruce followed him inside, eyes wide. "Woah." He walked over to an alcove with a massive set of Peacekeeper scout armor standing in the middle. The matte black suit looked like someone was standing there.

"Don't," Zephyr warned as she walked toward her own alcove. "He'll know."

Cynthia moved into her alcove. "Maxim is...particular."

"Dude comes down here and dusts his armor once a week." Wil slipped the torso armor over his head, locking the side clasps. "We're on a spaceship. There's no dust." He pulled a gauntlet off a shelf, snapping it over his wristcomm. After attaching the other gauntlet, he slipped off his shoes and stepped into a pair of boots. He tapped a command on his wristcomm, and the system activated. A thin, flexible material spread from each armor component, over his clothes, fully enclosing him in the light armor.

He leaned over to look past his lighter gear to the full combat armor suit. "Maybe next time."

Cynthia was donning much lighter armor components that wouldn't interfere with her mobility. She slid fingerless gloves onto each hand, flexing her fingertips to extend razor-sharp claws.

"What about us?" Bruce asked. He watched her claws retract, eyes wide.

Zephyr turned. "What about you? You're staying aboard the ship."

Bruce looked at his boss, pleading. The ambassador cleared his throat. "It would be instructive to experience the GC in full. Especially the parts that don't get as much attention."

Wil cocked his head. "Like crime?"

The ambassador smiled. "Like everything."

Zephyr looked at Wil, who pursed his lips. He looked at Cynthia, shrugged, and said, "Fine. You stay behind us at all times." The two men nodded. "Seriously. Behind us. I don't want to get sued or whatever if you get killed on my watch."

Bruce quirked a smile. "You think you'd be sued? If we died?"

Wil shrugged. "I dunno. I don't want to lose my Earth citizenship either."

Carlisle shook his head. "That's not a thing."

Wil shrugged again. "Either way. Stay behind us."

The two men nodded.

Cynthia watched the exchange, rolled her eyes, and said, "We have some spare armor pieces over there." She pointed to a closet at the end of the room. It was where everyone put pieces of armor they no longer wanted or needed. Eventually, Gabe would get around to recycling all of it.

Zephyr finished stepping into her Peacekeeper scout armor. Bringing its systems online, she raised each arm, making a fist and checking her range of motion. "All set."

Cynthia helped Bruce slide a piece of armor over his head. It wouldn't stop much more than a pulse pistol, but he wouldn't be stepping out of the airlock until they cleared the ship. Turning to Ambassador Carlisle, she held up a slightly dented piece of chest armor. He shook his head.

"Everyone ready?" Wil asked.

Cynthia looked at their guest and then turned to him and nodded. Zephyr did the same.

Wil grabbed a pulse rifle from the rack in his alcove.

WIL PUSHED HIMSELF UPWARD. "This would be easier with Bennie." He turned. "Don't tell him I said that."

They were all clustered outside the *Gaart Naarg*'s airlock, drifting in the zero gravity between the two ships.

Cynthia shook her head. "Don't you have the Bennie app?"

Wil made a face. "No. I assumed it was a virus or something. He'd use it to hack my private data stores or siphon money from my accounts."

She shook her head and moved him aside to float near the corvette's airlock control panel. "As if he can't do those things already."

"Your hacker has an app?" Bruce asked Wil.

Wil nodded. "Yeah, when he started getting more involved with the Knights, he packaged up a bunch of his hacking tools into a little animated him that supposedly can replace him. Basic AI and all that." He turned to Cynthia. "I still don't trust it on my wristcomm."

She shook her head. The airlock's outer doors cycled open

with a hiss. Cynthia adjusted her grip on the open hatch, pulling herself into the airlock. "Say what you will. But AI Bennie got us in."

Wil frowned.

One by one, the group guided themselves into the airlock, letting the ship's gravity assert itself, pulling them to the deck. The airlock was roomy as far as airlocks went—room enough for all five of them to fit inside. The outer doors closed.

Zephyr reached for a control panel, activating the entry cycle to fill the airlock with atmosphere. She looked at the two new humans. "You both did better in zero-g than I expected."

The ambassador smiled. "Believe it or not, zero-gravity training is required for all off-world positions."

Wil nodded his approval.

After a minute or two, the light over the inner hatch blinked from orange to blue.

Cynthia pushed the release, parting the inner doors.

"How did you know it was okay to open? What's orange mean?" Ambassador Carlisle asked.

"Or blue?" Bruce added.

Wil aimed his rifle the opposite way Zephyr was aiming hers as he stepped out into the corridor. "Malkorite blood is orange. So, for them, it's the same as red to us. Warning. Bad. Etcetera."

"Interesting," the older man said, adding, "Good to know."

Wil turned serious. "You two stay here. We'll clear the ship. Anyone that isn't us comes toward you, get back into the airlock, seal it, and get back to the *Ghost*. And call Gabe. He'll know what to do." He stared at the two men until they nodded. Then he said, "You're getting to see the GC few get to see, Ambassador." He smiled and closed the face shield on his helmet.

"Zee and I will head forward. Cyn, you go aft to engineering." He knew his wife—

both women, actually—were far more militarily capable than he was and would have preferred not to split their small team up, but there just weren't enough of them. "Be careful. No idea how many are aboard this thing." He turned to head forward and then stopped. "If anyone seems useful, keep 'em alive."

Cynthia grinned. "No promises." She turned and strode toward the ship's rear.

Wil and Zephyr started forward. The *Gaart Naarg* was three times the size of the *Ghost*. He was a little surprised they hadn't been met at the airlock by whoever was crewing the ship. After all, they'd had an hour to prepare for boarders.

The pair crossed an intersection, continuing forward. "Know where we're going?" Wil asked.

His blue-skinned first officer nodded. "I've been aboard a similar vessel before. The Malkorites always follow the same design principles. The bridge should be two more intersections forward and then up one level."

"I wonder where the—" Wil's question was cut off by a hail of plasma rounds slamming into the bulkhead ahead of them. Both of them dove for cover on either side of the corridor. "Never mind," he said as he leaned out to return fire up the corridor.

"Give up. You can't take the ship!" someone shouted from up ahead.

"Yes, we can!" Wil shouted.

"No, you can't!"

"Yes, we can!" He fired again.

Someone up ahead screamed. "Told you!"

Plasma splashed over their heads to rain molten metal on them.

"Hey!" Wil shouted. He looked at his second officer. "Why aren't they showing on our sensors?"

She shrugged and pulled a small sphere from a thigh pouch on her armor. He grinned and nodded. She slid the activation plate up with one of her thumbs, then rolled the device up the corridor.

Wil smiled as their friends up ahead shouted before a loud pop drowned their shouts out, followed by a blinding light that both his and Zephyr's armor compensated for.

The two of them stood and bolted up the corridor. There were three stunned beings staggering around the corridor: two Guldranii and a Malkorite. Pulse pistol blasts took care of all three.

"I thought you wanted to question some of them," Zephyr said.

Wil looked at the three bodies and shook his head. "Nah. These guys were cannon fodder." He nodded in the direction they wanted to go. "Come on." He tapped an icon on his armored wristcomm. "Cyn, we just encountered three hostiles. Stay sharp."

"Always, my love," she said.

At the landing to the deck above, Zephyr held up a hand. Her tactical sensors showed two contacts outside the bridge hatch. He looked at Wil and shrugged, having no idea why the two up ahead were showing up on her sensors when the first three hadn't.

FROM HIS PERCH halfway between the club's back door and its front, in a booth along the wall, Maxim wasn't sure where Bennie was but assumed it was somewhere along the opposite wall. At least he hoped so. Catching their attackers in a crossfire was their only hope.

The club's back door burst open, sending a shaft of dim light stabbing into the room. A large shadow stepped into the bright rectangle of light, then moved in and to the side, vanishing in the gloom. One at a time, seven other shadows appeared and then moved off to the side, out of view in the darkness.

Maxim was beginning to think Bennie had forgotten he was supposed to signal Nic when the entire room was flooded with light and noise. Nic must have been familiarizing herself with the controls because, besides the blinding light show, a cacophony of sound assaulted everyone in the club. He shook his head. Was that music?

Maxim rose and opened fire. His pistol wasn't great for long distances, but he made up for it by spraying energy bolts across the dance floor.

It turned out that Bennie wasn't where Maxim assumed he was. The nimble little Brailack had scaled the club's wall so that he could leap down on top of their pursuers from the ceiling. "Like a little guanjoo lizard," Maxim said with a smile as he dropped another Multonae man in a smoldering heap. Before the remaining goons could get a bead on him, he crawled to another booth. The one he'd just been using for cover exploded in a shower of stuffing and pieces of furniture frame.

Bennie put his beam saber hilt against the back of the man he was straddling and activated the weapon. The pale purple beam blossomed from the man's chest, the wound glowing as his tissues super-heated. The blade winked out of existence just as quickly as it had appeared. Bennie rolled off of the corpse before it hit the ground. He was on his feet in a flash, darting left and right to dodge the chaotic weapons fire that was flying in all directions.

From the small booth Nic was in, a bright red bolt of energy crossed the room to slam into another of the Multonae men, vaporizing most of his right arm and shoulder.

Their attackers rallied, two of them figuring out Maxim's

new hiding place, turning their weapons on his location. Like the last one, this booth didn't hold up long under pulse rifle fire. He dove out from cover, his pistol flashing as he sent his own return fire toward the dance floor. He heard a pained shout as he hit the floor to scurry behind another booth. With a grunt he heaved the table up over the back of the seat to give him some room to maneuver.

He rose and fired a few shots. Looking at his pistol's charge display, he asked, "How many are left?" His pistol was at ten percent.

The small control booth Nic was using as cover exploded. Maxim turned, worried for his small friend. He exhaled when the small furry young woman leaped from cover, sending another crimson bolt of energy into one of the Multonae men trying to kill or capture them.

"Three," she said. "Two Multonae and a Mald."

"I need answers from one of them," Maxim reminded.

Someone screamed and then cried, "My arm!"

"One less Multonae," Bennie reported. Over the channel, the sound of the Brailack hacker breathing hard and grunting was heard.

"What're you doing?" Maxim asked. He peeked over his cover to see Bennie wrestling with the much larger Mald man. The reptilian man was flailing, a pulse rifle, cut in two, at his feet.

Maxim headed toward the dance floor. He looked over to see Nic doing the same.

On the dance floor, Bennie and his opponent were stumbling around among the bodies and discarded weapons. The Mald man stepped on a pulse rifle, losing his footing. The pair went down in a heap.

"You little krebnack!" the Mald shouted, reaching to Bennie. He drew back. "You bit me!" He rolled away from

Bennie, struggling to get to his feet. He looked at Maxim. "That little krebnack bit me." He slurred before collapsing to the ground.

Maxim reached the dance floor. He nudged the Mald man with his boot, then turned to Bennie. "Now we have to wait for him to wake up."

Bennie shrugged. "He was gonna throttle me."

Maxim huffed, letting his hands fall to his side. Holstering his pistol, he said, "Let's get all these bodies into the alley. Least we could do. The person who owns this club is gonna lose their mind when they see this place. No need for it to smell like dead bodies."

Nic looked around, making a face. "They look heavy." She waved an arm. "Plus, this place is a wreck. Will bodies matter?"

Maxim shrugged.

CHAPTER FOURTEEN

CYNTHIA CREPT aft from the airlock. According to Zephyr, the engineering space should be two levels down. She reached a place where the corridor branched in a lopsided Y shape. Both branches led aft, but the rightward branch headed more starboard than the other branch, which kept a more aftward angle. She kept to the left.

Just as she was wondering why there were so few crew aboard the ship, a hatch opened ahead of her. *Should have known better,* she chided herself as she stopped dead in her tracks.

A pair of Rigellians rushed out. They obviously thought they were going to get the drop on someone right in front of the hatch. Cynthia, standing about a meter and a half away, caught them by surprise. She didn't miss a beat, leaping up onto the nearest man's shoulders, her legs wrapping under his long arms, squeezing his reproductive organs tightly.

"Get her off me!" the man under her shouted in a high-pitched voice, as he flailed his arms trying to get a grip on his attacker. Cynthia, squirming and wiggling, avoided his grasp as she raked his face with her extended claws.

"Stop moving, and I'll shoot her!" the other man said. He had a custom-looking rifle in his long arms, trying to track Cynthia as the man beneath her flailed and spun in circles. His large, pupil-less eyes narrowed as he tried to steady his weapon.

"Don't shoot, you'll hit me!"

"I will not!"

"Your aim is terrible! Just knock her off! She's squeezing my bebdaks!" Rigellians had disproportionately long arms, and he was waving his all around trying to get a grip on Cynthia.

She released her leg-lock, letting her body slide backward down her opponent's back. She grabbed his waist, putting all her weight into toppling him backward. She hit the deck on her back and used all her strength, and his momentum, to bring him up and over her to crash onto the deck head first. His body crumpled in an uncomfortable looking tangle of limbs.

She wriggled out from under him and up on one knee, pulse pistol in hand, before the second Rigellian could track what was happening. As he swung his rifle around to fire, her first pulse round hit the rifle, super-heating it and forcing him to drop it. Her second round hit him center mass, sending him flying backwards to land in a smoldering heap.

She turned to the other man, who was just regaining consciousness, and sent a bolt of energy into his chest.

"Not the best pirates I've ever seen," she said, reaching the hatch to the service stairs.

"Cyn, we just encountered three hostiles. Stay sharp," Wil said over her commset.

She looked behind her at the two dead Rigellians. "Always, my love." She took the stairs slowly, listening for any other defenders. Nothing. The engineering deck was also oddly silent. *Too silent.* Since she didn't wear an armored suit like the others, she didn't have sensors, just her own senses. This ship definitely seemed to be under crewed. She wondered if it had been dispatched to intercept them in haste.

She was just outside engineering when the attack came from out of nowhere. If she hadn't heard the slight click of a sticky trigger, she wouldn't have ducked a split second before a plasma bolt splashed against the bulkhead behind her. Several globs of molten metal splattered onto her, singeing her jumpsuit and exposed fur. Hatches on either side of her, what looked like storage rooms, opened, spilling eight assorted beings into the corridor.

"Oh, this will be fun," she muttered.

"SHOULDN'T we have heard from them by now?" the ambassador asked. He leaned out the airlock hatch to look up and down the corridor. He turned. The pistol in his hand bumped the hatch frame, causing him to jump.

Bruce put a calming hand on the other man's shoulder. "It's a big ship. I'm sure they're being thorough." He certainly hoped they were, but nothing Bruce had seen to date made him think thorough was something this team did.

A noise up the corridor made both men fall silent. Ambassador Carlisle turned to Bruce, who nodded, putting a finger to his lips. He raised his pulse pistol and moved closer to the airlock hatch. With his free hand, he guided his boss backward toward the still-open outer airlock door.

The ambassador's aide leaned out to see if anyone was up the corridor and nearly had his head blown off. He fell backwards as the plasma round struck the hatch, melting it.

"Oh, shit!" He raised his pistol and leaned out the hatch, opening fire. "Sir, need your help."

"Right!" the older man said, taking up a position behind Bruce. He kneeled down and fired in the same direction as Bruce.

There were five aliens up the corridor, using the intersection ahead as cover.

"I think those are Trenbal!" the ambassador said.

Bruce nodded as he ducked back, supercharged plasma scorching the airlock's frame. He leaned out, sending return fire up the corridor. One of the reptilian aliens screamed and fell to the deck.

"You got one!" the ambassador shouted. He scrambled backwards as a plasma blast nearly caught him in the shoulder.

Ambassador Carlisle moved closer to the outer hatch. He fished his CommPad out the thigh pocket of his trousers. "Gabe? Do you read me?" he shouted into the device. Several more plasma rounds splashed into the airlock, spraying molten polymers.

"Yes, Ambassador Carlisle. Is there a problem?" the droid answered.

"Yes! We're at the airlock. They're attacking!" He heard a faint beep and looked at the screen. The call had ended. Flustered, he was about to tap the icon for the droid again when he heard, "Get down!" from somewhere ahead of him.

Bruce spared a look over his shoulder and stepped away from the hatch, pushing the ambassador down to the deck.

The pair had barely hit the deck when a matte gray blur sailed overhead.

Gabe had launched himself off of the *Ghost*'s airlock hatch to sail through the boarding tunnel and into the *Gaart Naarg*'s airlock. He landed in a roll, coming to his feet, both forearm blasters already deployed. He turned to the airlock, his optic sensors glowing bright red. "Stay put." He turned and sprayed the corner ahead, charring the bulkheads on either side of the intersection. Several of the attackers fell in the first assault.

At times like this, Gabe missed his previous physical configuration. That design had far more weaponry and armor. He stopped firing to let the forearm blasters cool. He charged toward the remaining attackers.

When the weapons fire ceased, he three remaining Trenbal peeked around the intersection. "Oh, dren!" one of the reptilian aliens screamed a second before a matte gray fist slammed into his face.

Several energy bolts slammed into Gabe's back and the surrounding bulkhead. Without looking, he swung his arm backward in a wide arc, sending one of the aliens flying to strike the far bulkhead with a wet crunch. He turned to the other, cocking his head. "My blasters have cooled off."

The last Trenbal standing tossed his rifle to the ground. Gabe nodded, raising one arm, blaster deployed. "A wise decision." He turned to look down the corridor. "You may come out now."

Ambassador Carlisle and Bruce peeked around the edge of the airlock, mouths hanging open.

Gabe opened the team comm channel. "I am aboard the corvette with the Ambassador and Mr. Hawkins. A group of Trenbal were attempting to take the airlock. I have one in custody."

"EIGHT ON ONE." Cynthia cocked her head to one side, cracking the vertebrae. She cocked to the other side, the cracking less pronounced. "Not great odds." One of the crewers, an Elar Keeg, cracked the knuckles on his top set of hands and then those on the lower pair. Smiling, she added, "For you."

She fired the borrowed rifle at a Multonae man, catching him in the shoulder, before dropping the weapon and leaping at the nearest crew member, a Mald. While in the air she pulled a pair of knives from her waist band. The stubby reptilian man screamed, staggering backward. Cynthia landed on him, driving both blades into his shoulders. He screamed again, but she'd already pushed off, sending him to the deck in a heap, both arms incapacitated.

A barrage of plasma bolts few over her from the remaining six crewers, sending more molten metal and plastic raining down on her.

"Six now." She grinned, then rolled across the deck. She reached two more attackers, a Tygran and another Mald. She kicked the feet out from both of them as quickly as she could, before either recognized their danger. Both fell to the deck around her. She lunged for the Tygran, slamming a blade into his torso. The Mald recovered faster than she'd expected, reaching over to punch her in the face. She rolled backward from the blow. She stuck out her tongue, tasting blood on her nose. She rolled to avoid another blast that struck the Mald in the shoulder from behind. He screamed. She used the distraction to punch the Mald twice in the face. He slumped to the ground unconscious.

Cynthia stood, coming face to face with the remaining four crew members. "And then there were four," she said.

"Surrender," the Klini said. In one hand, she hefted the rifle Cynthia had dropped; the other was planted on her hip.

"I was about to say the same thing," Cynthia said with a smirk.

The other woman's face fell. "What?" She glanced at the three behind her.

Cynthia took advantage of the moment. She underhand hurled one of her knives at the Klini woman. The knife embedded itself in the yellow-skinned woman's collarbone. The rifle fell to the ground as her long thin fingers went numb.

While the remaining crew were distracted by the screams of the Klini woman, Cynthia slapped the access panel on the hatch to engineering. The thick hatch slid open and she ran inside, slapping the access panel on the inside. The door slid closed as plasma bolts streaked in, burning several consoles inside the large room. One caught her on the hip, spinning her in place with a grunt.

THE TWO GUARDS outside the bridge didn't put up much of a fight, due in large part to Wil accidentally rolling a plasma grenade at them instead of a flash bang. Stepping over the gore that plastered the deck, ceiling, walls, and bridge hatch, he looked at Zephyr. "We don't need to mention this to anyone else."

She smiled. "Oh, I think we do." She plugged her wristcomm into the access panel next to the reinforced hatch. While portable Bennie got to work on the panel, she said, "You know, it's a little weird we've seen so little resistance. Three goons plus these two. Plus whoever is on the bridge." She shook her head. "Something doesn't add up."

Wil shrugged. "Maybe the rest are in engineering?" He thought about that a moment. "Hope not."

"Cynthia can take care of herself," the first officer said. She looked down at her wristcomm when it beeped. A tinny voice said, "You're in!" The bridge hatch clicked. Zephyr quickly unplugged her wristcomm, stashing the data cables in a pouch at her waist. She looked at Wil and nodded.

He held up a hand with three fingers extended; lowered one, then another, then the last.

Zephyr pushed a button on the access panel and stepped back to make sure she was clear of the hatch's frame as the reinforced doors slid apart. Wil took up a position on the opposite side of the hatch.

The moment the hatch slid open, plasma rounds streamed through the opening, splashing against the far bulkhead.

Staying low, Zephyr leaned around the edge of the opening to fire into the bridge. Wil did the same from the opposite side, staying standing to take the high angle.

"I count five," Zephyr said.

Wil nodded. "I think I got one." Weapons fire was still pouring out of the open hatch. He leaned over again and fired. "Definitely only four now."

Zephyr leaned over to fire. "Three now."

"We can keep picking you off, or you can surrender," Wil shouted.

"You surrender!" someone inside replied.

"Not how this works," Wil answered, adding, "I mean, we really don't have a problem burning you down. I'm just hoping to get some answers, but I can live with disappointment."

"I am aboard the corvette with the ambassador and Mr. Hawkins. A group of Trenbal were attempting to take the airlock. I have one in custody," Gabe announced over the shared team channel.

Wil listened. "Copy that." He turned his attention to the bridge hatch. "Turns out we've got a prisoner; don't need any of you. Now where did I put that last plasma grenade?"

There was a moment of silence. They could hear hushed whispers mixed with an occasional expletive directed at someone named Gunjo.

"We surrender!" the first voice said.

Wil looked at Zephyr and shook his head. "No commitment to the cause. Whatever that is," he said in a low voice. Louder, he said, "Put down your weapons and kick them clear. If we see a weapon when we come in, we kill you."

"Okay, jeez," the owner of the first voice said. They heard several distinct thuds and clinks followed by the scudding sounds of things sliding across the deck.

Wil and Zephyr stepped through the open bridge hatch, rifles sweeping the room. Two Quillant and a Klini were standing near the small bridge's forward display, arms raised.

CYNTHIA SWORE as she limped around behind a console as more plasma rounds flew overhead. Her new friends got to the access panel before she'd had a chance to disable it. She tapped her earpiece. "Contact, more baddies." She rose up to peer over the console and then dropped back down into a crouch. "Four left: two Malds, a Palorian, and a Klini." More plasma rounds screamed overhead. She figured now that she only had one knife left, she'd have to use her pistol. She enjoyed using blades so much more. She pulled the gun from its holster and rose high enough to hold her pistol over the console, spraying the area with rounds. Someone screamed.

"Need us?" Zephyr asked.

Cynthia crept to the far side of the console. The plasma burn on her hip was screaming. Leaning out, she squeezed off another volley, blasting one of the Malds' knees apart. Between gritted teeth she said, "I'm good." She checked the charge on her pistol. Half charge remaining.

"Kill that flobin!" one of the attackers ordered the group.

"That's uncalled for!" Cynthia shouted. "What'd we do to you?" She heard three pairs of footsteps moving around, two on one side, one on the other. She was pretty sure the wounded Mald wasn't who she'd heard scream before, so one of the three by the door was wounded; even if just a bit, it was enough. Maybe she got the Klini woman twice?

Looking around, she didn't see a great many options for more cover. The corvette's engineering space was considerably larger than the *Ghost*'s, but hiding places were in short supply. She could hear all three beings moving closer. She pulled a panel off the back of the console in front of her. Time to work fast.

Thirty seconds later, she stood. "I surrender."

The remaining Mald was to her right. The Palorian, sporting a plasma burn on her shoulder, and the Klini were on her left. All of them held weapons that at once snapped to take aim at her.

"Who are you guys?" she asked. She looked at each of the ship's crew in turn.

The Palorian sneered. "Concerned citizens who don't like the company you're keeping."

Cynthia cocked her head. "Bennie's not so bad when you get to know him. I mean, for a Brailack." She shrugged. "I mean, sure, his farts are lethal and he's rude and self-centered." She nodded. "He steals stuff all the time, too." She made a show of slowly nodding. "I guess I see your point."

The Klini blinked all three eyes. "What? Who's Bennie?" The woman's pale-yellow skin rippled in a camouflage pattern that might have been anger or confusion. She raised a six-fingered hand, holding a pistol, pointing at her. "The humans. They're not wanted here." The deep basso rumbled from the woman's misleadingly slight frame. Her wounded shoulder had forced her to trade weapons with one of her colleagues.

"Where? This sector? Brai?" Cynthia was fishing and starting to get annoyed at how un-forthcoming these three were.

"The GC. They're not welcome," the Palorian woman said. "They're too chaotic."

Cynthia quirked a smile. "You've met the Brailack, right?"

The Palorian woman adjusted her grip on her rifle.

Cynthia opened her mouth to argue but closed it. The other woman and her friends were not wrong. Wil was surely the embodiment of chaos. Sexy chaos, to be sure, but...She shook her head. "Why do you think it's up to you? The GC Council has already voted on their provisional membership. Swearing in the ambassador is kinda just a formality."

The Palorian woman smirked. "We'll just make sure they don't want to join the GC. Maybe by not existing." She raised an eyebrow ridge. "Starting with you and your friends."

Cynthia nodded. "Gotcha." She slid her boot off the pistol she had quickly hacked to make a homemade grenade. The pistol's activation switch beeped. She counted to three, then jumped.

The Palorian woman must have been ex-Peacekeeper—she didn't flinch at the sudden movement. She tracked Cynthia's arc and fired a single shot that clipped the Tygran woman in the side, the same side she'd already been shot in. She roared in pain.

Cynthia landed in a heap. The three attackers moved towards her, the Klini moving around behind the console on her way to Cynthia. She looked up and grinned.

The console exploded. All three crewers flew in different directions. The Palorian woman struck the room's wall with a crunch. There wasn't much left of the Klini woman.

Cynthia pushed up to her hands and knees. She looked around for any threats. None presented themselves.

She stood and approached the Mald. He was dying; that much she could tell. What was visible of his skin was scorched black. It rippled and bubbled. She leaned down to pick up one of the discarded plasma rifles.

The wounded man made a gurgling noise. Cynthia shot

him. She turned to the Mald just outside engineering in the corridor and shot him, too. The Palorian was already dead. She tapped her commset. "Engineering is secured."

"Any trouble?" Zephyr asked.

Cynthia poked at the charred section of her jumpsuit gingerly. She'd need to see the *Ghost*'s autodoc. "All good."

CHAPTER FIFTEEN

CYNTHIA, Gabe, and the two humans stepped through onto the bridge. The former said, "This ship is not going anywhere anytime soon."

Zephyr looked up from the console she was bending over. "Gabe, didn't you have a prisoner?"

"We dumped him in their brig. It was near the airlock," Bruce answered.

Wil glanced at the new arrivals, turned back to what he was doing, then spun to look at his wife. "What the hell happened to you?"

Cynthia was resting most of her weight on her non-charred leg. Her jumpsuit and fur around the other hip were a singed mess. He moved over to stand next to her, taking some of her weight onto himself.

Cynthia gave him a kiss on the cheek, then said, "Want them to join their friend?" She pointed at the captured bridge crew.

Wil nodded. "Yeah." He rubbed his chin and then said, "Gabe, you and our guests stay up here. See what you can get out of the ship's computer. We'll take our friends to the brig and have a chat with all four of them."

Zephyr looked at the three bridge crew. "Come on, you three." She waved her pistol toward the hatch.

She led the prisoners off the bridge. Wil and Cynthia followed, the former calling over his shoulder, "You two, don't touch anything." He turned to Cynthia. "Didn't need our help, huh?"

She emitted a low purring noise. "You should see the other eight."

"Eight? You know I think you're badass already, right? No need to prove it."

Zephyr looked over her shoulder. "He's right."

"See," he said.

"I'm fine. A tock with the autodoc and I'll be good as new," Cynthia insisted. She kissed his cheek again, hoping he'd drop it.

He did.

The *Gaart Naarg*'s brig was fairly spacious for a ship of that size. There was a large security foyer twice the size of the *Ghost*'s entire brig space with two large cells. The right-hand cell had Gabe's Trenbal sulking in it.

Zephyr pointed to the cell. "Go sit with your friend." She tapped the control panel at the small security desk. The Trenbal's cell door slid open. The three other crewers entered. The door slid closed.

Wil looked at the four beings. "So, who wants to go first?" All four exchanged looks but said nothing. "No one? Come on. We're all," he made a show of looking first at Cynthia, then Zephyr, and then back to their prisoners. "We're very friendly."

Cynthia clucked. "It's you they don't like."

Wil's mouth fell open. "Me? What did I ever do to you? I don't even know you." He squinted at the Klini woman. "We haven't met, right?" He lowered his voice. "Did we date? I assure you I intended to call you. It's just that—"

The yellow-skinned woman lunged for him, her skin shifting from yellow to red to pale green to purple and then back to yellow. "We don't even know you, Multonae."

"He's human," Cynthia offered, knowing it would elicit a reaction.

One of the Quillant spit. "Of course, he is." He glared at Wil. "Humans will be the downfall of the Commonwealth."

Wil frowned. "That's a bit of a generalization, isn't it? I mean, shit. We've never tried to destroy the GC." He looked at the four aliens. "What's your problem with humans?"

"They're a destabilizing influence," the Trenbal man said, adding, "The GC has been through enough lately and needs to focus on repairing the damage. Adding new civilizations, especially ones as messy as these humans, is only going to make things worse for us all."

The Klini woman nodded. "I don't know if you human lovers have—"

"Whoa, whoa!" Zephyr interrupted. She pointed at Cynthia. "She's the human lover."

Wil turned. "You say that like she's got chicken pox."

Cynthia looked at her friend. "Hey!" She then turned to Wil. "Chicken what?"

The Klini woman screamed. "You see what we mean? The GC had thousands of cycles of relative peace. Since these pink monstrosities appeared, all wurrin has broken loose. The Peacekeepers can barely maintain a presence in the Tier 1 systems, leaving the rest of the GC to fend for ourselves. The corporations are doing experiments on citizens!"

The three Rogue Enterprises team members took that in. Cynthia finally said, "You may have a point."

"Hey!" Wil growled. He looked at the four aliens. "My wife

is kidding." He narrowed his eyes and glanced sideways at Cynthia. Turning his focus back to the prisoners, he asked, "One: Who are you to say who gets to be in the GC and not? Two: None of that shit you just listed off has anything to do humanity."

The Trenbal grinned, his tongue darting out between razor-sharp teeth. "The Coalition."

Wil looked at Zephyr, then Cynthia. "What the fuck is the Coalition?"

Both women shrugged.

BY THE TIME their Mald friend came to, Maxim and Bennie had tied his hands with a belt Nic found in the club's lost and found. He opened his eyes and looked around slowly. They'd wedged him into the seat of a booth in a section of the club that was the least scorched from weapons fire. "I think I need medical attention. Please," he croaked. Pale red blood dribbled from the corner of his mouth. He coughed, sending a spray of blood onto the tabletop in front of him. Nic made a face as she leaned back.

"How'd you know who we were?" Bennie demanded. He was sitting cross-legged on the table. He'd scooted backward to avoid the blood-laced spittle. He was fiddling with his beam saber hilt absentmindedly. The other man's eyes were fixed on the device.

"What is that?" the Mald asked.

"We're the ones asking questions," the Knight of Plentallus said. "How'd you know who we were?"

The Mald's eyes flicked from the lethal weapon in Bennie's hands to the angry Brailack's face. "I don't know who you are." He nodded toward Maxim. "We were given his image."

"Mine?" Maxim asked.

"That tracks," Nic said.

Maxim kneeled down next to the booth, looking the would-be assassin in the eyes. "Who gave it to you, my image? A Palorian man?"

The Mald shook his head. "I don't know. Yuvis took the job." He looked around the room and at the bodies littering the dance floor. "Bald Multonae."

Nic hopped out of the booth and trotted over to a bald man. She kneeled down. "This one is dead." She pulled the body up so the group could see the dead man's face.

The Mald shook his head. "Not him." He coughed again.

"Can you please stop that?" Bennie asked, brushing at his pant leg.

Nic looked around, spotting another bald Multonae. She kneeled down next to that one and shook her head. "This one is —" The man released a small breath. "Oh, he's alive!" She clapped her hands and then hoisted the wounded man up into a sitting position. "Hi!"

The Mald nodded once, coughed up more blood, and said, "That's Yuvis."

Nic eased the man back down to the dance floor and then tapped him on the forehead. "Hey. Wake up." More tapping. "Wake up, drennog. I know you're alive." She looked up at Maxim and Bennie.

Maxim looked at the Mald. "You know nothing else?"

"No. I swear."

Maxim rammed his fist into the reptiloid man's face, rendering him unconscious. He turned to Bennie. "Let's see what Yuvis has to say."

Bennie nodded and hopped off the table.

The two men joined Nic, kneeling on either side of Yuvis. Maxim nudged the man. Orange blood was splattered all over his face and the front of his shirt. A plasma round had scorched his shoulder. Dried blood and the remnants of his shirt were fused into the wound. Another plasma round had struck him in the abdomen. That wound was still oozing.

Nic tapped Yuvis' forehead again, harder. "Wake up, or he'll bite you." She jerked her head toward Bennie.

"I will not," Bennie said. He made a face at his apprentice.

Nic leaned over to whisper. "He didn't know that."

"He's unconscious," Bennie said. He poked the Multonae man in the ribs with the hilt of his beam saber.

"Ouch."

Bennie's eyes widened. "Or not." He nudged the man again. "Time to start talking, Yubis."

"Yuvis," Maxim corrected.

Bennie frowned. "You're sure? I thought that guy said Yubis."

Nic shook her head. "It's Yuvis."

"Really?"

The man on the ground between them whispered, "Yuvis."

Maxim looked down at Yuvis and pulled a water bulb from a thigh pouch and splashed the man's face. "How did you know to expect us? Who gave you my image?"

"Uhhh," the barely conscious man drawled.

Nic jabbed her beam saber hilt into Yuvis's ribs. "Come on, Yuvis."

"I think I'm bleeding internally," the man complained. He reached up and gingerly touched his wounded shoulder. "This feels bad."

"Looks bad, too," Bennie said.

"The sooner you talk, the sooner we call for medical help," Maxim said.

"I took the job on the dark nexus," the man wheezed.

Maxim glanced at Bennie, who nodded and got to work tapping on his wristcomm.

"More," Maxim urged Yuvis.

After a coughing fit, the Multonae man said, "Anonymous client. Payment in VortiCoin: half up front, half on completion." He looked at Maxim. "Any chance I could get a picture of you looking dead?" Maxim glared but said nothing. "Never mind."

Bennie reached down and plugged a cable from his wristcomm into Yuvis' device, thankful it hadn't been damaged in the various firefights. "Stop wiggling. This'll just be a few microtocks."

"I'm having a hard time breathing."

"Then stop. I don't care," the Brailack hacker said, his eyes glued to his device as lines of code scrolled by. He used his free hand to enter commands at a pace Maxim found astounding.

Maxim looked down at their new friend. "What else?"

Yuvis groaned. "I think I'm dying."

Nic leaned in. "You probably are. Answer him."

Yuvis swallowed. "I bribed someone at the spaceport with your pic. The client provided a likely timeframe for your arrival."

"Just him? Not us or the ship?" Nic asked.

Yuvis shook his head. "The client said maybe you'd arrive in an Ankarran Raptor but wasn't sure. Said it'd be you with or without a few extra people."

"How were you supposed to get the second payment?" Maxim asked.

"Log in, upload proof."

"Give me your credentials," Bennie said, looking up from his wristcomm.

"No."

"We'll kill you if you don't," Nic said.

"I'm dying already," Yuvis said before coughing up a glob of orange blood.

"It'll be slower," Nic said. She leaned in and bared her teeth. "And more painful."

Another bout of coughing preceded, "It's pretty painful now."

Nic growled.

"Fine, here." Yuvis raised his wristcomm, careful not to jostle the data cables Bennie had plugged in. "Unlock all files. Access code," he paused, looking at the others, "'I love my mom.'"

"Access code received. All functions unlocked," a tinny voice announced from his wristcomm.

"I'm in," Bennie said. "I'll clone his account. Once we're back on the *Nontee,* I'll hack into the nearest dark nexus server and embed a trace on your cousin's ID."

Yuvis looked over to Maxim. "Your cousin?"

Maxim sighed. "Long story." He turned to Bennie. "We good?" The Brailack hacker nodded. Maxim stood and walked away, placing a call on his wristcomm. "Hello. There's an assortment of bodies, mostly dead but at least two living in the," he looked around, "Uh, what's this place called?"

His colleagues both shrugged.

Yuvis coughed. "The Energetic Plin."

Maxim nodded. "The Energetic Plin." He didn't wait for a confirmation, ending the call. He turned to Bennie and Nic. "Okay, let's go."

They stood and walked away from Yuvis.

He raised his arm. "What about me?"

"Don't do crime," Nic said.

The three of them walked back to the spaceport.

"UNFORTUNATELY, the crew wiped most of the computer files," Gabe informed the others as they joined him and the other humans on the *Gaart Naarg*'s bridge. Bruce and Carlisle were sitting at powered-down terminals along the bridge's periphery.

"Nothing? At all?" Wil pressed.

Gabe shook his head. "Unfortunately, no." The droid turned to Zephyr and Cynthia. "Were you able to get anything from the prisoners?"

The Tygran woman shook her head. "Not much. They're part of something called the Coalition." She was leaning against the bridge hatch to ease the pain in her leg.

"I do not know what that is," the droid admitted.

"Makes four of us," Zephyr said.

Wil shook his head. "I swear to God, if some new random bunch of assholes is trying to destabilize or infiltrate or otherwise destroy the GC, I will..." He looked at the ceiling. "I don't know! Become a fucking hermit on a mountain or something." He threw his arms up into the air. "Every six months with this shit!"

"We should be so lucky," Zephyr said under her breath. He turned to glare at her, and she winked. She shook her head. "If those drennogs in the brig are to be believed, this isn't about the GC as much as it's about you."

"Wil?" Bruce asked. He was nodding slowly.

Wil looked at him, expression flat. "That's so believable?"

"Humans," both Cynthia and Zephyr said as one.

The other man's eyes grew large. "Humans?"

Ambassador Carlisle looked at his aide and then the others. "This Coalition is moving against Earth?"

Wil shrugged. "That's what the goon squad in the brig is saying." He looked around the *Gaart Naarg*'s bridge. "Whatever the hell that means. Other than attacking us, I guess."

"Any indication of what the goal was in attacking us?" Bruce asked.

Zephyr shook her head. "No. Apparently, the captain was one of those killed when we tried to take the bridge. His XO, too."

Cynthia looked at her friend. "Of the two goons you took out, both were command staff?"

"We're just that good," Wil chimed in. He held his fist out toward Zephyr. The Palorian woman looked at Wil, sighed, and bumped her fist against his.

Cynthia rolled her eyes. "The others didn't know anything, just crew. Recruited from all over the GC. All mad about some aspect of current events or another. The Klini did say that they were given the order to intercept us with very little warning, had to push the engines."

Wil sighed. "Okay, well, we're not likely to get much more out of them." He turned to Gabe. "You've got the comm system set up to call the PKs in?" The droid nodded. "Do it." Looking at the others, he added, "All right. Let's go. Brai awaits."

Ambassador Carlisle nodded. "Yes, indeed. I'm excited to continue our tour of the Commonwealth." He gestured around the bridge. "This has been exciting but well outside my area of expertise."

Wil nodded and pointed to the bridge hatch. "Then let's get to it."

Cynthia nodded. "I really do need the autodoc."

"NO, WE DON'T HAVE AN APPOINTMENT," Wil growled. He took a deep breath and then added, "We're family friends stopping by for a visit with a VIP guest in tow."

The overhead speaker was silent for a moment. "Sorry,

Ghost. Without an appointment, the best I can do is give you visitor clearance at the Daro Akkamm Spaceport. You can figure things out from there."

Wil looked over at Zephyr, who gave a shrug. "According to the data packet, it's a less affluent part of Pooraj, quite far from Bennie's parents' house. We'll need to rent an air-car."

"Castle, you mean," Wil said.

Zephyr frowned.

The speaker crackled. "Or you can stay in orbit while you work this out with the Vulvos, *Ghost*," the space controller offered.

Traffic over Brai was heavy. The *Ghost* was in the middle of a clump of freighters and personal transports waiting for landing clearance. They'd already been in orbit two hours just waiting for the opportunity to speak with space control. If they didn't take the offer, they'd be shunted to a higher orbit and would have to work their way back down.

Wil turned his attention back to the main display. "No, thanks, Brai Space Control. We'll take the slot at Daro... whatever."

"Daro Akkamm," the man at the other end of the call corrected.

"Yeah, that. We'll take it."

"Sending guidance data your way, *Ghost*."

"Thanks."

"Nav data received," Cynthia said. She sent the data to Wil's console.

"Have a pleasant day, *Ghost*," the space control operator said before cutting the connection.

Bruce, sitting at Maxim's console, said, "So, his family is super rich and powerful?" He shook his head and pointed at Bennie's station. "Him?"

Zephyr nodded. "Yup. Took us by surprise, too. His sister's also a popular vid-actor. They're a big deal among Brailack."

The ambassadorial aide shook his head. "But he's a hacker, and a—what was it—

Jedi something?"

Wil smiled. "Right? Should totally be Jedi. Not like they could sue him."

"Knight of Plentallus," Cynthia said. She looked at the others. "He told his parents about that, right?"

Wil nodded. "Yeah. A couple of months ago, he detoured to Brai on his way back from Nexum on his way to Fury."

"Sounds like they sell pens," Bruce said, adding in a lower voice, "Plentallus. Pentallus. Pens Are Us."

"Entering atmosphere," Wil announced.

The *Ghost* vibrated a little as she touched the planet's upper atmosphere.

"Entry shields up," Wil said as the shaking faded.

On the forward screen, streamers of plasma formed against the ship's shields.

"Does it ever get old?" Bruce asked.

"What? Being awesome?" Wil grinned. He turned to the other man and added, "No, it doesn't. Every planet is different. Every race is different." He turned his attention back to flying the ship but added, "We haven't even visited every planet or society in the GC."

"Just the profitable ones," Zephyr said.

Cynthia grinned. "And the ones that don't want any of us dead or in prison."

Ambassador Carlisle looked at her. "Is that a high number?"

Cynthia made a hand-wiggling gesture she'd picked up from Wil. "Non-zero."

CHAPTER SIXTEEN

THE WALK back to the spaceport was uneventful. From the next block up from the dance club, the trio watched as several emergency services vehicles descended on the club.

Apparently, the group that was hired to kill or abduct them was the only one, at least as far as they could tell; no one attacked them on their way back to the port.

The *Rocky Nontee* was exactly as they'd left her. No attempts at entering or hacking the small freighter's computers were detected.

Once Bennie was sure it was safe, they entered and locked up behind themselves before heading up to the bridge so Bennie could get to work on hacking the dark nexus.

"Why isn't there another chair in here?" Maxim asked. He was leaning against the bank of computer gear that lined the bulkhead opposite the station Nic used.

Bennie was sitting there at the moment, his wristcomm connected by a data cable to the station. He didn't look up. "Because I don't like guests."

"I'm your teammate."

The hacker waved a hand, saying nothing.

Maxim pushed off the wall, about to leave the small ship's flight deck. He'd tried sitting in the pilot's chair, but like the chair Bennie was in, it had been converted to fit a much smaller being and he could only sort of sit in it sideways with half his body on the chair's arm. After Maxim accidentally raised the shields, Bennie forbade him from further attempts at sitting in the chair.

"Wait," Bennie said.

Maxim stopped and moved to look over his little friend's shoulder.

"I'm in," Bennie leaned back, bumping into Maxim behind him. He glanced up, frowning. "Our friend Yuvis was telling the truth. I found the message board on the dark nexus server he said it'd be on. Which, I should add, was not easy." When the big Palorian said nothing, he continued, "Once I found the right server, it was easy to break through their firewalls. The posting for the hit was still live, but it doesn't look like anyone else has accepted the job." He tapped more commands into the console. "Okay, yeah, I have the unique identifier for your cousin's account." Again, he tapped at the keyboard for a moment. "Weird."

"What's weird?" Maxim asked.

"Your cousin's account is heavily secured. Like way more than your average user. Even your average dark nexus user."

"And?"

"And, that's suspicious." The hacker set about entering commands into his terminal.

Maxim watched until he couldn't take it anymore. "Do I need to be here?"

"I thought you'd left," Bennie answered without looking up from his work. He quickly added, "Since you're still here, though, I could use a snack."

Maxim smacked him on the back of the head.

"Ouch! Fine, never mind." He rubbed the back of his head. "I'll eat later, assuming my blood sugar doesn't bottom out." Before Maxim could strike him again, he added, "Any idea what the Coalition is?"

Maxim shook his head. "No, never heard of it. Why?"

Bennie gave a small shrug. "I've been digging around Tane's account, see if I could figure out why it was so well secured. I don't think it's his account at all, by the way."

"And?"

Bennie turned and looked at him. "Expand your vocabulary." When Maxim jerked toward him, he flinched.

"Continue," the big Palorian said.

"I think someone, maybe this Coalition, whatever it is, set up the account in his name and expanded the protections on his account about twenty days ago, give or take. Multiple layers of encryption, active ICE."

"Ice?"

"Intrusion Countermeasure Electronics," Bennie replied. "Super advanced programs that attack anyone that pokes around the account too deeply."

"Including you?" Maxim was suddenly worried.

Bennie turned to his friend, eyes narrowed and mouth pursed. "I'm insulted." Maxim rolled his eyes and Bennie continued, "No. I'm skirting the edges. I saw the ICE and pulled back in time. We shouldn't trigger that until we're ready." Switching back to the previous topic, he added, "I'd guess they set up the account, then gave it to him to arrange this little party."

Maxim nodded. "And when would that be? Us being ready, I mean." He cocked his head. "And why would they help him do this?"

Bennie ran a hand over his face, thinking. "I'll leave a couple daemons on this server to keep an eye out for the next time Tane or his handlers logs in. Since he's expecting Yuvis to report, we shouldn't have to wait long." He turned to look up at his friend. "As to the why, who knows? I'm still leaning towards you having pissed someone off."

Maxim nodded. "What's that get us?" Sometimes ignoring the team hacker's jibes was the fastest way to get to the end of a conversation.

The Brailack hacker huffed out a loud sigh. "What that gets us is that when Tane comes online, I'll know and can track his location. Once we're close enough to strike, I'll break through the ICE and get his exact location."

GABE REMAINED aboard the *Ghost* while the crew and their guests made their way to Bennie's parents' house. He had more than enough on his to do list to keep him busy while they showed the two humans from Earth around. It turned out that the repairs he and Nic had made on Fury, while more than suitable, did not hold up to the combat stresses the *Ghost* had recently experienced.

Standing in the ship's magazine as diagnostic data scrolled through his consciousness, showing the status of each missile in the room, he dedicated a few processing cycles to wondering how things were going on Arcadia. His recent chat with droids helping the humans on Oberon sparked his curiosity.

After establishing their homeworld, the droid nation had more or less kept to itself while building out their first cities. To see them, and especially former President Mitch, out in the galaxy—on a human colony world, no less—was surprising.

It had been several months since he visited the homeworld

of the society he helped create. After refusing, more than once, to put his name on the ballot, and seeing that the Mechnoid nation was well on its way to thriving, he devoted his attention to his friends. They certainly needed him more than his people did.

He had just activated a secondary diagnostic on a pair of variable output missiles when a noise somewhere in the cargo hold brought all of his attention back to the here and now. He looked around the magazine; nothing was out of place. They were in need of replacement shield buster missiles but otherwise were well stocked. He closed down all secondary and tertiary processes to focus.

Exiting into the cargo hold, he accessed the ship's internal sensors. Several blind spots that had not existed earlier in the day were now present. He cocked his head. "Interesting." One of the blind spots was moving. His optic sensors shifted to blue as he powered up his advanced sensor suite. "Even more interesting."

Sealing the ship's magazine behind him, Gabe headed into the center of the cargo hold. The large doors were still closed, the ramp raised. Another of the blind spots was moving, toward the common deck.

"Whoever you are, I am aware of your presence," he called out. Using his connection to the ship, he piped his voice through every speaker in the ship.

"Just your friendly neighborhood ghosts, here to liberate your ship," a voice called out, also using the ship's speakers. Gabe could not locate the source of the taunt.

He turned a slow circle. *Interesting,* he thought. *I will need to act fast.* Using his link to the ship's computer, he issued a series of commands. Thick bolts in the bridge hatch slid into place, securing it. The same happened one deck below, closing off the armory. Whomever these invisible intruders were, they were not getting into the ship's sensitive areas. *The hatch to the computer core did not respond.* That was worrying.

He did not have time to worry about the computer core. Two of the blind spots were in the crawlspace between the cargo deck and the common deck. As Gabe reached the stairs, two small forms dropped from open access panels to land on the midpoint landing of the staircase. Both were in head-to-toe matte black combat garments.

Both were obviously Brailack. *I suppose that tracks*, he thought.

He cocked his head. His optic sensors shifted to red as his forearms whirred and clicked, deploying a matched set of pulse blasters. In a fluid motion, he raised both arms, firing a single shot at each intruder. The blasts struck both small forms, dissipating across their bodies without harming them.

Interesting. I have never seen such an efficient energy web in such a small form factor.

One of the intruders chuckled before leaping from the landing, twisting in midair to plant both feet in Gabe's chest, sending him staggering backwards. He grabbed the small attacker's foot, flinging the nimble attacker across the cargo hold.

"How did you gain access to the ship?" Gabe asked. "Where did you acquire such advanced tech?"

The second attacker landed on his back before he could turn. "Can't give away our secrets," he said as he tried to plant a device on the side of Gabe's head. Before he could attach the device, Gabe's hand closed around his arm, pulling him up and over the droid's shoulders. He hurled the second Brailack in the same direction he sent the first.

While he stalked toward the two intruders, Gabe accessed the ship's sensors to locate the remaining two blind spots he'd found. Both were on B deck; one was in the computer core while one was making its way toward the bridge and armory below it.

Gabe raised both arms, firing several more shots at the two intruders, the plasma bolts fizzling against their suits. "Impressive." He wondered how many shots would be required to overload the energy web's dampening capabilities.

"Right? These cost a fortune," one of the intruders said, rolling to her feet and charging Gabe, a telescoping shock stick in one hand.

Gabe's sensors confirmed that the device was powerful enough to overload his power supply, at least temporarily. He sidestepped the diminutive attacker using an open hand to smack her to the ground. "I am trying to not harm you, but you have infiltrated my ship and seem intent on causing me harm."

The other intruder, the male, said, "Well, we can't really steal this thing with you on it."

"At least not with you on it, and operational," the woman added.

Raising his arm, Gabe didn't turn to look at the male intruder and fired three more blasts. Two struck. This time his sensors detected a reduced absorption level. He quickly fired twice more, tracking the small man as he ran across the cargo hold toward the training area the crew had set up in the corner. Adding his second arm to the barrage, he watched as the little man stumbled then collapsed to the ground, his suit sparking and fizzing.

Gabe immediately turned his attention to the woman; she was no longer sprawled on the ground where he'd last seen her.

From out of nowhere a surge of electricity poured through his frame. He quickly batted his attacker away, but the damage was done. Several internal alarms were scrolling through his sensorium. Several systems were rebooting, including his weapons and advanced sensors.

He spun quickly, locating the small attacker. She was already on her feet, charging toward him, shock stick held out in front of her.

"I am sorry," he said. She closed the gap, and he chopped down, snapping the shock stick in two while using his other hand to grab the back of her suit. He dropped to one knee and slammed the small being to the deck with a bone crunching thud. He rose and repeated the move, ensuring she was no longer moving. Or breathing.

He attempted to scan the other attacker who was still on the ground not moving. Their suits, even malfunctioning, blocked most of his sensors. Moving quickly, he grabbed a jump rope from the workout area and dragged the male attacker to the female, tying them both together as tightly as he could.

ACROSS THE CORRIDOR in the ship's small common area, Nic was on the sofa with her tablet. "So, after we followed a lead that Bennie got from the spaceport servers, we ended up on Jannav Kenu."

On the device's screen, C7K2, the droid that served as caretaker of the Tower of Plentallus on Nexum, said, "I am not familiar with that world." The glossy black droid cocked its head.

"Not much to talk about. I think Bennie said it was a Malkorite colony way back or something."

The droid nodded. "I see. And you are there now?"

She nodded. "Waiting for whatever the next move is. Maxim and Bennie are on the flight deck. Bennie's doing his code slicer thing. Boring to watch."

"Do you anticipate returning to the Tower anytime soon?" While C7K2 had served as sole occupant of the Tower for hundreds of years, now that Bennie had assumed the mantle of Knight of Plentallus, taking Nic as his apprentice, the droid felt they should be at the Tower more.

Nic's facial fur flattened. She didn't enjoy getting between Bennie and the snooty droid. She didn't mind being out and about. The Tower, even with new initiates in residence, was too stuffy for her tastes. "How are they doing?" she asked, hoping to change the subject.

"They are progressing. I had to expel Tarke Hrunorgk." The droid replied matter-of-factly. "DV-0 caught him attempting to sell beam saber parts on the internex."

Nic scrunched up her face. "Which one was that?" There were currently sixteen—or rather, she guessed, fifteen now—initiates in the Tower going through their first-year training, something C7K2 and DV-0 were more than capable of handling. Even if they didn't want to.

"The Ruknak boy."

"Oh, yeah," she said, nodding. "I don't know why Bennie thought he was a suitable candidate."

"Sir Ben-Ari Vulvo is a remarkably poor judge of character."

Nic chuckled. "True."

"Apprentice, prep for takeoff," Bennie announced from the overhead speaker.

Nic made a face. "Guess we found Maxim's cousin."

"Indeed. Good journey, Apprentice Thot'la. We look forward to seeing you and Sir Vulvo at the tower...someday."

"Thanks, C7." A pang of guilt washed over her. She added, "I'll see what I can do." She closed the communications app and set the tablet down as the droid was inclining his head in thanks.

THE COMMON DECK lounge was silent when Gabe stepped out of the stairwell hatch. He knew that there were at least two more intruders on this deck. Based on the sensor ghosts he was still registering, one was forward, probably attempting to gain access to the bridge. He turned aft; the other intruder was in or around the computer core. He hadn't been able to secure that space, so that was his first stop.

The *Ghost*'s computer core was in a small room next to engineering and across from the ship's small medbay. He stopped at the door, dialing up the sensitivity of his audio receptors. Nothing. He accessed the ship's computer wirelessly to open the door.

It did not open.

He cocked his head. He would have frowned if he had an expressive mouth. This was not good. The two downstairs must have been distractions. He had underestimated how quickly the two on C deck could break through his firewalls.

With all of his systems fully restored, he reached out, sliding his fingertips into the door seal. With one strong shove, he slid the door aside.

The sight that welcomed him was not was he was expecting. A Brailack was sitting in the middle of the room, his back to the door. Several data cables plugged into the base of his skull snaked across the room to ports in the computer. Data was pulsing between the computer and the small man across the myriad cables.

"I wouldn't take another step," the hacker said, not turning to look at Gabe. "I can activate the self-destruct with a thought."

"That is good to know," Gabe replied. He fired a single shot into the back of the intruder's head. In less than a second, metal and plastic melted as gray matter super-heated. The small intruder's head, or at least half of it, exploded in a spray of pale red and gray mist. The body tipped over, falling to the deck, the remains of data cables and a neural interface clattering to the deck, smoking.

Gabe spent three seconds looking at the mess on the deck in the middle of the computer room then turned and headed toward the bridge, leaving the door to the computer core open.

The last intruder was waiting for him in the foyer outside the bridge. The hatch showed signs of attempted entry but was still closed. As Gabe stepped out of the "neck" that connected the two sections of the ship, plasma bolts streaked toward him, scoring the port airlock hatch next to him.

He turned to the starboard bulkhead. "You are the last," Gabe called out.

"And the best," replied the intruder. Their voice seemed to come from all around the foyer.

"There is no way this ends with your taking possession of this vessel."

"Shows what you know." Another barrage of supercharged plasma splashed against the near bulkhead and airlock hatch.

Gabe shifted his position and then adjusted his legs to be longer. When the intruder stopped shooting, he quickly strode across the airlock foyer, reaching the bulkhead his attacker was hiding behind.

Except no one was there. Gabe spun just as a black clad Brailack fell onto his back. A shock stick stuck into his neck caused several systems to shut down immediately while several others stuttered and threw error codes.

I should contact the others, he thought, realizing that this final intruder may get the better of him. Accessing the ship's systems, he realized that the ship's communications array was offline. No doubt the work of the dead hacker in the computer core.

Gabe slammed his back against the bulkhead trying to

dislodge his attacker. The small being clung to him like a larba beetle, scurrying out of the way to avoid being crushed.

With a single command, Gabe deployed metal scales over his neck like a high collar.

"Not so fast," the little man said, jabbing the shock stick into Gabe's neck one more time, right where his servos went under his outer casing.

Several new alerts flooded Gabe's sensorium. Several key systems were shutting down or malfunctioning.

Sensing he had only moments left, Gabe leaned forward, squatting low. He pushed off the deck with all his power, launching himself toward the ceiling. He heard the crunch of his attacker as his back slammed into the ceiling. As he headed for the deck, he shifted his center of gravity, lining his back and the Brailack ship thief up for collision.

He crashed to the deck, crushing the Brailack man that was clinging to his back with a sickening crunch.

The little assailant gurgled.

Gabe shut down.

EVEN KNOWING Bennie's family name, it took a while to actually find their estate. They didn't appear in the public directories.

"You're sure this is it?" Cynthia asked.

The hover cab they'd hired was approaching the main gate of a castle that Wil swore looked right. The drive from Daro Akkamm felt like it had taken forever, and everyone was antsy.

"If it's not, we're still staying here. I'm getting carsick," he replied looking out the side window as the vehicle slowed as it lowered toward the ground. "And I have to pee."

"I'm pretty sure this is it. Matches Gabe's data," Zephyr said from the seat next to the ambassador. She held up a tablet to show the others.

The older man hadn't stopped looking out the window since they had departed the spaceport. "So, this is still the same city? That we landed in? Two hours ago?"

Zephyr nodded. "Yes. Pooraj is actually three large cities that over the centuries grew until they merged into this mega city. At that point, it just made sense to consolidate resources and management."

"And the Brailack are a founding member of the GC?" He finally turned, now that the landscape was just the outer grounds of the Vulvo estate.

She nodded. "When the Tarsi approached them, the Brailack were eager to sign on. They'd been in a few small-scale wars with neighbors, and while incredibly intelligent and clever, their size made combat difficult."

"Hard to bite your enemies when they're wearing armor," Cynthia said, nodding.

Bruce turned to her. "What now? They bite?"

She waved a hand. "Long story. Funny one, too."

The vehicle reached the gate and came to a stop. The speaker in the dashboard beeped twice. "Hello, how can we help you?"

Zephyr leaned forward. "Is this the Vulvo residence?"

"I'm sorry, who's asking?"

She rolled her eyes. "We're colleagues of Ben-Ari Vulvo. Forgive us for not calling ahead." She turned to Wil. "Maybe you should try sending a message to Len-Lu?"

Wil said nothing but raised one hand, middle finger extended. Bennie's sister had had a crush on Wil the last time they saw her. It had been awkward. "I dunno if that's a good idea."

"Oh?" Cynthia said, turning to her husband. Her ears twitched playfully.

"Sorry for the delay," the person on the other end of the comm channel said. "The family will see you." The speaker beeped twice.

"Thank God," Wil whispered.

The gates rolled open, allowing the hover cab to glide toward the house. Even having seen the place once before, Wil couldn't help but stare up at the massive dwelling.

When the car came to a stop, an officious blue-skinned Brailack man was waiting for the group. "Hello." He inclined his head. "I'm Fuso Tay. Head steward of the house." His skillfully tailored black suit complemented his deep blue skin.

Wil offered his arm. "Wil Calder. We met last time, I think."

The other man clasped Wil's forearm. "Indeed. Welcome back." He leaned to the side to look past Wil. "Is Master Ben-Ari not with you?"

"Afraid not. He was called away on another mission."

"I see. His parents will be disappointed. They were excited that he had dropped in." He raised a hairless eyebrow ridge. "I'm sure they'll be pleased to see you, however."

The group followed Fuso Tay inside to be met by the two older Vulvos and, to Wil's chagrin, his sister Len-Lu.

Po-Lu, Bennie's mom, clapped her hands together. "It's so good to see you all."

Carr-Ari, the team hacker's father, looked the group over. "Recruiting new team members?"

Wil smiled. "Carr-Ari, Po-Lu. Please meet Ambassador Branson Carlisle, Earth's first representative to the Governing Council." He pointed to Bruce. "His aide, Bruce Hawkins."

Both men nodded to the senior Vulvo. As they exchanged pleasantries, Len-Lu came around her father to look up at Wil.

"Hi, Wil. You're looking even more handsome than the last time I saw you." She winked.

Wil groaned. The two women on his team grinned.

AFTER INTRODUCTIONS WERE MADE, the elder Vulvo was incredibly excited to chat with Earth's first ambassador to the GC. He ushered the ambassador into his study, making sure Wil and Bruce knew they were not needed in the room before closing the solid wooden door on silent hinges.

Po-Lu and her daughter looked at the rest of the team. "So..." the former said.

"So, what do you all do for fun?" Cynthia asked.

Len-Lu's large black eyes widened. "Oh, fun. I know just the place." She turned and trotted down a side hallway. Wil thought it might lead to a garage but wasn't sure; he hadn't paid a ton of attention last time they were here.

Before Wil—or Bruce, for that matter—knew what was happening, the group was in an air car heading for what Bennie's sister assured them wasn't "just a mall," whatever that was.

"This is a nice ride," Cynthia said as the vehicle rose out of the ceiling hatch in the Vulvo estate garage. The vehicle was the size of a small school bus. Its exterior was drab and had several patches of worn paint along its side. The interior, however, was modern and plush.

Everyone spread out; Zephyr took a seat near the front of the large passenger compartment. Wil and Cynthia moved to the back of the space, followed, to Cynthia's delight, by Len-Lu, who somehow managed to end up seated between the husband and wife. Bruce sat by himself opposite Zephyr.

Threading her arm through Wil's, Len-Lu said, "You all

have had some amazing adventures since last we saw each other."

Bruce watched all of this before leaning over to Zephyr, eyebrows raised. She chuckled and shook her head.

Wil, his cheeks crimson, said, "Uh, yeah. Been a busy time." He looked at Cynthia, who leaned back, smiling, her hands behind her head. "Got married..." he threw out, hoping it would detour the small woman.

It was clear Len-Lu wasn't listening. "Oh, that sounds exciting."

Wil groaned.

Zephyr said. "Len-Lu, you said this place was more than a shopping center?"

The younger woman smiled, turning away from Wil. "Oh, yes. The Qilloppo Center is great! So much more than just a shopping center. It's one of Pooraj's oldest shopping districts. It used to straddle two of the old city lines and over the centuries expanded up and out."

"And sells things for spacers?" Cynthia asked. "We're not looking for luxury goods."

The other woman bobbed her hairless green head. Her large eyes blinked repeatedly. "Oh, yes. I like to go to Qilloppo and see how the other Brailack live." She turned back to Wil. "You'll love it."

Cynthia and Zephyr exchanged a look. The former said, "Explains your car."

Len-Lu nodded. "I had it specially made. It looks like any other readily available mid-range air car on the market." She waved a hand to encompass the luxurious interior. "On the outside."

Bruce watched all this and then asked, "Do we have Ms. Vulvo's works in your ship's library?"

Wil made a face. "I'm, uh, sure we do."

"We are arriving," the driver announced via a speaker in the ceiling.

Wil had assumed the car was driven by an AI. He should have known the Vulvos would employ drivers.

The air car eased down toward the shopping center below. "Massive" didn't do the building justice. It was several kilometers across and looked to be four or five stories at least. More in the center, where a thick tower rose another ten stories.

"The residential tower is one of the Pooraj's oldest tenements," Len-Lu offered.

Wil craned his neck. "A tenement?"

Len-Lu's head bobbed. She turned to point out other features of the shopping complex. The roof was lined with landing pads of various sizes. Several looked like they might be able to accommodate the *Ghost*. Most looked like they were designed for vehicles smaller than the one they were in.

Wil looked at the tower. It looked like any luxury condo tower you'd see in Earth's major cities.

The Brailack vid-star and author stood. "Excuse me, I need to get into my disguise." She looked at Wil. "Help me get dressed?"

He looked at his wife, eyes pleading. She made a noise he didn't hear often, then said, "I'll help you. He can barely undress a woman; dressing one is out of scope." It wasn't the save he was hoping for, but it'd do.

Bruce turned to watch as the car maneuvered around a similar vehicle that was rising from its landing platform. Their vehicle slid sideways, then centered on their assigned pad and lowered to the permacrete.

"We've arrived," the driver announced. Doors on each side of the vehicle rose up and out of the way.

Wil was out of the vehicle before the doors finished rising. "I'm gonna grab a coffee."

Zephyr and Bruce exited next, the latter asking, "Mind if I join you?"

Len-Lu and Cynthia exited the air car. The Brailack woman was nearly impossible to recognize. A simple headscarf covered her head, wrapping around her neck before trailing down her back. The elegant skirt she'd been wearing had been replaced by a pair of plain blue trousers. Her glittery tank top was replaced by a light brown crop top.

Wil looked at Bruce. "By all means." He waved. "Have fun, ladies."

CHAPTER SEVENTEEN

"THIS IS AMAZING," Bruce said. He and Wil were sitting at a café in the shopping center's main thoroughfare. Beings of all shapes and sizes wandered by the café. Wil had already had to explain that some Brailack were blue, due to specific things he didn't understand about their diet and genetics being from a particular island nation. The wide walkway was open to the roof with crisscrossing walkways at every level. The central tower's bank of lifts was in the distance, cars racing up and down delivering new shoppers while whisking those with full shopping bags back to their shuttles and aircars.

Bruce tapped a finger on the mug before him. "This is the same stuff you have aboard your ship?" He struggled to reconcile how bad the stuff on the *Ghost* tasted and how great the cup before him tasted.

Wil wiggled his free hand. "I mean, in the same way that hotel room coffee pods and Jamaica Blue Mountain are both coffee." He took a sip. "This shit is expensive, hence the space Folgers aboard the ship." He grinned. "Charging this to Len-Lu's account."

The other man smiled. "I was worried you were going to

expect me to cover it. The ambassador's expense account isn't that deep."

Wil looked at him. "I'd have thought since he is the first human ambassador to the GC, Earth would have pulled out all the stops."

Bruce shrugged. "How much attention have you paid to Earth lately?" When Wil wiggled his hand again, he continued. "The Earth Government Alliance has a lot on its plate; the new fleet, diplomatic corps, trade, colonization, a half dozen other things. Not to mention bringing existing military organizations under one banner. Oh, and the latest *Avengers* reboot is in reshoots, so there's that." He took a sip of his drink, savoring the rich nutty texture. It was so much like coffee and so different. "You'd be surprised how many other societies have started reaching out to Earth for this alliance or that trade partnership."

WIL NODDED ONCE. "Really? So not just the GC?"

The other man shook his head. "A couple of non-aligned societies have expressed interest in us."

Wil frowned. "I bet. I hope the folks in charge aren't rushing into anything. Lotta threats out here."

Bruce took another sip of his drink. From behind his mug, he said, "You seem to have come face to face with most of them."

The sudden change of topic caught Wil off guard. "I mean, sure..." He took a sip of his chlormax to buy time.

"Genetically manipulated monsters, galaxy spanning corporations waging war with each other, alien computer things," Bruce said, ticking each off on a finger. He added, "Rogue Peacekeepers, secret cabals..."

Wil leaned back, a wide grin on his face. "Oh, man. I'd forgotten about that! The Amalgamation of Parts." He shook his head. "Hope they stay wherever they are." The team was barely a team. They'd only known each other a few months when they answered a call from a friend of Zephyr's. Gabe died, sorta. He got better but the loss, brief as it was, shook the newly formed team. He shook his head to clear the memory.

He leaned forward. "And you think Earth is ready?" He waved his hand to take in whatever this giant mall was called. "For all this?"

Bruce sucked his teeth. "I don't think we have a choice anymore."

Wil gave a half shrug. "True." He hadn't expected Earth to move as quickly as it had when he gave them the archive he created. It had been his hope that the glimpse of the wonders within the archive, plus his own stories, would encourage the leaders of the world take a look at the state of the Earth and figure their shit out. Which he guessed they did, just much faster and in some cases more aggressively than he'd expected. He thought it would take decades. Instead, it took years.

Bruce was right, that ship had sailed now; Earth was building starships, colonizing other worlds. He was escorting Earth's ambassador on an unstructured tour of the GC before dropping him off on Tarsis to formally speak for the Earth.

Shrugging off those thoughts, he shook his head. "Galaxy's a big place. Just as many awesome non-evil things as there are evil things. Maybe more." He raised both eyebrows. "You know, there's a race in the GC, look just like chihuahuas. You know the little dogs?"

Bruce nodded.

"Just like 'em, but tiny little hands and feet. It's uncanny." Wil waved a hand. "Wonders everywhere."

"I'LL BE SO glad to get back to the *Ghost*," Maxim said. He was sitting on the couch in the *Nontee*'s common deck. Like the chairs on the bridge, most of the common deck furniture was geared more towards her smaller full time crew members than average sized guests. As such, he spent more time fidgeting and trying to get comfortable than sitting comfortably.

Bennie looked up from the tablet he was working on. "Welcome to our world. You know what it's like to sit in a chair and have your legs stick straight out like a pouchling?"

Maxim shook his head. "No, I've always been normal sized." He knew it would have the effect on Bennie that it did.

The small hacker's face flushed a deeper shade of green. "There are as many smaller statured races in the GC as not." He fumed.

"Yeah, and if three of them piled into one of Wil's long coats, they'd equal a normal sized person." Maxim grinned.

Bennie lunged across the room. "Why you!"

Maxim held an arm out, palming his small friend's face. "Calm down, I'm just messing with you." He waited for Bennie to calm down and step back before saying, "I'm happy the two of you have made this ship yours. I mean it's still ugly as sin, and the name is stupid, but otherwise..." He shrugged.

Nic watched the action, then said, "If he'd stop farting, it'd be nicer here."

Bennie scowled. "I have a delicate digestive system that is easily irritated."

The young woman folded her arms across her chest. "Uh huh. I've seen you eat."

Maxim pointed at her. "Point to the apprentice. I've seen you eat, too."

"I don't have to take this," Bennie said. He headed aft. "I'm going to bed. Don't wake me when you come in."

Maxim and Nic watched him go, the former saying, "It's amazing how easy he is to trigger."

The young woman nodded. "It's the only thing that's made my apprenticeship tolerable."

"How's that going, by the way?"

She shrugged. "It's going. I've learned a lot. It's nice that I don't have to be cooped up at the Tower all the time like the initiates."

Maxim raised an eyebrow. "So, there's a whole new class?"

She smiled. "Yeah. Sixteen." She shook her head. "Fifteen, actually. The Ruknak kid got the boot."

"If you and Bennie are out here, who's doing the training?"

"The droids. Turns out that DeVo, and a few other droids that aren't there anymore, did most of the initial training. Only once the initiates made it to level two did a knight take over their training." She smiled. "I was the exception."

Maxim nodded. "As you should be. You're quite the exceptional young woman." He thought back to when the team first met the young Olop woman, still a child then, aboard the *Galactic Empress* during the luxurious vessel's maiden, and only, voyage. She was traveling with her grandmother, who'd won some sort of contest.

Despite the ship being overrun with pirates, the young Olop woman had been determined to help the team as they worked to save the ship and its passengers.

He squinted. "So, when they reach level two, then what? Do you get promoted?"

She smiled. "Pretty much. According to the old manuals, an apprentice with as much experience as I've accumulated can be promoted to knight level one at their mentor's discretion."

"Think Bennie will do it?"

She grinned. "He doesn't have a choice. I made that clear."

"Kompromat?"

She grinned.

"He's trained you well, indeed."

Nic's facial fur flattened, an Olop blush. "Thanks."

Maxim nodded. "Warrior to warrior, you've earned your place in the galaxy. You'll make a fine Knight of Plentallus."

This time as she beamed, her small and incredibly sharp teeth bared. "Ah, thanks!" She moved to hug him.

Maxim held up a hand. "Uh, no. No hugging."

THE THREE WOMEN wound their way through the shopping center, Len-Lu leading the way. They'd stopped at a cafe to get some sort of crispy baked thing that Cynthia had already forgotten the name of and iced drinks that were immensely delicious.

"So, they saved you from Xelurians?" she asked. She'd heard the story, of course. Bennie liked to tell it because of Wil's panic attack on Xelur. That and the crazy war-machine they built out of a yacht and some spare parts. Ever since that job, Bennie always suggested some kind of epic build from whatever was nearby. She was interested in the team hacker's sister's version of events.

The Brailack celebutante shivered. "I know it's not kind to generalize, but Xelurians are just so creepy. All those legs and... fur."

Zephyr smiled. "We met a nice one a little while back. A scientist." She turned toward a store. "Let's go in there."

Cynthia looked to the indicated store, a grin spreading across her face. A boutique that specialized in formal occasions. A holo-sign floating in the window was advertising a bonding ceremony sale.

Len-Lu looked up at the two other women, first Zephyr then

Cynthia. "I thought you were already committed to Wil?" Her large black eyes narrowed.

Cynthia grinned, baring her teeth. "We are, joined, yes. He called it a marriage." She nodded to her Palorian friend. "Maxim is finally getting his dren together."

Len-Lu turned toward Zephyr, her previously squinting eyes now massively wide circles of ink. She clapped her hands. "Wonderful news!" She snatched Zephyr's hand and pulled her toward the boutique.

Cynthia fell in behind the pair, shaking her head and smiling.

The small Brailack woman behind the counter looked up at the newcomers. "Welcome to JeJe's. What's the occasion?"

"She's getting..." Len-Lu looked up at Zephyr. "What do you call it on Palor?"

"Joining," the *Ghost*'s first officer answered.

Len-Lu nodded and turned back to the store clerk. "Her slow-to-get-moving partner is finally ready to get joined."

The other small woman looked up at Zephyr. "That's wonderful news. Congratulations!" She clapped her hands excitedly.

Zephyr cleared her throat. "I actually have an outfit picked out already. I just wanted to look around."

Len-Lu made a rude noise. *Definitely Bennie's sister*, Cynthia thought. "Does your joining not include wardrobe changes?" When Zephyr opened then closed her mouth, Len-Lu looked at the clerk. "We'll need a suite."

"Of course," the clerk said. She hopped off the stool she'd been perched on and pointed them toward the back of the store. "This way, please."

Cynthia followed the group, grabbing a slinky low-cut number she thought Wil would appreciate. "Zee, you never mentioned you had an outfit picked out."

Zephyr raised her wristcomm and swiped through a few screens before holding it up for Cynthia to see.

"Dren. Is that a dress or battle armor?" It occurred to her that she didn't actually know what a Palorian joining ceremony entailed.

Zephyr turned, grinning. "Yes."

Cynthia laughed. "I should have known."

The group reached a luxurious suite with room enough for twice their number. The clerk gestured to a full-length mirror. "This ReflecTron 2000 will help you view any of our inventory as well as apply custom designs and alterations to anything you'd like to order." She pointed to an ottoman next to a chaise lounge. "Refreshments are in the cooler there."

Cynthia purred. "This is nice."

The clerk exited the suite, closing the door behind her. Len-Lu approached the mirror, tapping its surface. An interface appeared, as if floating in the air between her and the mirror. She waved Zephyr over. "Let me see what you're starting with."

From the mirror, a genderless voice said, "Please stand still while I take your measurements. To start, face forward." Zephyr did as the mirror said. A scanner beam shot out of the mirror and made its way from her head to her toes. "Thank you. Please turn around." She did and the beam repeated its scan. "Thank you. We are all set and ready to begin," the mirror chirped.

Cynthia watched the two of them start working through options on the mirror, the smaller woman using Zephyr's initial outfit for inspiration. She opened the ottoman. "Oh my." Zephyr and Len-Lu turned as she produced a chilled bottle of Gruke Nulimb.

Len-Lu bounced over. "This place is the best."

Zephyr shook her head. "I thought this was where the ordinary people shopped?"

The smaller woman shrugged. "Ordinary people can have good taste, too." She grinned. "Sometimes."

Cynthia distributed flutes of the pale blue drink, then dropped onto the chaise. "I'm gonna check on Gabe."

Zephyr and Len-Lu said nothing, focused on the mirror and the outfits already being displayed on its surface.

THE THREE OF them were crouched behind a shrub, looking at a dilapidated boarding house on the outskirts of the main business district of the colony. There wasn't much traffic, so no one had seen, let alone bothered, them while they lurked.

"Where are we again?" Nic asked.

"We've been here for five tocks. You don't know where we are?" Bennie replied.

The Olop girl shook her head. "I was just testing you." She wrinkled her furry brow. "Fine. I wasn't paying attention when we landed, and looking at this place, it's kind of a dump. The colony I mean."

Maxim shook his head. "Cadan Madak."

The young Knight of Plentallus looked at the much bigger Palorian. "That doesn't mean anything."

Maxim was about to reply when Bennie made a *tsk* sound. "His terminal just logged onto the dark net." He looked up from his wristcomm. "He's in there."

Maxim stood. He cracked his knuckles, adjusting the fit of the fingerless gloves he'd donned. He didn't have his full combat armor. There was no easy place to store it on the *Nontee*. But as a precaution, he grabbed some light armor pieces from the *Ghost* before joining Bennie and Nic. He tightened the straps holding his chest and back armor. "Then let's go." He didn't wait for the pair of knights. He strode across the road toward the ramshackle dwelling.

The boarding house was a three-story affair. According the city's information network, it was available to anyone struggling and in need of shelter. It was run by a religious order that operated several similar houses throughout the city.

Maxim reached the front door, pushing it open to reveal a dingy lobby. At the far end behind a small desk, a tired looking Tleb looked up from the tablet she was holding. "Help you?" she asked.

Maxim approached the tiny being. Wil was convinced that either chihuahuas were devolved from Tleb explorers or Tleb were uplifted chihuahuas. Maxim didn't care. He smiled. "I'm looking for my cousin." The little being stared at him, saying nothing. He put his hand out next to his head. "This tall. Palorian..." The tiny canine-esque woman kept staring. "Male?"

She nodded, baring her teeth. One of her incisors was bright silver. "Oh, yeah. Him. Second floor. Room 10."

Nic and Bennie watched the exchange, the latter whispering, "I hate Tleb."

Nic turned. "That's kinda general."

"You ever met one that wasn't a turd?"

She thought about it a while. "No."

Bennie nodded toward the front of the room. Maxim was moving toward the staircase. "This should be fun."

The two Knights of Plentallus followed their big friend up to the second floor.

"Don't break anything!" the Tleb lobby worker called after them.

Reaching the second floor, Maxim moved with purpose down the hall, stopping at the door that had "10" stenciled on it in galactic standard. At some point, someone had put a sticker with a cartoon Ruknak sticking its tongue out while making an obscene gesture over the zero.

Maxim took a deep breath and knocked on the door. There wasn't an electronic announcer panel next to the door.

Nic and Bennie moved to stand on either side of the door, both holding their beam saber hilts, thumbs hovering over activation switches.

No one opened the door.

"Maybe he's not home?" Nic offered in a whisper.

"I know he is. His terminal logged in just a few microtocks ago," Bennie whispered harshly.

"Maybe he uses one of those apps to trick employers?" Nic offered, moving her hand in random patterns. Both men turned to her, expressions flat. "What?" she demanded.

Maxim shook his head and knocked again.

"Who is it?" a voice asked from the other side of the door.

Maxim opened his mouth, but Nic spoke up in a low voice. "Building services." She looked at the big Palorian man and shrugged. "He might recognize your voice," she whispered.

The sound of bolts sliding out of locks came from the other side of the door. When it sounded like the last bolt was drawn, Maxim leaned back and kicked the door hard. It slammed into the room's occupant and bounced back to be stopped by Maxim's extended arm.

He stepped into the room and looked at the younger man sprawled on the floor. "Hello, cousin."

CHAPTER EIGHTEEN

Operating system re-initializing.

...

Running level one diagnostic.

...

Multiple sub-systems offline.

...

Communication systems experiencing intermittent phase discrimination.
Right arm mobility reduced by 35%.
Neck servos damaged. Mobility reduced by 10%.

...

...

Cognition function undamaged.
Starting up.

GABE'S optic sensors flickered to life. It took several seconds for his processing core to fully spin up. As it did, he took stock of his surroundings. He was aboard the *Ghost* in the foyer outside the bridge.

"Ga—come—u copy—" came over his built-in communication suite.

Accessing the comm software, he sent, "*I copy, Cynthia.*"

"Thank—I'v—ing to—you," she said. He prioritized a diagnostic of the comm suite. "Wha—status?" the Tygran woman asked.

Now that his processing core was fully online, he took in his full surroundings. There were plasma burns scattered around the space; several bulkheads exhibited melted sections. The hatch to the bridge also had several scorch marks on it. Obvious signs of a firefight. And there was a dead Brailack under him.

Oh, that is right.

The diagnostic on his comm suite completed. The software rebooted. A second later he heard, "Gabe? Are you there? Come in. Did I lose you?"

"Apologies, Cynthia. It has been an...interesting last tock." He accessed the ship's computer to confirm his internal clock's time. "...Or two."

"Everything okay?"

Gabe accessed the ship's internal sensors. No dead spots. No signs of further attempts to hack the ship's computers. The cargo hatch and airlocks were still secure. Accessing the internal cameras, he confirmed the location and status of each of the intruders. He still was not sure how the band of thieves entered the ship...The dorsal airlock. He scolded himself for not thinking of it earlier.

Clever, he thought as he sent a command to the dorsal airlock hatch, securing it and scrambling the access codes. "Yes. Everything is fine. There is some clean up required."

There was a pause on the other end of the line. Finally, Cynthia said, "Gotcha. Well, Zee and I can come back in a bit. We're at a shopping center with Bennie's sister while the ambassador and Bennie's dad are meeting."

"That would be appreciated."

He sat up, looking over his shoulder to ensure his opponent was indeed deceased. There was nothing there. Nobody. His arm rotated around to reach for his back to peel the body off. *I will need to clean myself when this is over.*

The bridge hatch whirred and clicked as the security bolts slid back releasing the hatch. Gabe entered the bridge and brought the ship's main systems online. He stood motionless waiting for the reactor to reach minimum power output before engaging the anti-personnel systems.

Once he was sure that Brailack ship thieves would not be an issue, he headed back down to the cargo deck to continue what he was doing. He carried the attacker from the bridge to the common deck, dropping the body near the stairwell access hatch. Then he retrieved the body from the computer core.

I am glad the attackers were Brailack. Very portable, he thought to himself. He picked up the first body and headed for the cargo hold.

Reaching the cargo deck, he turned to the two attackers he'd tied up. "Hello." He dropped the two bodies on the deck near the large cargo doors.

"You killed them?" the woman asked.

"Yes."

"You gonna kill us?" the male asked.

Gabe turned to the two surviving ship thieves. "No. I have called the authorities. They should be here in a few moments. I will release you to their custody." He considered the two beings. "Why did you attempt to steal this vessel?"

The female thief made a face. "Are you kidding? An Ankarran Raptor Model 89?" She shook her head. "Do you know what one of these, in this good of condition, goes for?" Gabe shook his head. "A lot. Buy-an-island-on-a-Tier-3-colony-world money."

Gabe cocked his head. "Interesting."

She nodded to the bodies. "Room to cut you in. All our cuts would be larger than our original plan." She winked.

He received a signal from the *Ghost*'s computer that a civil security vehicle had just arrived. He sent a command to the control pedestal next to the cargo door. The massive door split down the middle, the two sides sliding apart as the ramp lowered.

Gabe picked up the two bound Brailack. "Your ride is here."

"Last chance," the female thief said.

A quartet of Brailack in olive uniforms came up the ramp. Gabe looked at the two Brailack. "I shall pass." He lowered his charges to the deck. "These are the survivors." He gestured to the side. "Those were their colleagues."

The seniormost security officer nodded. "Thanks. We've been after this group for quite some time. They've stolen dozens of ships from spaceports across Brai and several neighboring worlds."

Gabe inclined his head. "I am happy to have helped."

"Lucky you were aboard your ship," one of the other security officers said as she shoved the two prisoners down the ramp.

The senior officer nodded his agreement. "She's right. I'm sure they assumed the crew was off ship." He pointed to one of his underlings, then the bodies. "You and Den-Dei take those." The security officers nodded. Turning back to Gabe, he said, "We thank you. I'll take my leave."

Gabe nodded. "Good day." He reached over and tapped the control pedestal, closing the heavy cargo doors.

MAXIM STEPPED FURTHER into the room.

His cousin clapped both hands together twice. The room

burst into blinding light and earsplitting noise. Maxim fell to his knees.

Before Bennie and Nic could move in from the hallway, the younger Palorian bolted through the door after vaulting over Maxim and knocking the two smaller team members aside.

Bennie was on his feet first, giving chase.

Maxim helped Nic up. "See what you can find in there. He went to the trouble to rig that countermeasure. Betting there's more in there he'd rather we not see."

She pursed her lips and nodded.

Maxim broke into a run down the corridor after Bennie and Tane. He tapped his earpiece. "Bennie, what's your location?"

"Just burst out into the back alley," the Brailack reported.

Maxim picked up his pace, taking the stairs three at a time to reach the ground floor in four strides. Grabbing the banister, he spun himself around to dash down the back hallway.

"I said, don't make a mess!" the Tleb woman scolded as Maxim headed for the building's rear.

"We've chased you. Halfway across. The GC. You drennog," Bennie said as he ran. Tane was almost as big as his older cousin, and his strides were at least four of Bennie's. The hacker and Knight of Plentallus was glad this little adventure was now instead of before he began his training as a knight. He had never been in as good a physical shape as he was now. Hacking didn't require a lot of moving.

Even so, he was getting tired. "Just. Stop!"

Maxim caught up to him, snatching up as he ran, not slowing down, securing Bennie in the crook of his arm.

Bennie flailed. "I'm not luggage!"

"Wasn't thinking you were," Maxim said, grinning. He was closing the gap on his cousin.

"Oh, no!" Bennie protested. "Don't you dare!"

Maxim smiled. He palmed Bennie and reared back. Bennie

was flapping both arms as Maxim hurled the angry Brailack as hard as he could.

"I hate you!" the team's hacker wailed as he arced through the air. He spied Tane below. "Incoming!" he screamed, pinwheeling his arms.

Tane turned just in time to see a flailing Brailack falling from the sky right at him. "What the—?" Bennie slammed into him.

The pair tumbled to the ground, rolling several meters in a tangle of arms and legs. Both men were screaming and shouting as they continued to strike things as they rolled.

Maxim caught up. "I wasn't sure that would work." He helped Bennie to his feet.

The little Brailack scowled. "I hate you." His eyes grew wide. "Wait. What the wurrin do you mean? You didn't know if it would work? You threw me! This isn't even the first time!" He stamped a foot.

Behind him, Tane rose to his feet. Maxim stepped around Bennie. "Cousin." He eased his pulse pistol, freshly recharged, out of its holster.

The younger Palorian scowled. "Maxim."

Maxim shook his head. "Explain yourself. We've chased you all over the GC. You broke into my home. Stole our family's colla band. Why? To keep me from joining with Zephyr?"

Tane looked at Maxim, then Bennie, then their surroundings. The chase had ended in a small park next to a multistory residential building.

"Don't," Maxim warned. Tane turned to look his cousin. Maxim was certain he was about to bolt. So, when he lunged to attack, Maxim was caught off guard.

Bennie took a step back, content to watch the fight.

The younger Palorian lashed out with repeated punches and jabs, mixed in with kicks. Maxim parried each attack but was unable to counter, barely staying ahead of his cousin's moves. He didn't think technicians got this much hand-to-hand training. Maxim gave ground slowly, letting Tane push him deeper into the park, away from the street.

Bennie followed, watching the two Palorians exchange blows and blocks in a blur of motion. "Max, you know you can fight back, ri—"

"Stay out of this!" Maxim ordered as he took advantage of Tane turning his focus briefly toward Bennie, to land a jab at the other man's chest, staggering him. "Talk to me, Tane." He ducked a right cross, landing another jab into his cousin's armpit. Tane stumbled backward, holding his right arm tight against his torso. Maxim moved in quickly, delivering a kick to his cousin's thigh and an uppercut that sent the younger man lurching.

"You disgraced our family," Tane said between rubbing his jaw. His pause caused Maxim to lower his hands slightly. Tane stepped in quickly to deliver a jab with his left fist and spin kick with his right leg. Maxim parried each, grabbing his leg and dropping an elbow on Tane's knee, shattering it.

"I did no such thing," Maxim countered. "Zephyr and I were framed and then fully exonerated." He shoved the other man away to put some distance between them.

Tane struggled to keep his balance, favoring his left leg. "You've aligned yourself with humans," he sneered. He nodded to Bennie. "And lesser beings like him."

"Hey!" Bennie shouted. "That's just rude."

Maxim dropped his hands to his sides. He shook his head. "That's what this is about? Some Palorian purity thing? Our being a part of the team...Wil?"

Tane kept his eyes on the ground but nodded. "It's embarrassing. It's beneath you! It's beneath us!" he snarled. He looked up to meet Maxim's gaze. "I'm not the only one who thinks this.

They said I could help you, and the Commonwealth, by keeping you busy. Away from the human." He shook his head. "I didn't know how at first, but then your father mentioned that you'd asked for the colla band during a visit with my father."

Maxim was stunned. He stood staring at the younger man.

Bennie came up beside Maxim. "What're you talking about? Who's they? Keep us busy? Why?" He squinted up at the man they'd been chasing. "Who helped you secure your dark nexus account?"

Tane turned to the Brailack. He shrugged. "They said they were the Coalition." He shrugged again. "They provided everything I needed."

Nic came around a corner. "Nothing of interest in his room." She held up a half-eaten candy bar. "Except this." She took a bite.

WAVING to the air car as it rose back into the air to take Wil, Bruce, and Len-Lu back to the Vulvo estate, Cynthia and Zephyr turned to the spaceport entry. Cynthia looked over her shoulder at the automated cargo bot. "Come along."

"You think he's safe? With her?" Zephyr asked. She chuckled remembering Wil's face when Cynthia told him she and Zephyr were going back to the spaceport to help Gabe.

Cynthia waved a dismissive hand. "He'll be fine. Probably."

They made their way through the lobby, swiping their wrist-comms over the reader granting them access to the inner lobby, a space reserved solely for crews of ships in the port.

Exiting the inner lobby onto the duracrete, the pair spotted civil security forces approaching in an air car with a pair of stealth-suit-clad Brailack in their custody.

"Are they wearing—?" Zephyr started.

"Yeah," Cynthia cut in. That couldn't be a coincidence.

The pair watched the authorities usher their charges into the waiting vehicle.

"Think that's what Gabe—" Cynthia started.

"Almost certainly," Zephyr said.

They both picked up the pace, leaving the small cargo bot and its cargo of bags from the boutique behind to catch up.

The pair reached the ship in short order. Both women offered thanks that the port wasn't one of the really big ones. The *Ghost* looked undamaged.

"It looks okay," Cynthia said. She raised her wristcomm. "Gabe, you there?"

"Affirmative, Cynthia," the droid replied.

At the top of the ship's cargo ramp, the large cargo doors ground open. The team's engineer was waiting for them at the top of the ramp. "Greetings."

The two women reached the top. Cynthia said, "You mentioned there being some clean up?"

He nodded. "Indeed. Where are the captain and our guests?"

"Wil and Bruce caught a ride back to the palace with Len-Lu," Zephyr said.

"Should be along in a tock or two. They wanted to sync up with the ambassador and Bennie's father."

The trio moved through the cargo hold and up the stairs to the common deck. When they reached C deck, Zephyr looked at Cynthia, who gave her a look back. She said, "You told Cynthia you needed help with cleaning something up?"

Gabe led them aft, stopping at the hatch to the computer core. The door slipped apart at the middle.

Cynthia leaned in. She spotted the gore covered deck and sniffed. "Is that brain matter?"

"Mixed with plastic?" Zephyr added.

Gabe nodded. "It is." He held up a hand to keep either of them from entering the room. "There is more." He gestured for them to head forward.

Outside the bridge, Zephyr sighed. "What the wurrin?"

Cynthia kneeled down. "Blood?"

The droid nodded. He pointed to the bulkhead behind them.

The two women followed his gesture, then turned back to Gabe.

"Okay. Spill," Cynthia demanded.

Gabe cocked his head. "I had...visitors."

Zephyr ran a finger along a section of plasma burned bulkhead. "Not friendly ones."

The droid shook his head. "A crew of Brailack ship thieves thought the *Ghost* looked like a promising target."

"Good thing you were here," Zephyr said.

"Indeed," the droid agreed. He gestured to the blood. "That one was their leader, I believe."

"Was?" Cynthia asked.

"I was able to secure two of the four thieves, alive."

Zephyr nodded. "Okay. Let's going."

"I will tackle the computer core," Gabe said.

Zephyr looked at the damage to the bulkheads and bridge hatch. "I don't think there's much we can do with this."

Cynthia headed for the stairs. "I'll get some rags from the head downstairs."

Two hours later, Gabe was crossing through the common deck lounge when the stairwell hatch opened. Bruce entered followed by Wil, then Ambassador Carlisle. He stopped. "Hello."

"Hey, pal. We ready to depart?"

Gabe nodded. "We can be ready shortly." He continued aft, then stopped. "Do not go in the computer core."

The three men exchanged a look. Wil shook his head. "Yeah, okay. The ladies back?"

"The bridge," Gabe said, reaching the hatch to engineering. He stopped. "Please keep in mind, I kept the ship from being stolen." He entered engineering, letting the hatch close behind him.

Bruce turned to Wil, who shrugged and headed for the neck and the bridge beyond. "You two might as well get comfortable."

Zephyr stood as Wil stepped through the hatch. "Everything good with Bennie's father and the ambassador?"

"What the hell happened here?" Wil asked, hitching a thumb over his shoulder and pointing through the bridge hatch.

Cynthia walked over and kissed his cheek. "Gabe decided to have friends over."

"YOU CAME IN THIS?" Tane asked as the group came around the tail end of a large Hulgian cargo hauler, and the *Rocky Nontee* came into view.

"You're welcome to walk," Bennie said without turning to face the young man he'd decided was one hundred percent unlikeable.

"Not yet, you're not," Maxim said. He had a hand firmly on his young cousin's shoulder. "Not until the colla band is back in my possession."

The *Nontee*'s forward cargo ramp dropped to the duracrete with a thud. The group had made their way from the park to the spaceport without incident. As a precaution, Bennie sent Nic ahead to ensure there weren't any surprises along their route. There had been none. The young Olop woman was waiting just inside the cargo hold.

Bennie walked to the ladder with the small built-in lift platform. As the device rose, he said, "I'll get the preflight started. We'll be in the air in half a tock."

"Copy that," Maxim said. He guided Tane to a small stack of crates near the rear of the small ship's hold. "Take a seat."

The younger man sniffed. "I believe whatever is in here has spoiled," he said.

Maxim moved a crate aside so he could sit opposite his cousin. "I think it's Fyolpi. He probably forgot it was here." He made a face, then tried to put the sour smell out of his mind. "What's going on with you, Tane? You've never been a populist. I didn't even think you paid attention to politics."

The younger man kept his gaze focused on the deck. Somewhere aft of them, the ship's reactor spun up, a slow thrum building through the deck plating. Tane took a breath, then let it go. "People are talking. A lot of them. Between the GC nearly collapsing and then these humans being welcomed in. You know there are trillions of them? All waiting to emigrate. To spread themselves throughout the GC, corrupting every planet they set foot on, taking work, sewing chaos."

Maxim listened to his young cousin, unsure what to say. To the best of his knowledge, Tane had been your average Palorian. He'd entered the Peacekeepers on his twentieth year. As far as Maxim knew, he was still in the service. "Aren't you still in the service?" He couldn't remember what the younger man did in the Peacekeepers, but he was reasonably sure it was technical or something else non-frontline—communications, maybe? Thinking back to their fist fight, maybe he was a frontline trooper.

Tane shook his head. "Discharged last year." He held up a hand to keep his older cousin from following up. "Between the Harrith incident and all the separatist stuff recently, the service has been scaling back. A lot of younger, newer service personnel were released from service. Keeping most of the more senior officers." He scowled. "Released from the one thing our people have been good at. The one thing that, for centuries, gave our people purpose." He looked up at Maxim, his eyes angry. "The GC encouraged us to be warriors. Now they're tossing us aside because it's bad optics."

The thrum of the *Nontee*'s engines rose in pitch. "We're cleared to depart," Bennie announced over the intercom. The deck shook and tilted as Bennie piloted the ship up and away from the spaceport.

Maxim looked at his family member. He and Zephyr tried to stay abreast of what was going on in the larger GC, especially after helping the Harrith come in to help stabilize the collapsing Commonwealth. That had been a challenging time. He'd known Palor was struggling. Knew that the Governing Council was scaling back Peacekeeper activities to look less like a military empire. To his chagrin, he had not paid enough attention, it seemed.

"Tane. The GC isn't perfect. That's more than obvious these days. But things change. The old structure was rigid and unable to change. It almost broke as a result."

Tane shook his head. "Change seems to be hurting some of us more than others, cousin." He stood. "This bucket have bunks somewhere?"

"We're out of atmo. FTL in ten," Bennie announced.

Maxim led Tane up the ladder pointing aft. "Bunks are that way." He watched the young man for a moment and then turned forward to enter the bridge. "Make sure the terminals and comms back there are cut off."

"Already done," Nic said from her console. Maxim nodded and patted her shoulder.

"So back to Lorstak Seven?" Bennie asked.

"Appears so. Said he stashed it there before leading us on

the chase. We should check in with the others. This Coalition thing doesn't sit well with me."

Bennie nodded. "You and me both." He adjusted their course data, then pushed the FTL control forward. The stars ahead of them stretched out into rainbow lines.

"Apprentice, contact the others." When he heard no reply, he turned in his seat to see Nic staring at him. "Please," he added.

She nodded.

THE *GHOST* WAS SITTING in orbit over Brai while the ambassador and his aide discussed next destinations with Wil and the crew.

"You're due on Tarsis in like," Wil looked at his wristcomm, checking the date. "Four days."

"Carr-Ari was rather insistent I visit Harrith Prime," the older man said. "Especially after everything that's happened of late."

Wil inhaled and blew out a breath. "Okay, that would make sense, but..."

"It's not close to Tarsis," Zephyr said.

"Plus, there's the new wrinkle of our friends the Coalition, whatever that is," Cynthia added. She did her best approximation of snapping her fingers. With her soft fur and pads on the undersides of her fingers, it was more of a muffled click than anything. "Crildon Three."

Zephyr shook her head. "No one cares about Crildon Three." Then it dawned on her. "Oh. Duch."

"Dutch?" Bruce asked. He'd been sitting silently watching the discussion since everyone had collected in the common deck lounge.

Wil tapped his fingers on the table absently while he thought it over. "He would know what's what. If we push it, we could be at Crildon Three in two days. Likely as safe a harbor as we're gonna get right now." He turned to Carlisle. "You may want to call Tarsis and let them know you might be late. Just a day or two."

The other man nodded. "The ceremony isn't for two days after our arrival, so there is some padding." He looked at the crew. "And who is this Dutch person on Crildon Three?"

Wil shook his head. "Duch is Rhys Duch. Crildon Three is the planet he's set up shop on." He held his hand out, just below his shoulder. "Home of the Goombans. Mushroom people, this tall. Very polite. You'll like 'em."

The ambassador looked at Wil. "And this will be a better use of our time than going to Harrith Prime?"

Wil shrugged. "You wanted to see the underbelly of the GC. Well, Rhys Duch is it."

"Is it safe?" Bruce asked.

Cynthia made a face. "You were the one trying to buy arms from him."

Bruce looked at her. "What do you mean?"

"That Hulgian woman. Worked for Duch."

He pursed his lips. "We thought so but weren't sure."

Wil perked up. "Who's we?"

Bruce crossed his arms over his chest. He looked around the space. After taking a deep breath, he said, "I was following a lead."

"A lead?" Zephyr asked.

Bruce looked at her, then his boss, then back to Zephyr. "I'm not just his aide."

"You don't say," Cynthia said in a low voice.

Bruce frowned. "I work for Earth Gov Intelligence."

"A spook," Wil said.

Zephyr made a face. "He's a ghost?" She reached across the table to poke his shoulder.

Wil shook his head. "A spy."

"Ah," she said.

The hatch to the computer core opened. "I have finished the repairs to the computer. Those thieves were quite adept at their work. Bennie would be impressed." Gabe looked at the others. "Did I miss something?"

"We're going to Crildon Three," Wil said.

"On purpose?"

"'Fraid so." Wil's wristcomm buzzed. He looked at the screen. "Good timing. Max is calling." He turned to the large bulkhead-mounted display screen, sending the comm request to it. The ship's computer handled accepting the communication request and routing it to the display screen. He glanced at Bruce. "Obviously not done."

The other man said nothing.

The display came to life. Maxim was looking at the others. "Hi."

"Hey, Max," Wil said. He waved.

Bennie and Nic crowded into view, the former saying, "Hi, everyone! Have we got news. We found Max's cousin, and we're heading to Lorstak Seven to get the band thi—" Maxim slapped Bennie out of the frame. The sound of a Brailack hitting the deck could just be heard over the line.

Wil pursed his lips and did his best not to look at Zephyr.

"Maxim's cousin?" Zephyr asked.

"We, uh," Maxim started. He schooled his expression and continued. "We tracked the thief to Jannav Kenu and ran into my cousin Tane."

"Tane? Really?" Zephyr said. "That's weird." She looked around the room, rubbing her chin.

Cynthia looked at Wil, who gave the tiniest wide-eyed shrug.

Before the other woman could continue with questions, Cynthia said, "What was little green talking about? News?"

Maxim nodded. "Oh, yes. We discovered something interesting. The thief was working for something called the Coalition."

"The Coalition?" Wil said. He looked around the common deck lounge at the others, then turned back to the screen.

Maxim made a face. "You know them?"

"We've met," Zephyr said.

CHAPTER NINETEEN

MAXIM RUBBED HIS JAW. "We should link up. This feels big."

Cynthia nodded. "He's right. This Coalition seems to know a lot about us. Enough to know to split us up for maximum effect."

Maxim inclined his head. "I concur."

Zephyr clucked. "Meet us on Crildon Three?"

Wil saw Maxim make a face. He knew Max wouldn't stop until he had his band-thing. "We should head for Lorstak Seven." Everyone turned to him. He could feel his cheeks flushing. Lorstak Seven wasn't that far from Tarsis. Maybe half a day's travel farther than Crildon Three, so not a major detour, but not a reason on its own to go there versus Crildon Three. Rhys Duch was on Crildon Three. There was nothing of value on Lorstak Seven other than Maxim's band doodad. "More scenic and interesting than Crildon," he said.

Zephyr nodded. "He's right. Duch is an asset, but there's not much else there." She turned to the ambassador. "Might as well give you one more view of life in the GC." She turned to

Wil. "A bit surprised you'd want to revisit it, though. Didn't you almost get eaten by a billabong?"

"Beachbong," Wil corrected.

"Baechoo," Cynthia said, turning around. "They're called Baechoos."

Wil shivered, remembering the experience. His inner thigh still had a few small scars. He and Cynthia had taken a vacation there a few years ago. They'd spent a great deal of time on the planet's many nude beaches—beaches visited by normally docile Baechoos that seemed to enjoy the smell or taste of human flesh.

"What is Lorstak Seven?" Ambassador Carlisle asked.

Gabe opened a new window on the display, blocking part of Maxim's face. "Lorstak Seven is a colony not far from Tarsis." The window showed a world orbiting a yellow star. The image zoomed in on the seventh planet. "Known primarily for its beaches, Lorstak Seven also boasts several robust industries, namely: consumer electronics, high-speed rail components, and —"

"Dude. No one cares," Wil said, interrupting the droid.

The inset window vanished.

Wil turned to the two additional humans. "Lovely place. Except for the sea monsters. Lots of industry." An idea came to him. "Neutral ground." He turned to Cynthia. "Think Duch will meet us there?"

"Longer trip for him, but I'll ask." She headed towards the bridge.

"What about Crildon Three?" Bruce asked.

"You'll like Lorstak Seven better," Wil said. He turned back to the bulkhead-mounted display where Maxim was silently watching the exchange from the bridge of the *Rocky Nontee*. "Get moving. Lorstak Seven."

Maxim nodded. "See you there." He turned to look toward a

muffled noise off-screen. "You'll heal. Set the course." The screen went dark.

Wil turned toward the hatch leading to the bridge. "I'm going to get us on the way to Lorstak Seven." He stopped and looked over his shoulder at Bruce. "Then we'll eat lunch. Then we'll discuss your occupation." He disappeared through the hatch.

Zephyr looked at the two humans and Gabe. "Something weird is going on."

"And water is wet," the droid replied in a monotone. Zephyr frowned at him.

"You're just now thinking that?" Bruce asked. He turned to the ambassador. "Maybe we should just go to Tarsis now?"

The thrum of the engines changed pitch.

"No real point. We won't get answers on Tarsis," Zephyr said.

Gabe nodded. "Indeed. If we hope to gain any clarity on what we are facing, Tarsis would not be the place to get it." He paused, accessing the ship's navigation data. "Plus, we are already en route to Lorstak Seven."

Bruce threw both arms in the air. "I need a drink."

Ambassador Carlisle nodded his agreement. Zephyr shrugged and headed for the food chiller.

The forward hatch opened, and Wil and Cynthia filed out. The latter said, "Duch was surprisingly amenable to joining us on Lorstak Seven."

From the chiller, Zephyr asked, "What did you have to offer him?" She stood, her arms loaded with several bottles of grum.

Cynthia made a face. "I promised we'd listen to his pitch for his new business idea."

Wil took a bottle from Zephyr, groaning. "Oh, come on, babe." He opened the bottle and took a sip. "Last time it was a three-hour pitch for that ridiculous emergency EVA suit idea of his. Damn thing nearly suffocated me." His nose wrinkled. "While you all watched and laughed, I might add."

From his place near the cooktop, Gabe said, "I believe several earlier test subjects did, in fact, die."

Cynthia looked at Gabe. "Not helping." Turning to her husband, she shrugged. "He's trying to diversify his business holdings. We should encourage it. The idea wasn't horrible, just poorly executed. But it was a legitimate and above-board business idea."

Wil took another sip of his drink and noticed Gabe. "Are you cooking?" he asked the ship's engineer.

"Yes," the droid said. "I have added some culinary routines to my base programming. I would like to try my hand. If that is okay?"

Wil inclined his head. "By all means. We've survived Bennie's cooking." He turned back to his wife. "If there's a live demo, you're doing it."

"Wuss." She raised her bottle of grum in salute.

Wil turned to Bruce and gestured to the lounge area. "Let's chat."

"LOOK AT THIS BRUISE," Bennie demanded, holding his elbow out for Nic to look at.

She shoved the thin arm away. "I don't want to look at your elbow."

"It might be broken." He turned to glare at Maxim.

The trio and their guest were in the *Nontee*'s lounge, the remains of dinner on the low coffee table before them. Maxim, sitting on the floor, watched them. For the life of him, he wasn't sure how they hadn't killed each other yet.

He turned to Tane, who was sitting next to him. The

younger man had said nothing since they left Jannav Kenu and had barely touched his meal. "Does your family know about all this?"

"It's not broken. For an adult, you're an enormous baby," Nic said.

Tane shook his head. "We don't talk much."

"Your father would want to know," Maxim said.

"Know what? That I've been released from the one job our people are naturally good at? From the one employer we're basically born to serve? The one job the Tarsi encouraged us to be good at?"

"I'm not being a baby. It's important for a Knight of Plentallus to be in top physical form, and this injury prevents that," Bennie said.

Maxim shook his head. "I was thinking more generally that you're struggling and need support. You could have reached out to Zephyr and me." He stared at the other man a long moment. "What did you think this Coalition would do for you that your family couldn't? Or wouldn't?"

"That's not even your sword arm," Nic said.

Bennie was curling and extending his arm slowly, experimentally.

Tane sighed. "Change. Not just for me. For everyone who's been left behind by the GC. The council cares more about itself than the average citizen. Now we've got these Earthers showing up, ready to take what little work there is." He looked at his cousin. "Have you even looked at the Palorian economy lately?"

Maxim shook his head. "That's what the Harrith are trying to do. That's why we brought them in. To help the Commonwealth get back to its roots, the core of what made it work. For everyone."

"We?" the younger man scoffed. "Who appointed you and

your human friend to be the arbiters of what's best for everyone in the GC?"

"It doesn't matter if it's my sword arm or not. It could still hinder my ability to execute my responsibilities," Bennie said. Now he was rotating his arm slowly while holding his elbow, testing his shoulder. With every rotation he made a small noise. "My shoulder might be bruised, too."

Nic made a face, crossing her arms over her chest. "Your responsibilities? Like scamming free meals from restaurants?"

Maxim looked at the smaller members of the group and sighed. Turning back to Tane, he said, "We all have to do what we can to try to make things better. Are we always right? No. Does Wil mess up more than he fixes? Not most of the time." He shrugged. "Okay, sometimes."

"The Coalition says you—well, mostly him, the human—are trying to undermine the GC. To disrupt the balance of power that's existed for centuries. They say the humans will flood the GC: taking work, asserting themselves into the government. Destabilizing industry." He jabbed a finger at his cousin. "Your friends are carrying their ambassador, are they not?"

Maxim nodded.

"I do not *scam* restaurants. They freely offer to feed a Knight of Plentallus because our cause is noble, and they do it, against my judgment, for free." Bennie snapped. He looked at the two Palorians. "What're you two talking about?"

Maxim looked at his cousin. "And you're concerned about the humans?"

"SO, YOU'RE A SPY," Wil said. He sat down on the lounge sofa, reaching across to offer Bruce a fresh bottle of grum.

The other man took a sip of his drink, his eyes never leaving

Wil's. Both men were sitting at opposite ends of the sofa, angled so that they could talk to each other. The rest of the group were doing their best to give the pair some room, which in the small common deck lounge wasn't easy. He set the bottle down on the small coffee table. "Sorta."

"Sorta?" Wil repeated with a smile.

"Okay, less sorta and more yes. You have to understand, this is a once in a lifetime opportunity. Earth's first foray into the wider galactic community. Earth Gov Intelligence needs to know what we're getting ourselves into."

The explanation made perfect sense to Wil. He was still a bit annoyed that no one had told him. "Good actor, too. The whole slightly-in-over-your-head aide."

"Part of the job," Bruce said with a smile. He leaned forward to grab his drink. "No offense was meant. The ambassador wasn't even read in until we were on Oberon. The fewer people who know, the better. We didn't want to risk the Peacekeepers getting wise to my true purpose."

Wil shook his head. "You're lucky Bennie isn't here. He's a blabbermouth." He took a sip of his drink. "So, what's the end goal here? Why were you trying to talk to arms dealers and such?"

Bruce looked at the ceiling. "My primary mission is collecting intelligence, from any and all sources. When you told us we were going to Genko Akdool, I did a little research and discovered Kela Telle's little operation."

"Then you'll love Duch," Cynthia said from the kitchenette where she was helping Gabe. She turned to the droid as the sound of something sizzling filled the room. "Watch your temperature."

"Thank you, I am aware of the temperature down to a tenth of a degree," the droid replied a bit more tersely than Wil would have expected.

"Just trying to help," Cynthia said.

Wil turned back to Bruce. "All right, so what do you know about this Coalition thing?"

Bruce shook his head. "Actually. Nothing. First I heard of it was the same time as you." He gave a one-shoulder shrug. "Which should prove my point. Earth doesn't know what's out here. And needs to." He cocked his head as he leaned forward. "And tells us a lot about this Coalition group. Avoiding scrutiny is no small task."

Wil nodded his agreement on that last point.

"For what it's worth, I wasn't in favor of all this when I found out, but by then it was too late," Ambassador Carlisle offered from the kitchen table. He had been nursing his own drink while working on a tablet and listening to the two men in the lounge.

The two men on the couch turned to look at the older man. Wil said, "Please tell me Earth is doing all this in good faith."

Cynthia turned slightly to watch the older human answer. Gabe didn't turn his head but adjusted his hearing to home in on the ambassador, while his hands remained a blur, working the two frying pans on the cooktop at the same time.

The older man looked at Wil. "Yes." He looked at Bruce. "The State Department is deadly serious about this. Earth wants nothing more than peaceful relations with the GC and all other member societies." He inhaled. "We just want to know what we don't know."

"Lunch is served," Gabe announced before anyone could say anything else.

Wil kept his gaze locked on the ambassador. Finally, he said, "Okey dokey." He stood; Bruce followed. Both of them made their way around the sofa. Wil tapped his wristcomm. "Zee, lunch is ready."

"Copy that," she replied. She'd retreated to the bridge to keep an eye on things.

Cynthia helped Gabe move plated food to the table. "Gabe might have a new calling."

Wil eyed the dishes. He whistled. "Wow, man." He looked at Gabe. "This all looks amazing." He sat down. "What is it?"

The forward hatch opened, and Zephyr entered. She inhaled deeply. "Is that..." She took another deep inhalation. "Glor So?"

Gabe nodded. "It is. I look forward to any notes you may have."

Behind the tall engineering droid, Cynthia shook her head, lips pursed. Zephyr saw her and smiled as she took her seat.

THE *NONTEE* CAME in low over the Bamston City Spaceport. Her repulsorlifts hummed as she slowed.

"Why did Wil pick this place?" Nic asked. She had the local newsnet up on one of her screens. "Bamston City is not exactly the nicest part of the planet." She scrolled to another screen. "It's not even on their recommended tourism list."

Maxim leaned over her shoulder. He looked at the details and nodded. "This is where he used to meet Xarrix when that slime-mold had work for him." He pointed to a low-resolution map. "It's an older city in the original colony section. No beaches. No tropical arboreal zones. Just duracrete, commercial buildings, and cold weather."

The young woman looked at another section of the display, which showed the local climate. "Felgercarb. Hope you furlesses brought coats."

Bennie made a groaning noise. "I hate the cold."

Maxim shook his head. "It's nowhere near as cold as Glacial was. You survived that."

The ship made a slow circle over the port, losing altitude as it did. On the transparent forward window, a green rectangle appeared, highlighting their designated landing pad.

"I almost died, and you had to wrap me up like a to-go order."

Maxim chuckled. "Good times."

The small freighter came to a stop over its assigned pad and descended. Moments before touchdown, four panels slid open to reveal her stubby landing gear. Once the gear locked in place, the ship settled onto the duracrete. Bennie set about flipping switches, putting the ship into standby. "I think we've got a tock or two before the *Ghost* arrives."

Nic was still looking at her console. "Oh. There's a Durbrillian restaurant on the second level, north side."

Maxim thought back to their time on Durbril Two. The small beings resembled something Wil called a Mogwai, whatever the wurrin that was. Their food was good, though. He exited the bridge. "First round's on me." Keeping close to the spaceport until the others arrived made sense.

Bennie leaped up over the back of his chair, executing a backflip and landing on his feet behind his chair. "Appetizers, too? Sounds good to me."

Maxim held up a hand. "I never said—" He gave up and followed the little hacker out of the bridge.

Nic listened to Maxim and Bennie down in the cargo hold arguing about the climate as she put her station into standby mode. Once everything was as it should be, she stood and crossed into the common deck, making her way to the single small berth at the rear of the lounge. When it was just her and Bennie, it was crowded. With Maxim aboard, every place felt cramped. After grabbing her sling bag, she pulled open a drawer in the small room's equally small desk. Her beam saber hilt was right where she'd left it. After checking the charge, she clipped it to her belt.

By the time Nic reached the cargo deck, the temperature had dropped several degrees. The port entry hatch was wide open. Maxim and Bennie were standing outside the ship. Her mentor turned. "Thought you decided to stay with the ship. Can we go already?"

Nic was about to make a biting retort when Maxim put his hand on Bennie's head and turned him toward the spaceport's north sector pedestrian lobby, a half plorith away.

Nic hopped out of the ship, then entered a command on her wristcomm, putting the ship in lockdown. The port entry hatch slid closed, a loud thud announcing that the locking bolts were in place. From under the stubby wings, a pair of antipersonnel blasters deployed, rotating this way and that as they scanned.

"Okay, let's go," she said.

Maxim had a firm grip on his cousin's elbow. "We'll meet up with you shortly." He looked at Bennie. "Behave." To Tane he said, "Lead the way."

"WIL, I've got a call coming in. For the ambassador. From Tarsis," Cynthia said.

Everyone was on the bridge, except Gabe, who was in engineering. The *Ghost* was about an hour from the Lorstak system.

Wil looked up from his flight console and turned to Ambassador Carlisle, who was sitting at Maxim's station. "Want to take it in your quarters?"

The other man shook his head. "No, that's okay. If they're going to yell at me for being late, you might as well hear it, too." He got up and moved to stand behind Wil.

Cynthia took that as her cue and accepted the comm request. The window appeared on the main display. A stern-faced Tarlak appeared. The man's pale brown skin was almost orange. The four eyes blinked. "Hello. I am Second Aide Iran ch'Aroon." Two of the eyes stayed fixed on Wil, while the other two moved to the ambassador. "I am assigned to your office while you get acquainted with council policies and procedures and work on finding your own staff."

Wil tried to keep his face passive. He knew he was on screen.

The ambassador said nothing for a moment, unsure of how best to reply. Finally, he said, "I wasn't aware I had been allocated resources."

The second aide inclined his head. "It is a new procedure." The Tarlak man scowled. "Our advisors from Harrith suggested it." The two eyes focused on Wil, squinted. "Hello, Captain Calder."

Wil gave a tight-lipped smile. "Hi. How's Blumtillithian?" He glanced at Zephyr to see her approving nod of his correct pronunciation.

The second aide stared at him for a minute. "He is fine. He's been promoted to chief administrator for the council's new committee on open governance."

Wil nodded. "Right on. Sounds cool."

"He hates it."

"Okay then." Wil looked and pursed his lips.

Ambassador Carlisle made a small noise, then said, "What is it you called to discuss?"

The officious Tarlak inclined his head, all four eyes turning to the ambassador. "My records indicate your planned arrival to be in 32 tocks. Is that still accurate?"

Wil raised his hand. "We're showing the ambassador around

Lorstak Seven but shouldn't be there long. It may be an extra day, no more."

Tarlak, being a genetic cousin to the Tarsi, often felt like they ran the GC. In many ways, they did. As administrators and low-level bureaucrats, they moved things along or stopped them dead in their tracks within the gargantuan galactic government of the Commonwealth.

Iran ch'Aroon made a grumbling noise that Wil assumed was Tarlak for sighing. "Very good. I shall update my plans. Please keep me abreast of your travel plans so that I can ensure the honor guard is present when you arrive."

Carlisle inclined his head. "Of course. Thank you for your efforts on my behalf. I look forward to meeting you in person."

"Indeed. I shall await you with baited breath."

The window blinked out of existence, the main display showing the rainbow streaks of FTL travel once more.

"Fucking turds," Wil said under his breath.

Ambassador Carlisle patted Wil's shoulder before heading back to his seat. "Seems you've made friends all over the Commonwealth, Captain."

Wil grinned. "Well, when you've saved it as often as we have..." He gave an exaggerated shrug.

Zephyr looked at Cynthia, who rolled her eyes.

THE MAGLEV TRAIN from Bamston City to the Loni Industrial Complex took just ten minutes. Maxim watched the run-down factory building grow as they neared the station.

He looked at his cousin. "This is where you stashed my colla band?" The younger man shrugged. Maxim turned back to the window as the train slid into the station. As far as he knew, the Loni Industrial Complex was one of Lorstak Seven's earliest industrial centers. It looked it; stained, graffiti-covered duracrete crumbled everywhere he looked. Several small commercial stalls were nothing more than dark caves, their wiring and equipment stripped. He spied a grime-covered face peak out of the gloom as the train slid into a silent halt.

Standing to exit, Maxim said, "If you pawned it, I—"

"I didn't pawn it," the sullen younger man said. He led them off the maglev train. "Come on."

The Loni Industrial Complex didn't get any cleaner as they exited the transit station. Maxim looked around. "Hard to believe this is the same planet that's home to pink sand beaches as far as the eye can see and resorts that cater to every lifestyle and then some."

Tane shrugged. "Only ever been to this part."

His older cousin eyed him. "I'm not the enemy."

The younger man grunted. "This way."

"How much further?"

"Four more blocks. A pawn—"

Maxim growled. "I just asked y—"

The younger man tsked. "A friend runs it. She's holding the colla band for me."

They continued on, Maxim scanning the area. "How'd you meet someone on Lorstak Seven?"

Tane shook his head. "We met on Palor, in secondary school. She chose to not enroll in the academy and," he shrugged, "you know how that goes. We stayed in touch. I knew she was on Lorstak Seven. Figured she'd be a good person to keep the colla band safe."

The pair walked in silence for a few minutes, each man lost in thought.

As they rounded the corner, Maxim's training instinct kicked in, jarring him from thoughts of his upcoming joining to Zephyr. In a low voice, he asked, "This isn't a trap, is it?" Tane frowned and moved to glance over his shoulder. "Don't," Maxim said, then added, "Five: two Harrith, a Hulgian, and two Tleb."

"Tleb?" the younger man scoffed.

Maxim clucked. "They bite." As they passed a closed down electronics repair shop, he looked in what remained of the glass frontage. Their friends were closing the gap.

"I don't know them. Star is the only person on this planet that I know," Tane insisted.

Maxim nodded. "Just had to be sure."

"Wouldn't I say the same thing even if it is a trap?"

Maxim growled. Tane smiled. "There."

Up ahead, a failing hologram proclaimed the Second Chance Pawn and Loan to be open.

The door slid open, letting both men in. The interior of the pawn shop was filled with overstuffed shelves. Maxim looked around; toys, home electronics, clothing, and what looked like sex toys were intermingled with each other in a dusty and disturbing clutter.

"Star! Starfire! You in here?" Tane called out.

Maxim picked up a tube-shaped device, its interior lined with spikes. His finger brushed the activation switch causing the rings of spikes inside to undulate rhythmically.

"Grolacking dren!" Maxim flung the device away.

"If you break it, you buy it," a voice drawled from the back of the store.

Maxim turned to see a young Palorian woman no older than Tane. Her jet-black hair was shaved to stubble. Earrings similar to those worn by Malkorites lined both of her ears. She was looking at Maxim, then turned. "Back already?"

Tane smiled. "Hey, Star." Maxim joined him. "This is my cousin, Maxim."

The younger woman eyed Maxim up and down, then turned to Tane. "His?" The other man nodded. "One microtock." She vanished into the back of the shop through a beaded curtain.

Maxim turned to look out the shop's window. "Not sure being in here will detour our friends."

The group that had been tailing them were approaching the pawn shop.

The beads rattled as Starfire returned. She held out a small wooden box. Tane nodded to his cousin; she turned the box to Maxim. He took the box and was about to open it when the shop's door opened.

"Who're your friends, Star?" one of the Tleb asked. The other, right behind him, had only one eye.

Each small canid alien had a wicked looking long knife in hand.

The young Palorian woman rolled her eyes. "What do you two drennogs want?"

The two Palorian men looked at each other, then their host, then the two diminutive intruders.

The still open door admitted two Harrith women while the Hulgian man stopped in the doorway, blocking it.

Maxim looked at the new arrivals. "Who are you?"

The Harrith man turned to Maxim. "The welcoming committee, of course."

The Tleb with both eyes rubbed his hands together. "Simple mistake—you forgot to pay your entry fee for the complex when you got off the train."

Maxim looked the new arrivals over, his gaze settling on one of the two Harrith, the one that looked more intelligent. "Have you all looked around?" He gestured around the space. "Three Palorians, in their fighting prime, against—no offense—two Tleb, a pair of scrawny Harrith, and a Hulgian. No offense to any of you, but come on."

The Hulgian crossed his arms over his massive chest. "I like our odds." Maxim guessed wrong, apparently, with the Harrith.

From behind Tane and Maxim, a low whine began to build. "I don't."

Everyone turned to see Starfire holding an evil looking energy weapon that was clearly building to a full charge.

The two Tleb growled.

Maxim turned back the Hulgian. "And now?"

The big man reached up slowly, palms out. "We won't forget this, Starfire."

She smirked. "I'd hope not, Turk. I don't want to have to remind you and your band of drongos in a week." She waved the menacing looking weapon. "Go on now."

One by one the thugs filed out of the pawn shop.

Maxim looked at his cousin. "I like her." Turning to the pawn shop's proprietor. "You going to be okay? When we're gone?"

Starfire made a face. "Them?" She clucked. "They're nobodies. They wander around the transit center seeing who they can shake down."

Maxim looked at his wristcomm, swiped the screen. Looking up to Starfire, he said, "If you ever need anything."

She smiled and nodded.

CHAPTER TWENTY

"OVER HERE!" Nic shouted, waving. She'd hopped up onto her seat to be seen over the other patrons.

Wil nodded and guided the group toward the rest of the team. Maxim, Bennie, Nic, and a Palorian Wil didn't know were all sitting at large round table with more than enough room for the rest of them.

Maxim rose and moved to embrace Zephyr. He looked at Wil. "Good to see you."

"Hurry up! Merriment tock ends in ten microtocks!" Bennie said, pointing at several flexis laying on the table. "Drink menus are blue."

Cynthia moved to sit next to Bennie. "Hey, little green." She plucked a flexi off the table. "What's good?"

The Brailack held up a half empty glass with a purple and pink sludge that seemed illuminated from within. "These are delicious." He squinted. "I've had four."

Everyone took a seat, snatching menus off the table.

Cynthia pulled the half empty glass out of Bennie's hand. "Maybe no more of these." She took a sip. "Dren. This is good."

"Give it back!" The drunk hacker reached for his drink.

Cynthia swatted his hands away with ease. "I used to like you," he said.

A Durbrillian man trotted up to the table. Like all Durbrillians, he had large hairless triangular ears that stuck out sideways from his fur covered body. He had brilliant blue eyes. "Hello, travelers. What can I get you? We've got a wide assortment of delicacies from Durbril Two as well as fare from around the GC."

"They have fried zerglings," Bennie said. He pointed to an empty basket in the center of the table.

Wil rolled his eyes. "Two more orders of zerglings." He looked around the table. "Grum all around."

Cynthia raised a hand. "Actually, I'll have whatever little green's been drinking."

The small furry man nodded, his large eyes blinking rapidly. "Very good; two orders of fried zerglings, one stellar bliss, and six grums." The little man looked around. "Anything else?" Head shakes all around. He nodded and departed.

Wil looked at Maxim, who smiled and nodded. He returned the smile and nod. He put his arm around his wife, glad that the team was back together again. They were stronger as a whole.

"Duch should be here in a few tocks," Cynthia said. She finished off her stolen drink, handing the empty to Bennie, who scowled at her.

The waiter returned, wordlessly distributing glasses of water, then vanishing.

Wil turned to Tane. "And you are?"

Maxim made a face. "This is...my cousin, Tane." He grabbed the glass of water in front of him.

Zephyr leaned forward to look past her partner. "So, you stole his colla band?"

Maxim spluttered, spitting his water out across the table, his free hand moving the small box on the seat next to him.

Zephyr patted his knee. "It's okay, my love. You did an admirable job keeping it under wraps."

The big man turned, glaring at Bennie. The drunk Brailack made a squeak noise, leaning closer to Cynthia for shelter.

Zephyr shook her head. "Can I see it?"

Maxim blushed, his cheeks turning a shade of deep blue. He picked up the box and held out to her, opening it. Inside was a light gray band of metal with several metals of other colors twined around it. She reached out and touched it.

"Kinda plain looking," Wil said. Cynthia elbowed him in the ribs, harder than was strictly necessary. "Ow! Just sayin'."

Zephyr was beaming. She reached up and closed the box's lid. "Don't lose it." Looking past Maxim to Tane, she said, "Okay. Spill."

The younger man looked down at the table. "What's spilled?" He looked under the table.

Zephyr chuckled. "It's an expression. From—"

Maxim clucked. "Not important."

Tane watched the exchange. "So, you're what? Going to fight the Coalition?"

Bruce leaned over to the Ambassador. "Doesn't it worry you that these are the people not only responsible for our safety but that have been representing Earth for the last ten years?"

The waiter returned with their drinks and appetizers.

Bennie stood on his chair and looked over at the two humans. "Try a zergling." He pushed one of the freshly arrived baskets toward them.

Bruce pulled the basket closer. He looked at Bennie. "What are they?" He held it out for the ambassador to see.

"Delicious," the team hacker said.

Wil turned to Bennie, waving a hand at him to shoo him away. He turned to the two humans. "They're fine. Like popcorn chicken." He turned to Tane. "I mean, yeah, it's what we do."

The younger Palorian stared at Wil without saying anything.

Wil sighed. "Why don't you catch us up on your part in the Coalition?"

Bruce made a face and popped the morsel into his mouth. He closed his eyes. "You're right. This is good." He picked up another piece and slid the basket over to his boss.

Bennie grinned. "Told you." He looked over at their new Palorian addition. "So, you got duped by this Coalition?"

"Duped?" Tane asked.

"Tricked," Zephyr offered.

Carlisle pushed the basket away. He looked at his aide, whispering, "Honestly. The longer this little adventure goes, the shakier my confidence is." He looked up in time to see Nic reach over to pinch Bennie's arm to deter him from taking something off her plate.

THE TEAM ENJOYED each other's company for a few hours, catching each other up on their various adventures before heading outside the spaceport district to a nearby vapor lounge that Bennie suggested.

Wil looked around again. "Space cigar bar. Neat." He spied Zephyr's disapproving look and winked. "You know we had a craze on Earth around things like this?" He held up the device he'd been handed when they rented the private room. It was chrome and had lights along its sides. "It peaked before I was born. These goofy little things were supposed to be safer than cigarettes. Turned out they were way worse, just bubblegum flavored."

Zephyr cocked her head. "Cigarettes?"

He held a hand up; his finger and thumb about four inches apart. "Little sticks packed with dried leaves. You'd light 'em on fire and inhale the smoke."

"Why?" Nic asked.

"Felt good," Wil said. He shrugged. "Oh, and they were super addictive and eventually killed you."

"That seems stupid," the young Olop said.

Bennie looked at Wil, then his apprentice. "You've met humans, right?"

Wil glared at the team's hacker and nodded to Nic. "Very. Eventually everyone came around." He waved a hand around the dark wood-paneled room they were in. "Places like this, folks would hang out and smoke cigars and sip brandy." Spotting the look on Zephyr's face, he said. "Fat cigarettes." She nodded. "Eventually even cigars faded. By the time I was old enough to smoke, they cost a fortune and were nearly impossible to get."

Cynthia took a hit from the small device in her hand; lights along the side blinked in a happy little pattern. "These are perfectly safe. No addictive compounds." She took another hit. "And tasty." She leaned back, releasing a cloud of flavored water vapor. "Aged Fyolpi."

Wil wrinkled his nose as the vapor cloud spread.

"Is that blue cheese?" Bruce asked.

In a pair of high-backed chairs, Maxim and Tane huddled in the room's corner. Cynthia was with Nic and Bennie on a sofa facing Wil, Zephyr, and Ambassador Carlisle. Bruce was sitting in another high-backed chair nursing a vaporizer of his own.

Across the room, the door to their private lounge opened to allow a massive, scowling, four-armed, red-skinned Elar Keeg to enter. The 2.2-meter tall wall of muscle looked around. When he spotted Wil and the others, his scowl turned into an ear-to-ear grin. All four hands rose to wave. "Hi, Wil! Hi, Zephyr! Hi, Cynthia!" He turned, two of his arms motioning for someone outside to come in. "They're here, boss. It's clear." He strode into the space, heading for the main seating area.

Bruce watched the big four-armed man approach, then turned his attention to the man who entered behind him. Leaning forward in his chair, he asked, "Is that guy human?"

Ambassador Carlisle craned his neck to look at the new arrival and shrugged. "Looks like it."

Zephyr leaned over. "Multonae. They look like humans on the outside. Nearly identical." She smiled. "Internally, not that similar."

Bruce made a face. "I'll take your word for it." He looked at the approaching muscle. "Elar Keeg?"

She nodded. "Zash. Rhys Duch's bodyguard and chef."

"Chef?" Carlisle repeated.

She nodded. "Long story. He's good, though."

The Multonae crime boss reached the seating area. He stopped next to a chair between the two sofas. "Hi, everyone." He beamed. "It's been too long." His floral print shirt was crisply pressed. He came around the chair and plopped into it. Zash moved around the group to squeeze into the chair opposite his boss' seat.

The crime boss looked around the room. "A lot of new faces." He lingered on Nic. "Is it Bring Your Niece to Work Day or something?" He grinned. "That'd be pretty neat."

Wil shook his head. "No, Duch." He gestured to Nic. "She's Bennie's apprentice."

The Multonae man nodded once. "Oh, yeah." He looked at Bennie. "Your wizard club."

Bennie scowled. "Not a wizard club, you drennog."

"Where's Grell?" Zephyr asked, hoping to head off whatever tantrum Bennie was about to launch into. The short, purple-skinned man wasn't that useful, but she enjoyed his presence.

"He and Tah'tu were finishing a renovation project on the estate," Zash offered.

Ambassador Carlisle rose. "Branson Carlisle. Earth's ambassador to the GC Governing Council. My aide, Bruce Hawkins." He offered his hand. Rhys Duch stood and grasped the outstretched arm. Bruce stood and offered his arm.

Once all three were back in their seats, Duch said, "So, the Earth people are moving fast."

Zephyr nodded. "Indeed."

Tane leaned over to Maxim. "Humans *and* criminals?"

The bigger man shrugged. "We do what we have to. Don't forget it was one of our own that framed Zephyr and me and tried to force the GC to invade the Harrith—and, oh yeah—used an illegal genetic engineering program to mutate the crew of his command carrier. Palorians aren't pinnacles of virtue." The other man pursed his lips and leaned back in his seat.

Duch looked at the two humans, then at Wil. "Congrats?"

Wil shrugged. "Nothing to do with me, really."

"On the contrary," the ambassador said. "If not for Captain Calder, humanity would still be divided and warring with itself. His actions directly led to Earth's first global government.

Wil pursed his lips. "Well, true."

Duch eyed him. "I'm sure that'll make you popular in certain circles."

"Already has," Cynthia said.

Wil clapped his hands softly. "Now we're getting off topic." He pointed at each new person in the room, introducing them. Once that was done, he leaned back in his seat. "Thanks for agreeing to meet us here. We had, uh, reasons to be here." He glanced toward the corner of the room where Maxim and Tane were sitting.

Duch gave a one-shoulder shrug. "Anything for my friends. It's nice to get off Crildon Three once in a while." He smirked. "Plus, I had business off-world, anyway." He grinned, leaning forward. "I'm taking over Blin Lergo's operations."

Cynthia made a noise. "What's Blin think of this?"

Duch shrugged. "I can ask her in the afterlife."

Ambassador Carlisle's eyes grew to the size of plates. "What? You killed this person? A rival crime boss?" He looked at Wil.

Ignoring them, Duch continued, "Plus, like I told Cynthia, I wanted to run my new idea by you."

"We told you he was a crime boss," Wil said, looking at the ambassador. He turned to Duch. "Better not be something stupid that's going to break my arm or leg."

"You'll love it! I met this Ruknak woman. She's invented this incredible process to increase the tensile strength of Kendrite."

Wil shook his head. "I don't know what that is."

Zephyr held up a hand. "Maybe we take care of business, then Duch can fill you on his latest venture?"

The Multonae man nodded. "Good idea." He leaned forward. "So, you've had some run-ins with the Coalition?"

BENNIE NODDED. "Led us on a wild Jibludo chase." He pointed to Wil. "Attacked them with some old Malkorite corvettes in the Parcaya Ulan Sector."

Duch nodded. "Sounds right." He shook his head. "They're bad news and well-armed."

In the room's corner, Tane nodded his agreement.

"Not that well-armed," Zephyr said with a smirk.

"How've we never heard of them?" Cynthia asked. Between

herself, Bennie, and the Palorians on the team, one of their connections should have alerted them to this Coalition group.

The door to their private vaping lounge opened, allowing a well-dressed Trollack man to enter. He was balancing a tray of drinks in one hand, using his stubby, little fishlike tail to maintain his balance.

Zash pushed up out of his seat to help the waiter distribute drinks. "We'd like two vapes: one dralberry and one smoked fyolpi." The vaguely catfish like man nodded and left the room.

Duch drummed his fingers on the arm of his chair while he took a sip of his drink. "You haven't heard of them because they don't want to be heard of. They loiter on the dark nexus recruiting dupes to—"

"Hey!" Tane was on his feet.

Duch held up his free hand. "No offense meant, my friend."

Maxim put a hand on his young cousin's arm, guiding him back down into his seat.

"Go on," Wil urged.

"I don't really know that much. The rumors are that they're well-funded and well connected. No real idea what their end goal is. Just that they're amassing an army. They don't really exist in the same circles as I do."

Wil looked at him. "Come on, man. You've taken over what? Fifty? Sixty percent of Xarrix's empire?"

"Closer to seventy," the blonde-haired man, who looked more like a surfer than a crime boss, said, pride in his voice.

Wil nodded. "Okay, seventy percent of the scaly slime bag's empire. And you mean to tell us you don't know what they're up to?"

The other man shrugged. "They reached out to me about a year ago, when you did that whole Harrith thing, the second Harrith thing."

Wil leaned forward. "And?"

The waiter opened the door. He smiled and handed a device to Duch and Zash each. "Enjoy, gentlemen."

Duch took a hit of his vape. "Oh, this is nice." He leaned back, his eyes closed.

Wil snapped his fingers. "Focus."

Duch turned his attention back to Wil. "Hmm? Oh! Yeah, so they reached out to me to join them. Probably wanted my money and shipping network more than anything."

"And you said no?" Cynthia asked.

The Multonae man nodded. "I did." His normally jocular expression turned serious. "Politics isn't my thing. I don't want to be noticed or known. That's too much spotlight."

"But what do they want?" Bruce asked.

Duch looked at the man. "Oh, they want to drive humans back to your world. Berf?"

"Turf," Nic offered.

"No, that's not right," Duch shook his head.

"Earth, you idiot," Bennie said under his breath. Nic reached over and pinched him. He flinched. "He is!" he hissed.

"So, what do we do?" Maxim asked from the corner of the room.

The waiter entered. "Would anyone like a refill or change of flavor?"

Wil nodded. "You mentioned a special flavor?"

The man nodded. "Yes, spicy ferio." He smiled. "Good choice. You're okay with some heat?"

Wil nodded. "Bring it."

"I'll do the same," Cynthia said.

Once the waiter left, Wil turned back to Duch but pointed to Bruce. "Like he said. What do we do?"

The human-looking crime lord shrugged. "Don't get on their bad side."

"I think it's too late for that," Zephyr said.

"But Earth is already a member of the GC," Nic said.

"Associate member," Bennie and Ambassador Carlisle corrected at the same time.

She looked at each of them in turn. "What's the difference?"

"Associate membership can be revoked by the Governing Council without explanation until such time as a majority certifies the full membership," Duch said. Everyone turned to him. "What? I don't want to get involved in politics. That doesn't mean I don't follow it."

Ambassador Carlisle cleared his throat. "The crime boss is correct. The swearing-in ceremony on Tarsis would precede a full vote by the council. Earth has been assured their membership would be made full at the next vote. This associate member step is really just a formality."

"And these Coalition drennogs could mess that up?" Nic asked.

Carlisle nodded. "Very much so. Especially right now." He looked around the room, his gaze settling on Tane. "The GC is still in much turmoil. The recent secessions, the Harrith, to name two. They could very well decide that now's not the time to rock the boat."

The door opened. Wil turned to thank the waiter for the vape device refill. Standing in the doorway of their private lounge were six beings. Each of them wore black one-piece tactical getups, with knives and pistols attached in several places.

He stumbled. "Oh, shit."

AS WIL DOVE to the side, the decorative planter separating the two sofas from the room's door erupted in flames as energy bolts tore into it. The plants caught fire; the planter glowed.

Zephyr pulled the ambassador to the ground before rising enough to return fire.

Maxim and Tane's chairs were in the corner along the wall with the entry. Maxim quickly took two of the attackers out before they realized they were under attack from the side. One of the attackers powered up a portable shield before taking aim.

The big ex-Peacekeeper pulled his cousin out of the way as blaster bolts shredded the chairs they had just vacated. The room didn't offer much in the way of cover. As he moved, Maxim pushed Rhys Duch's chair over, dumping the crime lord onto the ground.

Nic and Bennie sprang into action before Wil reached the floor, their beam sabers snapping to life with a *snap-hiss*. The room was bathed in crimson and magenta light. The two did their best to deflect the incoming weapons fire while their friends scrambled for cover.

"Your lives are never boring!" Duch shouted as he crawled behind the now-turned-on-its-side coffee table next to Ambassador Carlisle. Cynthia was next to them, leaning around the side to return fire. She reached over to the chair Duch had been in and turned it on its side to provide a small amount more cover.

Nic stayed balanced on the smoking planter, swinging her beam saber, keeping bolts from reaching her friends. While deflecting one blast, another struck her wristcomm. The device instantly grew hot, forcing her to wince. "Release, ten-ten-eight-break," she hissed. The device responded to her verbal command, loosening its grip on her forearm. She flicked her arm, sending the smoking wristcomm to the ground in a fluid motion as she used her other hand to deflect a blaster bolt meant for Zephyr. The Palorian woman looked up and nodded.

Zash had his own chair overturned. Two of his hands held

pulse pistols. "They've got personal shields." A bolt struck him, sending him sprawling to the ground.

Wil pulled the much larger man back behind the remains of the smoking planter. "Stunned," he announced to everyone before turning to fire, but a stun blast hit him right in the face. He collapsed on top of Zash.

Bennie leaped from his perch on the planter to dive between several of their attackers. One man was separated from his arm while another felt his leg give out at the knee because the leg below the knee was no longer connected.

Before the Brailack Knight of Plentallus could bring his blade to bear on another attacker, a stun blast struck him at point-blank range. He fell to the ground, his beam saber hilt rolling out of his limp hand. The beam cut off the moment he released the hilt.

Stun bolts found more and more Rogue Enterprises team members.

"We just need the two humans," one intruder called out over the din of weapons fire.

"There's like four humans in here!" another shouted over the noise of weapons fire and crackling actual fire. They looked over their shoulder at the crowd in the main lounge space.

A third looked at their wristcomm and added, "Hurry. Local security will be here in three microtocks."

"You can just leave if you like!" Maxim shouted before rising from behind his overturned chair enough to squeeze off two shots.

The room was filling with smoke. Chairs and decorative plants were aflame.

"Give me a gun!" Tane hissed.

"If I had an extra, do you think I wouldn't be using it?" Maxim hissed. He rose again but caught a stun blast in the face.

Tane tried to grab Maxim's sidearm but caught a blast as well. Both of them collapsed in a heap.

The fight was turning against her friends quickly. Nic deactivated her beam saber, clipping it to her belt. She heard Zephyr coughing and Bruce shouting. She glanced over and saw Ambassador Carlisle collapsed in a heap. Somewhere, Rhys Duch was shouting about their attackers not knowing who he was.

"Get all the humans; we'll sort 'em out later!" one of the intruders ordered.

A Ruknak man came around the sofa and plucked the ambassador off the ground. "Got one!"

Two Harrith came around the other side of the smoldering planter. Nic laid down and closed her eyes. The attackers looked around. They picked up Wil and headed for the door.

Somebody hit the ground with a thud.

"Don't bother with that one. The name he was shouting isn't on our list."

Nic wriggled around the edge of the overturned sofa to see Rhys Duch's unconscious form fall to the floor in a heap.

"I got the other one," someone said.

"Let's go!"

The remaining intruders filed out of the private vape lounge. Nic counted to three, then got up and followed.

The main lobby of the Vapor Lounge was littered with the bodies of customers and staff alike. Most had been stunned; the rest were cowering in fear in corners and under tables. She spied their waiter sprawled on top of his tray. A trio of vape devices lay nearby, their lights blinking.

The snatch team made their way out the front doors to a waiting cargo hauler that was hovering half a block away. Nic crept along behind them, ducking any time someone glanced backward.

She hid behind a trash bin while they tossed Wil, Bruce, and Ambassador Carlisle into the back of the vehicle.

"Meet us at the rendezvous point," a Harrith man told the trio of Ruknak and two Trollack. They nodded and headed off down the street. He moved into the vehicle's cab.

Nic waited until he was inside before sprinting for the vehicle. She reached the back hatch just as the vehicle's gravlifts powered up. She scrambled onto the roof, using her sharp climbing claws for purchase.

With a whine, the cargo hauler headed off down the street. Away from the spaceport.

PART 3

CHAPTER TWENTY-ONE

MAXIM SAT UP. The room was spinning, but he could vaguely make out several shapes moving around the smoky space. The fires he remembered seeing all over the room appeared to be out, based on the powerful aroma of flame retardant assaulting his sense of smell.

A small, blurry shape approached. "This one is awake. Sir? Sir, can you hear me?" A gray-furred Durbrillian woman reached over to poke Maxim's forehead. "Sir?"

He swatted away the little two-fingered hand. "I'm good. What happened?"

The small woman stepped back so he could get to his feet. "Well, you and your friends set the room on fire, for one."

Maxim shook his head. "No. That wasn't...We were attacked."

She nodded. "Yes, a regular cornucopia of GC races walked in and stunned everyone in the lobby." She smirked. "Some party."

Maxim spied Cynthia and Zephyr stirring. He looked around, counting bodies. "Where are my friends?"

The small security woman shook her head. "I don't know. How many are missing?"

A Malkorite medic came over. "You've been stunned—please take it easy."

Maxim waved him off. "Not my first time." He looked down and kicked his cousin's leg. "Wake up, Tane." The younger man stirred.

"What the grolack was that?" Cynthia said as she waved another medic away, claws out for emphasis.

"Guessing your friends from earlier," Rhys Duch said as Zash lifted him to his feet. The Malkorite medic spotted the Elar Keeg man's shoulder wound and rushed over.

"Friends? From before?" the Durbrillian security officer asked. Her large eyes moved from person to person. "You know your attackers?"

Cynthia shot Duch a look, then turned to the much shorter woman. "No. Never seen them before. We were meeting our old friends here," she nodded to Duch and Zash, "when they burst in, weapons blazing."

"You're lucky no one is dead," another security officer said, a Quillant man, from the doorway. "Looks like they switched to stun for you but kept their weapons at full power for everything else." He stepped forward. "Chief Investigator Chowfu. Looks like your side wasn't as amenable?" He nodded to two smeared blood trails leading out of the room.

Zephyr came forward, stepping over the blood. She offered her arm. "Zephyr."

Chowfu clasped her forearm in the GC handshake.

"I think Bennie and Nic each got one. They out there?" Zephyr asked.

"Already in custody on their way to a med center," the small law enforcement official said. "I'll question them when they're out of surgery." He squinted up at the tall Palorian. "You make a habit of cutting limbs off those who attack you?"

She looked around the room, spotting Bennie. "More often than you might think." She looked around the room again. "Where's Nic?"

"Who?" the stubby-tailed lawman asked.

Bennie stopped what he was doing. "Apprentice!"

Nothing.

"Where are you?" the Brailack demanded.

Cynthia looked up from helping Zash with a burn on his lower left arm. "Kid? You in here?"

Zephyr leaned around the door to look into the main lounge space. "Nic! Kid, you out there?"

Chowfu shook his head, fleshy whiskers twitching. "No kids out there." He cocked his head. "You brought a kid to," he looked around the complete write-off of a private lounge, "whatever this was?" Without waiting for an answer, he turned and said, "They're ready."

Zephyr looked over the investigator's head at a group of local security officers making their way toward the private room. "Ready for what?"

The little man looked up at her. "To go to the station. You didn't think you were just walking away, did you? You and your friends are one half of a shootout that left two people maimed and all of you, plus a room full of what I assume are innocent bystanders, unconscious."

He stepped aside to let his underlings enter the lounge. "Not to mention the completely over the top amount of damage to this room. The insurance adjuster will absolutely want to speak with you."

Zephyr held up a hand. "Well, actually we—"

The little man planted both hands on his hips. "This isn't a debate." He looked at the team. "No one is going to cause me any trouble, are they?"

Zephyr took a deep breath, letting it out slowly. "No." She reached her free hand over to her wristcomm and tapped the emergency icon in the screen's corner. A placement that didn't require her to see the screen to find. She just hoped Gabe was paying attention.

THE HOVER VAN was still winding its way through town. It was all Nic could do to stay atop the vehicle. Her fingers ached from the stress her climbing claws were under, holding her down. She glanced at her wristcomm-less arm, wishing she had some way to let the others know where she was. At least she had her beam saber; she could feel it bouncing against her hip every time the vehicle shifted.

Just as she was beginning to worry her strength would give out, the vehicle pulled into what looked like a small private spaceport and came to a halt.

"Thank the deities," she whispered. Her fingers ached so badly from the strain on her claws she wasn't sure she could retract them right then. She massaged each finger one at a time to ease the claws back into their sheaths.

"Okay, come on. We gotta get 'em off-planet. By now, local security is on the job. They'll lock the larger ports down first, but it won't take long before they get to the private ones," one of the snatch team members said. Presumably the leader.

"What about Frol and Sden?" another asked. Nic figured those were the beings currently missing a forearm and lower leg. She wondered if they were alive, then shrugged. She had more pressing concerns.

"Nothing we can do. They're on their own," the leader said.

"Harsh," Nic whispered.

"We keeping all three?" another asked.

"Yeah, they'll be out for a while still. No time to wait," the leader said. "Can sort 'em out later, get rid of whichever one we don't need."

Nic looked up. Sitting a half plorith away from the cargo vehicle was a freighter about twice the size of Bennie's *Rocky Nontee*. It wasn't any more attractive than the *Nontee*, however.

The vehicle shifted as the attackers opened the cargo area, pulling the three unconscious humans out. Each Ruknak slung a human over their shoulder and headed toward the unidentified freighter.

Nic waited until she saw the leader of the team follow his people toward the ship before she slid over to the edge and jumped off. "Wonder if I can get a wristcomm somewhere?" She looked around. The spaceport looked uninhabited, likely closed for the day. The main admin building would definitely be locked, and she couldn't see any retail stalls.

A loud hiss sounded from the ship ahead. It was starting its preflight warmup. She'd have to get one aboard the ship. She darted off toward the freighter after her friends and their attackers.

The ship's cargo ramp was still down, so she angled toward that. The attackers-turned-kidnappers had used the personnel hatch near the forward section of the ship. It didn't look like anyone was around the hold.

Coming up the ramp, she looked around. She was right, no one around, but the hold was quite full; cargo modules were stacked deck to ceiling. This was a working cargo ship. "Kidnapping and hauling cargo," Nic said to herself. She stopped next to a crate and lifted the lid. "Oh." She rose on the tips of her toes to reach into the crate, withdrawing a package of Crispy Yipsee strips. "Yum." She slid the pouch inside her tunic and then grabbed another before closing the container.

Behind her, the cargo ramp rose, closing off the cavernous space. The deck rumbled as the ship's reactor continued to power up, reaching liftoff levels.

Nic exited the cargo hold into a wide corridor that looked like it ran the entire length of the ship. Hearing voices up ahead, she moved to the first hatch on the right.

The hatch slid open. "Computer core. Lucky me," she said, looking around the room. It was larger than the *Ghost*'s computer room, though the actual processing core was about the same size as that of the *Ghost*. She moved to a terminal set in the bulkhead next to the processing core, intent on accessing the ship's communication system. She pressed a key, and the screen woke.

After several attempts, she swore. "Felgercarb." The ship's systems were better protected than she expected, and without her wristcomm and its current copy of E-Bennie 3.0, she had no hope of cracking the encryption.

A noise outside the room caught her attention. She spotted an air duct under the console and removed the cover. As the hatch slid open, she was pulling the vent cover back into place.

"No one here," a voice said. Nic couldn't identify it, not one of the grab team. The voice continued, "Musta been one of the new people. Probably thought any terminal was fair game. I'll remind everyone once we're underway."

"Sounds good. Bridge, all clear. No one here," a second voice said.

Nic couldn't tell what race either person was. One had a deep voice and big feet. The other's voice was androgynous, and the owner had hooves.

"Copy that. We'll be airborne in ten. The prisoners have

been secured," said a third voice, from the sound of it, over a wristcomm speaker.

Nic scooted further into the air duct as the rumble of the reactor rose a few octaves.

"THANKS, PAL." Maxim clapped Gabe on the droid's shoulder. "Can't believe they thought we were involved in all that."

Once he received Wil's distress call, the team's engineer tracked their wristcomms to the local municipal security precinct. It had taken him the better part of an hour to negotiate his way past the front desk.

"Yes, hard to imagine," the droid said, holding the door for the team as they filed out of the building.

"What did you tell the chief investigator? What was his name? Chow fun?" Maxim asked once everyone was piled into the ground vehicle Gabe rented.

"Chowfu," Gabe and Zephyr said as one. Without a word, they leaned towards each other to bump fists.

Gabe continued, "I was able to reach Second Aide Iran ch'Aroon, who forwarded an official letter reflecting our being hired to shepherd the ambassador and his staff to Tarsis."

Maxim smiled. "That worked?"

Gabe shook his head. "I also made sure the chief investigator was aware of our past good deeds on behalf of the GC."

Zephyr nodded. "That usually works."

Again, Gabe shook his head. "I also threatened to single-handedly bring the entire building down around them after expertly killing each person in the building that wasn't you."

Bennie clucked. "My man." He held his hand out for a high five.

Rhys Duch watched all of this and said to Zash, "And people think I'm ruthless." His four-armed employee shrugged.

At this time of night, the spaceport admin complex was on night shift, so there was only one attendant on duty. Zephyr smiled as they passed, swiping their wristcomms over the reader.

Once the group was outside the admin building and standing on the duracrete landing field, Zephyr said, "Let's regroup on the *Ghost*." She pointed at the waiting Ankarran Raptor, which, until Wil was recovered, she guessed she was in charge of.

"We could meet aboard my ship," Duch offered. He nodded to a ship just beyond the *Ghost*.

"Magnificent dren," Maxim said as he saw the ship Duch was pointing at. He turned to look at the team's sometime friend. "You came in that?"

The ship was at least twice the size of the *Ghost*, likely pushing the limits on ship size for this spaceport. It was painted light blue with gold and chrome highlights. Off the back, above the main engine cowlings, was what looked like a covered porch.

"My goodness," Zephyr said. "Is that a hot tub on the... porch?"

Cynthia looked from the heavily modified mid-size freighter to Duch. "Is that—"

"Xarrix's yacht?" The crime lord grinned. "Yes. The *This Won't Take Long*." He ran a hand through his mop of sandy blonde hair. "I found her."

"Wasn't easy," Zash added.

Duch nodded. "Tah'tu spent nearly a full cycle digging through that scaly drennog's records."

Bennie smirked. "Of course, it was the Brailack who did the work. Hope you paid that little blue grolack for his efforts."

Duch looked at Bennie, staring until the Brailack hacker

looked away. "Yes, my majordomo received a handsome bonus for deciphering Xarrix's records." He shook his head. "That man was not a trusting person."

Cynthia nodded. "No, he wasn't." She looked at the *This Won't Take Long*. "Let's go there. I always wanted to see the inside of the *Take Long*." She didn't wait, adjusting her course for the larger ship.

Maxim fell in next to Zephyr. "Did you know Xarrix had a superyacht?"

She shook her head. "No, but I tried to tune him out whenever we dealt with him. Wil usually did most of the talking." She shuddered. "Hated that guy."

Maxim's brow ridges rose. "You and me both."

It was Xarrix's intel that had led Wil to rescuing the two wrongfully imprisoned Peacekeepers so that they could be part of his crew. When Wil first arrived in the GC, Xarrix was the only person who would give him work, most of it illegal: smuggling, blockade running, light piracy. Even after Maxim and Zephyr joined the crew, the Trenbal crime lord continued to push the team into more and more dangerous jobs, while treating them worse and worse.

By the time Wil and the team had had enough and killed the detestable criminal, Xarrix's criminal empire had been massive. Several lieutenants, like Rhys Duch, had moved in to take over. The Multonae man, who looked more like a beach bum than a crime boss, somehow managed to take out most of his competitors in the first cycle, pulling their territories into his.

Bennie trotted up next to them. "We shoulda stolen this thing."

Maxim shook his head. "We didn't know it existed."

"I blame Wil for that oversight."

Zephyr sighed. "Cynthia, wait up."

NIC FINISHED the last of her Yipsee sticks and peered through the vent grate, watching the Quillant man she assumed was guarding her friends. The freighter had jumped to FTL an hour or so ago, and she'd spent that time exploring the ship's air ducts until she found what she was looking for.

"Flomurr," a voice said. Nic recognized it from the computer room. The hooved person.

The Quillant turned. He nodded. "Ugort."

The other person, a Crakim—now that she could see better—strode up to him. "I'll stand watch. Anything worth noting?"

Flomurr's thick, fleshy whiskers bobbed. "Nope. Not a peep."

The jackal-faced being nodded. "Maybe we'll get to base without trouble."

"Not now that you've jinxed it," the man joked. He chuckled and headed down the corridor. "Have fun."

From her perch in the air duct, Nic whispered, "Definitely jinxed it." She reversed back down the air duct to a junction she had already explored that she knew would take her up a level and closer to whatever was on the other side of the door Ugort was standing in front of.

"Shoulda grabbed more packs of Yipsee strips," she muttered to herself as she scrambled up an incline in the duct that took her over the corridor. As the duct cut through a bulkhead, it shrank by twenty percent. "Okay, two was enough," she mumbled as she squeezed herself forward.

"WE'RE GOING TO DIE," Ambassador Carlisle said for what Wil thought might be the fortieth time.

The three men were sitting on cots in three of the four rooms that made up the ship's brig. From the size of the space, Wil knew it was larger than the *Ghost,* but that was about all he could tell. The rumble of the engines also made him sure it was a larger craft.

Wil sighed. "We're not. Probably." They'd been in the brig of this mystery ship for who knew how long before they woke up, but it had been four hours since then.

"Probably?" Bruce said.

"For a spy, you're pretty easy to shake," Wil said. He shifted to lie down on his cot. "The others are looking for us."

"How would they find us?" the ambassador asked. "They took our comm units and your wristcomm."

Wil raised his left arm. "I need to take that thing off more." His forearm was paler than the rest of him.

"You're in luck then," the older man quipped, adding, "assuming there's sun where they're taking us."

Bruce stood and paced the width of his cell, which took all of six steps from wall to wall. "We can't just sit here."

Wil sat back up. "Look, man. Do you have any idea the number of times bad guys have captured me?" The spy stared at Wil, then shook his head. "A lot." Bruce rolled his eyes. "More than the average person."

Bruce turned to him. "The average person doesn't get abducted by..." He looked around, "galactic malcontents?"

Wil shrugged. "Then you're in good hands. I'm a pro."

The secure hatch leading out of the brig made a clank sound before parting down the middle. A pair of Trenbal entered the room. Wil spotted a Crakim standing guard outside. He hadn't had many dealings with them. They didn't leave their homeworld much, which he was glad for; they were hideous, like a jackal-centaur mashup with long orangutan arms that ended in claw-tipped, three-fingered hands.

The hatch slid closed behind the two visitors.

Wil waved. "Hi."

"Which of you is the Earth ambassador?" the taller of the two asked. A male with dark blue scales and a missing right eye.

Wil raised his hand. "That's me." The other two men turned to look at him.

The other Trenbal shook his head. "He's not. He's the kreb-nack that's been here for cycles. Works with the Palorians and that weird droid."

"You've heard of me? Cool." Wil grinned. "I'm happy to sign autographs."

One-Eye turned to Bruce, then Ambassador Carlisle. "Which of you?"

"What's it matter?" Bruce asked. "You're going to kill us both, anyway."

The reptilian man inclined his head. "True, but it can be quick and as painless as possible or, well, the opposite." He grinned, baring his razor-sharp teeth. He looked at Wil. "And for sure, all three of you are dying."

Wil made a face and said, "That didn't need to be added," under his breath.

"What do you want?" Ambassador Carlisle asked.

"For you to denounce the GC and ensure your world does not formalize its membership. End all expansion efforts."

Carlisle shook his head. "Why would I—we—do that?" One-Eye just stared at him. "Oh, the slow death part." The reptilian nodded.

The other Trenbal smirked. "I'm sure the hard way will be fun for us." The pair turned. One-Eye tapped the control panel, opening the brig hatch. "Think it over." They left. The hatch closed and locked behind them.

The ambassador turned to Wil. "You were saying?"

Wil opened his mouth to answer but stopped when

someone said, "Psst." The three men looked around their small spaces: under cots, pulling down the fold-out toilets. "Up here, drennogs."

Looking up, Wil saw a familiar slash of pink fur on a familiar face behind the grate of an air duct. He smiled. "Hi, kid."

CHAPTER TWENTY-TWO

"WIL IS GONNA BE SO MAD," Bennie said as he spun around in one of the chairs in the outrageously opulent lounge. The *This Won't Take Long*'s common deck was nearly three times the size of the *Ghost*'s. There was a full kitchen, hidden away from sight. A small bar in one corner of the lounge space, a dining table capable of seating twelve in the opposite corner with the lounge, complete with matching, not at all ratty, sofas and two ornate captain's chairs in the center. One of which Bennie was in, enjoying the full three-hundred-and-sixty-degree rotation capabilities.

Everyone else was seated at the large dining table. Except Zash. The big Elar Keeg was busy in the kitchen whipping up who knew what, but it smelled heavenly. He'd already deposited an expensive looking bottle of Gruke Nulimb and glassware that looked like it cost as much as the *Rocky Nontee.*

Zephyr took a sip. "This is good."

Duch grinned. "One of my favorites." He looked around the table. "So, what're you planning next? Your little child colleague hasn't called in yet. What if she doesn't?" He leaned forward.

"Is it legal to employ her? Child labor law was never anything I looked into, but if you can have kids doing this kind of work—"

Zephyr held up both hands. "No. She's not an employee." She narrowed her eyes. "Do not. Start hiring. Children."

"She will. Call, that is," Cynthia said. "She's probably lying low to avoid detection." She cast a look at Zephyr, who shrugged and shook her head.

"Do not forget. Nic does not currently have a wristcomm," Gabe offered, holding up the damaged device. "It took a direct hit."

Cynthia leaned toward him. "I didn't know a stunner could do that to a wristcomm."

"According to the local security force's database, at least one of the attackers did not have their blaster set to stun. They assume a mistake."

Duch nodded toward Gabe. "Useful, isn't he?"

Zephyr smiled. "Indispensable."

Tane made a noise. "Kid lucked out."

Maxim cleared his throat, nodding. "Nic will come through. She's a pro."

The hatch that led to the kitchen slid open. "Hope you're hungry," Zash said. Each of his four hands was balancing a serving tray. The big man made his way around the table, placing the serving trays. He sat down at the end of the table, picking up his glass of Gruke Nulimb. "Eat up."

Bennie hopped off the still-spinning chair and joined the team at the table.

Maxim sat his glass down. "We're going to need your help, Duch. Can we count on you?"

"No," the criminal said. He reached for one of the serving trays.

Cynthia lowered her fork. "No?"

Duch's eyebrows drew together. "It's too risky. These kreb-nacks are not messing around. As you've seen. They know me."

"Didn't seem like they knew you," Bennie said as he scooped something off one of the trays onto his plate.

"You're afraid of them?" Cynthia said.

"Felgercarbing right, I am." He met Cynthia's gaze and held it. "I can't get involved. I don't know much, but even that's enough to cause me trouble."

Bennie stabbed a breaded something or other off the nearest serving tray. "You're already involved. The attackers know you were with us. You screamed your name at them over and over." He made a face. "I'm Rhys Duch! I'm Rhys Duch!"

The crime lord frowned. "Regardless. I don't want to get any deeper into this." He looked at Cynthia. "I'm sorry." Before she could speak, he added, "I'll give you all the data I've got on them. It's not much." He took a sip of his drink. "Best I can do."

Cynthia nodded. "Fair enough."

"You could send food with us," Bennie offered.

Zash stood up. "Guess I should get to work."

"Word of advice. Get Wil and those other two back and lie low. Let this Coalition deal with Merth as—"

"Earth," Maxim interrupted.

Duch waved a hand. "Whatever. Their beef is with Earth."

BRUCE and the ambassador looked up at the vent grate. The ambassador's mouth fell open. "Nic?"

She waved. "Hi, Ambassador. Hi, Bruce."

"Nic, what're you doing here?" Bruce asked.

"Saving you," she said as if it was obvious.

"The others are with you?"

She shook her head. "Just me."

Bruce fell back onto his cot with an explosive sigh. "We're dead men."

"If you'd like, I can find an escape pod and get out of here," she said.

Wil glared at the other two men. "You got a plan, pipsqueak?"

She chewed her lower lip. "I figured you might have one."

Bruce let out a low groan.

Wil ignored him. "Do you know how many bad guys are aboard?"

"Twenty-one," she answered.

Wil pursed his lips. That was more warm bodies than were aboard the last corvette they encountered. "Know what type of ship we're on? Corvette?"

She shook her head. "Big freighter. Modified a bit, but a freighter."

He nodded. "Know where we're going?" She shook her head.

"Have you been able to reach the team?" He held out his left arm, where his wristcomm would be. "They took our comms."

She made a face. "My wristcomm got damaged in the firefight."

Wil turned to glare at Bruce before the other man could make a noise. Turning back to Nic, he said, "Okay. Here's what you have to do." He held up his hand to tick items off on his fingers. "First, figure out where we're going, or at least how long until we get there." She nodded. "Second, see if you can find a way to get a signal to the others." Another nod. "Third, find the armory. Fourth, bust us out of here."

"Why is bust us out of here last?" Ambassador Carlisle asked.

Wil looked at Nic and waved a hand, sending her on her

way. He then turned to the ambassador. "If there are twenty odd bad guys aboard, all armed, getting out without weapons does us no good."

"You really think she can do all that?" Bruce asked.

Wil looked up at the vent grate, seeing no sign that Nic was still there. "I hope so. She's had a lot of training."

"From the Brailack?" Bruce asked, skeptical.

"Don't hold that against her," Wil answered.

"Now what?" Ambassador Carlisle asked.

Wil fell back onto his cot and then lay back. "We wait." He rolled over to lie on his side. "Think President Douce would name a holiday after me?"

BENNIE HANDED Maxim a case full of bottles of grum. "We'll need to drink these."

"Why?" He set the case on the counter.

"No more room." Bennie closed the refrigeration unit door. "That four-armed goober sure can cook." He held a hand out. "Gimme."

Maxim rolled his eyes as he handed Bennie a drink.

The *Ghost* was still sitting on the duracrete on Lorstak Seven. Without a destination, the team agreed it made little sense to leave the planet. Duch and his people had taken the *This Won't Take Long* and departed a few hours ago.

Zephyr, Cynthia, and Tane were sitting in the lounge area. "Anyone want a drink? Before they warm up," Maxim said. He carried the remaining bottles of grum to the lounge.

Cynthia took one and offered it to Tane, who accepted. She took another and opened it. "So."

The young man looked at her, then at his drink, then back at her. "I might know where they're going," Tane offered.

"You do?" Bennie asked. He moved to perch on the arm of the overstuffed chair. "Really?"

"How?" Maxim asked.

"You think?" Cynthia asked, her eyes narrowing.

The younger Palorian shrugged. "It's not like they throw a party or induction ceremony or something. I've never been to a secret hideout."

Gabe cocked his head to one side, looking over the young Palorian man. "Then how do you know where they are?"

Tane took a long drink of his grum, draining the bottle. "Okay, well I don't know where they are. I meant I think I can find out where they are. I can reach out." He looked at his cousin. "I can tell them I finished the job. They don't know I've been captured."

Maxim looked as though someone had punched him in the gut. "Captured? I'm your cousin."

"You know what I mean."

Maxim's lips pursed. He nodded slowly. "Not sure I do." He shook his head. "That's good, though."

"The job?" Cynthia asked.

Bennie looked at Maxim. "Oh."

Maxim took a deep breath. "The Coalition planned Tane's theft of the colla band."

Zephyr's eyes widened. "Planned?"

Bennie leaned back, saying, "This should be interesting," under his breath.

Tane held up a hand. "They didn't actually specify that I take the band, that just came up on its own."

"Not helping," Cynthia said.

Maxim looked to Tane, who, after a deep breath, said, "They approached me to get between you," he nodded to Zephyr, "and my cousin. They wanted your team to be as split up and as distracted as possible."

"Why?" Zephyr asked.

The younger man shrugged. "Keep you all off-balance. Not working at your peak or whatever. They didn't tell me why, just what."

Bennie shook his head. "Back to the main point. You sure? That you can get us in? Wouldn't those goons that grabbed Wil and the others recognize you? Know that you're with us? They saw you sitting there, unbound."

Tane shook his head. "I don't know them. Didn't recognize any of them. I never worked with anyone else. Those people at the vape lounge were likely hired the same way the teams on Jannav Kenu were." His lip curled at that particular memory. He shook his head. "It'll work. I'm certain."

Cynthia looked at the eager young Palorian man. "I dunno."

He leaned forward. "I reach out to my contact. Tell them I got it done but need to lay low. Off the grid. Ask them to let me come in." He looked at Maxim. "I may need the colla band. To prove it."

Zephyr looked at Maxim. He met her gaze. She nodded.

He turned to his cousin. "Very well."

Bennie looked at Gabe. "We can route his signal through the *Ghost*'s comm system, so I can piggyback a tracer on his internex ID."

Gabe nodded. "That should allow us to locate the receiving connection."

Bennie nodded and pointed at his mechanical friend.

Cynthia looked at her teammates and then at Tane. "You'll need to sell it. Like, really sell it." She thought back to what Duch had told them about the Coalition. "These people are serious."

"You think I don't know that?" Tane's cheeks flushed a deep blue.

Cynthia stared at him until he looked away.

Zephyr stood. "This plan is the only one we've got. So, we go with it." She headed forward, toward the hatch that led to the ship's bridge. "I'll get us underway. No need to do this on the ground, paying docking fees." She turned to Bennie. "You and Gabe work with Tane to get things ready for him to make the call."

Tane looked at Maxim. "Do you have any fake blood around?"

NIC MADE her way through the ducts until she found a grate that looked out into a supply closet or something like it. Whatever it was, it was empty. She dropped to the deck without a sound. Shelves lined the room. Nothing that looked useful.

"What I wouldn't give for my grolacking wristcomm," she whispered. The room's hatch was a manual affair. She reached up and released the latch, pulling the door open just enough to peek out into the corridor.

"Here goes nothing." She opened the door just enough to slip out, closing it behind her. "First order of business. Where are we going, or how long until we get where we're going?" She headed forward.

Voices ahead of her sent her scurrying back up the corridor to find an alcove. She looked around her. Someone had stored rifles in the alcove, haphazardly at that. She leaned as far back as she could as a Harrith woman and Trollack man walked by the intersection. She bumped a pulse rifle knocking it over. It was a scramble to catch the weapon before it hit the deck. It didn't sound like either being heard anything. Their voices grew more and more distant.

She continued forward until she found another alcove, this one with a terminal instead of rifles. "Why isn't there a stool?"

she whispered. She looked around the corridor. Nothing. Reaching up on the tips of her toes, she was able to wake the terminal. It was unlocked. "Yes!" she said. She dropped to the ground and looked up and down the corridor in case she'd been heard.

It didn't take her long to find the ship's navigation subsystem. It was locked out. "Dren. How else can I figure this out?" she said. Gabe would know. Bennie would too, and he'd be smug about it. What would Wil say? She reached back up to see what other systems she could access when she heard someone clear their throat.

She turned to see a stocky Guldranii man standing in the corridor, his long arms crossed across his chest. He narrowed his forward eyes and stared at her. The eye on either side of his long skull moved around taking in the corridor in both directions.

She raised a hand. "Hello." He reached for the pistol at his hip. "Wait!" His hand stopped. "I'm new here."

"What do you mean, new here?" he demanded. "Were you with the group that came aboard with Natra?"

She smiled, nodding. "Yeah. Yeah, I came aboard with Natra."

He smiled wickedly. "Got you! There is no Natra. I made that name up." He pulled his pistol, taking aim on Nic.

She said nothing further. She leaped to the side, drawing his aim. Landing, she bent her knees to drive herself in a new direction right toward his midsection. His gun grossly out of position.

The worst part of fighting a Guldranii was their side-mounted eyes. Her new friend saw her coming and swung his free hand up to knock her aside.

At least that was what he intended. The moment his arm came in contact with her, she latched on with her razor-sharp claws. They dug into his arm as she spun around to reach his shoulder with her feet. Her climbing claws dug into his shoulder, causing him to release a guttural scream.

She released his arm with one hand, grabbing her beam saber hilt. "Sorry," she said before pressing the emitter against his torso, activating the weapon. The *snap-hiss* that normally announced the weapon's activation was muffled by his body. In the blink of an eye the blade burned through the other side of his torso. She snapped the weapon off, the holes cauterizing as the beam vanished.

A pained burble escaped his lips as he collapsed to the deck.

Nic looked around, hoping that no one had heard the struggle. She looked down at the body. "Now I gotta hide you," she groused. "Making up Natra, really! I bet no one likes you." She looked around the corridor. "I hope no one liked you; otherwise, I'm in trouble."

After dragging the body back to the storage closet she'd emerged from, she came back to the terminal, still unlocked, thankfully. She'd have to move the body eventually; someone would notice the smell. She wiped sweat off of her forehead. Moving it again wasn't high on her list. The body weighed nearly three times what she did. She made a mental note to look for a gravsled. Maybe during the night cycle, she could move it to the recycler. Thinking of that grisly task made her fur stand up on end, but there was nothing to be done about it.

She still wasn't sure how to tackle her first objective: where they were going or how long until they got there. Then it occurred to her. She couldn't access the navigation system, but most ships kept the crew up to date on travel times via other systems.

She tapped around until she found the cargo manifest. "Gotcha!" She pumped a fist in the air. The cargo management system said there were four hours until unload operations were set to begin, and cargo teams would be needed in the hold.

CHAPTER TWENTY-THREE

"HELLO, I'M GULBAR' Te. This is your GNO Morning Briefing." The lanky Burzzad turned to his cohost.

"And I'm Megan. Things are getting exciting in the world of politics. The human ambassador from Earth has apparently gone missing while being escorted on a tour of key Commonwealth systems."

"Puzzling, to be sure," Gulbar' Te agreed. "Hopefully, they find the new ambassador soon, and in good health. Surely that would make for an inauspicious start to Earth's tenure as a GC member."

The camera pickup moved back to Megan. "In other news, the missing Peacekeeper task force in the Ontruum Sara Sector has been found. It turns out they were exploring the Dostra Reach when they were set upon by a plasma storm that came out of nowhere, engulfing the entire task force, jamming their comms and sensors for nearly five days."

The camera moved to Gulbar' Te, who was nodding his head, his long neck swaying. "That's certainly good news. The Peacekeeper forces have been stretched thin of late. Losing a task force would have been a severe blow." He turned to another camera pickup. "In more positive news, the 223rd annual Finn Breton Invitational starts tomorrow on Chorwed Six and is expected to see record crowds. Ular Dale, the reigning champion, is expected to maintain her title, but upstart Kai Lya'Lya has shown remarkable resilience."

"If I was a gambling woman," Megan said, "I'd put my credits on Kai Lya'Lya."

Her cohost squinted. "Indeed."

ZEPHYR LOOKED around the *Ghost*'s computer room. She glanced down at the faint stain still visible on the floor from the dead Brailack ship thief. Shaking her head, she looked at whatever it was that Gabe and Bennie had cobbled together. "And this is what again?"

Bennie blew out a loud breath. "I already told you."

"Tell me again," she said. "This time, explain it like I'm Wil."

Gabe got out from under the console. "I have completed the rewiring of the secondary subspace transceiver. We will be able to piggyback a trace signal onto the comm stream without any links to this ship."

Zephyr nodded. "Okay. You're sure they won't know?"

The droid inclined his head. "That is what I just said." He turned to look down at Bennie.

"What're you looking at? My code is tight. They'll never know." He gave Zephyr a defiant look. "Tane will make the call using our secondary transceiver. It's not linked to us in any way. We've never even used it. While he's on with his friends, we'll use the primary transceiver to add a carry signal that will let us trace the call even while they're scrambling the signal between themselves and Tane."

Zephyr looked at the ceiling. "How smart do you think Wil is?" Before Bennie or Gabe could answer, she held up both hands. "Okay. Okay." She looked at the ceiling. "Cynthia. We're good to go down here." She frowned. "He's got me looking at the grolacking ceiling." Shaking her head, she looked at Bennie. "Can you monitor from here?"

He shook his head. "Better if I'm up on the bridge." As he headed past the ship's first officer, he said, "I'll open a channel, Gabe."

"Very good," the droid replied. He turned to Zephyr. "I may need your assistance." She nodded.

CYNTHIA WAS SITTING in the command chair when Bennie reached the bridge. Tane was at the comm station with Maxim sitting at his tactical console. "We're set down there. Just give me a millitock or two to get set up with Gabe."

Cynthia spun the chair around to face aft. "You ready for this?"

The younger Palorian man nodded. He glanced at one of the smaller displays on the console. He had images of dead Maxim queued up for transfer. They'd staged a scene in the corner of the cargo hold with fake blood and bruises that Cynthia had concocted.

"All set over here," Bennie said.

Cynthia nodded. "Do it."

The Brailack hacker started entering commands into his console. The communication station came to life. Tane watched as the system, remotely controlled from the annoying Brailack's terminal, initiated the call to the anonymous internex account his contact had given him.

"On your screen in ten," Bennie called out.

Tane counted down in his head. At zero, one of the screens on his station came to life. A digitally obscured head and shoulders appeared. "You did the job? We thought you might have lost your nerve."

At his station, Bennie whispered, "Rotate the frequency shift to match theirs. Tricky little flobins."

"Acknowledged," Gabe replied in Bennie's ear piece.

Tane nodded. "Yeah. Took a while. He had two of his friends with him." He reached over and triggered the data transfer. "Sending files."

The digitally blurred head nodded. "Well done. The other two?"

Tane shook his head.

"Then why are you calling?"

"Bennie, they are using a worm to attempt to track the signal," Gabe said over Bennie's commset.

"I'm on it. We trace you—you don't trace us." He tapped furiously at one keyboard then turned to another that he had epoxied to the side of his console.

The droid announced, "They are shunting their signal to a nearby freighter's comm ID. Zephyr, please adjust the data feed on the primary subspace transceiver. Thank you." Bennie watched the data flow dashboard he'd set up on another screen, seeing Zephyr's adjustment take effect.

Tane looked down. "I'm calling because it wasn't as clean as I expected. One of his friends was injured and the other one got the authorities on me. I need to come in. Let the heat fade."

The obscured head shook. "Too risky."

"Riskier than me being out here?" Tane insisted. "If his friends or the authorities catch up to me..." He let the idea hang there.

The blurred head released a loud sigh. "Fine. Come to Kuria Andron. Wait for instructions."

Before Tane could answer, the screen went blank.

He blew out a breath. "See?"

Bennie looked at his console. "Gabe, you get that?"

"Kuria Andron," the droid confirmed. After a minute the droid said, "Confirmed. The trace led back to the Musi system." Kuria Andron was the fourth planet in that system.

Bennie nodded, even though he knew his friend couldn't see him. "Confirmed on my end as well." He turned to Cynthia and nodded. "Kuria Andron it is."

Tane turned in his own chair. "So, we're going? To Kuria Andron?"

The Tygran woman nodded. "Don't see why not." She powered up the ship's flight systems. They'd been drifting in space several light days from Lorstak Seven, well out of any travel routes to the resort world.

The ceiling speaker crackled. "If I may." It was Gabe.

Cynthia started to look at the ceiling, caught herself, and remained staring at the forward display. "Go ahead."

"The *Rocky Nontee* is still on Lorstak Seven. It may be wise to make use of a second ship."

Cynthia ran a hand through her fur, smoothing one ear, then another. "Good idea." She adjusted their course to head back to the resort world.

From the ceiling, Zephyr said, "On my way up."

Cynthia nodded. "Copy."

THE TALL TRENBAL came back again to threaten the ambassador: some teeth baring, some weapon brandishing, and then he left. Wil still wasn't as worried as the other two men but understood their fear. It was clear the Trenbal man was deadly serious in his demands.

After the brig's hatch closed, the three men tried their best to get some rest. Something not easy in the brightly lit room. To Wil's chagrin, Bruce didn't seem to have any trouble falling asleep. He snored. Loudly.

Looking up at the brig's ceiling, Wil still couldn't figure out how something as organized as this Coalition seemed to have escaped everyone's notice. They had ships, at least three that he was aware of. They had people. What was their beef with humanity?

"Psst."

Was the GC simply doomed? Was he responsible? Thousands of years of stability, he shows up, and it's one thing after—.

"PSST."

"Huh?" Wil looked at the grate. "Oh. Hey, kid. What've you got?"

"Good news. I found guns," she reported.

He inched up onto his elbows. "That is good news."

"What's going on?" the ambassador asked, sitting up in his bed.

"Nic's back," Wil answered, not taking his eyes off the vent grate overhead. "What else?"

"Bad news. I don't know where we're going but found out we're almost there. Just a few more tocks."

Wil swore. "Bad news for sure."

"Why?" Carlisle asked.

Wil sat up. "Even if we could take the ship in that amount of time, we're closer to their reinforcements than we are to ours." He looked up at Nic. "What else? Were you able to call the team?"

Bruce stirred. "What's up?" He went from softly snoring to alert faster than Wil expected until he remembered that the man was actually a spy. He waved a hand to silence the newly awake secret agent.

She shook her head. "No. They did a good job locking things down. I could only access a few secondary systems. I was lucky I found a low-level system that had the countdown."

Wil thought for a moment. "Okay. Stay out of sight. See if you can find a way to get some of those guns you mentioned to a hiding place, in case we need them."

"Oh, on the good news front. One less bad guy."

Wil nodded. "You hid the body?"

He couldn't see her face very well but was pretty sure she was making a face at him. "Of course."

Bruce looked to his boss. "Is it just me, or is the casual way they're discussing killing someone and hiding the body a little off-putting?"

The older man shrugged. "I'm trying to think of other things."

"What about you guys?" Nic asked.

"I think we're okay for now. That Trenbal jackass would've killed us already if it was his call. Since we're alive and almost to wherever we're going, there must be someone there that wants to meet the ambassador."

"Lucky me," the older man said.

"I DON'T APPROVE OF THIS," Bennie said. He crossed his arms over his chest.

"You are the one that always wants to," Gabe held both hands up, making air quotes, "A-Team the shit out of something."

"Not my stuff!" the team's hacker protested.

The group was aboard the *Rocky Nontee*, standing in the cargo hold. The *Ghost* was parked nearby.

Cynthia leaned out from the small engineering compartment at the aft end of the cargo hold. "Oh, calm down, little green. We're not dismantling your smelly little home away from home." She winked, a gesture she'd picked up from Wil. "We're making her better."

"She's fine the way she is," he said.

"That is quantifiably not true," Maxim said. He made a point of turning away from the fuming Brailack. "We'll want to reinforce the bulkheads along the sides." He pointed to each side of the hold. "We'll block the side cargo doors to make it easier."

"We can affix the reinforced panels to the door tracks, adding cross bracing here and here." He pointed to different locations within the cargo hold.

Maxim nodded his agreement.

Bennie made a disgusted-sounding noise.

Zephyr nodded her agreement.

Gabe said, "I believe we can improve the maneuverability of the ship by routing secondary power buses to each of the reaction control thrusters."

"Wil would never let you do this to the *Ghost*," Bennie complained.

"The *Ghost* doesn't need it," Zephyr said.

"If the *Nontee* gets blown up, you owe me a new ship. This one wasn't cheap."

Cynthia emerged again from the engineering space. "You bought this ugly bucket with stolen money."

"I coulda bought something else with those credits!"

Cynthia rolled her eyes.

Gabe, ignoring his friends' banter, asked, "Bennie, do you think the dorsal struts would support a missile pod?"

Bennie's already large dark eyes grew larger. "A missile pod?"

The droid looked around the group. "Too much?"

Maxim grinned. "I have a better idea."

Bennie made another noise.

TWO HOURS LATER, the ship rumbled to a landing. The three men were led off the ship, surrounded by ten of the ship's crew. All of them were armed and had their weapons trained on the three humans.

Wil looked around as they descended the boarding ramp. They weren't at a spaceport. Rather, it looked like the ship—he glanced up and over his shoulder. Nic was right, a heavily modified mid-sized freighter—had landed in a clearing. What looked like an old-growth forest surrounded them on all sides. Next to the corvette they came in was a Harrith frigate.

"You all have some nice toys," Wil said.

The Trenbal who'd been tormenting them on the ship pushed him forward. "Shut up."

"Is there an Ewok village in there?" Wil nodded toward the tree line.

"Captain, is tormenting him wise?" Ambassador Carlisle asked.

Wil shook his head. "Probably not, but it's what I do."

"You'll all shut up, or we'll stun you and drag you the rest of the way."

The group moved to the tree line. There was a wide path through the trees. The path was wide enough for equipment and then some, and the dirt was hard-packed. These people had been here a while. They walked for ten minutes not seeing another being or any signs of life.

"Looks like Vancouver," Wil said under his breath. "Wonder if there's a Stargate around here?"

"What?" Bruce asked. He said it loud enough that it earned him a smack on the head from the Ruknak woman next to him.

A Crakim leading the way looked over their shoulder. "We really need them all?"

The Trenbal sighed. "For now." He nodded forward. "We're here."

The group emerged into another clearing, this one filled with tents of various sizes, arrayed in rough concentric circles. There were dozens; all different colors, some circular, some rectangular.

"Tents?" Wil blurted. "This is a damn set from a sci-fi show."

"If tents offend you so much, I can kill you. We really just need him," the Crakim said, pointing to Ambassador Carlisle.

Wil shrugged. "Tents are cool. I love tents. All the Jaffa I know, love tents. Hope to own one someday."

Bruce rolled his eyes. "You can't possibly think this will work. He's one man. Earth won't stop because he says so."

"So, we should just kill you. And then the next one they send, and the ones after that," the Trenbal man said, his hand resting on the pistol at his hip.

The Crakim rattled a laugh. "Maybe one of them will see our point of view."

The Trenbal shrugged. "Or not. Not like we'll run out of plasma rounds."

Wil gave his own laugh. "Hope you're not hoping Earth will run out of humans. We're...prolific."

Everyone, humans and alien, made a face looking at him. "What?"

NIC WAITED what felt like forever but was closer to half a tock after she heard the captain and the others being escorted out of the brig. From the sound of things, everyone had departed the ship. All she could hear were the occasional pops and pings of the ship's structure settling.

Landing in the corridor, she looked around. She couldn't see or hear anyone. It bothered her a bit that no one seemed concerned that they were missing a crew member. Not that she worried they'd find the body. They wouldn't, but still. She was pretty sure the team would miss her if she went missing. At least everyone that wasn't Bennie. He probably wouldn't notice if the whole team vanished.

Shaking the random thoughts away, she headed for where she'd hidden a few rifles and pulse pistols. She entered the small storeroom half expecting the weapons to be gone, but no, they were still there, in a laundry bag she'd found. As much effort as these people put into securing their computers, they put the exact opposite amount of effort into securing weapons, or the ship generally, for that matter. She grabbed the bag and exited the storeroom.

Before the door even closed, she heard voices and ducked back inside.

"Have you seen Trallo?" a voice asked, getting louder as it approached Nic's hiding place.

"No, he must have disembarked the moment we landed. Probably already two mugs in at the canteen," another voice replied, this one getting softer as the pair continued on past the storage room.

She smiled. Okay, someone might miss Trallo. Then she frowned, uncomfortable with liking the idea that her dead opponent would be missed. Shaking her head, she exited the storeroom.

Wherever they were, the bad guys must have felt pretty

secure. No one was standing guard at the bottom of the boarding ramp. The ship was powered down, and no one was around. She glanced toward the cargo hold. It was wide open, waiting to be unloaded.

There was no sign of anyone, but it wasn't hard to track the group. She knew Wil's scent anywhere. She made her way through the forest, staying off the well-used trail in case anyone was coming from the opposite direction. This forest reminded her of home on Olopnal and her grandmother.

After she hid the bag of weapons in a shrub near the makeshift compound, the nimble Olop woman scrambled up one of the trees. In her natural element, it was easy to move about unseen.

"Wow," she whispered. The compound was larger than she thought when she saw the tents from the ground. From above, it was three concentric circles with a single large hut in the center. She saw the Crakim she'd seen on the ship standing outside the central building.

"They must be in there." She leaped from her tree to another, closer to the edge of the clearing. She'd have to wait there.

CHAPTER TWENTY-FOUR

THE REFIT of the *Rocky Nontee* took nearly two days. Bennie complained the entire time. Everyone else was getting antsy to get underway. They knew where to go and where they thought Wil and the others would be.

"Are you looking at used starships?" Maxim asked, leaning over Bennie's shoulder.

Everyone was aboard the *Ghost,* with the *Nontee* being remotely flown in formation. Gabe had rigged up a full remote flight system for the smaller cargo ship.

"Just in case," the team's resident Knight of Plentallus said. He held up a tablet. "What do you think of this one?"

The big Palorian took the tablet and came around the sofa to sit next to his little friend. "Exactly how much do you think the *Nontee* is worth?"

On the device's screen was a light freighter similar in tonnage to Bennie's forty cycle old bucket but much newer and far better armed. He handed the device back.

"What about this one?" On the screen was a sleek pleasure yacht twice the size of his existing ship.

Maxim tsked. "What would you do with that? It has no

cargo space. You couldn't haul more than a few mid-sized crates."

"But I'd look good doing it," he said with a grin. He tapped the screen, zooming in on the luxury craft. "It has a Gal Dukat Mark 9 FTL generator. She's faster than the *Ghost.*"

Maxim shook his head. "The *Nontee* isn't going to get destroyed. And even if she did, who do you think is going to pay you out for it?"

Bennie scowled but said nothing.

Cynthia entered from the bridge. "Incoming call. Our friend Iran ch'Aroon is on the line. He's curious about our ETA."

Maxim nodded. "I'll get Zephyr." She was in their shared quarters.

Cynthia took the tablet from Bennie. She glanced at the screen and shook her head. "That's the last thing the galaxy needs. You strutting around in that shiny useless thing." She swiped away the ship brokerage site and brought up the ship's communication suite.

Zephyr walked in, followed by Maxim. Her hair was wet. "Give me a millitock." She shook her head and schooled her expression. "Grolacking functionaries," she said under her breath. She nodded to her friend. "Okay."

Cynthia chuckled, nodded, and tapped the control on the tablet to connect the call through the lounge's bulkhead-mounted entertainment display.

Zephyr stepped forward. "Greetings, Second Aide Iran ch'Aroon." She inclined her head respectfully.

"First Officer Zephyr." The Tarlak returned the gesture. "I am calling to inquire as to the current state of your itinerary."

Zephyr ran her tongue over her teeth. "Yes, about that." The officious little man made a noise that Zephyr took as disappointment. She continued. "The ambassador, his aide, and Captain Calder were abducted two days ago."

The antennae on the second aide's head bobbed up and down. "I see. I will have to apologize to Blumtillithian."

"Sorry?" Zephyr looked at the others, who all shrugged.

The Tarlak man's brown skin blushed to a lighter shade. "Blum forewarned me that you people were harbingers of chaos. I said he was being melodramatic."

Zephyr snorted. Blumtillithian wasn't wrong. She nodded. "We have our charms. Currently, we're en route to the planet we believe our people are being held on. We'll gather them up and be on our way to Tarsis shortly."

Iran ch'Aroon bowed his head. "Honestly, I do not care, so long as you do not embarrass the Commonwealth or the Council."

The screen went black.

Zephyr inhaled. "Always a pleasure." She turned to the others. "Did Wil ever say how much we're being paid for this? Whatever it is should be doubled."

Cynthia smiled. "I thought you were going to ask him about the Coalition if you had the chance."

Her friend looked at her. "Did it look like I had a chance?"

WIL LOOKED AROUND THE ROOM. For a tent, it was remarkably nice, like a tent he stayed in when his grandparents took him and his sister to Tanzania on a safari. That tent was something else: wood floors, electricity, plumbing, sorta. He grinned, remembering how showers required someone outside to hoist three gallons of hot water up over the back of the tent for a gravity-fed shower, and the toilet was likely flushing into a hole under the tent. This tent looked like it had actual plumbing.

"Gentlemen," a voice said from behind the three seated humans. All three of them turned, craning their necks to look at the new arrival. A well-dressed Elar Keeg woman in a bespoke suit came around the desk they were seated at. Two Trenbal had followed her in, taking up positions on either side of the tent door. *Or was it a flap?* Wil shrugged as he turned back around.

She eased herself into the chair opposite them. "Ambassador." She nodded to Carlisle.

Guess it was just the goons that didn't know who the ambassador was, Wil thought to himself.

The sharply dressed, four-armed woman turned to Wil. "I admit I wasn't expecting to see you here, Captain."

Wil inclined his head. "Wil Calder, agent of chaos, at your service."

She smiled, her black lipstick glistening in stark contrast to her deep red skin. "We weren't sure who'd end up with these two. My credits were on the Knights of Plentallus." She shrugged the top set of shoulders. "You win some, you lose some." She looked past the three humans. "Glirt, I owe you twenty credits."

The one-eyed Trenbal from the ship smiled. "Yes, ma'am."

She turned back to the humans. "So."

Wil held up a hand. "I got a question." She smiled, inclining her head. "Why did you split up the team? How does that help you?"

She looked at Wil as if he had just sprouted wings. "That should be obvious. Your reputation precedes you—all of you, that is. Rogue Enterprises—cute name, by the way. We knew you were hired to guide the ambassador and get him to Tarsis. All of you together is no small matter."

Wil leaned back in his chair. "Ah...thank you." He put both

palms against his chest. "That means a lot to me." He looked at the other men. "You heard that, right?"

She rolled her eyes. "You done?"

He turned back to her, deadly serious, giving a half shrug. "Continue."

She shook her head. "Once we decided that splitting the team up was to our advantage, it wasn't hard to find young Tane. A couple of well-placed calls at the right time made sure that when he found our dark internex message board, he'd be open to the idea of sending a message. That it was his own kin made it even easier. He knew just how to string Maxim along." Her self-satisfied grin made Wil's blood pressure rise.

"What are you even talking about?" Bruce asked.

"Tane? His cousin? That young man we met back on...?" the Ambassador asked.

Wil shrugged. "Lorstak Seven, yeah. That guy," Wil said. He took a deep breath. "That whole thief thing back at the office?" The two men nodded. "That was because the thief stole Maxim's wedding bracelet thing. He needs it to, you know, marry Zephyr."

"A wedding ring? You split your team—the team paid to protect us—over a wedding ring?" Bruce asked.

"You met Tane?" the woman asked.

Ignoring her, Wil cocked his head to one side. "It's more of a bracelet."

"Un-fucking-believable," Bruce said. He launched to his feet in irritation. He spied the armed guards reaching for their guns. Holding up both hands, he said, "Sorry." He sat back down. He looked at Wil. "You're not getting a good review."

Wil shrugged. "With whom? The space Better Business Bureau? Space Yelp—wait, that is a thing." He turned to their host. "Again. Why?"

She cocked her head to one side. "We needed you as off-balance as possible. Tane decided on the exact course of action himself. But you said you met him?" Her face scrunched up in thought. She motioned one of her henchmen over and whispered something in his ear. He hurried out after that.

Ambassador Carlisle released a loud breath, looking at the woman across from the trio. "Who the hell are you?" the ambassador asked, having no interest in the big Palorian man's wedding bracelet or whatever it was. Or why this well-dressed, four-armed woman wanted to split up the team being paid to protect and escort him.

She shook her head. Her black hair, cut in a high and tight pixie cut, bobbed slightly. "Names aren't needed." She shrugged. "I'm sure you understand."

"If this goes sideways, you don't want it blowing back on your real life," Wil offered.

She inclined her head. "Just so." She turned to Carlisle, meeting his gaze. "So, to answer your question, Captain Calder. Why is simple. We don't want Earth here. Or humans. You know what we expect of you. What say you?"

Bruce held up a hand. "Excuse me, but what exactly do you think will happen if the ambassador publicly withdraws Earth from the GC? I mean, the moment he gets back to Earth, the government will just replace him."

The mystery woman made a clicking noise. "Surely, Mr. Hawkins, you don't think our plan is that flimsy?"

He shrugged. "The fact that your plan seems to hinge on humans tells me quite a lot."

Wil pursed his lips and looked from Bruce to their host. "He's not wrong."

The woman scowled, leaning forward. "Don't worry, the ambassador's part is a small one. But important nonetheless."

Wil sat and watched the secret agent work. Would this

woman explain the entire plan just to prove how superior she was? *Is this what James Bond must have felt like?*

"The chaos that your declaration will cause will provide just the right window for those sympathetic to our cause to act."

Wil's eyes narrowed. "You want the GC to collapse. After all I—we—did to prevent that."

Another clicking noise. "What? No, why would we want that?" She shook her head. "Can you imagine? The GC goes away, and what? Every world for itself? We saw how that played out not too long ago on a small scale. Remember?"

Wil did. The team had—unintentionally, as always—found themselves in the middle of a plot to destabilize the GC, driving more and more systems away until the bleeding couldn't be stopped.

Their host continued, "No. We simply want the GC to remain how it is. Calm. Human free. That way, when the time comes, certain factions within the government can make the necessary moves without chaotic elements at play."

Wil turned to the ambassador. "That's us. Chaotic elements."

The other man frowned. "Yes, I figured that out."

Wil nodded. "You're gunning for the Tarsi. The ambassador publicly withdraws. The Tarsi look bad for having rushed Earth into the fold in the first place."

Their host turned to Wil, one black eyebrow raised. "You've been out here long enough. Surely you can see the value in a change of leadership. The Tarsi have ruled the GC for the better part of five thousand cycles."

Her upper left hand rose to tick items on her lower right. "The thing with Sub-Commander Janus. That big robot probe. The separatists."

Wil shook his head. "And the guy at the top takes the blame."

The mysterious woman gave her own shrug. "Why shouldn't someone else have a shot?"

"The Elar Keeg?" Ambassador Carlisle asked, leaning in.

She shook her head. "No. Though I don't see why it couldn't be my people. No, we're working with a group representing several Tier 1 and 2 societies that would make up a new governing council."

Ambassador Carlisle ran both hands through his salt and pepper hair. "But why me? Why my people? What would this mean for Earth?"

She pursed her lips. "Sacrifices have to be made. You'd be fine on your own, I'm sure." Her wristcomm beeped. After reading something on the screen, she looked up. "I have other business to attend to." Standing, she said, "I'll be back to get your answer."

When she reached the tent door, she spoke with the two Trenbal. She left, and they remained.

AN HOUR AFTER SHE LEFT, the unnamed Elar Keeg woman was back in the central tent. "I'm afraid time's up, Mr. Ambassador," the well-dressed, four-armed woman said as she leaned forward, two sets of elbows on the table between them.

The three men had been given an hour to discuss the Coalition's demands. To help enforce their point, the two Trenbal from the ship remained at the tent's door to remind them of their options.

Wil had argued in favor of refusing the demand. Bruce, in his role as a spy, argued for doing what the Coalition wanted in order to prolong their lives and possibly in order to gather intelligence.

The two men looked at the third. He opened his mouth, and an alert siren sounded. The ambassador's eyes widened.

So did those of the woman across from him.

The tent flap ruffled and split apart. The Crakim burst in. "We're under attack!" They waved their hands. "You must leave! Now! The *Tila Drado* is lifting now to assist the *Kha'Dak*."

The two Trenbal had their pistols out and aimed at the three humans. Another Crakim and a Trollack entered. The lead Trenbal issued several orders, then nodded to his superior. "Let's go." The pair left.

The Elar Keeg woman stood and looked at each human in turn. She sighed and turned to the exit with her entourage in tow.

The Crakim came forward, their hooves clopping on the tent's wooden floor. Wil thought it was the being from the ship but wasn't sure. They looked at each man in turn. "Guess we'll be finding another angle." Motioning the other three beings forward, they smiled. "Taking you out will look great on my resume." They looked right at Wil.

He put a hand over his chest. "Me? Really?"

"Attention, attention. The *Avan Lifa* will depart in one-half tock."

They raised their pistol, jackal-like muzzle pulled back in a snarl.

Wil turned to the ambassador. "Guess we won't be getting a five-star review?"

The other two men looked at him, mouths hanging open.

From above the tent came a faint *snap-hiss*. Everyone in the tent looked up in confusion. A red glow appeared a split second before a crimson-colored blade of coherent energy stabbed through the tent, instantly slashing a cut big enough for a small furry Knight of Plentallus to drop into the tent to land between the humans and Coalition aliens.

The gash in the tent from Nic's beam saber was flowing, the tent fabric smoldering.

Nic looked up at the Crakim. "Hi." She sprang into action; her blade sliced up through the other person's pistol barrel. She brought it down, cutting through the Trenbal man diagonally, shoulder to hip. He gurgled as he slumped to the ground.

The tent erupted in chaos after that. The remaining Coalition members all began shouting and screaming at each other and at the small Olop person who'd just killed one of them.

Wil pulled the other two men toward the table in a crouch. "Told you she'd come through!" he shouted over the pandemonium. He flipped the table over to create a barricade.

Nic used her smaller size to her advantage, darting between opponents, slashing weapons where she could and bodies where she couldn't. She and Bennie had both been making a concerted effort to kill fewer people when they could. She ducked under a wild swing from a Trollack man, swinging her blade up through her attacker. Sometimes killing was the only way.

The Trollack man fell to the ground, a glowing slash bisecting his torso. The wound was still smoking.

The two Crakim pulled long serrated blades and squared off in front of Nic. "You're dead," the one she'd seen aboard the ship said.

Nic cocked her head to one side. "No, I'm not."

The first jackal-faced being scowled. "You will be."

Nic grinned. "No, I won't."

"Yes. You will."

Nic shook her head. "No, I won't."

The first Crakim roared as they lunged for their smaller opponent. Nic grinned and met the attack. She raised her blade to block an overhead swing, assuming that, like most things, the other being's blade would be melted through by her beam saber.

When the Crakim's blade struck her beam saber blade, it stopped. The motion caught Nic by surprise. Her eyes widened when her blade stopped short.

The Crakim laughed, leaning back to plant a hoof in Nic's chest, sending her flying backwards. As Nic stumbled, the second Crakim dove in, their blade twirling in a blinding flash of silver. From the ground, Nic parried each thrust and slash one-handed while scooting backwards with her other hand and feet.

Wil looked over the table. The tent's roof was fully engulfed in flames now. Nic was doing her best to keep the two Crakim at bay from the floor. One of the tent's roof supports toppled, spreading flames to the floor. She needed backup. "Nic, guns?" he shouted.

"Oh, yeah!" She parried an attack and then swung her weapon in a wide arc to one side, then another, forcing both Crakim to take a step back. With her free hand, she reached into a pouch on her pant leg. She tossed something toward the table, then another and another. Three pistols skidded to a stop next to the overturned table.

"Pistols?" Wil shouted.

Nic ducked an overhead swipe from one of the Crakim, slashing at the second's leg. The second Crakim jumped back, so instead of losing their leg they found themselves hobbled. She rolled onto her back, pushing off with her free hand. Getting to her feet, she tossed a glance his way. "Rifles are heavy!"

"ONE MICROTOCK TO FTL EXIT," Zephyr announced. She was sitting at the flight command station that Wil usually occupied. She'd taken command of the *Ghost* many times over the last several years, on top of the times she'd been in command of small teams in the Peacekeepers. Sitting in the center seat of the *Ghost* never felt right.

Maxim looked up from his tactical station. "Shields are up and weapons are hot."

Bennie turned in his seat. "I have strong telemetry from the *Rocky Nontee.*"

"I am in engineering, and all systems are ready," Gabe announced from the overhead speaker.

Feeling left out, Cynthia said, "I'm just sitting here."

Her friend sitting in the center of the small warship's bridge looked over to her, smiling. Cynthia was sitting at the operations console that Zephyr normally occupied.

"Try sitting at a locked-out station," Tane groused.

Cynthia looked over at him. "Yeah, and don't get smudges on anything." She winked. He frowned.

"Here we go," Zephyr said as she pulled the FTL throttle control back to its base position.

On the forward display, the stretched rainbow lines shrank back into stars, with a mottled green and brown world directly ahead.

With a warship sitting in orbit.

"Dren," Maxim whispered. "One Quillant cruiser in orbit." He looked up and over at his partner. "She's old, but I'm betting her teeth are still sharp."

Zephyr nodded. She'd hoped that if it came to a fight in orbit, it would be against aging corvettes like those they'd already encountered. A cruiser? That was a whole other thing.

"*Nontee* is holding one light day out," Bennie announced.

"Have they seen us?" Zephyr asked.

Maxim shook his head. "Not that I can tell. She hasn't fired up her mains, and we're not being scanned."

"Check again," Cynthia said, eyes on one of her screens.

He checked his console. "Oh. Never mind. Her weapons are hot and she's maneuvering." He looked up. "Were they waiting for us?"

Zephyr tapped a few controls on her console. "Tane, comms is unlocked. Jam what you can!"

The young man turned from the forward display to look at the mostly unfamiliar console. "Uh. Okay."

On the forward display, the Quillant cruiser's main drive was powering up. Beam weapon turrets along its flank were swinging into position to take aim at the much smaller Ankarran Raptor closing on it.

"Any idea their weapon's range?" Cynthia asked. She was trying to access the specs for the class of ship ahead of them when the cruiser's forward batteries opened fire. Powerful bolts of energy splashed against the *Ghost*'s shields.

"Never mind," she said as the ship shuddered. Sparks rained down from a panel over her head. She closed the ship recognition database, having no need of it now.

"Returning fire!" Maxim announced. The sound of the forward missile launchers cycling a pair of missiles into the tubes echoed through the ship. A loud clang sounded a second before two bright objects streaked out from the bottom corners of the display. "Missiles away. Loading next round."

From the sides of the screen, bright green plasma bolts shot toward the cruiser. The *Ghost*'s energy bolts passed those of the cruiser between the two ships.

Zephyr was biting her lip. She pulled the flight controls hard to port while pushing them forward. Their shields flashed as the enemy ship's weapons fire struck them.

The small ship soared up and over to the left as it shook from the impacts. The cruiser's turrets tracked them, lighting up the *Ghost*'s shields. Their two missiles lit up the larger ship's shields, bathing the area in bright light. The cruiser kept firing.

The *Ghost* shuddered and rocked with each impact against its shields. One of the smaller sub monitors attached to the primary forward display exploded. Another was showing nothing but static.

The sound of the missile launchers cycling echoed again, then again. On the screen, two pairs of missiles shot out from the bottom corner of the main display.

Bracing herself, Cynthia studied the displays on her console. "Enemy shields at eighty-five percent." She looked at another display. "Ours are at seventy."

The *Ghost* passed under the cruiser, twisting to avoid the larger ship's blaster fire as best they could. The second pair of the *Ghost*'s missiles exploded against the cruiser's shields, bathing the small ship in bright light.

"Dropping two more," Maxim said. The sound of the missile launchers cycling echoed through the ship again. Instead of the sound of the acceleration rails sending the missiles speeding ahead of the ship, the missiles left the launcher just a little faster than the *Ghost* herself.

On the tactical sub-monitor, the two missiles, yellow triangles, fell behind the ship before activating and heading in the opposite direction the *Ghost* was moving. This close to the cruiser, they impacted within seconds.

As the *Ghost* put distance between herself and the cruiser, four, then six, then eight red triangles appeared on the tactical display, rocketing away from the larger red triangle that represented the cruiser.

"Eight missiles on our six. Closing fast." Cynthia looked up from the sensor display. "Upside, cruiser's number three and five shields are fluctuating wildly. I think we hurt them."

"Copy." Zephyr never took her eyes off the primary display and the tactical sub-monitor.

"Prioritizing the number three shield," Maxim said. He tapped a few controls. "Bringing aft point defense online."

As the aft disruptor powered up, a panel set between the ship's atmospheric engine thrust nozzles slid out of the way. The small weapon slid out of its enclosure, the ship's tactical computer taking over the aiming. The gun twitched and jerked, firing no more than a shot or two in any position before moving on to the next.

"One down. Two. Three." Maxim looked up, nodding. "Four down." He swore. "Last two got through. Brace!" He grabbed the edges of his console. The *Ghost* shook and lurched forward violently. Something deep inside the ship groaned and then gave a metallic snap. The bridge lights flickered.

The *Ghost* made a wide banking turn, Zephyr pulling the flight controls back and to the right. This time the controls felt a bit sluggish. "Gabe, I'm having trouble with the maneuvering thrusters," she said.

"Cruiser's turrets coming around," Cynthia reported.

Turrets along the other ship's top and facing side swung around toward the *Ghost*. Each turret was two barrels of potential supercharged plasma that were about to strike their shields.

"Launching two more missiles," Maxim said. This time, the pair of missiles leaped from the small ship at the regular launch velocity. Maxim peppered the enemy ship's shields with high energy plasma. He swore. "They tagged one of the missiles. Other got through."

Cynthia nodded. "Their number three shield is at thirty percent." The ship shook. "Not sure whose will go down first, but I'm liking our odds." The *Ghost* rattled. "Mostly."

Zephyr nodded. "Maxim, load one of the ship-busters."

Cynthia and Maxim both turned, the latter repeating, "A ship-buster. You're sure?"

She shook her head. "I don't think we can take that cruiser otherwise."

"Just one?" he asked.

She smiled. "They are rather expensive."

He nodded. "Good point. Loading one ship-buster in launcher two."

"Bringing us around for another pass. We'll come in at an angle to their number three shield."

"Uh oh," Cynthia said.

Zephyr turned. "Uh oh. What, uh oh?"

"Picking up a corvette leaving the atmosphere."

"That's not good," Bennie said. He turned to Zephyr. "Bring in the *Nontee*?"

He had been silent until then, and Zephyr nearly jumped out of her skin when he spoke. She nodded.

CHAPTER TWENTY-FIVE

"CORVETTE WILL BE in weapons range in five microtocks," Cynthia announced.

The *Ghost* was passing over the Quillant cruiser, her nose on the ship as she slid fore to aft, raining supercharged plasma on the larger ship's shields.

"Yes!" Tane slammed a palm on the console. "I've isolated their comm frequencies. We're jamming them all."

"Good job, Tane! Stay on it. They'll try cycling frequencies," Zephyr said.

Maxim turned to look at his cousin, nodding. The younger man's cheeks flushed. He nodded back, then turned to his console.

"Their number three is down to ten percent!" Cynthia shouted over the sound of the cruiser's return fire battering their shields. The smaller ship shook and rattled.

"Anytime now, Brailack!" Zephyr shouted.

"Just a microtock!" Bennie replied.

"The *Nontee* just dropped out of FTL!" Cynthia said.

The secondhand, or possibly thirdhand, Star Rambler 3400 appeared in local space twenty thousand kilometers from the cruiser. Several of the enemy ship's turrets turned on the small freighter.

"They're targeting her!" Bennie screeched.

"Then maneuver!" Zephyr scolded.

The flustered Brailack turned back his console. He had set up one section of his console to mimic the *Nontee*'s flight controls. One of his extra displays showed the sensor data and camera view from the small ship.

"Opening forward hold," he said. He was twisting his control interfaces this way and that to make the ship harder to target.

The sound of the *Ghost*'s ball turret blaster sounded as Maxim took whatever shots of opportunity he could as the *Ghost* maneuvered. The small turret wasn't as powerful as the nacelle-mounted weapons that could only fire forward, but it was better than nothing.

"Any time now," Zephyr said.

The *Nontee*'s forward cargo ramp lowered to reveal a missile launcher that took up the entire opening. "Eat this!" the little Brailack said as ten snub missiles leaped from the launcher.

They were smaller than the missiles the *Ghost* fired, but the launcher they'd purchased on Lorstak Seven came with nearly a hundred of the small, self-guided munitions. The autoloader fitting into the cargo hold behind the launcher immediately set to work replacing the spent missiles.

The *Nontee*'s missiles spiraled through the distance between her and the cruiser. The gap was small; it didn't take long.

"You targeted the cruiser's number three shield, right?" Zephyr asked.

"Oh. Uh..." Bennie looked over his cobbled together remote console, spotting the targeting parameters screen.

She rolled her eyes. "Really? You've been sitting here the whole time we've been trying to get through that shield segment."

"I was. Busy." He looked over his shoulder at the acting captain of the *Ghost* and said, "Locking on to shield three. Firing ten more."

"Make it twenty," Cynthia said from across the bridge.

Bennie inhaled. "Twenty missiles away. Two waves of ten."

"Good job," she said.

The first ten missiles impacted across several of the cruiser's shield segments, none of which was the weakened number three segment. Ten bright explosions flared to life, then vanished.

The *Nontee*'s shields flashed as the cruiser turned its focus entirely on the smaller craft. Dozens of blaster turrets took aim, raining supercharged plasma on the small freighter.

"No!" Bennie screamed. He was doing his best to juke his ship this way and that to shake the other ship's target lock. His console was throwing more and more errors.

The first batch of the second wave missiles began striking the cruiser.

"Moving to cover," Zephyr announced.

The *Ghost* banked, moving to put herself between the *Nontee* and the cruiser's fire.

"Can't hold long," Cynthia said as the ship began shuddering anew. A relay in the ceiling exploded, sending sparks raining down.

More than half of the first ten missiles made it through to strike the cruiser's shields; the number three segment vanished in a bright white energy wave that rippled across the neighboring shield segments.

Six of the second ten missiles made it through the cruiser's defenses. Two struck an intact shield segment, the remaining four ripped into the ship's hull, penetrating deep before detonating. Explosions tore large chunks of the ship apart, sending debris spinning off in all directions and kicking off secondary explosions.

Bennie squinted at his flight controls. The *Nontee* was now throwing several new error codes.

"Good job, little green," Cynthia said with a nod from her station. "I'm picking up power failures across the cruiser." She looked at Zephyr. "They're out of the fight for the time being." On the screen the enemy cruiser was spinning along her axis as atmosphere vented from the gaping wound in her side.

Bennie looked over and nodded before turning his attention back to the *Nontee*'s virtual flight controls.

The *Ghost* shook. Something over the communication console exploded, sending sparks and bits of electronics in all directions. Tane shielded himself the best he could. He grunted in pain as something struck his shoulder, drawing blood.

Bennie furiously entered commands on his virtual flight console. "I'm bringing the *Nontee* around behind the cruiser."

"Not too close," Maxim offered. "No telling when they'll get things back in working order."

Bennie nodded.

WIL SHOOK his head and distributed the pulse pistols. "Know how to use one of these?" Bruce nodded; the ambassador shook his head. Wil held his own weapon out, pointing at pieces. "Safety, power cell charge, power level setting, stun, kill, and trigger." He handed a pistol to each man, then stood up from behind the table. "Swords down!"

Bruce followed suit, taking aim on the Crakim Wil wasn't aiming at.

Nic stepped back, her beam saber humming between her and the two cloven hoofed Coalition thugs.

The ambassador rose up from behind the table. Releasing a bloodcurdling war cry, he pulled the trigger and held it down, his pulse pistol screaming as bolts of energy tore both Crakim to shreds. Their bodies flew backwards, landing in smoking heaps. Nic barely got out of the way, mostly because she was shorter than the ambassador's spray of plasma. The pulse blasts continued on, ripping into the tent, igniting the walls. Wil did not know who was beyond those tent walls but hoped they ducked.

Bruce put his hand on the other man's arm. "Sir." The other man released the trigger. Bruce cocked his head toward the remains ten feet away. "Good job, sir."

Wil looked at the two men and shook his head. "Time to go. This place is about to be ash." He nodded toward the only remaining wall of the tent that wasn't ablaze. He looked at Nic. "Good job, kid."

She beamed. "Thanks."

"What's it look like out there?"

"Two corvettes and the freighter we came in. Lots of tents and what have you. Bad guys everywhere." She did the best approximation of a finger snap her little furry fingers could manage. "Oh, and my bag of rifles is just outside camp in the trees."

Wil smiled. "Rifles. Now we're talking. Do you know what's going on? Why's everyone freaking out?"

She shrugged.

"Fair enough." He gestured toward the presently burning door of the tent. "Lead the way."

On their way to the door, Wil leaned down and scooped up one of the fallen Crakim's blades. "Neat," he said as he slid it under his belt.

As the foursome crept out of the central tent, Wil shook his head. The whole place was in chaos. Sure enough, one of the two corvettes Nic saw earlier was gone. "Let's find those rifles."

"How do you propose we get off this planet?" Bruce asked as they reached the tree line. Nic lead them to the tree where she'd halfway buried large bag. He accepted a rifle from Wil, looking it over. It wasn't a design he was familiar with, but it seemed pretty straightforward.

"There's still ships on the ground," Wil said as he took the ambassador's pistol and gave him a rifle. He paused. "No. Give that back." He held his hand out, fingers wiggling. His other hand had the pistol.

The older man slumped against the tree. "Thank God." He offered the rifle back, taking the pistol in a shaking hand.

Wil nodded. "I've been through worse. It'll be fine."

Bruce raised an eyebrow. "You have?"

Nic bobbed her head. "Sure. We get into this kind of scrape all the time." She looked at Wil. "That's kind of strange, isn't it?"

Ignoring her, Wil headed back into the camp. A Brailack emerged from around a nearby tent. He shouted an alert that fell short when Wil's pulse blast hit him square in the chest, sending the lifeless little green body flying ten feet into the wall of a tent. He looked at Bruce. "More or less." He looked down at Nic. "You know the lay of this place?"

She shrugged. "Sorta. Got a good view when was up in the tree." She pointed. "The landing field is over there." Pointing elsewhere, "I think there's an armory over there and what looked like maybe the tents for the big deal folks. Looked a little fancier, like the one you were in."

He nodded. "Okay then. We skirt the edge of camp. Something's going on that's got them all twisted up. One of the corvettes is already gone. I'm guessing they're packing all the important things up to load on to the other. Let's steal it before they can take off."

THE SHIP ROCKED AGAIN, a blaster bolt from the corvette making it through their weakened shields to strike the ship. A piece of scalding hot something or other hit Zephyr in the back of the head. She grunted, taking one hand off the controls to feel her head. Her hand came away covered in blood.

A small inset window appeared on the primary display showing a wireframe diagram of the *Ghost*. Several sections of the main body were bright red.

"Corvette's in range," Cynthia said.

Zephyr glanced at her. "Timely."

Her friend made a face. "Sorry."

The *Ghost* banked hard to starboard, the corvette's weapons tracking the smaller ship. Zephyr pushed the pocket warship hard, twisting and turning in space. A corvette would normally not be much of a threat to the *Ghost*, but after the beating they'd taken at the hands of the cruiser, Zephyr didn't want to take chances. Wil would kill her if she wrecked the ship.

Cynthia, an emergency med kit in hand, stepped up behind her friend. She looked over Zephyr's wound and gave it a quick spray of DermSeal. "That'll hold you over." She patted her friend on the shoulder.

She turned to Tane. He waved her off. "I'm fine."

"You sure?" He nodded.

"Okay, I underestimated that old bucket's capabilities," Zephyr said.

Smoke was billowing from a light panel overhead.

"Maybe it's time to waste some money on them?" Cynthia asked as she sat back down at her station.

Maxim looked at her. "Really?"

"That corvette's fresh and we're not. The cruiser's gonna be back in the fight eventually. Even at half strength, it's still a cruiser." She shrugged.

Zephyr pursed her lips. "Agreed." She turned to Maxim, who nodded both his agreement and acknowledgement that the ship-buster was still in the launcher.

The *Ghost* spun on her long axis, kicking her aft section in a wider arc than her forward. The ship's blasters and missile launchers remained aimed at the damaged cruiser.

Zephyr watched as the damaged cruiser filled their forward display. "Fire."

"Launching one," Maxim said. A lone missile, its drive signature visibly different from the previous missiles, streaked out from the bottom right corner of the screen. "Suck it, kreb-nacks," he added as four more missiles streaked out from the bottom corners of the screen. Hopefully, they'd provide cover for the ship-buster. The enemy cruiser was wounded, but it continued to fight.

Point defense turrets along the cruiser's hull came to life. Not all of them. The fire was intermittent.

"One missile down," Maxim reported.

On the tactical sub-display, the *Ghost*'s missiles—green diamonds—sped toward the red triangle that was the cruiser. Another green diamond winked out.

"Two down."

The ship-buster, similar to the XPX-1900s they used so many years ago in the battle at Harrith Prime, was a devastating and expensive weapon, more modern than those previous warheads. Wil would certainly question their use of one. Assuming they lived long enough for him to ask.

The remaining diamonds reached the triangle. The flash of

light on the primary display brightened the bridge until the built-in filters reduced the glare.

"Scratch one cruiser," Cynthia said. The ship's sensors worked to filter out the flare of radiation. Once the display cleared, they saw the cruiser was now in two pieces that were quickly moving apart from each other.

Zephyr took a deep breath, then released it. Her head was killing her. Before she could say anything, Cynthia shouted, "Two missiles inbound! From the corvette."

The *Ghost* spun like a dancer, a drunken one for sure, tipping on her wing before accelerating away from the oncoming missile.

"I'm getting warnings on the port maneuvering thrusters," Cynthia said. She tapped a control on her console. "Gabe, you seeing this?"

"I am working on the problem," the team's engineer replied. "I could use Bennie's help."

Zephyr looked at the team hacker. "Go. Send the *Nontee* to staging area delta." He nodded then hopped out of his seat. She looked over her shoulder. "Tane, take over Bennie's station in case we need the *Nontee*."

"Copy that," the young Palorian said.

CHAPTER TWENTY-SIX

THE HATCH TO ENGINEERING OPENED, allowing a plume of greasy smoke to escape into the corridor. Bennie waved both hands, trying to clear the air in front of him. The ship lurched, sending him stumbling into the room.

Hacking and coughing, he stood up. "Port maneuvering thrusters?"

The air circulators kicked in, pulling the smoke from the room. The power conduit, which ran across the ceiling on the portside from fore to aft, had scorch marks and had melted in several places, making the internal wiring visible.

Gabe pointed. "The port lateral power flow stabilizer is suffering power fluctuations. The controller's software is experiencing...glitches—"

"On it." Bennie cut him off, heading for the indicated piece of equipment. He pulled a data cable out of his wristcomm and got to work.

The ship shuddered; the reactor's normal thrum stuttered.

Bennie looked over his shoulder. "That didn't sound good."

"It is fine." Gabe had his attention on a piece of equipment near the ceiling where the damaged cable entered the device.

"Really?"

"Probably." He ripped the damaged whatever it was—Bennie had no idea—off the wall.

Bennie made a clucking noise. "Reassuring."

"Have we ever blown up?" The droid glanced over at Bennie as he dropped the thing he'd ripped off the bulkhead.

The Brailack made a face and gave a half shrug. "Good point." He turned back the misbehaving power flow stabilizer. "You know, I used to be the ship's engineer? Back before we found you in that box."

The droid made a kind of *grunt-clank* sound but said nothing. He went to a storage locker and removed a piece of equipment that looked similar to the one he'd ripped from the bulkhead.

Bennie shook his head, smiling. "Got it," he said as he disconnected his wristcomm. "A little surprised you had an older firmware on this."

Gabe reached up and attached the new device to the damaged power bus. He opened a small control panel and made a few adjustments, then closed the panel. The reactor was thrumming along like it should. The ship shook again. Gabe cocked his head, accessing the ship's diagnostics wirelessly. "I have been busy." He pointed to the hatch. "The starboard missile tube autoloader is throwing an error." He headed for the door.

Bennie watched him exit engineering and shrugged. "Field trip."

As Gabe exited the engineering space, he sent, "*Zephyr, the port maneuvering thrusters should be...mostly back to normal.*"

The pair made their way to the common deck lounge and stairs that led down to the cargo deck.

Reaching the cargo deck, they made their way to the control pedestal next to the heavy cargo door. Gabe tapped several commands into the pedestal. Normally, opening the cargo doors would also trigger the ramp to lower, something that would be disastrous in space. This time, however, the big door ground open, and the ramp remained raised, keeping the space beyond the cargo doors safe to occupy.

There wasn't much in the space between the cargo doors and ramp except for the access hatch to the crawlspace that ran the length of the ship's neck between the two missile feed tubes.

Gabe led the way, opening the secure hatch and crawling into the crawlspace.

"Lucky I'm here," Bennie said from behind the droid.

The ship rocked, and something back the way they came gave a distinct sound of snapping metal.

"That probably wasn't good," the hacker said.

"Probably not, no," the droid agreed. As they neared the forward end of the tunnel, the smell of burned insulation met them. "That is also probably not good."

Maxim's voice came through both of their comm units. "I've lost all function on the number two missile launcher."

"We are already on it," the droid replied as they reached the end of the crawlspace.

Gabe slid open the access hatch that led into the starboard missile launcher. Acrid smoke billowed out into the crawlspace. Bennie reached up and punched a small panel overhead between the port and starboard missile launcher access hatches. Three rebreathers fell out. He snatched one before it hit the ground, placing it over his nose and mouth, the flexible molecular bonding material forming around his features.

Gabe was already inside the cramped space. Bennie slipped in next to his friend. "What's the plan?"

Gabe had the access panel open on the launcher. "We fix it. That is the plan."

Bennie shrugged. "Tell me what you need."

Gabe pointed to a section near the back of the mechanism, where missiles slid into place. "The primary load sensor has fused to the housing. Cut it free." He extended his hand, holding a cutting torch in it.

"Copy that," Bennie said.

A PAIR of Sylban fell to the ground, smoldering.

"I'm getting the hang of this!" the ambassador shouted over the noise of the rapidly packing up camp. He spun toward the others, who all ducked and jumped clear of his line of fire.

"You're doing great!" Wil said. "Just keep aiming the business at anyone who isn't us."

"Oh, yes. Oops." He lowered his pistol.

Nic had broken off from the three men to range ahead. As yet, the group was still without wristcomms. Every unit they tried to remove from a corpse locked them out. Each one burst into sparks and smoke when they tried to override it.

"You there!" someone shouted.

Wil and Bruce spun, opening fire. The quartet made up of two Klini and two Tragalallan attempted to return fire. Wil dropped to one knee behind a cargo module. Bruce shoved the ambassador behind a tent.

"This won't help!" the older man argued.

Bruce kept pushing. Bolts of energy burst through the fabric, setting it ablaze.

One of the Tragalallans fell, his head mostly charred. His friend's fire was melting Wil's cover.

From around another tent, energy blasts ripped the remaining Coalition members to pieces.

Standing, Wil said, "Nicely done, secret agent man."

Bruce inclined his head.

"What about me? I think I hit one of them," the ambassador said. He was holding his pistol in what Wil figured he must have thought was a heroic stance. Behind him, Bruce was slowly shaking his head.

Nic came around the side of a tent opposite them. "If you're done taking a breather, I think the corvette is powering up." She was hiding something behind her back.

"We weren't taking a breather," Wil said. He nodded to her, eyes on the arm behind her back.

She smirked. "Uh huh." Then produced his wristcomm. "Look what I found."

"Where?" Wil asked.

She jerked her head to the tent she had come around the side of. "I heard voices in this one, so took a peek. Two Tleb were trying to crack Bennie's encryption." She smirked. "They failed."

Wil took the device, swiping through screens to confirm the device's functionality. "No comm network to join. Even if they're up there, we can't reach them. Probably lots of jamming and radiation."

Bruce eyed the young woman. "What about our CommPads?"

She shook her head. "Guessing they tossed them once they got anything of value off them."

"Anything else of value?" Wil asked.

"If we had time and a cargo ship, sure, but otherwise, no," the Olop answered.

Wil looked at the other man with a look of mock sympathy on his face. "Come on."

The foursome made its way closer to the path that led to the makeshift landing field and the idling *Avan Lifa*. The freighter they had arrived on was also powering up. It looked like most of the camp was heading for the corvette.

"I'll scout ahead," Nic said before splitting off from the humans again.

The three humans stayed behind a thick stand of treelike things ten meters from the path. Beings were coming and going. Going from the camp with carts and armloads of cargo. Coming back empty-handed to gather more.

"How are you going to steal that ship?" Bruce asked.

Wil shrugged. "Something will come to me."

The ambassador's eyes grew. "Something will come to you?"

Wil smiled. "Usually does."

"Except for that one time on Clymene Six," Nic said as she stepped out from behind a tree a few feet away.

The other two men looked at Wil, whose mouth was hanging open. "We agreed no one would speak of that."

She gave him a one-shoulder shrug. "They've got a few guards at the main ramp. Your four-armed friend is already aboard with those Trenbal krebnacks."

Wil checked his rifle's charge. "And the one we came in on?"

She shook her head. "Looks like cargo and extra personnel for the most part. Everyone seems to be heading to the corvette."

"Any idea what's going on?" He jerked his head upward.

Another shake of her head. "Just that someone's here and they're freaking out. I heard someone mention," she rubbed her chin, "I don't recall the name, but something up there was taken out."

The ambassador looked at the two of them. "Freaked out enough to launch both of their warships and strike camp?"

"We have that effect on people," Wil said.

"Those aren't warships. Not exactly. Just corvettes. Old ones at that," Nic offered.

The older man looked at her as if she'd grown an extra head but said nothing.

"Let's go," Wil said with a smile.

The foursome made its way to the landing field without incident. The last corvette was sitting just as Nic said, readying for takeoff. Exhaust vents around the ship's rear were hissing out steam as the engines warmed up.

Unfortunately, it looked like a good chunk of the Coalition camp was also already at the landing field. People were standing around the two large vessels waiting their turn to board.

Bruce tapped Wil's shoulder. He made a buzzing noise, waving the other man's hand away. "I'm thinking."

"Wil," Nic said.

He shushed her.

"Captain Calder," Ambassador Carlisle added.

Wil turned to them. "I am trying to think of a way to get aboard one of those ships so we can steal it, and you three won't give me a moment's peace. What in the name of all things holy is so important?"

All three pointed.

Wil followed their gestures to a small craft parked just beyond the two larger vessels. There was no one around the small vessel, some sort of personnel shuttle.

"Oh," he drew out the syllable. "That looks like a more promising option."

They headed for the small shuttle. Likely it didn't have FTL capability, but if he was right and the *Ghost* was up there, it wouldn't matter.

"You can hotwire it?" Bruce asked.

Wil nodded. "Probably easier to hotwire than the corvette." He waved them on. "Let's go."

THE *GHOST* ROCKED VIOLENTLY, tossing Cynthia and Tane from their stations. She scrambled back into her seat. "Hull damage, A deck." She looked at Zephyr. "The port fresh-water tank." She read her screen. "That secondary sensor array, too."

Tane leaped out of his seat. "I'm on it!"

"Be careful," Zephyr and Maxim said at the same time.

"Of course."

The bridge hatch closed behind him.

"Corvette is closing," Cynthia said.

"Bring us around. Please," Maxim said.

Zephyr nodded. She pulled the controls over while giving the sub-light engines more power.

"Bridge, repairs to the missile launcher are complete," Gabe announced from the overhead speaker.

Maxim beamed. "Good timing, my friend!"

On the forward screen, the corvette was sliding in from the left. A pair of missiles, followed by another, streaked out from the bottom of the screen, accompanied by blaster bolts from the ship's main energy weapons.

The corvette's shields lit up as the energy bolts slammed into them. The ship's two forward turrets returned fire, lighting up the *Ghost*'s shields. It followed the blaster barrage with six missiles.

"Shield strength down to forty-five percent," Cynthia announced.

Zephyr pushed the controls forward, sending the *Ghost* into a spiral as she closed the gap with the enemy ship. Two more missiles streaked out ahead of them.

The *Ghost*'s missiles crossed paths with those from the corvette.

"Hold on!" Zephyr shouted as she yanked the controls in the opposite direction.

The *Ghost* spun and twisted in a way that Zephyr wasn't sure it was meant to. She didn't have time to think too hard about it right then. Metallic groans rang through the ship as the structure torqued this way and that.

Two of the missiles streaked past the *Ghost* as she spun. The other two were intercepted by Maxim's deft control of the bridge-mounted blaster turret.

"Good work, Max!" Cynthia said through gritted teeth.

The *Ghost* came around again to fire on the corvette, which, for its part, wasn't sitting idle. The other ship, while not as maneuverable as the *Ghost,* was no slouch, pivoting on various axes as incoming missiles targeted it.

WHEN BENNIE and Gabe reached the A deck hatch, the former said, "This doesn't look good." The hatch wasn't closed. It didn't look like it would be closing again anytime soon.

"Indeed," Gabe agreed, pushing the deformed hatch open.

The forward section of the deck was a ruined mess. That the inner hull hadn't been breached was a minor miracle. Tane was standing in the doorway of the forward equipment space in an emergency vac suit, the hood retracted. "Hi."

"Hello." Gabe pushed past the younger man into the small room. The forward bulkhead was caved inward; several conduits were split, their ends sealed with spray foam. Gabe examined the young Palorian's work. "Well done."

Tane's cheeks flushed deep blue. "Thanks." He stepped out into the corridor.

Bennie emerged from his quarters. "Looks like my room is fine."

Tane cocked his head. "Was that a worry?"

The Brailack shrugged. "I have a lot of irreplaceable stuff."

"Uh huh."

The ship shook, forcing both men to reach for the nearest bulkhead for stability.

Gabe leaned out of the equipment room. "The secondary sensor array is too damaged. I have shut off the power but could use your," he turned to Bennie and pointed, "assistance."

The little green Knight of Plentallus nodded and headed into the small room. Gabe watched him enter and then accessed the internal communication system. "The secondary sensor array is damaged. We are attempting to make repairs. Even if we are successful, it will not be fully functional."

"Do what you can," the ship's acting captain replied.

Gabe turned to Tane. "I could use your help as well."

The young man nodded. "How can I help?"

The engineering droid pointed to a piece of equipment that was bellowing smoke from a crack in its housing. "Remove that."

CHAPTER TWENTY-SEVEN

THE SMALLER SHIP turned out to be an assault shuttle.

"Okay, I like this," Wil said as they approached. The Coalition beings in the landing area were so focused on the remaining corvette and freighter that the shuttle, likely to be abandoned anyway, was unguarded.

He looked at Nic then the other two men. "I'll go first, make sure it's clear." He pointed to the other humans. "Then you two. Nic, you secure the rear and keep an eye out while I get her ready for takeoff." Nods all around. "Okay then." He rose, looked around, and darted for the waiting assault shuttle.

Bruce turned to Nic. "How will we know when it's okay to go?"

Without taking her eyes off the shuttle, the young apprentice Knight of Plentallus said, "If there isn't weapons fire and screaming in the next, say, two microtocks, it's clear. If he comes running out, not clear."

"Crack operation," the younger of the two said.

Nic turned. "We try. Go." Bruce stared for a moment. "Go," she hissed, waving a hand at him. "Up."

It dawned on him. "Oh, now? It's clear?"

She looked over to the shuttle. "No screaming or gunfire. So, yeah." She made a shooing motion.

Watching the two men do their best to creep to the assault shuttle, she sighed. "Should have just let them get captured or whatever." She counted in her head, and when she got to forty, rose and headed for the shuttle.

Reaching the shuttle's boarding ramp, she felt the rumble of the small ship's reactor powering up. From up ahead, Wil shouted, "We're out of here in three!"

"Copy that!" Nic turned to face out, crouching next to the bulkhead to present as small a target as possible if seen. The hubbub outside the second corvette was slowing down. "Hey, Wil! I think the bad guys are getting closer to leaving."

"Copy," Wil said from deeper inside the ship. "Closing her up!"

Nic walked up the ramp into the small ship's equally small cargo hold. From a side hatch in the cargo hold, Bruce said, "People just leave these things sitting around unsecured?"

Nic nodded. "I dunno. Do you lock your hovercar when it's in your parking bay?"

The human man shook his head. "I don't actually know what you just asked me."

"Alright, button it up!" Wil shouted from the forward section.

Nic reached for the control to raise the ramp. A blaster bolt struck the bulkhead over her head. She crouched. "The jog's up."

"The jog...what?" Wil asked. More weapons fire splashed against the assault shuttle's hull and cargo hold interior.

Nic brought her beam saber to bear, deflecting the blaster bolts that came closest to her. "You know, the bog, or hog, maybe? Fig? Jig?" The ramp finished closing, sealing off the incoming fire.

"The jig is up," Wil said. Then added, "We're leaving."

Nic turned, deactivating her weapon. Bruce was watching. "You're good with that thing."

She gave a half shrug. "The farce flows through me."

He barked a laugh. "It's force. Not farce." He nodded to her beam saber hilt. "May I?"

She unhooked the device from her belt. "You sure? Farce feels right." She handed it to him, emitter pointed toward her. "Be careful. The beam will stab right through the hull in a blink."

The shuttle tilted and rumbled as it rose off the ground.

Bruce held the hilt up, turning it to look down the barrel. Nic rolled her eyes. Holding the device out at arm's length, he said, "I wanted one of these as a kid, so badly."

WIL HAD his eyes on the flight dynamics display as handheld weapons fire splashed against the assault shuttle's hull. He glanced over at the ambassador, sitting in the copilot seat. "Buckle up."

The assault shuttle shot forward, still only a few meters off the ground. Wil pulled the flight controls toward him. The assault shuttle roared over the tops of the nearby trees.

"See if you can find weapons control," he said.

"What?" the older man asked.

"And shields."

"What?"

"Weapons. This is an assault shuttle. It'll have shields and weapons." Wil didn't turn to look at him. "This thing flies like shit."

"I don't know what I'm looking for!" the other man complained.

Wil glanced at the console. He pointed. "Those."

The ambassador started wildly flipping switches.

Wil nodded and then jerked his hand toward another set of controls. "I think those."

The ambassador moved his hand toward the indicated switches.

"Just don't dump the cargo bay, please," Wil said without glancing over. Out of the corner of his eye, he saw the other man's hands pause, hovering over the controls. He smiled.

Nic and Bruce entered the small shuttle's cockpit as the view outside the glass was moving from pale blue to black.

"Can we keep this thing? It's kinda nice," Nic said. She looked around the small cockpit. "Needs more seating, though."

Ignoring her, Wil said, "Picking a lot of debris." He nodded out the forward window to hundreds of pieces of slowly spinning debris.

Ambassador Carlisle whistled. "That's a lot of debris."

Wil smiled. "More than a corvette, for sure." He looked over the sensor display between him and the ambassador. "Got two more ships further out." He studied the screen. "One's bigger. Gotta be the corvette from the camp." He tapped the screen. "Which means: *Ghost*, that you out there?"

Silence.

"Maybe it's not—" Bruce started, but Wil waved a hand wildly.

Wil pushed the small ship's throttle toward the stops. He couldn't imagine why the *Ghost* wasn't answering. Must have something to do with the debris they'd seen.

"Uh, what's that?" Bruce was pointing at the sensor screen.

Before Wil could look, Nic said, "Guess the other corvette lifted off."

"Will they catch up?"

Wil nodded. "Be surprised if they didn't." He was scanning the flight console, getting familiar with it.

Nic poked the ambassador in the ribs. "Move." She hopped into the vacated seat. "Looks like we've got one small turret aft and a pair of forward plasma beam generators."

Wil stopped looking at the controls and turned to her. "Plasma beam generators?"

She nodded.

"Two of 'em?"

Another nod.

"What's a plasma beam generator?" the ambassador asked from the back of the small cockpit.

"Incredibly powerful weapons. Not usually found on a craft this size," Bruce answered.

Wil snapped and pointed at him. "The spy got it in one." He glanced at the assault shuttle's sensor display. "Start firing the aft gun. It won't do much but might slow the corvette down." He turned back to piloting the shuttle. "Hopefully."

"On it."

The sound of the aft-mounted blaster firing filled the shuttle's interior.

Bruce leaned over the two forward seats. Their stolen assault shuttle was closing on the other two ships while the corvette was closing on them. Will was right; the fire from the small aft turret didn't seem to deter the larger ship.

"How are we supposed to get aboard the *Ghost* if it's fighting the other corvette and we've got the another one on our ass?"

"That's future us's problem," Wil answered without taking his eyes off what he was doing.

THE *GHOST* WAS DOING her best to dance with the larger corvette. The small ship was more maneuverable, by far, but her claws were all forward facing. The corvette was designed to work in a fleet. Her weapons were along her top and sides. No matter what Zephyr did, they were always in range of one of the corvette's turrets or another. Add to that the fact that the *Ghost* and her crew weren't fresh. They'd already been fighting for a while before the corvette arrived.

"I'm picking up another ship. No, two," Cynthia said. She leaned closer to her console's screen. "One is small. I think it might be a shuttle." She looked at Zephyr, who shrugged.

"Maybe they're throwing everything they've got at us?" Maxim offered.

"That's a cheery thought," Cynthia replied.

"We can't keep this up," Zephyr said, her shoulders slumped. "I'm not the pilot Wil is." The ship rocked as a missile from the corvette struck its weakening shields. "We don't even know if they're down on the planet or on one of these corvettes, so we can't just fire more ship-busters."

"Hopefully, they weren't on the cruiser," Tane said. When everyone turned to glare at him, he held both hands up. "Sorry." He turned back to the comms station, adding, "Just saying," under his breath. He turned back to Zephyr. "Hey, I think this console is busted. There's a lot of error codes on the screen."

Cynthia pulled up the ship's communication systems. "He's right. Short-range comms are grolacked." She glanced at the ceiling. "Gabe, short-range comms are damaged. Can you repair?"

"Bennie and I have been looking the system over. We do not believe the damage is addressable in situ. Most certainly not while in combat. Long-range comms are functional. Marginally," the ceiling answered.

"So, even if they're on one of those ships, we wouldn't know it," Maxim said.

Tane had turned back to his console, studying it more intently than he had before. "You all use a closed mesh for local comms, right? Your wristcomms?"

Cynthia, the least busy of the three Rogue Enterprises team members, looked at the man occupying her station. "Yeah." She nodded. "Why?"

"I might be able to use the long-range antenna to piggyback your mesh. It wouldn't be great, might burn out the receiver's comm circuits, and ours maybe, but might give you a window to at least figure out where they are."

Zephyr glanced over her shoulder. "Get on it."

He nodded and turned back to his station. Mimicking what he'd seen the others do, he looked at the ceiling. "Uh, Gabe? Did you copy all that?"

"I did. How can I help?"

Zephyr tuned out the young man as he explained his idea to the team's engineer. Whoever was piloting the corvette was giving her a run for her money, not that piloting was even in her top five skills. Okay, maybe not even top ten. More than once she'd thought about tapping Bennie. He at least had experience with the *Rocky Nontee.*

"The *Nontee*!" she shouted, causing both Maxim and Cynthia to jerk in their seats. She looked at the ceiling. "Bennie, we need the *Nontee.*"

"For what?" the Brailack hacker asked.

"Now, felgercarbit!"

"Fine," he said. "She's on her way. Two microtocks. I'm transferring control to your station."

"Send it to Cyn—" She looked at her friend, who was vigorously shaking her head. "Maxim's station."

"Done."

The ceiling beeped twice.

"Sure, I can manage our weapons and fly a whole other ship," Maxim said under his breath.

"We all heard you. Wil and his weak ears aren't here," Cynthia said.

"I HAVE AN IDEA," Nic said.

The shuttle rocked. Something overloaded above their heads rained sparks down on them. Acrid smoke followed, puffing out between two panels.

"I'm open to suggestions," Wil said. He yanked the controls over, forcing the small ship into a roll.

"I'm gonna puke," the ambassador said from behind Wil's seat. There were only two seats in the small cockpit and just enough room for two others to stand. The bulkhead and hatch were barely four feet behind the pilot and copilot seats.

"Please don't," both Wil and Nic said as one. The young woman added, "I've been looking over this thing's specs."

"And?" Wil demanded impatiently. He knew they would not last long. The corvette was closing, and no amount of wild maneuvering was going to keep them from getting blasted to atoms. The other ship's forward weapons were far more powerful than the small assault shuttle's shields.

"The cockpit is a lifeboat," the young Olop woman said.

Wil turned. "What? Really?" He looked around the cramped space.

She nodded.

"What's that mean for us?" Ambassador Carlisle asked.

Wil turned back to his console, twisting and turning the controls this way and that. "It means if that's the *Ghost*, we can try a barn swallow."

"That sounds...not good," Bruce said. "A barn swallow?"

Nic turned in her seat. "It's easy. We get in close to the *Ghost*; they open the cargo hold and line up on us. We blow this thing's ejection system, and pop's your buncle—"

"Bob's your uncle," Wil interrupted.

"Yeah, that." Nic nodded her head. "Easy."

Bruce looked at Wil. "Easy?"

"Mostly," he said. He looked at his wristcomm. Still no response. If it was the *Ghost*, their comms must be out. "I've seen it done on TV."

The two human's eyes bulged. "On TV?" they asked in unison.

Wil nodded.

CHAPTER TWENTY-EIGHT

"TEN MILLITOCKS," Maxim warned.

"We're almost there," Zephyr said.

She had the *Ghost* limping along to lure the enemy corvette into position.

Tane was nearly finished modifying the communication system. She was really hoping that was Wil in the assault shuttle that was rapidly closing on their position. If it was, getting rid of the corvette that was harassing them was paramount.

"Five," Maxim said.

"Here we go," Zephyr said under her breath. She pushed the sub-light throttle all the way forward again. The timbre of the ship's power plant changed as the powerful engines cycled up to full power.

The *Ghost* jumped, putting distance between itself and the corvette that undoubtedly thought it was moving in for the kill.

In a flash, the *Rocky Nontee* dropped out of FTL barely two thousand kilometers from the enemy corvette. The small freighter's forward cargo door was already open. Within seconds of the ship's arrival, thirty stub missiles had leaped from the launcher. The side doors opened, exposing a matched set of blaster turrets. Bennie had resisted the idea of them, but Gabe assured him that the small freighter's power plant could support them.

The two ships' close proximity meant that the *Nontee*'s missiles weren't in flight long. Ten missiles pounded the other ship's shields as blaster bolts struck at the same time. Ten more caused the weakened shields to overload. The final ten ripped the side of the corvette open. The *Nontee's* blasters continued to power explosive energy into the wounded ship.

Secondary explosions blew out sections of the hull; short-lived flames burst forth. The corvette's engines sputtered out, going dark.

"Corvette's out of the fight!" Cynthia shouted, pumping a fist in the air.

Tane turned around. "I think I'm ready."

"It'll work?" Maxim asked.

His younger cousin shrugged. "Probably. Maybe?"

"We've got maybe two, three microtocks before that shuttle and the other corvette are in weapons range," Cynthia said.

Zephyr looked at Tane. "Do it."

Cynthia stood and joined him at her station. "May I?"

Tane nodded. He rested his finger on a button. When she had the commset securely in her ear, he pressed the button.

"*Wil*, do you copy? That you, babe?" Cynthia said.

WIL SCREAMED when his wristcomm's speaker blared to life. First a startling burst of static, then, "That you, babe?"

"Cyn! Yeah, it's us. We're on the—"

"This is gonna burn your wristcomm out. We have to be quick," she interrupted.

Wil glanced down at his wristcomm. That explained why it was getting warmer. "Okay, here's the plan. Barn swallow. The shuttle's cockpit is a lifeboat."

"Cop—" Cynthia started to answer, but Wil's wristcomm's speaker burst into sparks.

Flapping his arm to cool the device, he said, "Hope they can figure it out." He pulled the device off his arm, tossing it to the deck.

He watched the sensor screen as the *Ghost* turned onto a heading that would bring her around on an intercept course for their ship.

Bruce leaned forward between the two seats. "You're sure they understood?"

Wil shrugged. "I think so." Under his breath, he said, "She watched *Serenity* with me a dozen times. Give or take."

"Do any of them even know what a barn is?" Ambassador Carlisle asked.

Wil looked over his shoulder. "Not a fan of the classics, I see."

"WHAT'S A BARN?" Zephyr asked after bringing the *Ghost* around on an intercept course.

Maxim shrugged. "Earth thing?"

"Well, obviously," Cynthia scolded. Maxim glared but said nothing.

"I think a barn is a big mammal. They're gray and swim around," Bennie offered. He was back at his station, trying to coax the *Nontee* to a safe location. She'd taken a few hits from the corvette before it died. "They're huge. Could eat a Brailack whole," he added.

"A barn is a large storage structure. Typically built on

farms," Gabe said from the ceiling. "Typically used for equipment or livestock storage."

Zephyr rubbed her forehead. The headache from her wound was still a throbbing reminder of their current situation. "What's that mean, then? A barn swallow?"

"A swallow is an avian creature. Native to Earth. Very small," Gabe offered.

Zephyr shook her head. "A building and a bird?"

"Wait!" Cynthia said. "He said the shuttle's cockpit was a lifeboat. That has to mean something." She did her best impression of snapping fingers. "We're the barn. He wants us to swallow," she pantomimed swallowing something, "the lifeboat. In the cargo hold!" A memory popped into her head. "Yes, that's definitely it. It was in a movie he made me watch way too many times."

"On it," Gabe said.

"Good job," Maxim said before turning his attention to his console. They were heading straight for another corvette, with the small assault shuttle bobbing and weaving between them.

Zephyr focused on her flight controls and the image on the forward screen. The small shuttle was hurtling towards them, with the second corvette hot on their heels. She doubted their trick with the *Nontee* would work twice.

Cynthia sat back down at Zephyr's usual station. She scanned the assault shuttle, making note of its dimensions. It wasn't a model that the ship's computer had in the database, so she had to guess where the cockpit might separate from the rest of the ship. Pulling up the *Ghost*'s specifications, she swallowed hard. There was next to no margin for error. The cockpit-turned-escape-pod would *just* fit.

She tapped an icon to open a private channel. "Gabe. I'm sending the specs for the shuttle over. I can only guess at the exact plane of separation for the cockpit, but no matter what, it's going to be a tight fit."

A second passed. "You are correct. I have moved what little was currently in the hold to the sides and rear of the space."

"Will it be enough?"

"It will have to be."

In the hold, Gabe turned to look around. He was not optimistic about this plan working. Wirelessly, he disengaged the cargo hold's gravplating, then cycled open the heavy inner cargo bay doors. As the thick metal plates slid apart, he lowered the cargo ramp.

Stopping the door level with the hold, he quickly set up a program that would gradually increase the artificial gravity starting at zero at the end of the ramp and reaching fifty percent in the center of the hold. With luck, that would help slow the escape pod before it rammed into the rear of the hold.

As a precaution, he had also activated the emergency netting—something they had never used and he was not entirely sure was in good repair. It had escaped his notice all these years that the ship even had such a feature. The previous crew must have added it as it was not a standard feature of this particular model of Ankarran Raptor. It was doubtful Wil even knew about it. Gabe had only discovered it a few months ago; it wasn't listed in the computer. He had discovered the out-of-the-way receiver near the top of the hold by accident.

Turning to look out the open cargo hold doors, he spied the assault shuttle. "The cargo hold is as ready as it is going to be."

From Bennie's station, the team hacker said, "Sending in the *Nontee*!"

Maxim glanced over. "You sure? She's pretty beat up."

Bennie looked at his friend. "Wil and the others aren't going to make it otherwise."

"Bennie being selfless?" Cynthia said.

"Not normal?" Tane asked.

She shook her head.

"THE CORVETTE IS GAINING," Nic announced. She looked up and pointed off to the side. "The *Nontee!*"

"You go, Bennie," Wil said in a low voice. He didn't spare the small, ugly cargo hauler a glance, all his focus on lining them up with the *Ghost*'s open cargo hold. Without comms, they couldn't get telemetry from the *Ghost*'s computer, which would be really helpful right about now.

The ship shook, and the small—mostly useless, in his opinion—tactical display blinked twice. The aft shields were almost gone. "See if you can reroute the shield power, send it all aft."

Carlisle looked at him. "How do I do that?"

"Oh no," the young Olop woman said as the *Nontee* took several repeated direct hits, her shields flashing with each one. Two bolts of energy made it through, ripping into the small craft's cargo hold. The port blaster turret exploded, taking a large part of the aft hold with it. She made a face. Bennie wasn't gonna like that. The *Nontee* spun away, trailing debris.

"Okay, you two. Grab on to something, tight," Wil said as he watched the range finder count down to what he felt was a safe distance for them to travel without being vaporized while giving the shuttle's main body time to maneuver out of the *Ghost*'s way.

"Three." He flipped the protective cover on the eject button up.

"Two." He confirmed that the autopilot would engage the moment they separated.

"One." He slammed his fist down on the eject button.

The hatch connecting the cockpit to the rest of the small assault shuttle slammed shut a split second before the explosive bolts went off, driving the cockpit-turned-escape-pod forward, away from the shuttle's main body. Every console went dark.

"Is it supposed to do th—" Wil started.

Powerful rocket motors kicked in, pushing the occupants of the lifeboat into their seats. Wil forced his mouth closed.

Slowly, a single display came back to life, showing their life support as a countdown and the status of the pod's emergency beacon. Not that it mattered, but whatever had been done to the ship's comm system hadn't extended to the emergency systems—at least its beacon; it was working, for all the good it was.

The *Ghost*'s cargo hold was looming larger ahead of them.

"Can you maneuver?" Ambassador Carlisle asked.

Wil shook his head. "Nope. This thing goes in a straight line."

Ahead of them, the *Ghost*'s blasters opened up in earnest, and first one pair, then another, and another pair of missiles leaped from the forward launch rails. The light from the energy weapons and missile drives lit up the mostly dark cockpit as they passed.

The *Ghost*'s cargo hold continued to grow, looming larger and larger until it was all they could see.

"Is it just me or are they going really fast?" Bruce asked.

"No, they're going pretty fast," Wil agreed. "And so are we."

CHAPTER TWENTY-NINE

"OOPS," Maxim muttered. The *Nontee* was spiraling out of view on the main display, trailing debris. Her engines sputtered and then went cold. He made a face. "Maybe he won't notice."

"Yeah, that seems likely," Tane offered.

"You're going pretty fast," Cynthia warned, ignoring the younger Palorian man. She glanced over at Zephyr.

The other woman's brow ridges were furrowed. "I know that." She pulled back on the sub-light throttles.

Once the escape pod separated from its mother ship, the rest of the assault shuttle went dead, its momentum carrying it along the same path as the escape pod.

Zephyr toggled through options on her console until a windowed view from a camera in the cargo hold was floating in the primary display. They could clearly see the assault shuttle's cockpit speeding toward them, with the rest of the vessel behind it. Several bolts of energy struck the shuttle, causing it to drift off its terminal course.

Maxim, with the help of the *Rocky Nontee,* had forced the enemy corvette to slow down, giving the escape pod a chance.

Cynthia looked up. "No offense, but you're still going pretty fast."

"And we should do something about the rest of the shuttle," Maxim offered. The now-damaged shuttle body was twisting in space as it angled slightly off its original course. "Never mind," Maxim added as the body took another hit from the corvette, a sizeable chunk of it breaking off. He looked at Zephyr. "That corvette, though."

The look she gave him made him turn his attention back to firing on said corvette. They were rapidly using up their missile supply.

The cockpit-turned-escape-pod was closing fast, growing to fill most of the visible opening of the cargo bay. The enemy corvette loomed behind it, taking fire from the *Ghost* while it fired back.

Zephyr spared a glance at her friend, more of a glare really. "Yes, all true."

Cynthia turned back to her console and gave Maxim a small head shake.

On the display, the cockpit crossed the threshold of the static atmosphere barrier that covered the cargo bay entrance and then slammed into the recovery netting, stretching it to the breaking point. The variable gravity plating kicked in, dragging the pod to the deck, slowing it down as it did.

Zephyr slammed the sub-light throttle all the way back, pressed the button on the handle that changed modes from forward to reverse, then pushed the control all the way forward to the stops.

The *Ghost* lurched violently as maneuvering thrusters fired at full power. The docking thrusters under the forward section fired as well, adding their power to the braking maneuver.

It was all Zephyr could do to keep her upper body from slamming into her console.

On the display, the escape pod raced toward the camera and the deck in equal measure, before striking the rear of the cargo hold, destroying the camera. Static replaced the image. The corvette was still bearing down on them, weapons shaking the smaller *Ghost* more and more violently.

Over the intercom, Gabe announced, "They are in. Closing cargo bay."

"Acknowledged," the current commander of the ship said as she twisted her controls to bring the *Ghost* onto a course that would put what little remained of the assault shuttle between them and the corvette as they continued to bleed off forward velocity, the reverse thrusters howling.

"I'm losing my angle," Maxim warned.

Zephyr pulled the throttle control back toward her before switching back to forward mode at the same time she yanked the flight controls to the left, forcing the already straining maneuvering thrusters to push the ship to port.

The remains of the assault shuttle exploded, sending flaming debris against the *Ghost*'s already weak shields. The forward display dropped into static for a moment, something behind it making a popping noise.

"That could have been worse," the woman at the *Ghost*'s controls said.

"Could it?" Tane asked. He'd been mostly silent, so Zephyr almost forgot he was there. Maxim turned and glared at his cousin. "I'm just saying." The glared deepened. "Never mind."

The ship rocked as the corvette continued to fire. Maxim was doing his best to return fire and keep the rear shields up.

Ignoring them both, Zephyr said, "FTL in one microtock." The view on the primary display was clear. The hostile corvette was almost behind them and falling further and further away as the small warship's sub-light engines flared as bright as a sun, pushing the ship ever forward and away from harm.

Maxim tried to access the *Nontee*'s systems. The remote connection was unstable, to say the least. When the smaller ship was able to connect, his screen was mostly error codes and warnings. He sent the command to send the *Nontee* into FTL, hoping the small ship was even still FTL capable. He then dropped two missiles at their slowest speed so that they could fall behind the *Ghost*. Hopefully, they would keep the corvette busy.

"Here we go," Zephyr said. She pulled the sub-light throttle back toward her, cutting all thrust, then pushed the FTL lever forward. On the primary display, the stars stretched into wavy rainbow lines.

Zephyr slumped in her seat. "I need a nap."

THE ASSAULT SHUTTLE'S cockpit rocked back and forth, its entire front end crumpled from the impact with the cargo bay's aft bulkhead. The escape pod had slid the last twenty feet before striking the wall, leaving wrecked deck plating in its wake. The wreckage was draped in tangled emergency netting.

Gabe and Bennie approached the twisted wreck. "This doesn't look great," the latter said.

Gabe nodded, his optic sensors in their purple sensors-at-full-power mode. "I am detecting four life signs." He turned and looked down at his friend. "That is good."

Bennie nodded as he activated his beam saber. The bright magenta energy blade came to life with a *snap-hiss*. "I'll cut open the hatch."

"Be careful," the droid warned. "My sensors cannot discern the internal layout. It would be unfortunate if you cut someone in half."

The Brailack shrugged. "Only if it's someone we care about. Fifty-fifty on that."

Gabe stared at the team hacker—and, when it suited him, champion of justice—but could come up with nothing other than, "Fair."

Bennie stepped over a deep gouge in the cargo bay's deck and used the emergency netting to climb up onto the ruined metal hulk of the escape pod. "Hey, in there! If you can hear me, get back from the hatch!" He didn't wait more than a few seconds before plunging his blade into the hatch. He made a slow circle around the hatch, his blade hissing and sparking as it sliced through the metal of the hatch and the fabric of the thick netting.

He slowed as his blade reached the point where he'd started. The hatch sagged inward before falling into the pod's interior.

"Hey! That almost hit me!" Bruce shouted from inside the cockpit escape pod.

Bennie hopped down. "They're fine!"

Nic hopped out first, followed by Bruce, the ambassador, and then Wil.

Once all four of them were on the deck, Wil asked, "Status?" He looked around. "Please tell me the rest of the ship is in better shape than," he waved his hand to encompass the cargo hold, "this."

Gabe cocked his head. Holding up a hand, he raised a finger as he ticked off: "We are in FTL. We are presumably en route to Tarsis. I cannot."

Wil made a pained face, huffing out a breath, then nodding slowly. "And that other corvette?"

"In pursuit. The *Rocky Nontee* attempted to delay it but was damaged."

Wil rocked back. "The *Nontee*? We saw her out there. Bold

choice bringing that bucket into the mix. She's got pretty weak weapons."

"She's not a bucket! And she's got teeth now!" Bennie shouted from the stairs. He turned to Gabe. "What do you mean, damaged? No one said anything to me."

Gabe cocked his head but said nothing. Turning back to Wil, he said, "We retrofitted the *Nontee* to be a missile delivery vehicle. She performed admirably until..."

Wil whistled. "Okay then."

From the hatch to the common deck at the top of the staircase, Bennie shouted, "Of course, she did!" adding, "Until what?"

Wil looked around. "Okay. Well, we're not on fire at the moment, so that's good." He headed toward the stairs.

"I'd like to take a shower," Ambassador Carlisle said.

Wil nodded. "Good call. We're all a bit ripe, and nothing is likely to happen in the next thirty minutes."

"I wasn't going to say anything," Nic said, taking a few steps away from the humans.

From the hatch at the top of the stairs, Bennie shouted, "Until what, Gabe?"

THE *GHOST* and *Rocky Nontee* were drifting in deep space dozens of light years from the nearest star. Zephyr had given their pursuers the slip, even if only temporarily.

Circling back the way they had come helped throw their enemies off the track. At least, that was the hope. The *Nontee*'s FTL system was so damaged, she only made it a few light years before it gave out.

The smaller freighter sustained heavy damage. A boarding tunnel extended from the *Ghost* to the *Nontee*'s topside emergency hatch and connected the two ships. The newly installed blasters had replaced the side entries, and the missile launcher was meant to slide toward the cargo hold's aft section to allow entry, but the damage was too severe.

Aboard the *Ghost*, Wil finished drying his hair and sat the towel down on the dining table. He looked at the young Palorian man standing off to the side of the group. "So, let's take things in the order they happened. Tane?"

The younger man looked at Wil, face blank. Wil made a *go-on* motion with his hand. Tane took a breath. "I, uh. Stole Maxim's Colla band?" Wil nodded. The younger man continued, "to, uh, distract you," he nodded to everyone in the room, "all of you from what the Coalition had planned."

Wil nodded again. "Exactly." He smiled. "Just making sure."

Everyone except Bennie and Gabe was in the *Ghost*'s lounge on the common deck. The team hacker and engineer were aboard the *Nontee* attempting to make as many repairs as they could in what they all assumed was limited time.

Maxim cocked his head toward his young cousin. "Was that necessary?"

Wil shrugged and turned back to Tane. "For what it's worth, they're good. The Coalition. Now that I've met their leader, I get why Duch, that pussy, was afraid to get involved. The things that happened to you. All of them. They're good."

The other man's cheeks flushed dark blue. "Grolacking krebnacks," he hissed. "They ruined what little I had just to ensure I'd be willing to go against you?" He looked at his cousin. "I'm sorry."

Maxim nodded. "It's fine."

Wil nodded his agreement. "Damn right." He shrugged. "But they're a problem for another day."

Bruce's eyes grew. "Really?"

Wil shrugged. "I know we have this reputation for saving the GC every other Tuesday and all, but we can't tackle every issue that comes up." He pointed to the ambassador. "We gotta get you two to Tarsis as soon as we can. That won't make these turds go away but will force them to figure out a new strategy."

"And that buys everyone time," Cynthia said. She nodded her agreement of the plan. "Plus, Bennie would be pissed if we saved the GC again without a contract and a purchase order."

Zephyr pointed at her friend, nodding her head.

Maxim nodded as well. "True."

"Maybe that assistant, whatever his name is, can help?" Cynthia offered. "On Tarsis."

"Iran ch'Aroon," Zephyr said.

Wil looked at her. "Nice."

She winked as she tapped her forehead.

"Let's call him."

"If it matters," Bennie said from the ceiling.

Wil jumped. "Jesus. How long have you been on comms?" He waved a hand, not that Bennie could see it, adding, "and it doesn't." He moved to the low coffee table in front of the sofa. Picking up the tablet that controlled the bulkhead-mounted display, he checked the ship's communication suite. "What the hell?"

"Does it matter now?" Bennie asked. Wil could hear the smirk.

Zephyr rubbed one hand across her forehead. "We had to make some adjustments to the comm system."

"The long-range comms should still function as expected, Captain," Gabe said over the ceiling speakers.

"Should?" Wil asked.

"Yes."

Wil gave a one-shoulder shrug. "Okey dokey." He tapped a few commands into the tablet.

The screen mounted on the lounge bulkhead immediately came to life and then flashed the logo of the Galactic Commonwealth Governing Council. Soft music filtered through the ceiling speakers.

"Space Muzak," Wil mused.

Before Zephyr could open her mouth, the screen changed. The pale brown face of Iran ch'Aroon took in the lounge. "I see you're all together again. Yay." He shifted his gaze. "Hello, Ambassador Carlisle."

The older man smiled. "It's been an interesting few days."

Iran ch'Aroon looked to Wil. "As I understand it, that's generally how this group operates."

Wil smiled. "We're exciting to be around. Can't argue that."

The Tarlak's two pairs of eyes narrowed. "Indeed." Turning his attention back to the room as a whole, he continued, "What can I do for you? Please tell me there will be no further delays. I already owe Blumtillithian quite a lot."

"We need an escort to Tarsis," Wil said. He chose to ignore the last bit.

"Maybe a Command Carrier or two?" Maxim asked.

"No."

Wil had turned to Maxim, nodding, then spun back to the screen. "No? What?"

"No." The officious Tarlak shook his head. "Not only do I have no authority to authorize something like that, but the Council would never approve it. The Peacekeepers are still stretched thin. You likely haven't been watching the news of late."

Wil squinted. "Not another rogue commander?"

"Nothing so serious as that, thankfully."

Maxim leaned forward in his seat. "I'm not certain we'll get there on our own. The *Ghost* is pretty beat up, and the *Nontee* is in worse shape."

The Tarlak on the screen cocked his head. "What's a *Nontee?*"

"Our second ship. Rogue Enterprises is growing, don't you know." Wil smirked.

"With all due respect, Second Aide Iran ch'Aroon," Ambassador Carlisle cut in. "Could you possibly spare something? Anything? I don't think my dying on the way to Tarsis would be a good look." He put his hand on his chest. "And it would be unpleasant, you know, personally."

"Yes, I'm sure it would be," the second aide said. "I'll see what I can do. Send me your current coordinates and flight plan."

Before anyone could answer, the screen went black.

"WE'VE GOT COMPANY," Zephyr announced. She was, happily, back at her station on the *Ghost*'s bridge. "They must have a tracker on one of you." She turned to look at Wil.

He held up both hands. "No probing took place." He looked over his shoulder at Cynthia. "Babe, get Bennie and Gabe back over here, pronto." She nodded. He turned back to Zephyr. "Probably something in the food. That's a thing, right? Molecular tracers and such."

She shrugged. "Probably. Would explain why it's taken them six tocks to find us. They probably had to go slow, looking for a low-level signal. We'll run you all through the autodoc later."

Wil grimaced. The *Ghost*'s autodoc was a surly old piece of equipment that, despite not speaking Galactic Standard—or any other language—aloud, issued angry-sounding beeps when issuing diagnostic details via its screen. "Something to look forward to."

He looked at his first officer. "Let me know when you retract the boarding tunnel."

She nodded. "They're closing the outer airlock now." She watched one of her screens for a few seconds. "Okay. Outer airlock sealed and boarding tunnel retracting. Ten millitocks until secure separation."

Wil interlocked his fingers, palms out, cracking his knuckles. He looked at his navigation display. They were eight hours from Tarsis at maximum FTL. He wasn't sure the *Ghost* could maintain max FTL right now after the battle over Kuria Andron.

"We're clear," Zephyr announced.

A moment later, the bridge hatch slid apart to let Bennie walk in. "She's not back to one hundred percent. Gabe and I did what we could. The cargo hold is still open to space, and the remaining blaster is probably going to burn out after a few shots." He said as he took his seat at his station. A candy wrapper fell from wherever it had been stuck on his console. He brought the remote piloting interface up on one of his displays. Turning to Wil, he said, "We're ready."

Wil nodded then looked at the ceiling. "Gabe, you all set?"

"I am as ready as I can be. Please be aware that the ship is not in peak condition," the team engineer answered.

"I'll be gentle," Wil lied.

"They'll be on us in five microtocks," Zephyr said.

Wil pushed the sub-light throttle forward. "How many missiles does the *Nontee* have left?"

Bennie double-checked his display before answering. "Forty."

Wil nodded. "I kinda like having a dedicated missile frigate."

Bennie turned to him. "Don't get used to it."

Wil winked.

Bennie frowned.

THE SHIP ROCKED; the overhead lighting flickered.

"I'm not sure what's worse: watching a space battle from the bridge or doing it from a sofa," Ambassador Carlisle said.

He and Bruce were sitting on the sofa in the common deck lounge. Nic was keeping an eye on them from the overstuffed chair. The *Nontee* was still too damaged for a crew, so there wasn't much she could do aboard the *Ghost* in a battle.

"You get used to it," she said. She offered the tablet she had been reading on. "Periodical?"

"How can you be so calm?" Bruce asked. "This is nuts. We're about to be in a goddamn space battle!"

She shrugged. "You get used to it."

"I don't think that's true," the ambassadorial aide and spy for Earth Gov Intelligence replied.

The ship lurched, and a conduit overhead broke loose over the sofa. In the blink of an eye, Nic was on her feet, beam saber in hand and humming. The crimson blade slashed through the conduit, the loose end falling to the side before it could land on the two men.

With a snap, the blade of coherent energy vanished, and Nic dropped back into her seat as if nothing had happened.

The two men's eyes were wider than she thought human eyes could get. She reached up to touch her nose. "Do I have a booger?"

"You just kept that from—" The ship shook again, forcing the two men to clutch their respective edges of the sofa. "That pipe thing crushing both of our skulls," Bruce stammered.

"Before we even flinched," the ambassador added.

The young woman shrugged. She turned her attention back to

the tablet she'd offered Bruce, bringing up the book she'd been reading. When the two men's eyes finally moved off her, she reached up to check her nose. Just in case.

CHAPTER THIRTY

THE LIGHTS in the lounge flickered. Nic unfastened her restraints, letting them snake back into the large chair's cushions. "We need to help Gabe."

Both humans looked at her. "What?" Ambassador Carlisle asked.

"Damage control. He needs our help." She hopped out of the chair, then looked at the two men. "Now!" Both scrambled to unclip their own safety restraints.

She still didn't have a wristcomm, but hoped Gabe could hear her. "Gabe, where do you need us?"

There was a pause, then the overhead speaker crackled. "I could use your assistance in engineering. The other humans can be useful in computer core."

Nic reached the hatch that closed off the service corridor, letting the doors slide apart. She turned. "You heard him." She pointed down the short corridor. "On the right." She didn't wait for them, heading straight for the engineering hatch.

When the heavy doors slid apart, thick, acrid smoke wafted out. Nic crouched low and inhaled.

To the left of the main reactor, Gabe had the FTL system's

cowling raised and was bent at the hips, his upper half hidden inside the machine. He rose out of the machinery. "You are small." He pointed at the opening.

She wasted no time hopping up to the open FTL field generator housing. "What am I looking for?"

"Approximately twenty-two centons straight in and seven to the right is a small round device."

She wiggled around. "I think I see it. Is it blue?"

"Do not touch the blue one," Gabe said, his voice doubling in volume.

Nic's hand paused a fraction of an inch from the round blue whatever-it-was.

"It should be dark gray. I believe it will be stamped with the logo of Xorillian Blooj on the top."

Nic squinted. "Oh. I see it."

"Remove it."

The room rattled and shook as the ship took a hit. The reactor made a noise that Nic thought it wasn't supposed to make.

"Should it sound like that?" she shouted.

From somewhere further than he had been previously, Gabe said, "It is fine. Focus on your task." In a lower voice, he continued, "Mr. Ambassador and Bruce. The cabinet to the left of the entrance has a series of fuses. Please find the one that is tripped and reset it."

Nic turned her attention back to the task at hand. She pulled on the component. It was stuck fast. "It's stuck."

"I would imagine so. Pull harder." Gabe was back to standing nearby.

Scowling, she mimed Gabe's last sentence while pulling on the damaged whatever-it-was. It came free with a pop and a few sparks.

"Got it!"

"Well done. I have a replacement for you," Gabe replied.

"Okay, it's getting warm in here. Is that normal?"

"No, you've removed the partially functioning thermal management module. Heat is no longer being shunted away from vital components."

Nic reached back, offering the broken thermal whatsit to Gabe. When it left her hand, she wiggled her fingers. "Well, that explains it."

"It does."

She felt the new module drop into her palm. She was squeezing her arm back in beside her when the ship lurched hard. The gravity plating fluctuated, allowing more of the ship's movement to impart momentum on her, jarring her. The new thermal thing slipped from her grip to clatter deeper into the machine. "Dren!"

The shaking hadn't stopped.

"You did not drop it, did you?" Gabe asked.

Nic pursed her lips. She could see the errant piece of equipment, but there was no scenario in which her short arms would reach it. "I dropped it."

"Can you reach it?"

"No."

"That is not good. Come out."

When she hopped down to the deck, the team's engineer was reconfiguring his arms amid a series of clicks and whirs. "Go help the humans. I am receiving diagnostic errors from the flight assist module. It is—"

She headed for the hatch. "I know."

Gabe turned to the FTL mechanism. "Captain, the FTL drive is suffering thermal fluctuations. I have to take it offline to effect repairs."

THE *GHOST* and *Nontee* had spread out, both moving at their best possible speed toward their enemies.

"I've got two ships," Zephyr announced. She looked at Wil, concern on her face. "How many ships do these krebnacks have?"

"Too damn many," the ship's captain answered without taking his eyes off his console. "Either of them the one from Kuria Andron?"

Zephyr shook her head.

On the forward display, a corvette and cruiser dropped out of FTL directly ahead of them.

"Fire!" Wil shouted.

Ten thousand kilometers to port, the *Nontee* fired ten of her remaining stub missiles.

Maxim counted to ten before sending two of their expensive ship-breaker missiles: one per ship, streaking out of the forward launchers. He followed the missile attack up with energy bolts from the nacelle-mounted blasters and the smaller ball turret blaster above the bridge.

Both enemy ships scrambled, pivoting away from each other. The stub missiles didn't pack much punch, but five per ship still lit up the corvette's shields, making entire sections nearly opaque as they spread the destructive energy out as much as possible. The cruiser fared better. Her shields cover a larger surface and had more emitters. The five impacts barely affected her shields, but they did distort her sensors.

Which allowed the two ship-busters to reach their targets without any trouble. The corvette's shields failed spectacularly moments before the ship broke in half. The other ship managed to only lose its port shields.

On the tactical sub-display, one of the red triangles blinked then faded away.

"Yes!" Bennie shouted.

The surviving ship spun on its axis to bring more of its guns to bear on its attacker.

"Oh no. No, no, no," Bennie said, his hands flying across his console to get the *Nontee* moving. He tried to get a target lock on the enemy ship, but it was driving down on the *Nontee* too fast.

"Oh no. Nooooo," he drawled.

The corvette opened fire. Four missiles, then eight, then twelve. Energy bolts struck the small freighter before the missiles, causing her shields to flare brightly.

The *Nontee*'s shields flared again, brighter, then failed. Bennie made a small, sad noise. The *Rocky Nontee* exploded.

"I'M PICKING up three more signatures on long-range sensors." Zephyr looked up from her sensor screen. Worry was written across her face. She truly felt bad for the team hacker. Her friend. But there wasn't time.

"PKs?" Wil asked. "Please let it be the PKs." He, too, felt for Bennie. He knew what losing the *Ghost* would do to him. The *Nontee* was an ugly piece of junk, but it was Bennie's ugly piece of junk. He glanced at the team hacker's station. Bennie was sitting motionless, staring at nothing.

Maxim turned in his seat. "Bet you never thought you'd say that."

Wil looked at his friend. "You know, that's right."

Zephyr shook her head. "No transponders." The *Ghost* had a dozen or two transponder IDs that they rotated in and out of use at the touch of a button or two, thanks to Bennie. But she always had a transponder active. Every ship did.

Not broadcasting an ID was a sure sign the incoming vessels weren't friendly.

Wil looked at the ship's status on one of the floating windows on the primary display. The picture it presented wasn't a positive one. Several shield emitters were on the verge of overload. The number two missile launcher was slowly flashing an angry orange color. It was working, but for how long was anyone's guess.

He glanced at the tactical display. The cruiser was circling around to give them a wide berth.

"Captain, the FTL drive is suffering thermal fluctuations. I have to take it offline to effect repairs," Gabe said over the intercom.

"Not a great time, Gabe," Wil said, keeping one eye on the primary display and another on the small tactical sub-display in the corner.

"I could do nothing, and we explode, if that would be more convenient."

Wil groaned. "Hurry." He pulled the controls to dodge a volley of blaster fire. The controls felt weird. He glanced at his flight information display. Several icons were flashing yellow, and a few were blinking red. That probably wasn't good. The flight dynamics display was also awash in colors it shouldn't be.

He glanced up. "Uh, Gabe? Controls are wonky."

"Acknowledged," came the terse reply.

Wil glanced at Zephyr. "Guess he's busy."

She gave him a look.

NIC WALKED into the *Ghost*'s computer core. The room was much smaller than engineering. Most of the space was taken up by the computer. Three people were a tight fit.

"What's going on?" Bruce asked.

Nic shoved past him toward one of the banks of interface

modules. She opened the cabinet and found the flight assist module. Several red lights were flashing.

"We're getting our asses kicked," she said as she pulled the module out of the rack. The blinking lights went dark. She started counting in her head.

"How bad is it?" the ambassador asked. The ship shook again, forcing him to reach out to clutch one of the interface racks.

She turned. "I'm counting."

"Counting what?" Bruce asked.

After tossing a glare at the man, she sighed and slotted the flight assist module back into its bay. The previously red blinking lights all came to life, green. One flashed to yellow and then back to green.

The immediate crisis averted, she turned to the two men. "I don't know. We get shot at, and shot up, a lot." She shrugged. "If we die, we die."

The ship shook again, the artificial gravity fluttering.

Ambassador Carlisle looked at the young woman. "I'm not sure it's good for you to be hanging out with these people."

CHAPTER THIRTY-ONE

"OH, NO YOU DON'T," Wil growled. He adjusted their course to intercept the other ship. "I need everything we have left. If we can take that ship out, it might make the new arrivals think twice."

"That seems likely," Bennie said.

"You shut up," Wil scolded.

The *Ghost* had a much tighter turning radius than the cruiser—an advantage Wil planned to exploit if he could. Unfortunately, what the cruiser lacked in maneuverability against the *Ghost*, it made up for in firing arc and sheer number of guns. Unlike the *Ghost*, the cruiser could fire its main weapons from any angle because they were mounted on turrets.

"Three FTL events!" Zephyr shouted. She brought up an inset window in the corner of the main bridge display showing the silhouettes of three ships: two corvettes and another cruiser.

Tane watched the *Ghost*'s crew work; facing incredibly uneven odds, they were calm and professional. Bennie said something about dying and haunting the others. Okay, mostly calm and professional.

Blaster bolts began splashing against the *Ghost*'s shields, rocking the smaller ship, causing things throughout the hull to pop and fizz. The ship rocked.

"They're locking on missiles," Zephyr warned, adding, "New contacts are eight microtocks out."

On the cruiser, a pair of top-mounted missile launchers spun to face the small oncoming threat.

Three missiles leaped out of the forward launcher straight for the *Ghost*. Another two leaped from the aft launcher.

"Incoming! Five targets. Impact in fifty," Zephyr called out.

Wil looked at the tactical display. Five red diamonds were closing in on them. "Max?"

"On it," the tactical officer said.

Wil couldn't tell if that sentence ended with a period or a question mark. He twisted his flight controls this way and that, sending the *Ghost* spinning and pirouetting through space, still mostly toward their target. The controls were sluggish, but the ship had been through a lot in the last few hours.

The forward ball turret spun to face the oncoming missiles and opened fire. Bolts of energy spat out of the barrel in rapid succession.

"It'd be easier to aim if you stopped moving us around so much," Maxim said.

"And if you miss, we eat a missile," Wil retorted.

"Boys," Zephyr scolded.

Wil evened out their flight. Maxim opened fire. The small ball turret spun and twitched, taking aim over and over until finally the last two missiles exploded, the last just seconds before impacting the *Ghost*'s shields. The explosion was close enough to still rock the small craft.

Wil turned to Maxim. "Take her out!"

A pair of missiles leaped out from the bottom corners of the primary display.

Wil brought the *Ghost* around to follow the missiles so that

Maxim could fire their more powerful engine nacelle-mounted blasters.

"Number two missile launcher is offline," the team tactical officer reported. He looked at Wil and shook his head. He didn't think Gabe would be able to fix the launcher.

"Two more contacts just appeared," Zephyr announced as the ship rocked under the enemy cruiser's fire. "And those kreb-nacks are locking missiles again," she added. Then her face paled. "Two more contacts."

The *Ghost*'s missiles struck the damaged cruiser's side, ripping into it. Secondary explosions followed, doing even more damage. Lights along the ship's side flickered and then went out.

"You already said that," Maxim said.

She frowned. "I know. Two *more* contacts. Four new hostiles."

Wil sighed. "On top of the existing hostiles. Yay."

"Maybe we should—" Tane started.

"New arrivals are splitting up to try to flank us. Cruiser is losing power," Zephyr interrupted.

Wil pulled the controls back, swinging the *Ghost* into a wide arc up and away from the damaged ship. "That's it. We're out of here." He gripped the FTL control lever, pushing it forward.

Nothing happened.

"Dren," several people on the bridge said at once.

"Gabe!" Will bellowed.

"Wait!" Zephyr looked up from her console once again. "The other contacts. They're Peacekeepers!"

On the tactical sub-monitor, the four new contacts flipped from orange to green, moving apart with military precision to encircle the *Ghost* and her tormentors.

"Peacekeepers to the rescue," Tane drawled.

Maxim turned. "Really?"

The younger man held both hands up in surrender.

A WINDOW POPPED into existence on the main display showing a view from one of *Ghost*'s cameras. Each pair of Peacekeepers was a corvette and a cruiser. The corvettes in particular looked like they had just come out of the assembly yard.

"Bet those still have that new spaceship smell," Will said.

Ignoring him, the others watched as the first pair of PKs effortlessly put themselves between the *Ghost* and the two hostile corvettes while the other two continued along their wide arc toward the three new arrivals.

The three new hostiles slowed.

Wil reached out to his console, enlarging the windowed view to full screen. He whistled. The Peacekeepers lashed out with energy weapons and missiles. The enemy corvettes had nowhere to go. Their weapons fired wildly, trying to intercept missiles and occasionally strike their attackers.

"Sucks for those guys," Bennie said.

On the screen, one of the enemy corvettes exploded.

The bridge hatch opened to allow Ambassador Carlisle, Bruce, and Nic to enter, the latter saying, "We're not dead. That's good."

Cynthia nodded to the new arrivals. "Looks like you've had fun."

"Captain, FTL is back online," Gabe reported.

Wil looked at the others. "Good job, pal."

Nodding to the screen, the ambassador asked, "Peacekeepers?"

Maxim nodded. "Two cruisers. Two corvettes. Chewy Acorn came through for us."

"Iran ch'Aroon," Cynthia corrected.

Wil turned to his big friend. "That's my thing. Get your own."

Maxim grinned.

"We're being hailed," Cynthia announced.

"Oh, goody," Wil drawled before nodding to her.

The main screen cleared, and then a window appeared with a stern-faced Palorian woman staring out of it. "Captain Calder. I'm Commander Stalo of the *Peace Through Strength*." She inclined her head. "Second Aide Iran ch'Aroon sent us. Looks like we got here just in time."

Wil smiled. "You could say that. Glad you could make it, Commander." He glanced at the tactical display, seeing one of the red triangles blink and then vanish. "We appreciate the assist."

"If you're able, I can escort you to Tarsis." She looked off screen. "I was told there would be two ships?"

Wil pursed his lips and glanced at Bennie. "Just the one," he finally said.

The Peacekeeper commander nodded. "I'll transmit the priority approach vector." The window closed when Commander Stalo closed the channel.

Wil looked at everyone on the bridge before stopping with the Ambassador. "Ready to get this over with?"

The older man smiled. "I was ready several days ago. No offense."

Wil smiled. "None taken. Time to go."

Bennie turned. "Think we can bill the Earthers for the *Rocky Nontee*?"

"I'm right here?" Carlisle said, crossing his arms.

Bennie looked at him. "And?"

"He bounced back fast," Cynthia said.

Wil turned to the Brailack hacker with a flat look on his face.

"That's a no?"

Wil maintained his glare.

"Okay, okay." Bennie turned to his station. "Seems reasonable to me, but whatever."

Wil slowly shook his head. He accepted the incoming nav data from the Peacekeeper cruiser.

"I'm getting another hail," Cynthia said, a puzzled look on her face.

Wil turned his head slightly. "The commander forget something?"

Cynthia gave him a small headshake. "Not the PKs."

Wil had a feeling he knew who it was. "On screen."

HE WAS RIGHT.

"Captain Calder," said the Elar Keeg woman he had met on Kuria Andron.

"Mystery lady," he nodded.

Maxim, Tane, Zephyr, and Cynthia all turned to look at the screen. Bruce and the ambassador crossed their arms.

"This doesn't change anything," she said.

Wil shrugged. "Seems like it does. You lost. The ambassador is going to be sworn in and establish Earth's presence on the GC council."

Cynthia stood. "Head of the Coalition?"

Wil didn't take his eyes off the screen at the front of the bridge. "Yup."

The red-hued woman smiled. "Captain Calder's life partner, Cynthia, yes?" Cynthia's tail swished back and forth in jerky motions. She nodded. "A pleasure to meet you." She turned her attention back to Wil. "I have to admit, I underestimated you," she looked around the bridge, "all of you. A mistake we won't make again, I assure you."

"I take it you're not anywhere near here right now," he said.

She smiled again. "Of course not. With Kuria Andron burned, we're in need of a new place to gather our forces. I'm overseeing that effort."

"You're welcome," Nic chimed in. Several faces turned toward her. "What? Everyone else gets to quip."

Wil gave a half nod, half shrug. "Fair. So, is there a reason you're calling? We've got to get moving. Places to be and all that."

The mysterious woman, who ran what was apparently a well-funded and semi-well-organized-maybe-legal group bent on keeping Earth out of the galactic community, smiled. "Just wanted to acknowledge your win. Enjoy it." Her pleasant smile vanished, and her eyes grew hard. "It won't last."

The screen went black and then resumed displaying a view from the forward camera, with the waiting *Peace Through Strength* looming ahead of them.

"She hung up on me. Rude." Wil leaned forward, elbows on his knees. "I hate that."

"Commander Stalo is asking if we need assistance," Cynthia said after glancing at her station before sitting back down.

Wil sat back and shook his head. He brought the flight controls online and confirmed their course. "Tell her we're good."

He looked over his shoulder to the ambassador and his aide. "Let's get you two to Tarsis."

The older of the pair nodded.

Zephyr watched the two men exit the bridge. "This feels decidedly...not settled."

On the forward screen, the *Peace Through Strength* leaped

to FTL. Wil pushed the FTL throttle forward, sending the *Ghost* after the Peacekeeper cruiser.

"That had to be bravado," Maxim said. "We know what she looks like. The Peacekeepers will have no shortage of debris to sift through, plus whatever is left of the base on Kuria Andron. They'll find her and her friends."

"They better. We're busy."

"We are?" Cynthia asked.

Wil looked at his wife. "God, I hope so."

"I'll be in my quarters," Bennie said as he hopped out of his seat.

Everyone watched him go. Wil looked at Nic, who looked back at him. "What?" she asked.

"Go, and you know, console him." He made a shooing motion.

"Do I look nurturing?" She crossed her arms.

Zephyr rose. "You've known him longer than the rest of us. I'll take the bridge."

Wil sighed, rising from his seat, letting the flight controls slide into standby. "Fine."

WIL PRESSED the button next to Bennie's door. There wasn't a reply. He pressed it again. "I know you're in there, dummy!" he shouted.

The hatch slid open.

Bennie was at the small workstation next to the bed. Wil came up behind him. On the workstation screen was a listing of ships for sale from a ship broker in the Tlanb system.

"You aren't wasting any time."

The small hacker didn't turn. "The *Nontee* won't replace herself."

Wil nodded, his hand hovering over the Brailack's shoulder. He made a face, then patted Bennie's shoulder. "There, there."

Bennie turned in his seat. "What the wurrin is wrong with you?"

Wil dropped down onto the edge of the bunk. "What?" He reached under himself and pulled out a tablet. Tossing it onto another part of the bed, he said, "I'm trying to comfort you."

"You suck at it!"

"You suck!" Wil snapped, then rubbed his face. "I get it, dude. I know how I'd feel if the *Ghost* were destroyed."

Bennie slumped in his chair. "Would you? I certainly wouldn't have thought I'd care about a ship until recently." He pulled his beam saber hilt off his belt, mindlessly twirling it in one hand.

Wil leaned back. "Could you?" He nodded to the hilt.

"Sorry," Bennie replied, setting the device on the desk behind him.

"I should have brought some alcohol with me," Wil said under his breath.

Bennie nodded. "That would have made sense." He sighed. "The *Nontee* was mine. She was freedom to do what I wanted, when I wanted."

Wil cocked his head. "The *Ghost* is always available to you. To everyone." Wil had never, that he recalled, refused to take any of the team anywhere.

"So, I can take the *Ghost* if we don't need it, do Knight of Plentallus stuff?" Bennie leaned forward.

"Oh, hell no." Wil shook his head. "Never in a million years would I let you borrow the *Ghost*." He smiled. "I get what you're saying." He shrugged. "But you only bought the *Nontee* because you needed to get off whatever world you were on. I didn't realize you'd grown so attached to it."

Bennie pursed his lips. When he did that, you could almost

forget he had a mouth at all. "I didn't realize I had either. Until she exploded."

Wil looked past his friend to the screen. "Why don't you come out to the lounge? It's almost dinnertime. We can help you pick out a smaller replacement for the *Nontee.*"

Bennie hopped off his chair. "Sounds good."

"You had her insured, right?" Wil asked as he reached the door, letting it slide open.

"Insurance?" Bennie asked.

"Oh, boy."

CHAPTER THIRTY-TWO

"IN HONOR of this being the last dinner our guests will have aboard the *Ghost*, we're having an Earth specialty," Wil said to the gathered group spread around the kitchen table and lounge seating. He and Gabe were in the kitchen area preparing the meal.

Bruce perked up. He was sitting in the overstuffed chair in the lounge. "What do you have in mind?"

"Tacos, of course," Wil replied.

"Just so you know, I'm lactose intolerant," the spy said.

Wil grinned. "That's fine. The cheese isn't dairy." He used air quotes when he said *cheese*.

The other man's eyes narrowed. "Why did you put *cheese* in quotes?"

"Have you seen any coos anywhere we've been?" Maxim asked.

"Cows," Wil corrected. Maxim pointed at him, nodding.

Bruce made a face. "Fair." He turned back to Cynthia, who was on the side of the sofa nearest him. "So, they take children and train them to be assassins?"

She nodded. She had been telling him all about her

upbringing as a tangent to the question of how the team met each other. "Yup. Real messed up stuff. I thought they'd been shut down when I was young, but we discovered that wasn't the case a few cycles ago." She grinned, baring her sharp incisors. "We took care of that once and for all though."

Maxim and Zephyr were bent over the dining table, a tablet between them. The former said, "I think this is it."

Zephyr looked up from the tablet, smiling. She asked, "You're sure?"

He nodded. "I am."

She reached over the device, putting her hand on his. "If you're sure, I'm sure." She smiled.

Bennie reached up between them, grabbing the tablet. "You done with this? I need to bring up the ship broker page." The two Palorians' mouths fell open. He looked at the screen. "Is this...?" They nodded slowly. He smiled. "About felgercarbing time." Before either could say anything, he shouted, "Gather round. I need your help picking a new ship." He trotted into the main seating area, waking the bulkhead-mounted display screen.

At the cooktop, Wil said, "You're going to burn it."

Without looking at his human friend, Gabe said, "No, I am not. The internal temperature is still seven degrees from safe serving temperature."

Wil eyed the skillet. "You know there's a level of gut, of intuition, to cooking. Something sensors can't convey."

"Of the four thousand and twenty-seven meals you have prepared, that I am aware of, you have objectively burned five hundred and twelve. That is a —"

Wil held up both hands. "Okay, okay." He smiled. "It's burning now."

Gabe made his exasperated mechanical rattle sound. "That is not my fault."

Wil tossed a small cup of seasoning onto the mix followed by a smaller cup of water. "It's okay, pal. This covers a multitude of sins."

"I believe you intentionally distracted me to prove a point," the droid protested.

"Would I do that?" Wil asked, smiling, as he grabbed two packages of tortillas from the food chiller. Keeping meat and dairy products on the ship was tricky, but the food chiller kept Earth store-bought tortillas fresh longer than he thought was possible.

"Yes," the droid replied, moving the skillet from the burner as he used a slotted spoon to stir the mixture, ensuring it was properly covered with seasoning.

"Five minutes!" Wil shouted.

In the lounge, Bennie was saying, "I think something like this." On the large entertainment screen, a sleek craft that clearly made for speed over cargo hauling capacity was rotating.

Ambassador Carlisle, the only person giving Bennie their full attention, said, "That's pretty. Your previous vessel was capable of carrying cargo; is that not something you wish to continue doing?"

Bennie shook his head. "No. We made use of the *Nontee* as best we could for what she could do. But Knights of Plentallus don't haul cargo."

From her perch on the arm of the overstuffed chair, Nic said, "We have much more important things to do, like score free meals."

Bennie frowned. "This time, I want to focus on speed. Getting my soon-to-be ex-apprentice and I where we need to be quickly."

The ambassador nodded. "That makes sense. You and your apprentice, and I think I heard you have a few new apprentices?" Bennie nodded. "You should be more visible throughout the GC."

Bennie looked at Wil. "I assumed all humans were dumb. It's just you?" He ducked a ladle and stuck out his tongue.

THE *GHOST*, flanked by four Peacekeeper corvettes, descended through the clouds over Thurquar, the home city of the Galactic Commonwealth Governing Council.

Wil followed the faint green arrow on his nav display toward the half-kilometer tall metal and glass mushroom that was the regional spaceport. No duracrete rings for the Tarsi.

"Sure looks like they coulda spared a few more ships," Bennie said.

"Right?" Wil eased the ship to port. The four corvettes slowed and then rose as the smaller ship lined up for VIP docking bay thirteen.

"This place looks amazing," Bruce said. He and the ambassador were standing on either side of the bridge hatch. "The intelligence reports don't do it justice."

Ambassador Carlisle nodded. "Nor the State Department briefings." He turned his gaze to Cynthia. "And you all don't like it here?"

She shrugged. "Tarsis and the Tarsi are an acquired taste."

"Don't forget the Tarlak. Little ass-kissers," Bennie said.

Bruce looked at the team hacker. "Who hurt you?"

Wil barked a laugh. "Sorry." He turned his attention to his flight controls, missing the look his little green friend gave him. "Touch down in five."

Maxim turned in his seat. "So. You keeping him as your aide?" He nodded to Bruce.

Bruce turned. "I'm right here."

Maxim shrugged.

The ambassador chuckled. "Yes." He turned to Bruce. "It'd be a lot of paperwork to replace him, and I think, at least for now, having someone with his skills on my staff will be useful." He leveled his gaze at the other man. "So long as he remembers I'm the only thing keeping him here on Tarsis."

Bruce crossed his arms. "Understood."

The *Ghost* settled on her landing gear in the ornate VIP landing bay in the Galactic Commonwealth governance center's spaceport. Thurquar was a sprawling metropolis of glass and steel towers dominated by a two-kilometer diameter dome. The tower they'd visited on their first trip had been visible in the distance on their approach, the landing bay ring glittering in the fading daylight.

"Think that restaurant we ate at last time is still around?" Wil said, putting his station into standby.

Bennie's eyebrow ridges rose. "Oh, I hope so."

Cynthia turned. "Second Aide Iran ch'Aroon is waiting for us outside." She powered down her station and stood.

The ambassador and Bruce were waiting in the common deck lounge, both in bespoke suits, with their luggage next to the stairwell hatch.

"You two clean up nice," Wil said.

Cynthia nodded. "Looking good, Secret Agent Hawkins."

Bruce rolled his eyes. "Obviously, if you could keep my second role to yourselves, the United Earth Government would appreciate it."

Cynthia's tail swished playfully. "Pum's the word."

"Mum. Mum's the word," Wil said.

She shrugged. "The welcoming party is waiting for us outside." She gestured to the hatch.

Wil led the way, stooping to pick up the ambassador's bag. Maxim followed him, grabbing Bruce's bag.

Second Aide Iran ch'Aroon was standing with an honor guard of a dozen Peacekeeper centurions. The Tarlak official bent his front legs in a bow. "Greetings, Ambassador Carlisle of Earth. The Galactic Commonwealth Governing Council welcomes you."

The ambassador bowed his head. "Thank you. It's an honor, for myself and the people of Earth, to be welcomed to the beating heart of the Galactic Commonwealth."

Bennie looked up at Wil. "Are they flirting? Is this how humans flirt?"

Wil looked down at him, face scrunched up. "What? No, you weirdo. Now be quiet."

The ambassador and Iran ch'Aroon continued to exchange political pleasantries for a few more minutes. The officious Tarlack finally turned to the crew of the *Ghost*. "Well done, Rogue Enterprises. I had my doubts—"

"We're used to it," Wil said, interrupting the smaller being, with a smile.

Iran ch'Aroon pursed his thin lips to stifle a rude noise. "Indeed. Well, you once again have the thanks of the Commonwealth Governing Council."

Bennie leaned forward. "Do you have the banking details of the Commonwealth Governing Council?"

Zephyr groaned. Their Tarlack contact closed his eyes. Ambassador Carlisle sighed.

Iran ch'Aroon opened his eyes. "Your payment has been processed."

Shaking his head, Wil said, "Thank you, Second Aide." He looked at the two other humans. "When's the ceremony?"

"Tomorrow morning," Bruce answered.

Wil smiled. "We'll see you then." He turned to his crew. "Let's get drunk!" He clapped his hands and pointed toward the spaceport's bank of lifts.

The Peacekeeper honor guard snapped to attention, spun ninety degrees, and formed up around Iran ch'Aroon, Ambassador Carlisle, and Bruce.

As the lift raced down to the pedestrian levels closer to the planet's surface, Zephyr said, "Looks like we'll be here a few days." She raised her arm to show Wil the wristcomm screen.

Wil shrugged. "Can't be helped. The *Ghost* is too banged up to get back to Fury if our four-armed friend makes an appearance between here and there."

From the back of the group, Gabe said, "I have been in contact with the repair team assigned to the *Ghost*. They will arrive tomorrow around midmorning."

"Need help?" Nic asked.

The droid inclined his head. "That would be acceptable."

The young woman bounced on her heels.

"So, you don't think that's the last we'll see of that Elar Keeg woman?" Bennie asked.

Cynthia shook her head. "No way. She means business. Whatever this Coalition is about, they're not done. This was just a setback."

"Pleasant thought," Zephyr said.

The lift doors parted, allowing the noise of the public street to fill the lift car.

Wil stepped out. "Anyone remember where that restaurant is?" He turned to the others. "The Coalition is a problem for another day. Today we're in Tarsis, surrounded by Peacekeeper command carriers and thousands, probably hundreds of thousands, of Peacekeepers on the ground. The Coalition isn't getting anywhere near us, and it's gonna take them some time to regroup." He made a slow circle, arms raised. "So, let's find that place we ate at that one time and enjoy the fact that Mr. Bridezilla over here," he pointed at Maxim, "has finally gotten his shit together so he and she," he pointed to Zephyr, "can do whatever it is Palorians do when they get married."

"Hear, hear!" Maxim shouted, draping his arm around Wil's shoulder.

Nic leaned over to Bennie. "Do our outfits have a formal version?"

He shrugged.

"GOOD EVENING, this is GNO News Break," Klor'Tillen, the pale green Brailack, said. "The Earth is now a member of the Galactic Commonwealth." He smiled. "For better or worse, depending on who you ask."

The Brailack journalist turned to another camera pickup. "A recent GNO/Strelly poll shows that forty-three percent of those surveyed were either completely against, or at least unsure of the value of, welcoming the Earth into the Commonwealth."

He paused, looking over to his cohost. "Only time will tell whether those fears are warranted or not."

Xyrzix turned, his large compound eyes glittering under the studio lighting. "I don't know. They seem chaotic." He shrugged. "We'll find out soon, I'm sure."

EPILOGUE

EPILOGUE

"GABE CALLED. The *Ghost* is all patched up," Zephyr said after finishing her drink. She and Wil were in a bar at the top of one of the buildings near the Thurquar Spaceport complex. The glimmering glass and metal mushroom of the government building spread out beneath them. Overhead, thousands of vehicles sped this way and that in an intricate dance, forming a patchwork of lights in the sky.

Wil nodded. "Good. Four days is four days too many on Tarsis."

The server came over to their table. "Another round?"

Wil looked up. "No, we'll cash out."

The Tarsi rolled their eyes. "Very good." They swiped up on their tablet, sending the bill to Wil's wristcomm. Before Wil could even acknowledge the bill, they turned and walked away.

Zephyr gave a weak chuckle. "Yeah, this place does suck."

"Our glorious rulers," Wil said absently, trying to remember the override code Iran ch'Aroon had given him to transfer bills to the Governing Council's discretionary account. He looked up. "Do you remember the code? You know, to put the bill on Itchy's accounts." He looked at his wristcomm. "I thought it was eight-zero-zero-eight-one-three-five, but it's—"

"Four-four-one-nine-six-six," Zephyr interrupted.

Wil grunted. "There it is. Thanks." He tapped a few more things on the screen of his wristcomm and then grabbed his drink, finishing it off. The bill immediately showed as paid in full. "You good?"

She eyed her drink. "Where's everyone else?"

He shrugged. "I know Cyn is checking in on Bruce. Apparently, he's already putting his fingers where they don't belong. She made a face. He ignored it. The others..." He shrugged again. "Who the hell knows about the others? I'll call everyone back when we get to the ship. Might as well let them enjoy whatever it is they're doing a little longer. We'll need to run diagnostics on everything before we lift off."

"Except Bennie. He's for sure committing crime."

Wil frowned, then tapped an icon on his wristcomm. "Bennie, get back to the ship. Now."

"Now?" came the tiny Knight of Plentallus' voice from the wristcomm.

"Yes, now."

"I'm busy. I'll be there in two tocks."

"Now, stop whatever shady shit you're up to and get back to the *Ghost*."

"You suck. I'll be right there." The wristcomm beeped. Channel closed.

Wil looked up. "Let's go." He nodded toward her drink.

She downed it and stood.

THE *GHOST'S* cargo ramp was down and waiting when the pair reached the ship.

"Something's not right," Zephyr said. Her hand drifted to where she normally kept a pulse pistol. Tarsis had strict rules regarding weapons; only Peacekeepers got to carry them.

Wil rolled his eyes. "We're on Tarsis. The most dangerous things here are service charges and paperwork."

Zephyr visibly relaxed, her hand falling to her side. She nodded.

They walked up the ramp into the dark cargo hold. Wil was struggling to keep his composure. He said, "Did Gabe not fire up the reactor?"

The lights in the hold jumped to full intensity to reveal a decorated cargo hold full of people who all shouted, SURPRISE, all at once.

Zephyr sprang into action, grabbing the nearest person to her, throwing them to the ground, and planting a knee against their throat. She couldn't carry a pistol, but she produced a long knife that she held by the blade, ready to hurl at anyone who came close.

"Are you insane?" Iran ch'Aroon tried to shout, but it came out as a strangled gurgle.

Wil put a hand on her shoulder. "Whoa, girl."

Zephyr looked around. "Oh," she whispered. Looking down at the Governing Council's second aide, she said, "Sorry." She stood. She spun the knife to grasp it by the handle, sliding it into her boot. Then she offered the frightened Tarlak her hand.

Iran ch'Aroon accepted her hand, standing. "I didn't even want to be here." He stormed aft toward the rear of the hold. "Blumtillithian was right. These people are savages."

Zephyr looked around, spying Rhys Duch and his entourage. Her friend Prathea. Ambassador Carlisle and Bruce

Hawkins were standing off to the side, both smiling. The pair of scientists from the team's first real mission: Xan and Jor'Lu.

She spied Maxim standing in the center of the group surrounded by the rest of the team and his cousin Tane, a big grin on his face, his family's colla band in one outstretched hand. She shook her head. "You."

He inclined his head. "I recently learned that perfect is the enemy of good." He glanced over at his cousin Tane, who did his best not to smile.

Wil, in a bespoke suit that Bruce and Ambassador Carlisle assured him was the height of fashion right now on Earth, clapped his hands. "Let's do this, people! Space wedding time!"

Zephyr looked at Wil, who winked, then turned back to Maxim. "He seems more excited than I'd have expected." Her eyes narrowed. "You didn't—"

Leaning in close, he whispered, "Didn't tell him about Anat Utu? Nope. Figured it'd be a fun surprise."

Zephyr smiled. "Okay, this should be interesting. Come on, lover."

The pair headed for the corner of the cargo hold, where a small altar was set up, surrounded by chairs. She started to remove her top.

Wil saw this and asked, "Wait, what're you doing?"

Maxim smiled. "Anat Utu." He let his trousers fall to the deck.

Bennie reached over to cover Nic's eyes. She shoved his hand away.

THANK YOU

Thank you so much for reading this latest Rogues Enterprises adventure

If you enjoyed it I'd love it if you left a review. Seriously, reviews are a big deal. They help readers find authors. They help authors show how awesome they are.

Reviews are social proof and go a long way to encouraging other readers to take a chance on an unknown author.

STAY CONNECTED

Want to stay up to date on the happenings in the Galactic Commonwealth?
Like free short stories and more?

Sign up for my newsletter at
johnwilker.com/newsletter
Visit me online at
johnwilker.com
Or the Wilker-verse Discord

If you like supporting things you love by sporting merch or buying direct, well you're in luck! I've launched a Shop, take a look. **Use, discount code "Ghost" and you'll save %15!**

ACKNOWLEDGMENTS

I couldn't do this without an amazing group of people who sign up to beta and/or ARC read for me. The Beta readers in particular have to suffer through an early draft to help shape the story.

Below are some of these awesome people (If I missed your name, email me and you'll be in the next one :D)

- Rick Lindsay
- Marcus Zarra
- Chris Boyd
- Roger Gilmartin
- Scott Jann
- Steve Rakoczy
- Vickie Grider

Thank you so much, all of you!

ABOUT ME

I've loved writing since I was a kid. I entered writing contests in 2nd and 3rd grade. I won an award even (The only one to date) and got my story in an anthology. I was a big deal!

I read books and wrote book reports for my parents (It helped that I got a new G.I. Joe for each book report). From that point on I've read books and told stories wherever I could.

I hope to keep telling Wil and the team's story for as long as people enjoy reading them. They bring me so much joy and I hope they have that effect on you!

Tell your friends, tell your family, tell the person next to you on the plane that just looked at you funny for laughing out loud. You see where I'm going with this. :) Word of mouth is so incredibly potent, especially for folks not getting talked about on Oprah or NPR.

OFFER

As they say, there's no harm in asking, so here we go.

If you can help connect me with someone who can get Space Rogues on a screen (Big or Little) I'll cut you in for 10% (Up to $10,000) of whatever advance is paid.

Send me an email and we can discuss.
rights@johnwilker.com

OTHER BOOKS BY JOHN WILKER

Like your snark coming from sapient droids and ships that hate being left in parking lots? The Grand Human Empire Series may be up your alley. Jax, Naomi and the droids are just trying to get by. New droid parts ain't cheap after all.

Like Big robots fighting giant alien plants and animals set on taking over Earth? Check out the Invasive Species series. Monsters came from space and we nothing to fight them with. Until we did.

Prefer something more action/adventure, and set right here on Earth? The Expedition, Inc. team is worth a look. I write them under my pen name, J. Beckett. They're adventurers for hire. Like Indiana Jones and the A-Team.

www.ingramcontent.com/pod-product-compliance
Lightning Source LLC
LaVergne TN
LVHW050918080826
845145LV00001B/130

* 9 7 8 1 9 5 1 9 6 4 2 9 0 *